D0436238

NIGHTWORLD

ALSO BY F. PAUL WILSON

Repairman Jack*

The Tomb	Infernal
Legacies	Harbingers
Conspiracies	Bloodline
All the Rage	By the Sword
Hosts	Ground Zero
The Haunted Air	Fatal Error
Gateways	The Dark at the End
Crisscross	

Young Adult*

Jack: Secret Histories
Jack: Secret Circles
Jack: Secret Vengeance

The Adversary Cycle*

The Keep	Reborn
The Tomb	Reprisal
The Touch	Nightworld

Other Novels

Healer	Mirage (with
Wheels Within Wheels	Matthew J. Costello)
An Enemy of the State	Nightkill (with
Black Wind*	Steven Spruill)
Dydeetown World	Masque (with
The Tery	Matthew J. Costello)
Sibs*	The Christmas Thingy
The Select	Sims
Virgin	The Fifth Harmonic
Implant	Midnight Mass
Deep as the Marrow	

Short Fiction

Soft and Others*
The Barrens and Others*
Aftershock & Others*
The Peabody-Ozymandias Traveling
Circus & Oddity Emporium*
Quick Fixes*

Editor

Freak Show
Diagnosis: Terminal

* See "The Secret History of the World" (page 399).

NIGHTWORLD

F. PAUL WILSON

TOR®

A TOM DOHERTY ASSOCIATES BOOK • NEW YORK

NIGHTWORLD

Copyright © 2012 by F. Paul Wilson

A Tor Book
Published by Tom Doherty Associates, LLC
175 Fifth Avenue
New York, NY 10010

www.tor-forge.com

Tor® is a registered trademark of Tom Doherty Associates, LLC.

ISBN 978-0-7653-2167-1 (hardcover)
ISBN 978-1-4299-4801-2 (e-book)

First Edition: May 2012

Printed in the United States of America

0 9 8 7 6 5 4 3 2 1

ACKNOWLEDGMENTS

Thanks to the usual crew for their efforts: my wife, Mary; my editor, David Hartwell; Steven Spruill; Elizabeth Monteleone; Blake Dollens; Alex Cameron; and my agent, Albert Zuckerman. And as always, special thanks to Becky Maines.

AUTHOR'S NOTE

Nightworld ends the Secret History.

The novel picks up a couple of months after the horrors of *The Dark at the End*. I hope you've read the rest of the Adversary Cycle by now. The two story tracks—Jack's tale and the Cycle—have merged and this is the grand finale. (See "The Secret History of the World" at the end of this book for how everything fits together.)

I have extensively revised *Nightworld* since its initial publication in the early '90s. Jack's role has been expanded—he is now a major player—but he remains one of many. Characters who didn't exist when I wrote the original must be dealt with. *Nightworld* is an ensemble novel with characters drawn from across the Secret History. It ends both narrative tracks, as well as the Secret History itself. More stories remain to be told, but the timeline stops there. I will set no stories after *Nightworld*.

However . . .

In response to pleas (and occasional threats) from readers (you know who you are), I've agreed to write three more Repairman Jack novels from the period between his arrival in NYC and *The Tomb*, just to fill in those gaps. They'll trace how he comes to know Abe and Julio, and how he becomes the guy you meet in *The Tomb*. After those books, it is *over*. You will then know all I know about Jack and I'll have nothing left to say. I need to move on.

—F. Paul Wilson
the Jersey Shore

NIGHTWORLD

Rasalom went to the mountain.

Rasalom is not his birth name, not the one his mother bestowed on him. He discarded that back in the First Age when the Otherness held more sway in this sphere. When he tapped into that mother lode of power and strangeness he took on a new name, a True Name he had protected like a wolverine guarding her young. But the time for secrecy is past. He can now shout his True Name anywhere on the planet and it will not matter.

From here atop Minya Konka, through a break in the clouds, much of what is now called China spreads out four and a half miles below him in the darkness. His birthplace is not far from here. It is bitterly cold on the mountaintop. Gale-force winds shriek and howl as they swirl the frozen air about his naked body. Rasalom scarcely notices. The power within protects him, fed by the delicious woes of the world below.

The horizon brightens. Dawn does not break at this altitude—it shatters. Rasalom stares at the glint of fire sliding into view and focuses the power he has been storing since his most recent rebirth. Eons of frustration fall away as he finalizes the process to which he has devoted the ages of his existence. No gestures, no incantations, just elseness, otherness, vomiting out of him, spreading out and up and around, seeping into the planet's crust, billowing into its atmosphere, saturating this locus in the multiverse.

Soon all shall be his. No one and nothing opposes him, no power on earth or elsewhere can stop him.

He drops to his knees, not in prayer but in relief, elation.

At last, after so many ages, it has begun.

Dawn will never be the same.

PART ONE

SUNSET

WEDNESDAY

Nicholas Quinn, Ph.D.

Manhattan

On May 17, the sun rose late.

Nick Quinn heard the first vague rumors of a delayed sunrise while filling his coffee mug from the urn in the lounge of Columbia University's physics department. He didn't pay them much mind. A screwed-up calculation, a missed observation, a malfunctioning clock. Human error. Had to be. Old Sol never missed appointments. It simply didn't happen.

But the rumor continued to echo through the halls all morning, with no offsetting rumor of explanation. So at lunch break, when Nick had settled his usual roast beef on rye and large cola on his tray in the faculty cafeteria, the first thing he did was hunt up Harvey Sapir from astrophysics.

Nick looked for the hair. Harv's hair was always perfect. It flowed back seamlessly from his forehead in a salt-and-pepper wave, so full and thick it looked like a toupee. Close up, if you looked carefully, you could catch a glimpse of pink scalp through the mane. A running joke around the physics department was guesstimating how much time and spray Harv invested in his hair each morning.

Nick spotted him at a corner table with Cynthia Hayes. She was from astrophysics too. The two of them were in deep conversation.

Harv's hair was a mess.

Nick found that unsettling.

"Mind if I join you?" he said, hovering over the seat next to Cynthia.

Both glanced up and nodded absently, then immediately put their heads back together.

Beneath his uncombed hair, Harv's face was haggard. He looked all of his fifty-five years and then some. Cynthia too looked disheveled. She was younger—mid thirties—with short chestnut hair and glorious skin. Nick liked her. A lot. She was the main reason he'd put aside his Coke-bottle lenses and got fitted for contacts. Years ago. Still hadn't found the nerve to ask her out. With his pocked skin and weird-shaped head, he felt like a warty frog with no chance of ever changing into a prince, yet still he pined for this princess.

"What's all this I hear about the sun being late?" he said after swallowing the first bite of his sandwich. "How'd a story like that get started?"

They both glanced at him again, then Cynthia leaned back and rubbed her eyes.

"Because it's true."

Nick stopped in mid bite and stared at them, looking for a smile, a twist of the lips, a hint of the put-on.

Nothing. Two deadpan faces.

"Bullshit."

Instantly he regretted it. He never used profanity in front of a woman, even though many of them had no reservations about swearing like sailors in front of him.

"Sunrise was scheduled at five twenty-one this morning," Cynthia said. "It rose at five twenty-six. Five minutes and eight-point-two-two seconds late."

Her husky voice never failed to give him a warm feeling.

Except today. Her words chilled him. She was saying the unthinkable.

"Come on, guys." He forced a laugh. "We set our clocks by the sun, not vice versa. If the clock says the sun is late, then the clock needs to be reset."

"*Atomic* clocks, Nick?"

"Oh."

That was different. Atomic clocks worked on nuclear decay. They were accurate to a millionth of a second. If they said the sun was late . . .

"Could be some sort of mechanical failure."

Harv shook his head. "Greenwich reported a late rise too. Five minutes and a fraction late. They called us. I was here at four thirty A.M., waiting. As Cynthia told you, sunrise was late here by exactly the same interval."

Nick felt a worm of uneasiness begin to work its way up his spine.

"What about Palo Alto?"

"The same," Cynthia said.

"But do you know what you're saying? Do you know what this means?"

"Of course I know what it means!" Harv said with ill-concealed annoyance.

"This *is* my field, you know. It means the earth has either temporarily slowed its rate of spin during the night or tilted back on its axis."

"But either would mean cataclysm! Why, the effect on tides alone would be—"

"But it *didn't* slow. Not the slightest variation in axial rotation *or* axial tilt. Believe me, I've checked. The days are supposed to be getting progressively longer until the equinox in June, but today got shorter—or at least it started out that way."

"Then the clocks are wrong!"

"Atomic clocks? *All* of them? All experiencing precisely the same level of change in nuclear decay at the same time? I doubt it. No, Nick. The sun rose late this morning."

Nick's field was lasers and particle physics. He was used to uncertainties at the subatomic level—Heisenberg had seen to that. But on the celestial plane, things were supposed to go like . . . clockwork.

"This is all *impossible*!"

Harv's expression was desolate, Cynthia's frightened.

"I know," he said in a low voice. "Don't I know."

And then Nick remembered a conversation he'd had with a certain Jesuit a couple of months ago.

It will begin in the heavens . . .

After years of hiding in the South, Father Bill Ryan had returned to the city, but was still lying low. Only a handful of people knew he was back. After all, he was still wanted by the police.

Poor Father Bill. The years of seclusion had not been kind to him. He looked so much older, and he acted strange. Simultaneously jumpy, irritable, frightened, and angry. And he talked of strange things. No specifics, just cryptic warnings of some sort of approaching Armageddon. Nothing involving Islamic crazies. Something else . . .

One thing Father Bill had been fairly positive about was where it all would start.

It will begin in the heavens.

He'd told Nick to keep his ears open and to let him know if he heard of anything strange happening in the skies, no matter how insignificant.

Well, something more than strange had happened. Something far from insignificant. Something impossible.

It will begin in the heavens.

The unease in Nick's spine stopped crawling and sprinted up to the back of his neck, spreading across his shoulders. He excused himself from the table and pulled out his cell phone as he headed for the hallway.

William Ryan, S.J.

"Ask him about tonight," Glaeken said, close by Bill's side. "Do they think the sun will set *ahead* of schedule tonight?"

Bill turned back to the phone and repeated the question. Nick's reply was agitated. Bill detected a tremor weaving through the younger man's voice.

"I don't know, and I'm sure Harv and Cynthia don't know, either. This is terra incognita, Bill. Nothing like this has ever happened before. All bets are off."

"Okay, Nick. Thanks for calling. Keep me posted, will you? Let me know about sunset."

"That's it?" Nick said. *"Keep you posted? What's this all about? How did you know something was going to happen? What's it all mean?"*

Bill sensed the fear, the uncharacteristic uncertainty in Nick, and wished he could say something to comfort him. But Bill had nothing comforting to say.

"You'll know as soon as I know. I promise you. Get back to me here tonight. I'll be waiting for you. Good-bye."

Bill hung up and turned to Glaeken, but the old man was over by the picture window, staring down at the park. He did that a lot.

Glaeken looked eighty-something, maybe ninety, with white hair and wrinkled olive skin; blue eyes shone above high cheekbones. Though slightly stooped, he was still a big man, and his frame blocked a good portion of the window. Bill had been living here in Glaeken's apartment building for the past couple of months, helping him with his ailing wife, driving him around town while he did his "research," but mostly waiting.

A huge apartment, occupying the entire top floor of the building, filled with strange curios and even stranger paintings. The wall to Bill's left was mirrored and he started at the stranger facing him in the glass, then realized he was looking at himself. He'd shaved his beard and cut his hair. He missed his ponytail and still wasn't used to seeing himself with bare cheeks. Or looking so old. The hair had been gray for years, but the beard had hidden all the lines in his face.

He moved up to the window and stood beside Glaeken.

The months of waiting since March were apparently over. In a way he was glad for that. But an icy tendril of dread slithered through his gut as he realized he had traded one uncertainty for another. The apprehension of wondering *when* it would start had been replaced now by a greater worry of *what* was starting.

"You didn't seem too surprised," Bill said.

"I sensed the difference this morning. Your friend confirmed it. The Change has begun its march."

"You wouldn't know it from the looks of things down there."

Across the street and a dozen stories below, the high spring sun spread a palette of greens across Central Park as the various species of trees sprouted this year's leaf crop.

"No. And you won't for a while. But now we must lower our watch. The next manifestation will occur in the earth."

"Like what?"

"I don't know. But if he follows his pattern, that is where he'll make his next move. And when he has reached his full powers—"

"You mean he *hasn't?*"

"He must go through a process before his power is complete. Plus, there's a purpose to playing with the length of our days. It's all part of his method."

"Not at full power," Bill said softly, his mind balking. "My God, if he's able to alter the time the sun rises when he's *not* up to speed, what'll he be able to do when he is?"

Glaeken turned and pinned him with his deep blue gaze.

"Anything he wants, Bill. *Anything.*"

"Nick says it's impossible for the sun to rise late." Bill knew he was grasping at straws. "It breaks too many physical laws."

"We'll have to learn to forget about physical laws—or any laws, for that matter. The 'laws' we have created to explain our existence and make sense of the universe around us are about to be repealed. Physics, chemistry, gravity, time itself will be reduced to futile, meaningless formulae. The first laws were broken at sunrise. Many more will follow until they all lie scattered about in ruins. As of this morning, we begin a trek toward a world and a time without laws."

An old woman's voice quavered from the master bedroom.

"Glenn? Glenn, where are you?"

"Coming, Magda." Glaeken gripped Bill's upper arm and lowered his voice. "I don't think we can stop him, but we may have a chance to impede him."

Bill urged his spirits to respond, to lift, to cast off the pall of gloom that enveloped him. But his mood remained black.

"How? How can we hope to stand against a power that can alter the path of the sun?"

The old man's expression turned stern. "We can't. Not with that attitude. And that's just the way he wants us to react—with despair and hopelessness. 'He's too powerful. Why even try to resist?'"

"Good question."

"No." Glaeken tightened his grip. "*Bad* question. That way, he's already won, without a fight. He *may* win. In fact, I'm pretty sure we haven't got a chance. But I've fought him too long to sit around and simply wait for the end. I thought I could. I wanted to sit this out, sit everything out. That was why I took the name Veilleur. For once I'd be involved in nothing; I'd simply sit back and watch. And I have watched."

He released Bill's arm and turned back to the window.

"And all that time I've waited for someone to come along and be given the power to stand in Rasalom's way. I found that someone, but he hasn't the power. And he'll not be endowed with that power because Rasalom has succeeded in convincing the Ally that this world is non-sentient—dead. And the Ally has no interest in dead worlds." He looked at Bill again. "We're on our own here."

If he was trying to bolster Bill's spirits, he'd failed.

"So we're screwed."

"So it would seem. But despite my vow, I find I can't sit by and let everything fall into Rasalom's lap. I want that bastard to have to work for it. If he wants this world, he's going to have to *earn* it!"

Something in Glaeken's words, his manner, his flashing eyes offered a hint of hope.

"I'm all for that, but can we do enough to let him know he's even been in a fight?"

"Oh, yes. I'll see to it."

Magda's voice intruded again, trailing in from the bedroom.

"Doesn't anybody hear me? Isn't anybody there? Have I been left here alone to die?"

"I'd better go to her," Glaeken said.

"Can I help?"

"Thanks, no. She simply needs a little reassurance. But I'd appreciate it if you could be around tonight while I go out. I've got a little errand I must run."

"If you need anything, I can—"

"No. I have to meet with Jack."

Jack . . . they'd met a few times. Bill had even patched up a wound on the younger man. He and Glaeken had some sort of bond Bill couldn't fathom. He called Jack his "heir," but to what?

"Okay. I think I'll stop in on Carol. To tell her it's started."

"Good. Do that. And keep emphasizing to her that none of what has happened or is about to happen is her fault."

"Will do." Bill started to turn away, then stopped. "Can we really give Rasalom a fight?"

"If I can gather together the proper elements, we may have ourselves a weapon."

"Really?" Bill was almost afraid to yield to the hope growing within him. "When do we start this gathering?"

"Tomorrow. Will you drive me out to Long Island? And would you wear your cassock?"

What a strange request. Why did Glaeken want him to look like a priest?

"I don't have one. I . . . I don't believe in any of that anymore."

"I know. But I must be at my most persuasive. And the presence of a Jesuit at my side might lend some weight to my arguments. We'll fit you for a new cassock."

Bill shrugged. "Anything for the cause. Where on Long Island?"

"The North Shore."

A familiar pang stirred within Bill.

"I grew up in that area."

"Yes. In the village of Monroe."

"How did you know?"

Glaeken shrugged. "That is where we're going."

"Monroe? My hometown? Why?"

"Part of the weapon is there."

Bill was baffled. *In Monroe?*

"It's just a little harbor town. What kind of weapon can you hope to find out there?"

Glaeken turned and walked down the hall to attend to his wife. He cast the reply over his shoulder.

"A small boy."

In the East Eighties, Bill knocked on an eighth-floor apartment door. It opened and a slender woman with ash blond hair, fine features, and a pert, upturned nose stared at him. Carol. Their decades apart had been kinder to her than to him. But now her face was tight, her eyes haunted, her usual high coloring blanched. She knew.

"It's begun, hasn't it?"

The afternoon sun filled the room behind her with golden light, lending her an almost ethereal quality. The sight of her disturbed once again the old feelings he tried to keep tucked away.

Bill stepped across the threshold and closed the door behind him.

"How did you know?"

"I heard about the late sunrise on the radio." Tears filled her eyes as her lips began to tremble. "I knew right away it was Jimmy's doing."

Bill reached out and folded her in an embrace. She trembled as she leaned against him. Her arms locked around his back and she clung as if he were a tree in a flood. Bill closed his eyes and let the good feelings wash through him. Good feelings were so hard to come by these days.

He'd been moving through a black fog since the deadly events in North Carolina.

Three times his world had been all but torn apart.

First, the violent death of his old friend and Carol's first husband, Jim Stevens, followed by the bizarre murders in the Hanley mansion and Carol's flight to parts unknown; he'd recovered from that.

Then, years later, his parents' death in a fire, Danny Gordon's mutilation and all the horrors that followed, capped by his own flight and years of hiding.

He'd dragged himself from that well of despair and was just settling into a different sort of life when he'd had to face Renny Augustino's brutal murder, Lisl's suicide, and the exhumation of Danny Gordon's living corpse.

Bill wasn't bouncing back this time. He wasn't sure he had any bounce left. He'd dragged himself back to New York but it was no longer home. No place was home. In this entire teeming city, Nick Quinn and Carol Treece were the only people left alive from his past that he dared approach.

"You've got to call him Rasalom and stop calling him Jimmy. Got to stop thinking of him as your son. He's not. There's nothing of you and Jim in him. He's someone else."

"I know that," she said, holding him tighter. "In my mind I know that. But in my heart is this feeling that if I'd loved him more, if I'd been a better mother, he'd have turned out differently. It's crazy, but I can't get away from it."

"Nothing anyone could have done in his childhood would have made the slightest bit of difference. Except maybe strangling him as an infant."

He felt Carol stiffen against him and was sorry he'd said it. But it was true.

"Don't."

"Okay. But stop calling him Jimmy. He's not Jimmy. Never was. His name is Rasalom and he was already who he was long before he took over the baby in your womb. Long before *you* were born. He didn't develop under your care. He was already there. You are *not* responsible."

He stood there in the middle of her tiny living room, holding Carol's thin body against him, breathing the scent of her hair, spying the streaks of gray nestling in the ash blond waves. Trickles of desire ran down his chest and over his abdomen. With a start, he felt himself hardening. He became aroused so easily these days. Sex had been no problem when he'd still considered himself a priest. But now that his lifelong beliefs had been reduced to ashes, buried with the charred remains of Danny Gordon, everything seemed to be slipping out of control. Here he was, his arms wrapped around Carol Treece, formerly Carol Stevens, née Carol Nevins. His high school sweetheart, his best friend's widow, now another man's wife. Priest or ex-priest, this wasn't right.

Gently, Bill put some space between them. *Room for the Holy Ghost,* as the nuns used to say when he was a kid.

"Are we straight on that?" He gazed into her blue eyes. "You're *not* responsible."

She nodded. "Right. But how can I stop feeling like his mother, Bill? Tell me how I can do that?"

He saw the pain in her eyes and resisted the urge to pull her into his arms again.

"I don't know, Carol. But you've got to learn. You'll go crazy if you don't." They looked at each other for a moment, then Bill changed the subject. "How's Nelson? Does he know yet?"

She shook her head and turned away.

"No. I haven't been able to tell him."

"Don't you think—?"

"You've met Nels. You know what he's like."

Bill nodded silently. He'd met Nelson Treece a number of times—he'd even been invited over here for dinner twice—but always as a priest and an old friend of the family. Nelson was a straight arrow, a comptroller in a computer software firm. A man who dotted all his *i*'s, crossed all his *t*'s, and whose numbers always added up. A good man, a decent man, an *organized* man. The antithesis of spontaneity. Bill doubted whether Nelson had ever done anything on impulse in his entire life.

So unlike Jim, Carol's first husband. Bill couldn't see Nelson Treece and Carol as a loving couple, but maybe that was because he didn't want to. Maybe

Nelson was just what she needed. After the way chaos had intruded repeatedly on Carol's life, maybe she needed the structure, stability, and predictability a man like Nelson offered. If he made her happy and secure, more power to him.

But that didn't make Bill want Carol any less.

"How can I tell him what we know?" she said. "He'll never accept it. He'll think I'm crazy. He'll have me going to psychiatrists. I wouldn't blame him. I'd probably be doing the same if positions were reversed."

"But now with the sun playing tricks, we've got an indisputable fact on our side. Carol, he's got to know sooner or later. I mean, if you're going to be involved—"

"Maybe if he met Glaeken. You know how persuasive he is. Maybe he could convince Nelson."

"It's worth a try. I'll talk to him about it. Maybe tonight—"

"Maybe not tonight. He's been away on a trip."

"Since when does he travel?"

"Just the past month or so. The company's been sending him. And when he comes back he crashes. I don't think he's built for travel. It . . . changes him."

What was she saying? Or rather, what was she *not* saying?

"I'm not following."

A shrug and a shy smile. "It's nothing. Just stress."

Bill glanced at his watch. "When's he due in?"

"Any minute. His flight from Denver should have landed about an hour ago."

"I'd better go."

"No, Bill." She took his hand and squeezed it. "Stay. Please."

Her touch shot a bolus of tingling warmth up his arm.

"I can't. I've got a bunch of errands to run for Glaeken. Now that Rasalom's made his first move, the old guy's looking for countermoves. He needs me to be his legs."

Bill gave her a quick hug and fled the apartment.

He hated lying to Carol. But how could he tell her that it ripped his heart out to see Nelson Treece stroll in the door and give her his usual casual hello kiss? Didn't Nelson realize what he had? Did he have any idea what Bill would give—*do*—to take his place?

He had another reason for wanting to leave. He was afraid to get too close to Carol, afraid to care too much. First and most obvious: She was married. But, more important, terrible things seemed to happen to people he cared about. All his emotional investments crashed.

Bill began looking for a place where he could have a quiet beer and sit alone in the dark.

Repairman Jack

Jack sat at his back-against-the-rear-wall table in Julio's, apart from the evening regulars, nursing a Stella and fuming.

Some low-rent scumbag had tried to put the moves on Gia this morning while she was waiting with Vicky for the school bus. At seven in the morning. Right in front of Vicky.

He couldn't get it out of his mind. Hoped the creep tried it again tomorrow. He planned to be across the street. Watching. Waiting.

Everything seemed to be going to hell. After a long period of relative peace, the city was becoming unmanageable again. Same all over the world. During the past year or so he'd witnessed a slow unraveling of the social fabric. He had a pretty good idea what was behind it. Or rather, who.

It had started last year with the advent of the Kickers, but had spread from there, going into overdrive since March. As if the worst sensed that something was coming and they'd better grab what they could while they still had time.

Too many people had begun acting as if nothing was beneath them. Rip off an old lady's handbag or a toddler's candy bar. No item too small, no deed too low. Everything up for grabs, anything okay if you got away with it—that was the operating ethic.

Mine was anything I could take and keep. If you put something down and left it unguarded, it became *mine* if I could snatch it and make off with it. Civilized folk were on the run. Those who could afford to were leaving, others were withdrawing, tightening their range of activities, limiting their hours in public. And those unfortunates who had to be out on the streets and down in the subways were fodder. And they knew it.

Like the city had gone back in time to the seventies and eighties.

On the way over tonight he'd passed car after car with "No Radio" signs in the windows. Every street was flanked with them. A symptom of the city-dwellers' response to the predators. With failing faith in City Hall's ability to make the streets safe, they retreated. When they parked their cars they removed their satellite units and took them into the steel-doored, barred-windowed fortresses they called home. One more piece of ground surrendered. They'd pulled all their belongings in from the street; after having shrubs and small trees repeatedly dug up and carted off from the fronts of their apartment houses, they'd stopped planting them, and they'd chained—*chained*—the trunks of the few larger ones that remained.

The Taint was taking over.

It all sickened Jack. He'd had it up to *here* with watching the good folks retreat. But maybe it served them right. They'd allowed themselves to be disarmed, surrendered all responsibility for their own safety until they'd been reduced to rabbits cowering in their burrows, praying the wolves wouldn't find them.

Jack sighed and sipped.

"Is this seat taken?"

Startled, Jack looked up and saw Glaeken standing across the table, one big hand holding his cane, the other resting on the back of a chair.

"How *do* you do that?"

The man could slip through a room like a ghost.

"Years of practice."

Years . . . right. More like millennia.

Julio ambled over, wiping his hands on a towel.

"Hey, G. The usual?"

"If you'd be so kind."

"Comin' up, meng."

"Make that two," Jack said.

Glaeken sniffed the air as he watched the muscular little man hustle back to the bar.

"I do believe he's managed to find a cologne worse than the last."

Jack nodded. "I think this one's Eau du Wet Stray Dog."

The old man looked older than ever as he dropped into the chair and stared at the tabletop.

"Something wrong?"

Glaeken looked up. "Wrong? Of course there's something wrong. Have you been in a cave all day?"

The snapping tone was uncharacteristic. Glaeken upset . . . not good. He never got upset.

"Let's pretend that's just where I've been. What's up?"

"The sun rose five minutes late this morning and set ten minutes early tonight."

The words hit him like a bucket of ice water.

It will begin in the heavens.

Rasalom's warning back in March.

March . . . the horror of that night in Glaeken's apartment. Weezy, Eddie, the Lady . . .

"Oh, hell."

"Exactly: Hell. How could you not have heard?"

Jack had glanced through Abe's newspapers at the shop this morning and spent the rest of the day setting up a fix over in Brooklyn.

"Guess it happened too late for the morning papers and I'm not much for radio and TV."

"It's all everybody's talking about."

Jack gestured to the crowd of Julio's regulars, yakking and yukking it up like any other night.

"Not here."

"This place has its own consensual reality. It doesn't count. But you know now, and I think you know what it means."

Jack nodded, feeling a little sick. "He's started his final moves, his end game."

"Yes, the Change . . ."

Why now, damn it? This conflict had been running for ages. Why did the final showdown have to come at a time when Gia and Vicky would be caught in the fray?

Julio returned with two pints of John Courage. He'd put it on tap for Jack a few years ago. Jack had moved on to other brews but Courage Amber had become such a hit with the regulars that Julio kept it running with privately imported kegs.

Glaeken lifted the glass with a big, scarred hand, quaffed about a quarter of its contents in one gulp, then loosed an appreciative burp.

"Not as good as when they first made it back in oh-two, but still tasty."

Jack knew he meant *1*902. He leaned forward. "What are our options?"

Glaeken sighed. "I'd hoped not to live to see this day. But ever since . . . that night, I've been doing some research, trying to prepare."

"And?"

"And I've found some of what we'll need, but not all."

"What have you got?"

Glaeken leaned back in the chair.

"Nothing yet. One is a person—a boy. I could not very well go to his mother and tell her our story without something tangible—without evidence that I'm not simply a crazy old man. What is happening to the sun will lend credence to what I must tell her."

Jack shook his head. "If she's got even one skeptical neuron in her brain, some fluctuations in the sun's timing aren't going to be near enough. A cosmic shadow war . . . that's going to be one hard sell."

"Not as hard as the one I'm going to ask of you."

Jack stiffened. "Don't like the sound of that. I'm not exactly the salesman type. Who's the projected sellee?"

"Someone you know: Kolabati Bahkti."

Kolabati . . . as much as Jack was devoted to Gia—now more than ever—unbidden memories of Kolabati's long, dark, slender body occasionally floated back to him.

Glaeken was eyeing him. "I'm trying to locate her."

"Can't help you there. Haven't seen her in years."

"Oh, I realize that. I'll find her eventually. And when I do, that's when I'll need your help."

"What for?"

"I need the necklaces."

"You're talking plural? As in *both*?" Jack shook his head. "You don't know what you're asking. Kolabati will never give them up. Not in a million years. I might talk her out of one, but never both."

"I'll need both. And soon."

"Then forget it. The necklace keeps her alive, keeps her young. She's on the downslope toward the end of her second century. But she looks only thirty or so. All because of the necklace. You think she's going to give that up?"

"That's why I've come to you. So you can convince her once I've located her."

"She'll die without it."

"I have faith that you'll return with both necklaces."

Jack stared at him. "You asking me to kill her?"

"I hope it won't come to that."

"But if it does?"

Glaeken didn't blink. "Then I'll leave that decision to you."

"News flash," Jack said, feeling a burst of heat. "That's the kind of decision that never was and never will be anybody else's."

"Of course. But will you go to her when I find her?"

Tough question.

"Depends."

"On what?"

"On where she is. If she's still in New York, sure. I'll do my best."

The thought of facing Kolabati . . . they had a history, but he'd locked it away. He didn't want her thinking he was back looking for a key.

"And if she's not nearby?"

"Well, then . . . I don't know."

Glaeken spread his hands. "With the stakes what they are, how can you refuse?"

"*Because* of the stakes—because I have no idea what Rasalom's got planned. If Bati's back in India, I'll have to leave Gia and Vicky here. What if the Change kicks in full speed while I'm away and I can't make it back?" The thought of those two facing the apocalypse without him . . . He shook his head. "Can't risk it."

"They can stay with me."

"Oh, swell. You're right in Rasalom's crosshairs—*numero uno* on his extermination list. That would really put my mind at ease." He noted Glaeken's steely gaze. "Don't take that personally. It's just that I don't consider camping out on a firing range the best way to keep from getting shot."

Glaeken sighed. "Point taken. But you can't believe you're the *only* one who can protect them."

"That's not the point. When they need me, I want to be there."

"Short term, that makes sense, but in the long term Kolabati's necklace might be a greater help to them."

"'Might' be."

"Yes. Might be. I can offer a little hope, but sadly, no guarantee. You must—"

Jack raised a hand. "Let's table this for some other time. If you find her and she's living in Hoboken, then this is all wasted air: Of course I'll go."

"And if she's in India?"

"Isn't there another way? What about the *Compendium*?" Immediately Jack wished he hadn't brought that up.

Glaeken lowered his gaze. "We lost our interpreter."

The words were a gut punch, bringing back the aching sense of loss he'd managed to hide from . . . well, most of the time.

"I miss her, Glaeken." His throat felt thick.

"So do I. The Lady too."

"Yeah. The Lady too."

He did miss the Lady, but nowhere near the way he missed Weezy. A hole in his life. Not the gaping chasm the loss of Gia and Vicky would leave, but a hole nonetheless.

"They made the ultimate sacrifice. So . . . if Kolabati's back in India?"

Jack's teeth clenched. "I told you—"

"Will you reconsider if Central Park shrinks?"

"Sure." That seemed a safe bet. "If you find her in India or someplace else on the far side of the globe, I'll go see her when Central Park shrinks."

"Fine," Glaeken said, nodding. "It's a deal then."

"Deal."

"Wonderful."

The old man finished off his Courage, rose, and dropped a Hamilton on the table.

"My treat. See you soon."

As Jack watched Glaeken make his way to the door, he thought about Kolabati and wondered how she was. Where she was. And what she was up to these days.

Kolabati

Maui—upcountry

The wind stopped.

Kolabati put down her book and rose from her chair. Not sure at first what had happened, she took her coffee cup and stepped out on the lanai where she stood for a moment, listening. Something was wrong. Too quiet. In her time on Maui she could not remember a truly silent moment. She had no neighbors to speak of, at least none within shouting or even bullhorn distance, but even when the birds and insects were silent, the Maui breeze whispered. Child of the tireless trade winds rolling from the northeast, its constant sussurrant undertone varied in pitch but never ceased—perpetual, interminable, timeless, relentless.

But it paused now. The ceramic wind chimes hung silent on the corners of the unscreened lanai. The air lay perfectly still, as if resting. Or holding its breath.

What was happening? First the news of the late sunrise this morning, and now this.

Kolabati looked down the slope of Haleakala past the rooftops of Kula to the valley spread out below in the late afternoon sun. A gently curved, almost flat span between the two volcanic masses that defined the island of Maui, the valley's narrow waist was checkered with the pale green squares of sugar cane, the darker green of pineapple plants, the rich red-brown of newly tilled earth, and the near black of a recently burned cane field. She spent part of each day out here staring across the valley at the cloud-capped West Maui Mountains, waiting for her daily rainbow, or watching the cloud-shadows run across the valley floor thousands of feet below. But no shadows ran now. The streaming trade winds that propelled them had stalled. The clouds and their shadows waited.

Kolabati waited too. The air should have grown warmer in the wind's absence, yet she felt a chill of foreboding. Something was wrong. The Maui breeze occasionally changed its pattern when the kona winds came, but the air always moved.

Krishna, Vishnu, she said, silently praying to the ancient gods of her youth, please don't let anything spoil this. Not now. Not when I've finally found peace.

Peace. Kolabati had searched for it all her life, and it had been a long life. She looked thirty, perhaps a youngish thirty-five, yet she had been born in 1848. She had ceased counting her birthdays after the one hundred fiftieth.

A long time to be searching for contentment. She thought she'd found a chance for it a few years ago with a man named Jack but he had spurned her and the gift of longevity she'd offered him. She'd left him sitting in a pool of his own blood, dying. He was probably dead, and the thought saddened her. Such a vital man . . .

But I'm different now.

The new Kolabati would have stayed and helped Jack, or at least called a doctor for him despite the cruel things he had said to her.

Maui had worked a change in her. Maui and Moki. A place and a man. Together they had given her what little peace could be found in this world.

Here on Maui, clinging to the breast of the world's largest dormant volcano, she had all the world within reach. If she tired of watching the valley below, cloud-dappled on sunny days, lashed by rain and speared by lightning when storms marched through, she could travel to the mountain's windward east coast and visit the jungles above Hana; farther around on the south slope she could pretend she was in the savannas of Africa or the plains of North America, grazing cattle and all; or she could travel across the valley and wander among the rich Japanese and American vacationers in the resorts at Ka'anapali and Kapalua, or travel into the Iao Valley and beyond to the rain forests of the second wettest spot in the world, or return to Haleakala itself and walk the floor of its desolate crater, wandering among its thousand-foot cinder cones and imagining she was exploring the surface of Mars.

Wonders were close at hand too. Directly below the lanai her silversword garden grew. She had transplanted the seedlings culled during her explorations of Haleakala's slopes and was perhaps unduly proud of her collection of the rare spiky clusters. Each would grow for twenty years before producing its one magnificent flower. Kolabati could wait. She had time.

She glanced down at the cup in her hands. Oh, yes. And coffee from the big island's Kona Coast—the richest coffee in the world. She sipped.

No, she could not see herself tiring of living here, even if she didn't have Moki. But Moki *was* here, and Moki gave meaning to it all.

She could hear him in the back now, working in his shop. Moki—her *kane*, her man. He carved driftwood. Together they would scour the beaches and the banks of Haleakala's countless streams and waterfalls, searching for branches and small trunks, the long-dead pieces, bleached and hardened by time and the elements. They'd bring these gnarled, weathered remains back to the house and set them up around Moki's workshop. There he would get to know them, live with them. And gradually he would spy things in them—the wrinkles around the eyes of an old woman's face, the curve of a panther's back, a lizard's claws. When he'd spied the form hiding within, he would bring his small ax and array of chisels into play, working *on* the wood and *with* the wood to expose the hidden form to the light of day.

Moki was modest about his art, never taking credit and refusing blame for the nature of the works he produced. His stock phrase: "It was already there in the wood; I simply cleared away the excess and set it free."

But he deserved far more credit. For Moki wasn't content to leave his work as simple sculptures. They were Hawaiian wood carved by an almost full-blooded Hawaiian, but that wasn't quite Hawaiian enough for Moki. When each was finished he shipped it to the big island and carried it to the fiery mouth of Kilauea, the active crater on the southeastern slope of Mauna Loa. There he trapped some of the living lava, poured it into a shape that complemented his sculpture, allowed the lava to cool to a point where it wouldn't damage the wood, then set his sculpture into the gooey stone.

Kolabati had first seen Moki's work with its intricate cuts and swirls and unique lava-rock bases in a Honolulu gallery. Fascinated, she had asked to meet the artist. She commissioned a piece and visited Moki many times during its fashioning. She found herself as taken by the man as by his work. His intensity, his passion for living, his love of his native islands. He was complete. In that sense he reminded her a little of her dead brother, Kusum.

Moki wanted her, but he didn't need her, and that made him all the more attractive. Theirs was a relationship of passionate equals. She didn't want to own Moki, didn't demand all his passion. She knew some of that had to be funneled into his art and she encouraged it. To dominate him, to possess him would risk destroying a wild and wonderful talent. By demanding all of him, she would wind up with less than she had begun with.

Moki needed his art, needed to be Moki, and very much needed to be Hawaiian. He would have loved to have lived and worked on Niihau, the forbidden island, oldest of the Hawaiian chain, but had not been able to wrangle an invitation from the last of the purebred Hawaiians living there in the old, primitive ways. Like most Hawaiians, Moki was not purebred—traces of Portuguese and Filipino slunk through his bloodline.

But he remained pure Hawaiian in his heart, dressing the part around their *hale* or house, speaking the old language and teaching it to Kolabati.

His pieces, the graceful and the grotesque, were scattered about the islands, in galleries, museums, corporate offices, and on every available surface in their house. Kolabati loved the clutter, which was unusual for her. As a rule she preferred an ordered existence. But not in this case. The clutter was Moki. It put his stamp on their home, made it truly theirs. No other place on earth was quite like it.

Kolabati did not want that to change. For the first time in her many years the nattering inner voice of dissatisfaction had fallen silent. For the first time she no longer hungered for new people, new sensations, new feelings, the Next New Thing. *Continuity* counted most now.

"Bati! *Hele mai!*"

Moki's voice, calling from his workshop, telling her to come to him. He sounded excited. She started toward the rear of the house but he was already coming her way.

The old Kolabati used to tire of a man after two weeks. They were all the same; so few had anything new to offer. But even after more than a year with Moki, the sight of him still excited her. His long, wild, red-brown hair—he was considered an *ehu*, a red-haired Hawaiian—his lean, light brown, muscled body, and his eyes as dark as her own. An artist, a sensitive man, as attuned to the mysteries of the wood he worked as to the mysteries within her own psyche. And yet he still retained an untamed quality, as witness the brief, loincloth-like *malo* he wore now. No two days were alike with Moki.

Which was why Kolabati called him her *kane* and allowed him to wear the other necklace.

And she loved his lilting accent.

"Bati, look!"

He held out his left palm to her. A ragged red line ran across it.

"Oh, Moki! What happened?"

"I cut myself."

"But you're always cutting yourself."

She looked at the cut. It was barely bleeding. He'd done worse to his hands before. What was so special about this?

"Yes, but this was a deep one. I slipped badly. I thought the chisel went halfway through my palm. Blood started spurting a foot into the air—and then it stopped. I squeezed it for a few minutes, and when I checked again, it was half healed. And in the time it took me to come in from the workshop, it's healed even further. Look at it. You can almost see it closing before your eyes!"

He was right. Kolabati watched with uneasy fascination as the wound stopped oozing and became shallower.

"What's going on?" he said.

"I don't know."

He touched the necklace around his throat—a heavy chain of sculpted iron, each crescent link embossed with pre-Vedic script; centered over the notch atop his breastbone lay a matched pair of bright yellow elliptical stones, like thumb-sized topazes, each with a black center. Moki's necklace perfectly matched her own. They'd belonged to her family for generations . . . since before history.

"You said these things would help heal us, keep us young and healthy, but I never—"

Unease tugged at her. "They don't work like this. They've never worked like this."

The necklace could heal illnesses, prolong life, stave off death from all but the most catastrophic injuries. But it worked slowly, subtly. The healing of Moki's hand was crude, garish, like a sideshow trick.

Something was wrong.

"But they work like this now," Moki said, a wild light in his eyes. "Watch."

That was when she saw the wood knife in his other hand. He jabbed it through the skin on the underside of his left forearm and into the tissues beneath.

"No! Moki, don't!"

"It's all right. Just wait a minute and I'll show you what I mean."

Wincing with the pain, he dragged the blade upward until a four-inch wound gaped open. He watched the blood spurt for an instant, then squeezed it shut. He smiled crazily at her for a moment or two as he pressed the skin edges together, then he released it.

The wound had stopped bleeding. The edges were adhering as if they'd been sutured. And the wild light in his eyes had brightened.

"See? The necklace has made me almost indestructible. Maybe immortal. I feel like a god—like Maui himself!"

Kolabati watched in horror as Moki cavorted about the great room. First the sun, then the wind, and now this. She could not fend off the feeling of impending doom. Something was happening, something had gone terribly awry, and the necklaces were responding. Their powers were increasing, as if in preparation for . . . what?

And then she heard it—the ceramic tinkling of the wind chimes on the lanai. She turned and hurried to the railing. Thank the gods! The wind! The wind was back!

But the wrong wind. This blew from the west. The trade winds came from the east, always from the east. Where did this wind come from? And where was it blowing?

At that moment Kolabati knew beyond a doubt that the world was beginning a change. But how? And why?

Then she felt rather than heard a deep seismic rumble. The lanai seemed to shudder beneath her feet.

Haleakala?

Could the old volcano be coming to life?

THURSDAY

WFPW-FM

FREDDY: Hey! What's going on up there, man? It says here sunrise was late again this morning. C'mon, sun! Get your act together. You were fifteen minutes late this morning. Get a new alarm clock already!

The Village of Monroe

Bill barely recognized his hometown.

He stared in awe as he cruised Monroe's morning-lit harbor front behind the wheel of Jack's Crown Victoria, borrowed for the trip. New condos crowded the east end, the trolley tracks had been paved over, and all the old Main Street buildings had been refurbished with nineteenth-century clapboard façades.

"This is awful," he said aloud.

In the passenger seat, Glaeken straightened and looked around.

"The traffic? It doesn't look so bad."

"Not the traffic—the town. What did they do to it?"

"I hear lots of towns are trying to attract tourists these days."

"But this is where I grew up. My home. And now it looks like a theme park . . . like someone's idea of an old whaling village."

"I never saw a whaling village that looked like this."

Bill glanced at Glaeken. "I guess you'd know, wouldn't you."

Glaeken said nothing.

Bill drove on, shaking his head in dismay at the changes. At least they'd left the old bricks on Town Hall, and hadn't changed the high white steeple of the Presbyterian church. He noticed with relief that Crosby's Marina was still there, and Memison's was still in business. *Some* of the old town was left, so he didn't feel completely lost.

But he'd come here today hoping for a burst of warmth, for a sense of belonging, a place to call home. He knew now he wasn't going to find it in Monroe.

Still, better than sitting around waiting, letting the unease within bubble and stew. Probably nothing he could do would block out the growing dread, especially after hearing that sunrise had been even later this morning.

"I still don't know why you need me along, other than as a driver."

He was uncomfortable wearing a cassock and collar again. The clothing fit, but only physically. He no longer considered himself a priest, not in his mind, not in his heart, not in his soul.

"Your mere presence will help me."

"But you're going to do all the talking and what am I going to do? Stand around and look holy?"

"You may say anything you wish."

"Thanks loads. But I'll be afraid to open my mouth because I don't know what's going on. You're playing this too close to the vest, Glaeken. You ought to know by now you can trust me. And maybe if I knew a little bit more about what we're doing here, I might be able to help."

Glaeken sighed. "You're right, of course. I don't mean to keep you in the dark. It's just habit. I've kept so many secrets for so long . . ." His voice trailed off.

"Well?"

"We've come to Monroe for the *Dat-tay-vao*."

Bill had to laugh. "Well! That clears up everything!"

"The name is Vietnamese. In truth, the *Dat-tay-vao* has no name. It is an elemental force, but it has wandered around Southeast Asia for so long that it's convenient to refer to it by the name the locals have used for centuries."

"*Dat-tay-vao*." Bill rolled the alien syllables over his tongue. "What's it mean?"

"Loosely translated, 'to lay a hand on.' There's an old Vietnamese folk song about it:

> *It seeks but will not be sought.*
> *It finds but will not be found.*
> *It holds the one who would touch,*

Who would cut away pain and ill.
But its blade cuts two ways
And will not be turned.
If you value your well-being,
Impede not its way.
Treat the Toucher doubly well,
For he bears the weight
Of the balance that must be struck.

It has better meter in the original language."

"A bit ominous, don't you think?"

"The song is a celebration and a warning. Twice a day, for an hour or so at a time, the one who possesses the *Dat-tay-vao*—or is possessed by the *Dat-tay-vao*, depending on how you look at it—can heal wounds, clear cancers, and cure illnesses with a touch."

Not too long ago, Bill would have scoffed. Today he remained silent, listening. His scoffing days were over.

"The *Dat-tay-vao* came to Monroe last year and became one with a local physician, Alan Bulmer."

"Sounds vaguely familiar. Wasn't he associated with Doc Alberts for a while?"

"Possibly. He's on his own now. Out of practice since the *Dat-tay-vao* enabled him to heal with a touch."

"That's it—*People* did an article on him last summer." He remembered leafing through the issue during a work break at Darnell U. "Hinted that he was a charlatan."

"He wasn't. And isn't. His cures were very real. He lives now with Sylvia Nash and her adopted son."

"Out on Shore Drive, you said?

Glaeken nodded. "Two ninety-seven."

"The high-rent district."

The old Hanley mansion was out on Shore Drive too. Bill repressed a shudder as memories of the horrors he'd witnessed there in 1968 flashed within his brain like distant lightning.

"The estate is called Toad Hall."

"Never heard of it. Must be new."

But as soon as he saw Toad Hall, Bill knew that it wasn't. Only the brass plaque on the right-hand brick gatepost was new. He recognized the place as one of the Preferred North Shore's most venerable mansions: the old Borg Estate. Three acres on the Long Island Sound surrounded by a stone wall and dense, insulating stands of white pine.

He turned into the driveway. The house itself was set far back, close to the water; a many-gabled affair, flanked by weeping willows. He hated the thought of someone renaming the old Borg place, but as he turned off the ignition and heard the briny breeze whisper through the swaying willow branches, he conceded that the new name might be right on target.

He accompanied Glaeken to the front door.

"It's a household of four," the old man said as they walked. "Mrs. Nash, Doctor Bulmer, a Vietnamese houseman named Ba Thuy Nguyen, and Jeffrey, Mrs. Nash's adopted son."

"You said yesterday we're looking for a boy. Is he the one?"

Glaeken nodded. "He is. And his mother is not going to like what I have to tell her."

"Why? What's he got that—?"

The front door opened as they stepped onto the porch. A tall, gaunt Asian towered in the doorway. This had to be Ba. His age was hard to judge: might be fifty, sixty, maybe older. His high-cheekboned face was expressionless, but his eyes were alert, active, darting back and forth between Glaeken and Bill, picking up details, assessing, measuring, categorizing. Bill knew someone else with eyes like that: Glaeken.

"Yes, sirs." His voice was thickly accented. "May I be of service?"

"Yes, you may." Glaeken fished a card out of his pocket. "My name is Veilleur. I believe Mrs. Nash is expecting me."

Ba stepped aside and ushered them through a marble-tiled foyer and into the living room. Doo-wop was playing softly through hidden speakers. A wave of nostalgia swept Bill away as he recognized "Story Untold" by the Nutmegs. He and Carol had danced to that song at CYO dances in the gym of Our Lady of Perpetual Sorrow, not a mile from here.

Ba's voice yanked him back to the present.

"I will tell the Missus that you are here. Do you wish coffee?"

They both agreed and remained standing by the cold fireplace as Ba turned and left them alone.

"That's one powerful-looking fellow," Bill said. "I don't think I've ever seen a Vietnamese that tall."

Glaeken nodded. "A one-man security force, I would say."

A slender woman with short black hair, blue eyes, and finely chiseled features strode into the room. She wore loose black slacks and a white blouse buttoned all the way to her throat. She moved with complete self-confidence.

"I'm Sylvia Nash. Which one of you is—?"

"I'm Veilleur," Glaeken said, stepping forward and offering his hand. "And this is Father William Ryan."

Her handshake was as cool as the rest of her. A striking woman.

Bill was making connections now. He'd heard of her. Greg Nash's widow. Bill had gone to high school with Pete Nash, Greg's older brother. Greg had been in the Gulf War. He'd come back in one piece, but then he'd been killed trying to break up a convenience store robbery. Sylvia had become a renowned sculptress. And obviously a very successful one if she could afford this place.

"Please sit down," she said, gesturing to the couch. She seated herself across from them. "You said you had something of a personal nature to discuss with me. I hope that wasn't a scam to get in here and try to sell me something."

Bill glanced up at Ba as he returned with a silver coffee service set on a huge silver tray; he pitied anyone who tried any tricks in this house.

"I assure you I have nothing to sell," Glaeken said. "I've come to talk to you about the *Dat-tay-vao*."

The big Vietnamese started as he was setting down the silver tray. He almost spilled the coffeepot but righted it in time. He stared at Glaeken but his eyes were unreadable. Bill glanced at Sylvia. Her face was ashen.

"Ba," she said in a shaky voice. "Please get Alan."

"Yes, Missus."

Ba turned to go but at that moment a man in a wheelchair rolled into the room. He looked lean, pale, with gray-flecked brown hair and gentle brown eyes. He paused on the threshold, staring at Glaeken, a puzzled look on his face, then he came the rest of the way in. As the wheelchair rolled to a stop beside her chair, Sylvia reached over and grasped the man's hand. They shared a smile. Bill immediately sensed a powerful bond between these two. Sylvia introduced him as Dr. Alan Bulmer.

"They want to talk about the *Dat-tay-vao*, Alan."

Bill felt the weight of Bulmer's gaze as he stared at them.

"You'd better not be reporters."

Bill recognized a deep loathing in his tone as he spoke the last word.

Glaeken said, "I assure you, we're not."

Bulmer seemed to accept that. The old man had a gift for speaking the truth in a way that *sounded* like the truth.

"What do you know—or think you know?" the doctor said.

"Everything."

"I doubt it."

"I know that your present condition is a direct result of your association with the *Dat-tay-vao*."

"Really."

"Yes. I know that the *Dat-tay-vao* left Vietnam in late nineteen sixty-eight within a medic named Walter Erskine who couldn't handle the responsibility and became a derelict alcoholic—"

A flash of memory strobed Bill's brain. Years ago . . . the parking lot of Downstate Medical Center . . . two winos, one was Martin Spano, the other a bearded stranger named Walter . . . *Walter was a medic once* . . . repeatedly asking, *Are you the one?* Could it have been . . . ?

"—but before he died, Erskine passed the *Dat-tay-vao* on to you. You used the power of the *Dat-tay-vao* to cure a great number of people—too many people for your own good. As a result—"

Bulmer looked uncomfortable as he held up his hand.

"Okay. Score one for you."

"May I ask if you regret your time with the *Dat-tay-vao*?"

Bulmer paused, then: "I've thought about that a lot, believe me. It left me half vegetable, but that appears to be only temporary. With therapy I'm working my way back to full function. My arms and hands are as good as they ever were, and my legs are starting to come around. The *Dat-tay-vao* helped me cure—*cure*—a hell of a lot of people with an incredible array of illnesses— acute, chronic, debilitating, life-threatening. And in the process Sylvia and I found each other. A year or two of rehab is a small price to pay for that."

Bill knew then and there that this man operated on a different plane from most—and he liked him enormously for it.

"May I ask then—?" Glaeken stopped speaking and looked to his right.

A small boy stood in the living room entryway. He looked about nine; a round face, curly blond hair, and piercing blue eyes. He reminded Bill of another child from what seemed like another epoch . . . Danny.

The child's gaze roamed over the occupants of the room . . . and came to rest on Glaeken.

"Hello, Jeffy," Sylvia said. She obviously didn't want him listening to this. "Is anything wrong?"

"I came to see who was here."

He walked past Bulmer and his mother and stopped before Glaeken where he sat on the couch. For a long moment he stared almost vacantly into the old man's eyes, then threw his arms around Glaeken's neck and hugged him.

Sylvia found herself on her feet, stepping toward Jeffy and Mr. Veilleur who was returning the hug, gently patting the boy's back. This wasn't like Jeffy at all. He was usually so shy. What had got into him?

"Jeffy?" She restrained her hands from reaching for him. "I'm very sorry, Mister Veilleur. He's never done this before."

"Quite all right," Veilleur said, looking up at her over Jeffy's shoulder. "I'm rather honored."

He gently pulled Jeffy's arms from around his neck, engulfed one of the child's little hands in his own, and patted the couch cushion next to him.

"Want to sit here between me and Father Bill?"

Jeffy nodded, his eyes huge. "Yes."

He snuggled between them.

"Good."

Sylvia sat again but remained perched on the edge of the chair. She tried to catch Jeffy's attention but he had eyes only for Veilleur.

This whole scene made her uneasy.

"He used to be autistic," she said.

Jeffy had made such strides since his sudden release from autism, but he was still backward socially. He was learning, but remained unsure how to act, so he wasn't comfortable with strangers. Until now, apparently.

"I know," Veilleur said. "And I know that Doctor Bulmer's final act with the *Dat-tay-vao* was to cure Jeffy."

Sylvia glanced at Alan. His expression mirrored her own alarm and confusion. How did this stranger know so much about them? It gave her the creeps.

"All right," Alan said, shrugging resignedly. "So you do know about the *Dat-tay-vao*. But I'm afraid you're too late. I don't have that power anymore. The *Dat-tay-vao* is gone."

"The *Dat-tay-vao* has left you," Veilleur said, "but it is not gone."

Sylvia sensed Ba stiffen where he stood behind her. Why was he suddenly on the alert?

"That may be," she said. "But I still don't see what we can do for you."

"Not what you can do for me—for everyone. We are entering a time of great strife, of darkness and madness. The days are getting shorter when they should be lengthening. The *Dat-tay-vao* can help forestall that. Maybe even prevent it."

Sylvia glanced at Alan again. He nodded imperceptibly. This poor old man had blown a few fuses. She darted a glance at the priest—a good-looking man, older than Alan, with graying hair, a scarred face, and a nose that looked as if it had been badly broken. She wondered if he'd ever been a boxer. She also wondered how he could sit there with a straight face. Unless he was as crazy as the old fellow. Ever since yesterday's news of the sun's erratic behavior, the kooks had been coming out of the woodwork, predicting the end of the world and worse. And to think she had let two of them into her house.

And then she saw something flash in the priest's eyes. A look of tortured weariness, as if he'd seen too much already and was dreading the time to come.

"But I told you," Alan said. "The *Dat-tay-vao* is gone."

"Gone from you, yes." Veilleur put his arm around Jeffy. "But it hasn't traveled far."

Sylvia shot to her feet, fighting the panic vaulting within her. She let anger take its place.

"Out! I want you out of here! Both of you. *Now!*"

"Mrs. Nash," the priest said, rising. "We mean no harm—to anyone."

"Fine. Good. But I want you both to leave. I have nothing to say to either of you, nothing more to discuss."

The priest pointed to Veilleur. "This man is trying to help you—help us all. Please listen to him."

"Please leave now, Father Ryan. Don't force me to have Ba eject you."

She looked at Ba. Over the years she'd learned to read his usually expressionless face. What she saw there now was reluctance. Why? Did he want them to stay? Did he want to hear them out?

No. It didn't matter what Ba wanted in this situation. She had to get them out of here. Now.

She strode through the foyer and opened the front door. With obvious reluctance, the old man and the priest made their exit. On the way out, Mr. Veilleur left a card on the hall table.

"For when you change your mind," he said.

He sounded so sure, she found herself unable to frame a reply. As she slammed the door behind them, she heard the sound of Alan's wheelchair rolling toward her.

"Kind of rough on them, weren't you?"

"You heard them. They're crazy." She stepped to one of the sidelights flanking the front door and watched the old man and the priest stand by their car in the driveway. "They might be dangerous."

"They might be. But neither of them struck me that way. And that old fellow—he knew an awful lot about the *Dat-tay-vao*. All of it accurate."

"But his end-of-the-world stuff . . . about a time of 'darkness and madness.' That's crazy talk."

"I recall someone who reacted exactly the same way when I told her that I had the power to heal with a touch."

Sylvia remembered how she'd thought Alan had gone off the deep end then. But this was different.

"You weren't talking about doomsday."

The priest and the old man were getting into the car.

"True. But *some*thing's happening, Sylvia. It's spring, yet the days are getting shorter, and the scientists can't say why. Maybe we are heading for some sort of apocalypse. Maybe we should have listened a little longer. That man *knows* something."

"He doesn't know anything I care to hear. Certainly not doomsday nonsense."

"That's not what you're afraid of, is it, Sylvia?"

She turned and faced him. She still wasn't used to seeing Alan in a wheelchair. She *refused* to become used to it. Because Alan wouldn't be in it forever. The *Dat-tay-vao* had left him in a coma last summer, but he had fought back. And he was still fighting. That was why she loved him. He was a fighter. His will was as strong as hers. He'd never admit defeat.

"What do you mean?"

She knew exactly what he meant, and because of that she had trouble meeting his gaze.

"We've skirted around this for months now, but we've never really faced it."

"Alan, please." She stepped up beside the wheelchair and ran her fingers gently through his hair, then trailed them down to his neck, hoping to distract him. She didn't want to think about this. "Please don't."

But Alan wasn't going to be put off this time.

"Where's the *Dat-tay-vao*, Sylvia? Where did it go? We know it transferred from Erskine to me as he died. We know I still had it when it cured Jeffy of his autism. But when I came out of the coma in the hospital, it was gone. I can't cure anymore, Sylvia. The tide comes in and my touch is no different from anybody else's. So where'd it go? Where's the *Dat-tay-vao* now?"

"Who knows?" she said, angry that he was pushing her like this, forcing her to face the greatest fear of her life. "Maybe it died. Maybe it just evaporated."

"I don't believe that and neither do you. We've got to face it, Sylvia. When it left me it went to someone else. There were only three other people in the house that night. We know you don't have the Touch, and neither does Ba. That leaves only one other possibility."

She wrapped her hands around his head and pressed it against her abdomen. No! Please don't say it!

The possibility had kept her awake far into so many nights, and it skulked through her dreams when she finally did manage to drop off to sleep.

"You saw how Jeffy responded to Mr. Veilleur. He's attuned to him. So am I, I think. I just didn't happen into the living room earlier. I was *drawn.* And when I saw that old man I felt this burst of warmth. I can only guess at what Jeffy felt."

She heard a noise over by the window and looked.

Jeffy was there, pressing his face and hands against the glass.

"I want to go with him, Mom. I want to *go!*"

Bill was disappointed and found it difficult to hide his irritation. This whole trip had been for nothing.

"Well," he said, glancing at Glaeken, "that was a fiasco."

The old man was staring out the side window at the house. He did not turn to Bill as he spoke.

"It didn't go quite as I'd hoped, but I wouldn't say it was a fiasco."

"How could it have gone worse? She kicked us out."

"I expect resistance from the people I must recruit. After all, I'm asking them to believe that human civilization, such as it is, is on the brink of annihilation, and to put their trust in me, a perfect stranger. That's a difficult pill to swallow. Mrs. Nash's dose is doubly bitter."

"I gather you think this *Dat-tay-vao* is in Jeffy."

"I know it is."

"Well, then, I think you've got a real selling job ahead of you. Because it's pretty clear that not only does that woman not believe it, she doesn't *want* to believe it."

"She will. As the Change progresses she will have no choice but to believe. And then she will bring me the boy."

"Let's hope she doesn't wait too long."

Glaeken nodded, still staring at the house. "Let's hope that the *Dat-tay-vao* and the other components are enough to make a difference."

Bill fought the despondency as he felt it return.

"In other words, all this—everything you're trying to do—might be for nothing."

"Yes. It might. But even the trying counts for something. And I met the boy today. Contact with him will help me locate someone I have been searching for. That was a good thing."

"He took to you like I've rarely seen a child take to a strange adult."

"Oh, that wasn't Jeffy himself responding to me. That was the *Dat-tay-vao* within him." Glaeken turned from the window and smiled at Bill. "We're old friends, you see."

Over his shoulder, in the window next to the mansion's front door, Bill spotted the little boy's face pressed against the glass, staring at them.

WFAN-AM

Well, for those of you keeping track, the sun set early again tonight. Should've gone down at 8:06 but it was gone by 7:35. That means the lights'll come on a little earlier tonight here at Citi Field as the Mets meet the Phillies. A lot of our listeners are concerned as to how all this will affect the playing season . . .

The First Hole

Rasalom stands on the plot of grass in the heart of the city and looks up at the surrounding buildings. Their lights blot out the wheeling stars overhead, nearly blot out the rising moon. He stares at the top-floor windows of a particular building in the nearest row to the west. Glaeken's building. Glaeken's windows.

"Do you see me, old man?" he whispers to the night. "Or if your feeble, failing eyes can't penetrate the shadows, do you at least sense my presence? I hope so. I began in the sky where all could see. Now I move to the earth. Here. Under your nose. I don't want you to miss a thing, Glaeken. I want you front-row center from the overture to the final curtain.

"Watch."

Rasalom spreads his arms straight out on each side, forming a human cross. The left is truncated, missing the hand, but that is only temporary. He faces his right palm down. With a basso rumble, the ground begins to fall away beneath his feet, plummeting as if dropped from a cliff. But he does not fall. The opening widens beneath him yet he remains suspended in air as more earth, tons of earth crumble and tumble . . .

. . . down . . .

. . . down . . .

. . . out of sight.

Yet there is no sound of any of it striking bottom.

And when the hole has reached half of its intended width, Rasalom allows himself to sink into the abyss. Slowly. Gently.

"Do you see me, Glaeken? Do you SEE?"

Manhattan

The city was getting nuttier by the minute.

Jack ambled past the darkened Museum of Natural History and headed south on Central Park West. On the corner of 74th a bearded guy dressed in sackcloth stood holding a placard. Straight out of a *New Yorker* cartoon. His laboriously hand-printed sign bellowed "REPENT!" in giant letters at the top followed by a biblical quote so long you'd have to stop and read for a good three minutes before you got it all.

Yeah, the world might be coming to an end, but spring had sprung, and spring meant baseball, and the start of the baseball season meant it was time once again for the annual Repairman Jack Little League Park-a-Thon. Time to stroll Central Park and tempt the muggers out of hiding so they could give to the local Little League equipment fund. Give till it hurt.

Come to think of it, he'd met Glaeken during last year's Park-a-Thon.

As he crossed CPW he heard a deep rumble. Thunder? The sky was clear. Maybe a storm was gathering over Jersey.

He entered the Park at 72nd Street, got on the jogging path, and continued south. A young teenage couple, certainly not seventeen yet, appeared, faces pale and strained, running like the girl's father was after them. They weren't joggers—weren't dressed for it. In fact, they seemed to be buttoning up their clothing as they ran.

Jack stepped off the path to let them pass.

"S'up?"

"Earthquake!" the boy said, his voice a breathless whisper.

Jack walked on. He'd heard of making the earth move—he'd had it move for him a couple of times—but it was nothing to panic over. The quake in 2011 had been a nonevent.

Half a minute later another guy ran by and said the same thing.

"Where?" Jack hadn't felt anything.

"Sheep Meadow!"

"But what—?"

The guy was gone, running like a madman.

Curious now, Jack broke into a loping run and cut off the jogging path. He skirted the lake until he reached the wide expanse of grass in the lower third of the park called the Sheep Meadow. He'd heard that real sheep used to graze these fifteen acres as late as the 1930s. In the wan starlight he could make out a ragged, broken line of murmuring people rimming the area. And smack in the center of the meadow, what looked like a pool of inky liquid. But nothing reflected off its surface. A huge circle of empty blackness.

Tar?

Jack paused. Something about that black pool raised his hackles. An instinctive fear surged up from the most primitive parts of his being. He'd experienced something similar when he'd seen his first rakosh. But this was different. This was a hell of a lot bigger.

He forced his feet to move, to carry him toward the pool. He could make out the figures of a couple of people at the edge and they seemed all right, so he guessed it was safe.

As he neared, Jack realized it wasn't a pool at all. A huge sinkhole, a good hundred feet across, had opened in the middle of the meadow.

He skidded to a halt on the grass.

A hole . . .

He had a bad history with holes in the earth during the past couple of years. One in Monroe had almost swallowed him, and another in Florida had released some nasty creatures into the Everglades. Both had been connected with the Otherness, and now the Otherness was on the march.

Maybe this was something else, something innocent.

Yeah, right.

Two guys there ahead of him stood on the edge, laughing, jostling each other. Jack could see they were young, dressed head to toe in black, with spiky hair. He stopped behind them. No way he wanted to get that close.

One of the guys on the rim turned and spotted him.

"Hey, dude, c'mon up here. You gotta see this. It's fuckin' *awesome,* man!"

"Yeah!" said the other. "The *mother* of all potholes!"

They started laughing and elbowing each other again.

Wrecked.

"That's okay. I can see all I want from here."

Which was mostly true. In the wash of light from the tall buildings ringing the lower end of the park, Jack could make out a sheer wall on the far side of the hole leading straight down through the sod, the topsoil, and the granite bedrock. The edge of the hole was clean.

He'd seen pictures of sinkholes before on the news, from places like Guatemala where the underground water had been tapped out. But he'd never seen one so perfectly round. This looked like it had been made with a King Kong cookie cutter. Manhattan's bedrock—he could almost hear his dear, lost Weezy correcting him that it was called "schist"—was near the surface here. Could sinkholes occur in solid granite? Didn't think so.

Otherness . . . definitely the Otherness.

The two kids were still fooling around, dancing on the edge, playing macho games. Jack was moving to his right, away from them, trying to position the light-bleed from Central Park West behind him for a better look, when he heard a yelp of terror.

He saw one of the kids leaning forward over the edge, his arms windmilling. Even from Jack's distance it was plain he was overbalanced and no longer fooling around, but his buddy only stood beside him, laughing at his antics.

His laughter died with the first kid's scream as he toppled headfirst into the hole.

"Jason! Oh, shit! Jason!"

He lunged for his friend's foot, missed it, and Jason disappeared into the blackness. His scream was awful to hear, not merely for the blood-chilling terror it carried, but for its length. The cry seemed to go on forever, echoing up endlessly from below as Jason plummeted into the depths. It never really ended. It simply . . . faded . . . out . . .

His friend was on his hands and knees at the edge, looking down into the blackness.

"Oh, fuck, Jason! Where are you?" He turned to Jack. "How deep *is* this fuckin' thing?"

Jack didn't answer. If this one held true to the others he'd seen, it was bottomless.

He stepped to within half a dozen feet of the kid, got down on his belly, and crawled to the edge. He'd seen light deep down in the others—not a bottom, just light . . . a hazy violet glow. Maybe he'd see that—

Vertigo hit him like a gut punch as he peeked over and saw nothing but impenetrable blackness.

Jack closed his eyes and hung on. And as he did he thought he could still hear Jason screaming down there . . . way, way down there . . . fading . . .

He felt a slight breeze against the back of his neck. Air was flowing into the hole. *Into* the hole. That meant it had to go somewhere, be open at the other end. He had a good idea where that might be.

And then the earth began to slide away beneath his fingers, beneath his wrists, his forearms. Christ! The rim was giving way.

Jack rolled to his left and back, away from the edge, but he wasn't fast enough. A Cadillac-sized wedge of earth gave way and crumbled beneath him. He slid downward toward the black maw. With a desperate, panicky lunge he managed to grab a fistful of turf and hang on. His feet kicked empty air and for one breathless moment he felt eternity beckoning from below. Then the toes of his sneakers found the rocky wall. He levered himself up to ground level and scrambled away from the edge as fast as his rubbery knees would carry him.

When he'd gone a good fifty feet he heard a terrified cry and risked a look back. Jason's buddy had stayed behind and the edge had given way under him. Most of his body had dropped into the hole. Jack could see his head, see his arms and hands tearing at the grass in a losing effort to hold on.

"Help me, man!" he cried in a voice all tears and terror. "God, *please!*"

Jack started to unbutton his shirt, thinking he might be able to use it as a rope. But before he was halfway done, a huge clump of earth gave way beneath the kid's hands and he was gone, leaving behind only a fading high-pitched wail.

More earth sloughed off and fell away, narrowing the distance between Jack and the edge. The damn hole was getting bigger.

He looked around. The few people who had been scattered around the perimeter of the Sheep Meadow were now fleeing for the streets. Good idea, Jack thought. A *fine* idea. He broke into a headlong run and followed them.

And as he ran it occurred to him that a big chunk of Central Park was missing. What was it Glaeken had said last night?

Will you reconsider if Central Park shrinks?

Sure, he'd said.

Jack didn't remember his high school geometry, so he couldn't even guess the surface area of that hole, but a helluva lot of the Sheep Meadow was missing. Which meant the park was smaller by that many square feet.

. . . if Central Park shrinks . . .

Jack picked up his pace. How had Glaeken known?

He shook his head. Stupid question.

Arms limp at his sides, Rasalom floats within a tiny pocket in the bedrock, a pocket he has made. When he descended approximately a hundred feet into the pit, he stopped and hovered as a passage into the stone opened before him. He followed it to this spot.

Yesterday he began the Change without. Now to begin the Change within.

He hesitates. This is a step from which there is no return. This is a process that once begun cannot be reversed, cannot be halted. When it is complete he will have a new form, one he will wear into eternity.

He will be magnificent.

Still he hesitates. For the shape of his new form will not be of his own choosing. Those above—those puny, frightened creatures milling on the surface—will determine his countenance. He shall be an amalgam of all that they fear. For as their fear feeds him, so shall it shape him. His form shall be the common denominator of all that humanity loathes and dreads most, the personification of all its nightmares. The deepest fears from the darkest recesses of the fetid primordial swamps of their hindbrains. Everything that causes the hairs at the back of the neck to rise, makes the flesh along the spine crawl, urges the bowels and bladder to empty. He shall be all of them.

Fear incarnate.

Rasalom's body tilts until he is floating horizontally in the tight granite pocket. He spreads his legs and rams his feet against the stone wall. He screams as they fuse with the living rock, screams as all the fears, the angers, the hatreds, hostilities, violence, pain, and grief from the city surge into him. He stretches his arms and fuses his right fist and the stump of his left wrist to the stone, and screams again. A scream of ecstasy as new power surges through him, but a scream of agony as well. For now the Change within has begun.

He swells. His skin stretches, then splits along his arms and legs, tears from his genitals to his scalp. As he continues to swell, the skin sloughs off and falls to the floor of the stone pocket like a discarded wrapper.

As the night air caresses his raw flesh, Rasalom screams again with what remains of his mouth.

FRIDAY

In Profundis

WNYW-TV

—the sun's behavior continues to baffle astronomers, physicists, and cosmologists. We've been informed that it rose at 5:46 this morning, late again, this time by almost nineteen minutes.

And from Central Park, startling news of a huge hole opening in the Sheep Meadow during the night. We have a camera crew on the scene and you'll see live footage as soon as it is available . . .

Manhattan

Glaeken stood at the picture window and looked down on the hole. Flashing red lights lit the tardy dawn as police cars and fire trucks ringed the lower end of the park. A barricade had been set up around the entire Sheep Meadow to keep out the curious throngs. Television vans and camera trucks spewed miles of cable and aimed lights that lit the area to noon brightness. Dominating the center of the scene was the hole. It had grown to two hundred feet across and stopped.

He closed his eyes to shut out the sight of it—just for a moment. He swayed with fatigue. He ached for sleep, but when he lay down it spurned his bidding.

So tired. He'd thought he'd freed himself from this, escaped the burden of responsibility for this war. But it wouldn't go away. Only when his successor was empowered would he truly be free.

Jack was the successor, the Heir. The Lady had known it, and Glaeken had no doubt of it. Even Rasalom knew.

Under the old rules—when the Ally was still present—the succession would have occurred automatically with Glaeken's last breath. But now, with the Ally turned away, his death would accomplish nothing.

He needed the weapon.

He'd expected some difficulty in reassembling its components, but the task was proving to be more formidable than he'd imagined.

The weapon would empower Jack and pass the reins to him.

That was the hope: first the weapon, then the succession, then the battle. A battle that, from the looks of things, would be lost before it was begun. But he had to go through the motions, had to try.

Behind him he heard Bill hang up the phone and approach the window. Glaeken opened his eyes and rubbed a hand across his face. Had to appear calm and in control at all times. Couldn't let them see the doubt, the dread, the desperation that nipped at his heels. How could he exhort them to maintain belief in themselves if he didn't set the example?

"Finally got through to Nick," Bill said, coming up beside him. "He's on his way down to the park with a team from the university."

"What for?"

"To find out what caused the hole."

"I can save him the trip. Rasalom caused the hole."

"That's not going to do it for Nick." He gazed down at the park. "I guess this is what you meant when you said his next move would be in the earth."

Glaeken nodded. "And its placement is not random."

"Really? Central Park has some significance for Rasalom?"

"Only so far as Central Park is located right outside my window."

Going to rub my face in it, aren't you, Rasalom?

"It doesn't look real," Bill said. "I feel like I'm in a movie looking at some sort of computer-generated effect."

"It's quite real, believe me."

"I do. They've got close-ups on the TV, by the way. Want to take a look?"

"I've seen others like it close up before, although never one this big."

"You have? When?"

"Long ago." *Ages.*

"How deep is that thing?"

"Bottomless."

Bill smiled. "No. Really."

Apparently he'd misunderstood, so Glaeken spoke slowly and clearly.

"There is no bottom to that hole, Bill. It is quite literally bottomless."

"But that's impossible. It would have to go all the way through to China or whatever's on the other end."

"The other end doesn't open on this world."

"Come on. Where then?"

"Elsewhere."

Glaeken watched the priest's eyes flick back and forth between him and the hole.

"Elsewhere? Where's elsewhere?"

"The place has no name. We call it the Otherness, but I don't believe there's any way to describe in human terms what the other end of that hole is like."

"I believe I'll change and go down there for a closer look."

"No need to rush. The hole isn't going anywhere. And it's only the first."

"You mean there's going to be more?"

"Many. All over the world. But Rasalom has honored me by opening the first outside my front door."

"I'll see if I can hook up with Nick down there and find out what he knows."

"Just be sure to be back before dark."

Bill smiled. "Okay, Dad."

"I'm quite serious."

His smile faded. "Yeah. I guess you are. Okay. Back before dark."

Glaeken watched Bill hurry to his room. He was fond of the man. He couldn't ask for a better houseguest. Always willing to help around the apartment or with Magda when the nurse wasn't around.

As if sensing her name within his thoughts, Magda called from the bedroom.

"Hello? Is anybody there? Have I been left alone to die?"

"Coming, dear."

He took one final look at the hole, then headed down the hall.

He found Magda sitting up in her bed. She'd been losing weight and her eyes were starting to retreat into her skull. Her face was as lined as his, her hair as white. But her brown eyes were bright with anger.

"Who are you?" she said, switching to her native Hungarian tongue.

"I'm your husband, Magda."

"No, you're not!" She spat the words. "I wouldn't marry such an old man like you! Why, you're old enough to be my father! Where's Glenn?"

"Right here. I'm Glenn."

"No! Glenn's young and strong with red hair!"

He took her hands in his. "Magda, it's me. Glenn."

Terror flashed across her face, then her features softened. She smiled.

"Oh, yes. Glenn. How could I have forgotten? Where have you been?"

"Right in the next room."

Her expression hardened as her eyes narrowed.

"No you weren't! You've been out seeing other women! Don't deny it! You're out with that nurse! Don't think I don't know what the two of you are up to when you think I'm asleep!"

Glaeken held her hands and let her ramble on. He wanted to cry. After two years he'd have thought he could have adapted to anything, but he couldn't get used to Magda's dementia. None of her ravings were true, yet Magda fully believed the delusions floating through the expanding vacuum of her mind, truly meant the hurtful things she said as she spoke them. They never failed to cut him deeply.

Oh, Magda, my Magda, where have you gone?

Glaeken closed his eyes and recalled her as she had been when they'd met in 1941. Her soft, even features, her fresh pale skin, glossy chestnut hair, and wide dark eyes filled with love, tenderness, and intelligence. It was the love, tenderness, and intelligence he mourned for most now. Even after her physical beauty had faded, his love for her had not. For she had remained Magda the poet, Magda the singer, Magda the mandolin player, Magda the scholar who so loved art and music and literature. Her compendium of Romanian Gypsy music, *Songs of the Rom,* was still in print, still gracing the shelves of finer bookstores.

Three years ago she started to slip away, infiltrated and irreversibly replaced by this mad, incoherent stranger. Her mental status deteriorated first, but soon she became physically enfeebled as well. She could not get out of bed by herself now. That made caring for her easier in a way because she could no longer wander at night. In the early stages of her decline Glaeken had found her searching the street below, calling for their pet cat, dead since 1962. After that he'd had to deadbolt the apartment door and remove the knobs from the stove to prevent her from cooking "dinner" at two in the morning.

The old, buried Magda occasionally flickered back to life. She couldn't remember what she had for breakfast—or if she'd even *had* breakfast—yet now and then she'd recall an incident in their life together from thirty or forty years ago as if it were yesterday. But instead of buoying Glaeken, the brief lapses in her dementia only deepened his despair.

It wasn't fair.

Glaeken had known and loved so many women through the ages, yet each relationship had ended in bitterness. Each love had, in her own way, ended up hating him as she grew old while he stayed young. Finally he had found Magda, the one woman in his seemingly endless life that he'd be allowed to grow old with. And they'd had a glorious life, a love that could not be tainted even by the pain of these past few years.

Maybe it was for the best. Magda would spend her final days immune to the horror stalking the world. Her body was as vulnerable as everybody else's, but her mind was impregnable to reality.

He glanced over and saw that she'd fallen asleep again. This was her pattern—a reversal of day and night. Catnaps throughout the day, awake most of the night. Even with the hired nurse and Bill to help, Glaeken existed in a state of constant exhaustion. His heart went out to all the unfortunate spouses of Alzheimer's patients throughout the world who did not have his financial resources. Unless they had a large family of willing helpers, their lives were an endless nightmare.

Nightmare . . . soon everyone across the globe would know what it was like to live a nightmare.

Gently he laid Magda's head back down on the pillow and tucked the covers in around her. He would not allow a deterioration of her brain to lessen his commitment to her. If their conditions were reversed, she'd be at his side whenever he needed her. He was sure of it. And he would do no less.

All morning he had debated whether or not to warn the media about the hole. Finally, he'd decided against it. He didn't want to attract attention to himself. Besides, they'd write him off as just another doom-monger. The end result would be the same: They'd have to learn the hard way.

CNBC

—on the commodities exchanges, due to uncertainties about the upcoming growing season, prices are up sharply, especially October beans and orange juice futures, in brisk trading around the globe . . .

Nick felt someone tugging at his arm. Reluctantly, he turned away from the hole to face one of the park cops.

"You Doctor Quinn?" the guy said, shouting over the rattle and roar of the generators.

"Yeah. What's up?"

"Got a priest back in the crowd says you asked him here to say some prayers."

"Priest?" Nick said, baffled. "I didn't ask for any—" And then he knew. He almost laughed in the cop's face. "Oh, yeah. I've been waiting for him. Can you bring him over?"

The cop turned and waved to someone along the barricade. Nick saw a lone figure in black break from the crowd and approach at a quick walk.

He shook Father Bill's hand when he arrived. He'd seen the priest a couple of times since his return from North Carolina but still couldn't get used to how he'd aged during his years in hiding. Before he disappeared, Nick had got to the point where he'd been calling the priest simply "Bill," but since his return he'd fallen back into the practice of prefixing the name with "Father." He pointed to the cassock and Roman collar.

"I thought you weren't going to wear that anymore."

"So did I. But I've decided the uniform has its uses. Especially when you want special treatment in a crowd."

"So what are you doing here?"

Father Bill smiled. "I came to perform the exorcism. To close this thing up."

"Very funny."

The smile faded. "Seriously, Nick. I would like to get a close-up look at the hole."

"Sure. But stay on the platform. The dirt tends to crumble at the edges."

Nick felt the excitement build all over again as he led Father Bill to the edge of the wooden platform. He still couldn't get over it. Something like this—a mysterious two-hundred-foot-wide hole appearing here, practically in his backyard. It was wonderful.

They stopped at the railing and looked down. He heard Father Bill catch his breath.

"Incredible, isn't it?" Nick said. "I can't believe my luck. And that's all it is. Luck. If I'd been out getting coffee when the boys from geology called this morning, someone else might have picked up the phone and he'd be calling the shots here now instead of me. Being in the right place at the right time. That's all it takes."

But Father Bill said nothing. He seemed to be mesmerized by the hole.

Nick knew what the priest was feeling. He'd looked down into that opening a good hundred times since he'd arrived and still couldn't shake how unnatural it seemed.

The walls did it. Too sheer. They didn't look fallen away—more like *scooped* away. He could see the layers of earth and schist stacked like the cut edge of a trifle. When he'd first looked down he'd expected to see a sort of inverted cone with a rubble-filled bottom. But he couldn't see the bottom. The hole was much deeper than he'd imagined. Half a mile down, he guessed. Maybe deeper. Straight down into darkness. Maybe when the sun got higher they'd be able to see more, but right now it was night down there.

Nick had visited the Grand Canyon last summer and still remembered the vertigo he'd experienced standing at the edge of the lookout for the first time. The giddy, vertical descent of these walls gave him a similar sensation. But he'd been able to see a ribbon of water at the base of the Grand Canyon. Here, with the gentle downdraft flowing around him, he could see only blackness.

The downdraft had bothered him at first. Where could it be going? Then he realized that the air was probably sinking into the cavity at the edges, and then reversing and flowing out straight up through the center. Like the bubbles in a glass of Guinness. That had to be the explanation. It couldn't all be flowing continually downward. It had no place to go.

He straightened and turned to the priest.

"Well? What do you think of our little sand pit?"

The priest tore his gaze away and looked at him. He looked frightened.

"How'd it get here, Nick?"

"Don't know. That's for the geology boys to figure out. But already people are making comparisons to those crop circles in England. The tabloids will have a field day. I think *The Light* has got its whole staff here already."

"Any idea how deep it is?"

"We don't know yet. Geology rigged up a sonic range-finder first thing this morning and pointed it at the bottom, but couldn't get a reading."

"No bottom?" The priest's voice suddenly sounded a little dry.

Nick laughed. "Of course there's a bottom. It's just that echoes from the side walls were interfering with the readings. Geology was stumped, so they called physics—*moi*. We could wait till the sun hits zenith and do a sight measurement, but why wait? We've got a new laser that'll bounce a beam off the bottom and give us a distance reading accurate to within a centimeter."

Father Bill was staring into the hole again as he spoke.

"I have it on good authority that it's bottomless."

"Well, it *is* deep, but not *that* deep. Guarantee it." And then a thought struck him. "This authority wouldn't be the same one that told you about something happening 'in the heavens' now, would it?"

As Father Bill nodded, Nick felt a cold weight settle between his shoulder blades. He gestured toward the hole.

"Come on, now. Bottomless? You can't really believe that."

"I never believed the sun would be rising progressively later each day in mid spring either. Did you?"

"No, but . . ."

Bottomless? No way. Patently impossible.

Someone tapped him on the shoulder. He turned and found one of the grad students.

"We're ready to shoot."

"Great." He turned to Father Bill. "The laser's set. Wait here. In a few minutes we'll have a reading from the bottom—wherever it is."

Bill watched a moment as Nick hurried away toward some odd-looking contraption suspended on a boom over the hole. He was proud of him. He'd come a long way from the bratty little nine-year-old orphan he'd played chess with back in his early days at St. Francis Home for Boys. He was mature and self-assured— at least in the field of physics. He wondered how he was faring socially. Bill knew Nick was more than a little self-conscious about his appearance—the misshapen skull from when he was abused as an infant, the old acne scars. But worse-looking men had found the girl of their dreams and lived happily ever after. He hoped that would happen for Nick soon.

He turned back to the hole and stared into its black depths.

What was that Nietzsche quote? *If thou gaze into the abyss, the abyss will also gaze into thee.*

That was how he now felt—as if he were gazing inward at his own reclusive darkness. The abyss expanded before him, beckoning. What mysteries, what horrors were sequestered in those misty, chaotic depths? For an instant he was gripped by a mad impulse to step off the edge and let himself fall. If it was truly bottomless as Glaeken had said, he would keep falling. And falling. Imagine the vistas, the wonders he'd see. What would he find? Himself? An endless voyage of self-discovery. How wonderful. How could anyone resist? How on Earth could anyone with an iota of character refuse? How—?

"Better be careful, Father."

The voice jolted him out of the reverie. To his horror he found himself sitting astride the platform railing, readying to swing his other leg over. The depths loomed below. With a convulsive lunge, he hurled himself back onto the platform and squatted there panting, sweating, and shaking. He looked up and saw one of the city workers standing nearby, looking down at him.

"You okay, Father?"

"I will be in a minute."

"Hey, I din't mean t'scare ya, but I mean we built that railing as sturdy as we could, but it ain't gonna hold a guy your size, know what I mean?"

Bill nodded as he rose shakily to his feet.

"I realize that. Thanks for the warning." *Thanks more than you know.*

The workman waved and ambled off, leaving Bill alone on the platform. He pulled himself together and moved away from the edge.

What had happened a moment ago? What had he been doing sitting on that railing? Had he actually been readying to jump? What could he have been thinking?

Or had he been thinking at all? More like reacting—but to what? To the abyss?

He shuddered. Maybe coming down here hadn't been such a good idea. He'd now seen the hole up close. He could watch further developments from Glaeken's window or on the tube. He looked around for Nick and saw him walking his way, his expression troubled.

"What's wrong, Nick?"

" 'Technical difficulties,' as they say on TV. We'll have it straightened out in a few minutes."

Bill watched Nick's face closely. His upper lip was beaded with perspiration.

"You didn't get the reading you expected, did you."

"We didn't get *any* reading. A glitch in the receiver, that's all."

Bill allowed himself a quick shot of relief. He wanted very much for Nick to find the bottom of that hole. He wanted Glaeken to be wrong, just once. Not out of animosity or envy, but because Glaeken had been right about everything so far, and everything he was predicting was bad. Bill felt he'd be able to rest a little better at night if just once Glaeken was proven wrong.

And then a thought struck him like an icy wind, carrying off any sense of relief.

"Wait a minute, Nick. You said you didn't receive *any* signal. Isn't that what would happen if the hole was bottomless?"

"It's not bottomless, Fa—"

"*Isn't* that what would happen?"

"Well . . . yes. But that's not the only reason. There are scores of reasons why we wouldn't get a signal back."

"But one of them is that the beam didn't find anything to bounce off, and so therefore it never came back. Am I right?"

Nick sighed. "Technically, yes, but . . ." Suddenly he sounded tired. "But the hole's not bottomless. It can't be. Nothing's bottomless."

One of the grad students rushed up to Nick with a green-striped printout. Bill could tell from Nick's expression that he didn't like what he saw there. He handed the slip back to the student.

"Do it again. And do it right."

"But we are," the student said, looking offended. "Everything checks out a hundred percent. The beam and the receiver are working perfectly."

Nick tapped the printout. "Obviously not."

"Maybe something down there's absorbing the beam."

"Absorbing the beam," Nick said slowly. He seemed to like the idea. "Let's look into that." He turned to Bill. "I'm going to be tied up for a while, Father, but hang around. We'll crack this yet." He winked and walked away.

At midafternoon Bill headed back to the apartment to grab a bite and make a pit stop before Nick started his descent.

He had to hand it to Nick—he was as inventive as he was stubborn. Wouldn't admit defeat. When he'd learned of a working diving bell on display down at South Street Seaport, he made a few calls and arranged to rent it. His plan was to get in that thing and ride it as far into the hole as the cable would allow, then take another laser reading from down there. Bill wanted to be back in time to see him off.

He had to fight through the crowd on Central Park West. The area around the lower end of the park had become an impromptu street festival. Well, why not? The sun was out and the area was jammed with curious people. Anyone with anything to sell, from hot dogs to shish kebab, from balloons to knock-off Rolexes was there. The air was redolent of an array of ethnic foods wide enough to shame the UN cafeteria. He spotted someone hawking "I saw the Central Park Hole" T-shirts, still wet from the silk screener.

In the apartment he found Glaeken, as expected, at the picture window.

"What have they decided down there?" the old man said without turning.

"They've decided that due to various technical glitches they can't figure out how deep it is at this time."

Even at noon, with the sun shining directly into the hole, they hadn't been able to see the bottom. The blackness had been driven farther down, but it remained, obscuring the bottom.

Now Glaeken turned. His smile was rueful.

"They've constructed these fabulous instruments for exact measurements, yet they refuse to believe the data they're receiving. Amazing how the mind resists the truth when the truth conflicts with preconceptions."

"I can't really blame them. It's not easy to accept the impossible."

"I suppose. But impossible is a useless word now." He turned back to the window. "What's that they're rigging up?"

"A derrick. Nick's going down into the hole to—"

Glaeken spun and faced Bill, his eyes wide.

"You're talking about your young friend? He's going down into the hole?"

"Yes. As soon as the bell is set up."

Glaeken grabbed Bill's upper arms. His grip was like iron.

"Don't let him do it. You've got to stop him. Don't let him go into that hole!"

The look on his face made Bill afraid for Nick. Very afraid. He turned and ran for the door. Out in the hall, he pressed the elevator button. When the doors didn't open immediately, he ran for the stairs. No time to wait. He made it down and out to the street in a few minutes, but there his progress came to a grinding halt. The crowd had grown even thicker. Pressing through them was like wading through taffy.

He fought a rising panic as he roughly pushed and shoved people aside, leaving an angry wake. He hadn't waited around to ask Glaeken what might happen to Nick down in that hole. The look on the old man's perpetually dead-pan face told him more than he wanted to know. He'd never seen Glaeken react that way.

As he inched toward the Sheep Meadow he remembered Nick saying how lucky he felt to be here. But Bill couldn't help thinking about the awful fates that had befallen all those other people he cared about.

His gut writhed with the thought that perhaps luck had nothing to do with it.

"Lights, camera, action!" Nick said as the diving bell lurched into motion.

Dr. Dan Buckley gave him a wan smile and gripped one of the hand rungs. Buckley was an older gent from geology, balding, white-haired, sixty at least. He had his camcorder hooked up and directed out one of the forward ports; a digital Nikon hung from his neck. He was sweating. Nick wondered if Buckley was prone to panic attacks. The bell, named *Triton,* was the size of a small, low-ceilinged bathroom. Not a happy place for a claustrophobe.

His stomach did a little spin as the bell swung out over the hole. He'd never liked amusement park rides and this was starting out like one.

He peered through the aft port to his right to double-check the laser range finder mounted there. Everything looked secure. He glanced out the other port toward the crane and the crowd of cops, workers, various city officials, and the other members of the teams from the university. He saw Father Bill push his way to the front and start jumping and waving and shouting. He'd been late coming back but at least he'd made it. Nick was glad to have him here to see this. He waved back and gave him a thumbs-up through the glass, then settled down for the ride.

This was great. This was fabulous. This was the most exciting thing that had ever happened to him.

"All set in there?" said a tinny voice from the speaker overhead.

"All set," Nick said. Buckley echoed the same.

A sick second of free fall, then they were on their way, sinking into the depths on a steel cable. The sunlight changed to shadow. The alternating floodlights and spotlights ringing the bell's equator were already on, illuminating the near wall. Buckley pressed his camera against his porthole, snapping shot after shot of the passing strata with his Nikon.

"Can you hear us up there?" Nick said.

"Loud and clear, Triton," came the reply. *"How's it going?"*

"Smooth as can be. And fascinating. The city ought to consider buying this rig and making it into an amusement ride. Might keep taxes down."

He heard appreciative laughter from above and smiled. That sounded pretty cool and collected, didn't it? He hoped so. Cynthia Hayes was up there, watching and waiting with the others from the department. He hoped she'd heard it, hoped she was impressed.

This little jaunt was going to make a name for Nicholas Quinn, Ph.D. The press would see to that. A mob of reporters was waiting up top, and he knew as soon as he stepped out of the bell they'd be all over him with a million questions. He'd be on all the news shows tonight, both the early and late. Maybe even the networks. Most guys in his spot—Nick could think of three from his own department right off—would be figuring out how they could parlay this into a major step up in their career. He almost laughed at his own narrow vision. He was wondering how to parlay it into an opportunity to ask Cynthia out. If he was famous, how could she say no?

The intercom popped him out of a Cynthia daydream.

"You're at the halfway mark, Triton. *How're you doing?"*

Halfway. They had ten thousand feet of cable up there. Almost a mile down and still no bottom. This was incredible.

"Fine," Nick said. "Can you still see us?"

"Yeah, but you're just a little blob of light down there now."

What could have caused a hole like this? Could it be natural? Something extraterrestrial maybe? Say, that was a thought. It did seem like an artifact. What if—?

Buckley's voice drew him back to reality again.

"Can we get these lights any brighter?" he said to the intercom.

"They're at max. What's the problem, Triton?"

"The wall's fading from view."

"You're out of sight now. Want to stop?"

Nick looked out his port. Black out there. The beams from the floodlights didn't seem to be going anywhere; the blackness swallowed the light within a few yards of the bulbs. The spots weren't doing much better—bright shafts poking a dozen or so feet into the darkness and then disappearing.

No, wait—ten feet into the darkness. No . . .

Nick swallowed hard. The darkness was edging in on the lights, overcoming, *devouring* the illumination.

"What's wrong with the lights?" Buckley said, his voice tremulous.

"I don't know." His own voice didn't sound too steady either.

"They're losing power."

Nick didn't think so. The darkness . . . something about it was overpowering the light, gobbling it up. Something thick and oily about it. The blackness seemed to move out there beyond the ports, almost seemed alive. Alive and hungry.

He shook himself. What kind of thinking was that?

But this blackness was certainly unusual, and probably the reason the laser signal had never returned. He smiled. Bottomless indeed! This weird old hole was deeper than it had any right to be, but it wasn't bottomless.

"We need more power to the lights!" Buckley said to the intercom.

Pure black out there now. All illumination was *gone.*

"You got it all, Triton. If there's an electrical problem we'll bring you back up and try again tomorrow."

"Not till I get at least one reading off the laser," Nick said.

He started flipping switches on the controls and noticed that his hands were trembling. Had the temperature dropped? He glanced at Buckley as he fastened a flash attachment to his camera.

"You cold?"

Buckley nodded. "Yeah, now that you mention it." His breath steamed in the air. "You get your reading, I'll try a couple of flash shots through the ports, then we'll get back upstairs."

"You've got a deal."

Nick suddenly wanted very much to be out of this hole and into the sunlight again. He adjusted the laser settings, triggered it, and waited for the readout. And waited.

Nothing.

Buckley tried a few flash photos out his port while Nick rechecked his settings. Everything looked fine.

"This is useless!" Buckley said, irritably snatching his camera away from the glass. "Like black bean soup out there."

Nick glanced out his port. The blackness seemed to press against the outer glass, as if it wanted to get in.

Nick fired the laser again. And again nothing. Nothing was coming back. Damn! Maybe the laser wasn't getting through the blackness or maybe the hole was indeed bottomless. Right now he was too cold to care.

"That does it," Nick said. "I'm through. Let's get out of here."

"Take us up!" Buckley shouted.

"Say again, Triton," said the speaker in the ceiling. *"We've got static on this end."*

Buckley repeated the message but no reply came through. The bell did not halt its descent.

Nick was frightened now. The walls of the *Triton* seemed to close in on him. And it was colder. And . . .

. . . darker?

"Did the lights just dim?" Buckley said.

Nick could only nod. His tongue felt glued to the roof of his mouth.

"Take us up, goddammit!" Buckley screamed, banging on the steel wall of the bell with his fist. *"Up!"*

"Okay, Triton," came the matter-of-fact reply. *"Will do."*

But they didn't stop, didn't even slow their descent. They continued down, ever downward.

And it was getting darker by the second.

"Oh, my God, Quinn!" Buckley said in a hushed voice teetering on the edge of panic. "What's happening?"

Finally Nick found his voice. He tried to keep it calm as the cold and the darkness grew . . . and Buckley began to fade from view.

"I don't know. But one thing I do know is we've got to stay calm. Something's wrong with the intercom up there. But they've got only so much cable. They can send us down just so far, and then they'll have to bring us up. So let's just be cool and hang in there and we'll be okay."

Darkness had control of the *Triton* now, within and without. Nick couldn't see his hand in front of his face. He was losing his sense of direction, of up and down. His stomach threatened to heave.

"Quinn?" Buckley's voice seemed to come from some point outside the walls of the bell. "You still there?"

Nick forced a laugh. "No. I just stepped outside for a cigarette."

And suddenly he sensed more than darkness between them. Something solid. An entity, a *presence*. Beside him, around him, touching him. And it was cold and evil and filled Nick with an unnameable dread that threatened to kick his bowels loose in his pants. He wanted to cry, he wanted Father Bill, he wanted to go home, he wanted the drugged-up mother who'd tried to kick his head in when he was three months old, *anything* but this!

And then Buckley's flash went off and they both screamed out their souls when they saw what had moved in to share the bell with them.

"Everything's fine. Don't reel us in yet. Play the cable out to the end."

Bill heard the voice over the loudspeaker and froze. That wasn't Nick's voice. And it wasn't the other scientist's either. It was a new voice—different.

He scanned the faces in the control area. No one was reacting. Someone replied, "Okay, *Triton*. Will do."

What was wrong with them? It was a different voice! Couldn't they hear that?

Something familiar about it too. He'd heard it before, but where? The answer was tantalizingly close. And then he heard it again.

"That's it," said the loudspeaker in that same voice. *"Just keep us going down."*

Suddenly Bill knew. And the realization nearly drove him to his knees.

Rafe! It was Rafe's voice! Rafe, Jimmy Stevens, Rasalom, whatever his name was, it was *him*! The one Glaeken called the Adversary. The one who was shrinking the daylight, who'd dug this huge wormhole in the earth. He'd tortured Bill for years in many forms and many voices, and the voice on that speaker was the one he'd used as Rafe Losmara. No mistake. Its sound still echoed through his dreams. Rasalom was controlling that diving bell—and God knew what he was doing to Nick!

Bill forced his wobbly legs into a run toward the control area.

"Bring them up! Bring them up now!"

The scientists and technicians started at the sound of his shouts. They looked at him as if he were crazy.

"Who the hell are you?" someone said.

"A friend of Nick Quinn's. And that wasn't his voice just then. Couldn't you hear that?"

"Of course it was Nick's voice," said a thirtyish woman with short brown hair. "I've worked with him for years and that was Nick."

Beside her, an older man with perfectly combed hair nodded in agreement.

"That was Nick, all right."

"I'm telling you it wasn't. Reel them back up, dammit! Something's happening in there! Get them up!"

Someone grabbed his arms from behind and he heard a mix of voices talking over and under each other: *Who is he? . . . Get security . . . Says he's a friend of Nick's . . . I don't care if he's Quinn's mother, get him out of here!*

Bill was hustled away from the control area. The security guards were going to take him back to the edge of the Sheep Meadow but he pleaded with them to let him stay near the hole, swore that he wouldn't say another word or go near the control area again. The Roman collar and cassock paid off again. They let him stay.

But it was torture to stand there and listen to that voice tell them to send the bell deeper and deeper into the hole. Did it sound like Nick to everyone else? Was he the only one who could hear the Rafe voice? Why? Another game being played with his head?

He wanted to scream, to charge the derrick cab and wrest the controls from the operator and drag that bell back up to the light. But he had about as much chance of succeeding in that as he had of leaping to the far side of the hole itself. So he stood among the crowd of privileged onlookers and silently endured the clawed terror that lacerated the inner walls of his heart.

Finally, the cable reached its end. No matter what the voice told them now, the bell could descend no farther.

But the voice was silent.

Bill noticed a flurry of activity in the control area. He sidled in that direction through the crowd. He intercepted a student hurrying away from the area and caught his arm.

"What's happening?"

"The *Triton*—they're not answering!"

Bill let him go and stood there feeling cold and frightened and useless as the derrick reversed its gears and began to reel in the *Triton*. The rewind seemed to take forever. During the interval an ambulance and an EMS van roared into the Sheep Meadow with their howlers going full blast. Finally the bell hove into view again. When it was swung away from the hole and settled onto the platform near the edge, the people from the control area surged toward it.

Bill pushed his way to the front of the crowd until his belly pressed against one of the blue "Police Line" horses that rimmed the area. He stood next to a dark-haired man in a white suit who carried a walking stick wrapped in some sort of black hide. Together they watched the workers spin the winged lug nuts on the hatch, swing it open, and peer inside.

Somebody screamed. Bill clutched the rough wood of the horse and felt his heart double its already mad pounding. A flurry of activity erupted around the bell, people grabbing their phones, frantically waving the EMS van forward.

Good God, something had happened to Nick! He'd never forgive himself for not getting here in time to stop him.

A pair of EMTs, stethoscopes around their necks, drug boxes and life packs in each hand, rushed forward as a limp figure was eased through the hatch. Bill craned his neck to see through the throng. He sighed with relief when he saw that the injured man was white-haired and balding. Not Nick, thank God. The other one. They stretched him out prone on the platform and began pumping on his chest.

But where was Nick?

Bill spotted more activity around the hatch. They were carrying—no, *leading*—someone else out. It was Nick. Nick, thank God! He was on his feet, coming out under his own steam.

Then Bill got a look at his face. Red—blood on his face, on his lips, dribbling down his chin. He'd cut his lower lip—looked more like he'd *chewed* it.

But it was Nick's eyes that drove the air from Bill's lungs in a cry of horror. They were wide open and utterly vacant. Whatever he'd seen down there, whatever had happened, it had driven away all intelligence and sanity, sent it fleeing into the deepest, most obscure corners of his mind.

"Nick!"

He bent to slip under the barricade but one of the security cops was watching him.

"Stay back there, Father!" he warned. "You come through there an' I'll have to toss you in the wagon."

He ground his teeth in frustration but straightened up behind the barricade. He'd be no help to Nick in jail. And Nick was going to need him.

"Do you know him?" the white-suited man next to him said with a slight German accent.

Bill only nodded and stood quietly as they led the stumbling, drooling young man to the waiting ambulance. Those mad, empty eyes. What had he seen down there?

And then, as Nick came even with him, his eyes suddenly focused. He turned his head to stare at Bill. Then he grinned—a wide, bloody-mouthed rictus, totally devoid of humor.

Bill started in horror, pressing back against the people behind him. And then as suddenly as it had appeared, the grimace was gone. The light faded from Nick's eyes and he stumbled away toward the waiting ambulance.

"Most entertaining," said the man in the white suit, then turned and walked away.

Bill fought an urge to take a swing at him. Instead, he watched, weak, trembling, as they loaded Nick in the back of an ambulance. Then he fought through the crowd and began to follow the rig on foot as it headed east across the grass. Finally he saw the name on its side: *Columbia-Presbyterian*. He ran for Fifth Avenue, looking for a cab to take him to the hospital, all the while fighting the feeling that he'd lived through this horror once already. He didn't know if he could survive a second round.

WFPW-FM

FREDDY: Bad news from Central Park, folks. Those two guys who went down into that big hole in a diving bell ran into some trouble.

JO: Yeah. One of them had a heart attack and the other got pretty sick. They're saying they think there was some problem with the air supply. We'll let you know more about it as soon as we hear.

FREDDY: Right. Meanwhile, here's a classic Beatles tune for all those people working out there in the Sheep Meadow.

<cue "Fixing a Hole">

"When's this other guy arriving?"

"I'm not sure," Glaeken said.

He looked up from the couch to where Jack stood at the picture window staring out at the park. Everyone who came to this apartment was drawn to that window, including Glaeken himself. The vista had always been breathtaking. With that hole in the Sheep Meadow now, it had become captivating.

Jack wore slightly wrinkled beige slacks and a lightweight Jets shirt hanging down to the tops of his thighs—loose, Glaeken knew, to hide the pistol holstered in the small of his back. Average height, brown hair with a low hairline, and deceptively mild brown eyes. You would not pick him out of a crowd; in fact his manner of dress, his whole demeanor was geared toward unobtrusiveness. This man could dog your steps all day long and you'd never notice him.

Glaeken liked Jack. More than liked. He'd known him only a year or so but felt a rapport with him on a very fundamental level. Perhaps because Jack reminded him of himself in another era, another epoch, when he was that age. A warrior. He sensed the strength coiled within the man; not mere physical strength, although he knew plenty of that hid in his wiry muscles, but inner toughness, a resolve to see a task through to the end. He had the strength, too, to question himself, to examine his motives and actions and wonder at the wisdom, the sanity of the life he had chosen for himself.

The Heir.

But he saw a downside to Jack taking his place. He was unruly and untamed. He recognized no master, no authority over himself. He followed his own code. And he was angry. Too angry, perhaps. At times the cold fire of his rage fairly lit the room.

Still, Glaeken desperately needed his services. Jack was the only one in this world who had any chance of retrieving the ancient necklaces. Glaeken knew he had to be at his most convincing here.

"How long are we going to wait for him?" Jack said, turning from the window.

"He should be here. I have a feeling he might have been delayed by a sick friend."

Glaeken had watched on TV as the diving bell returned from the depths. It continually amazed him how much one could experience through television without ever leaving the living room. When the first footprints were stamped into the surface of the moon, he had been there watching via television, just as he had been watching an hour or so ago when Bill's friend and the other scientist had been removed from the bell. The other man, a Dr. Buckley, was dead of cardiac arrest, and Dr. Quinn had been rushed to an emergency room in shock. Glaeken assumed that Bill had followed.

Too bad—for Bill's friend, and because Glaeken had wanted Bill present.

Jack dropped into a chair opposite Glaeken.

"Let's get on with it. You mentioned the necklaces again. You're not still set on getting hold of them, are you?"

"Yes. I'm afraid they're an absolute necessity."

Jack jumped from the chair and stepped to the window again.

"Well, the damn park *is* smaller, isn't it? I mean, it's lost whatever amount of surface area that hole swallowed, so it *has* shrunk, just like you said." He turned and stared at Glaeken. "How did you know?"

"Lucky guess."

"Yeah. Right. But you're going to need more than a lucky guess to find Kolabati and those necklaces."

"I've learned exactly where she is."

Jack sat down again.

"Where?"

"She's living on Maui, on the northwest slope of Haleakala, above Kula. And she has both necklaces with her."

He shook his head. "Too far."

"You can make the round trip in two days. The sooner you leave, the sooner you can be back."

He drummed his fingers on his thighs. "I don't know . . ."

"Jack—"

"How'd you find out? Two nights ago you hadn't the faintest idea where she was."

"I ran into an old acquaintance who happened to know."

"How convenient."

"Not really. I sought out this acquaintance."

Glaeken allowed himself a tight little smile and said no more. Let Jack assume that the acquaintance was a person. The truth was that when he had touched that boy Jeffy yesterday, he made contact with the *Dat-tay-vao*, and in a flash that contact revealed the whereabouts of the necklaces. For the *Dat-tay-vao* always knew their location. They had been intimately linked once. He hoped, with the cooperation of men like Jack, he could soon reunite them.

"And you want me to go there and convince Kolabati to give them up so she can turn into an old hag and die."

"I want you to get them. Simply get them."

"Killing her is out."

"Even if it means the destruction of life as we know it?"

"If she were doing the destroying it would be a different story. No problem. But her life's on the line too."

Glaeken pointed to the window. "That hole out there is only the first. Many more will follow—*countless* holes. Sooner or later one of them will bring about the death of one you love. Those necklaces will go a long way toward stopping that."

Jack blew out a breath. "You don't have to remind me. But putting a bullet through her brain and then looting her body?" He shook his head. "Can't see it."

Glaeken hadn't liked mixing Gia and Vicky into the conversation, but he wanted to see how Jack would react. He was pleased. Jack had lines he wouldn't cross. Now to try another tack.

"You've been known to steal things back for people, I believe?"

Jack drummed his fingers on the arms. "On occasion."

"Very well: Those necklaces—or rather, the metal they were made from— originally belonged to me."

Jack shook his head slowly. "I know for a fact that those necklaces date from pre-Vedic times, and that they've been in her family for generations. And believe me, hers is a family with *long* generations."

"Still, it is true. The source material was stolen from me long, long ago."

Jack rubbed his eyes and shook his head as if to clear it. "Yours, huh. Well, you do have a few years behind you."

"A few. I need that metal."

"Is this like the metal in the katana?" The word seemed to taste bad to him. "That belonged to you too originally."

Glaeken understood Jack's reaction. That blade had killed the Lady and Weezy and her brother as well.

"Yes, and we need it too. But though its metal is not of this Earth, it lacks qualities unique to those necklaces."

After a lengthy pause, "All right, I'll think about that angle. I'm not committing to running off to Maui yet, but in the meantime I could use some detailed drawings of the necklaces."

"You know what they look like."

"Yeah, but I might have to flash them around. Got any?"

"I can have them for you tomorrow."

Jack rose from the chair. "Let me know."

"It's almost sundown," Glaeken said as Jack headed for the door. "Go straight home."

He smiled. "Why? Vampires on the loose?"

"No. Worse. Do not go out after dark, especially near that hole."

Jack waved as he went out the door.

Glaeken hoped he heeded. He truly liked the man; and he needed him. He didn't want him hurt.

De Profundis

WNYW-TV

This is Charles Burge reporting live from the Sheep Meadow in Central Park. It's been quiet here since the tragedy this afternoon, but that doesn't mean nothing's been happening. If you look behind me you'll notice that the crowds are gone. That's because along about 5:30 or so, the downdraft that's been flowing into the hole changed to an updraft. And boy, let me tell you, it doesn't smell good here. A rotten odor permeates the air. Anyone who doesn't have to be here has gone. And I'll be going too. See you in the studio soon, Warren.

Washington Heights

"Physically, he checks out fine," the neurology resident said. "Overweight, cholesterol and triglycerides on the high side, otherwise all his numbers, scans, and reflexes check out."

Bill swallowed and asked the dreaded question that had plagued him since he'd seen Nick's blank expression and empty eyes. It reminded him too much of a similar sight years ago.

"He's . . . he's not hollow, is he?"

The resident gave him a funny look. "*Hollow?* No, he's not hollow. Where'd you get an idea like that?"

"Never mind. Just a recurring nightmare. Go on."

"Right. As I was saying, he checks out physically, but"—he waved his hand before Nick's unresponsive eyes—"the Force is definitely not with him."

The nametag read *R. O'Neill, M.D.* He wore an earring and his hair was braided at the back.

Not exactly Marcus Welby, Bill thought, but he seemed to know what he was about.

"He's in shock," Bill said.

"Well . . . shock to you isn't shock to me. Shock to me means he's prostrate, his blood pressure's hit bottom, his kidneys are shutting down, and so on. That's not our friend here."

Bill glanced over to where Nick sat on the edge of the bed. The emergency room physicians and the consultants had unanimously recommended that, at the very least, he be kept overnight for observation. The university had wrangled a private room for him, very much like a sitting room, with a small picture window, a sofa, a couple of chairs, and of course a hospital bed. Nick looked a lot better. His lower lip had been sutured; he'd been cleaned up and fitted into a hospital gown. But his eyes were still as vacant as a drive-in theater on a sunny afternoon.

"What's wrong with him, then?"

"Hysteria? Acute withdrawal? That's for the psych boys to figure out. I'm here to say it's not medical, not neurological. It's the windmills of his mind—they aren't turning."

"Thank you for that astute observation. How about the other man who went down in the bell with him?"

Dr. O'Neill shrugged. "Haven't heard a thing."

Nick said, "He's dead, you know."

Bill started at the sound. Nick's eyes weren't exactly focused, but they weren't completely empty. And he wasn't grinning as he had before when they were leading him to the ambulance. His expression was neutral. Still, the sound of Nick's voice, so flat and expressionless, gave him a chill.

"Great!" said Dr. O'Neill. "He's coming around already." He picked up Nick's chart and headed for the door. "I'll make a few notes and let psych know."

Bill wanted to stop him, make him stay, but didn't know how. He didn't want to be alone with Nick.

"Doctor Buckley's dead," Nick repeated.

Bill came around the bed and stood before him—but not too close.

"How do you know?"

Nick's brow furrowed. "I just do."

The fact didn't seem to bother Nick and he sat silent for a long moment. Abruptly he spoke again in that affectless voice.

"He wants to hurt you, you know."

"Who? Doctor Buckley?"

"No. *Him*."

The room suddenly seemed cooler.

"Who are you talking about? The one you . . . met down there?"

A nod. "He hates you, Father Bill. There's one other he hates even more, one he wants to hurt more than you, but he hates you terribly."

Bill reached back, found a chair, and lowered himself into it.

"Yes, I know. I've been told."

"Are you going to stay with me tonight?"

"Yes. Sure. If they'll let me."

"They'll let you. It's good that you're going to stay tonight."

Bill remembered the bespectacled nine-year-old orphan who used to be afraid of the dark but would never admit it.

"I'll stay as long as you need me."

"Not for me. For you. It's going to be dangerous out there."

Bill turned and looked out the window. The sun was down, the city's lights were beginning to sparkle through the growing darkness. He turned back to Nick.

"What do you—"

Nick was gone. He was still sitting on the bed, but no longer *there*. His eyes had gone empty and his mind had slipped back into hiding.

But what *of* his mind? What did it know about Rasalom? And *how* did it know? Was Nick somehow tapped into a part of Rasalom as a result of whatever happened in that hole?

Bill shuddered as he rose and gently pushed him back to a reclining position on the bed. He didn't envy Nick if that were true. Simply to brush the hem of that sickness would mean madness . . .

And that was precisely where Nick was now, wasn't he?

Bill stood over the bed, wondering if he should stay. How much could he do for Nick? Not much. But at least he could be here for him if he came around again, or came out of this mental fugue and wanted to know where he was and what had—

Something went *splat* against the window.

Bill turned and saw what looked like a softball-sized glob of mucus pressed against the outer surface of the glass. It began to move—sideways.

Repulsed but curious, he stepped closer. As he neared he heard an angry buzzing. The glob appeared to be encased in a thin membrane, red-laced with fine, pulsating blood vessels. It left a trail of moisture as it slid slowly across the glass. But the buzzing—it seemed to be coming from the glob.

Bill picked up a lamp from an end table and held it close to the window. He spotted a fluttering blur on the far side of the glob. Wings? He angled the lamp. Yes, wings—translucent, at least a foot long, fluttering like mad. And eyes. A cluster of four black, multifaceted knobs at the end of a wasplike body the size of a jumbo shrimp, lined with rows of luminescent dots. Eight articulated arms terminating in small pincers stretched across the mucus-filled membrane.

"What the hell?" Bill muttered as he followed its progress across the pane.

He'd never seen or heard of anything like this creature. He felt his hackles rise. This thing was alien, like something out of an H. R. Geiger painting.

It reached the end of the picture pane and slid over the frame toward one of the double-hung windows that flanked it. Bill realized with a start that the side window was open. He was reaching out to close it when the creature lunged toward him. Bill snatched his hand away and watched as it buzzed furiously against the screen, as if trying to squeeze itself through the mesh. A foul, rotten odor backed him up a step. He slammed down the inner sash and watched through the glass. The creature hung on another minute or so, then dropped off, swooping away into the night, leaving a wet spot on the screen that steamed slightly in the cooling air.

Shaken, Bill shut the other double-hung and turned down the lights. He pulled a chair up next to Nick's bed and readied himself for a long, uncomfortable night. He'd decided to take Nick's advice and stay. At least until sunrise.

WFPW-FM

—now official that the sun set early for the third day in a row. It dropped below the western horizon at 7:11 P.M., robbing us of nearly two hours of daylight. The scientific community is becoming increasingly alarmed about the environmental effects of the shortened days. In a statement . . .

Sutton Square

Gia kissed him at the door to the town house.

"Sure," she said with a sardonic smile. "Eat and run."

Jack returned the kiss and ran his fingertips through her short blond hair. "I've got an appointment at Julio's."

Her clear blue eyes flashed. "A new customer?"

"An old one." She opened her mouth to speak but he pressed a finger across her full lips. "We just need to settle up."

She kissed his finger and pulled it away.

"I was just going to say that Vicky wants you to stay."

Vicky. The other bright spot in his life. The skinny little ten-year-old who'd wormed her way into his heart years ago and refused to leave.

"Really?" Jack slipped his arms around her waist and pressed her slim body against him.

"I wish you'd stay too."

He ran his hands over Gia's back and noticed the tight muscles. He knew she was a high-strung sort, but tonight she seemed unusually tense.

"Something wrong?"

"I don't know. I feel jumpy. Like something's going to happen."

"Something already has. You saw the news: The sun set even earlier and a big chunk of Central Park fell all the way to hell."

"That's not it. Something in the air. Is it what I saw in the coma, do you think?"

"I hope not."

Ever since the near-fatal accident last year she'd become . . . he guessed "sensitized" was the best word for it. She'd seen a landscape of the future while she was out, and it had ended in impenetrable darkness this spring.

"Don't you feel it?"

Jack did feel it. A pervasive imminence in the still darkness at his back. The very air seemed heavy, pregnant with menace.

"It's probably all these strange things that've been happening."

"Maybe. But I don't want to be alone with Vicky tonight. Can you come back later?"

"Sure. Be glad to. I shouldn't be too—"

"Jack-Jack-Jack!"

Over Gia's shoulder Jack could see Vicky running down the hall, a piece of paper in her hand. She had her mother's blue eyes and her late father's brown hair, tied back in a long ponytail that flicked back and forth as she ran. Bony limbs and a dazzling smile that could pull Jack from his blackest moods.

"What is it, Vicks?"

"I drew you a picture."

Vicky had inherited her mother's artistic abilities and was increasingly into drawing. Jack took the proffered sheet of paper and stared at it. A swarm of tentacled things filled the air over the Manhattan skyline. It was . . . disturbing.

He smiled through his discomfiture. "It's great, Vicks. Is this from *War of the Worlds*?"

"No. It's raining octopuses!"

"Yeah . . . I guess it is. What made you think of that?"

"I don't know," she said, wrinkling her brow. "It just came to me."

"Well, thanks," Jack said, rolling it up into a tube. "I'll add it to my Victoria Westphalen collection."

She beamed and flashed him that smile. "Because it's going to be worth a lot when I'm famous, right?"

"You got it, kid. You're gonna help me retire."

Jack gave her a kiss and a hug, then another quick kiss for Gia.

"Be back later."

Gia gave his hand a squeeze of thanks, then he was out on the street, walking west.

As he headed up 58th, Mr. Veilleur's final words of the afternoon echoed in his head.

Do not go out after dark, especially near that hole.

Why the hell not? The warning was like a waving red flag. And since he'd have to pass the park on his way to Julio's . . .

Ernst Drexler smiled as he turned off Allen Street toward the Order's downtown Lodge.

The last twenty-four hours had been quite entertaining. Quite entertaining indeed. Not if you didn't understand the portent of the events, of course. Then you were baffled, perhaps even frightened. As well you should be.

No doubt about it—the Change had begun.

Ernst had been anticipating it since the death of the Lady. Two uneventful months had passed, leaving him wondering at the delay. But he supposed these things took time. The One had to give the Enemy time to conclude that sentience here had died and to move on to greener pastures, so to speak. Maybe the stars had to align or the spheres of the multiverse had to rotate into a certain configuration. Who knew? All that mattered was that it had begun.

The One's time, the Order's time, and most important, *Ernst's* time was at hand.

He just wished he'd been given some warning.

He'd consulted the head of the High Council as soon as he heard about the late sunrise. But the Council had been given no prior notice either.

Despite the One's saying he would not be contacting him if his plans bore fruit, the lack of warning bothered Ernst.

He replayed the moment on that frigid night back in March when he had dropped off the One in midtown, near Central Park. He remembered his words exactly.

Events will reach a head in the next few hours or days or . . . they will not. If they go our way, phones and money will be irrelevant. If they do not, you will hear from me.

If they go *our* way . . . Ernst had spent the ensuing weeks clinging to that pronoun.

The brothers of the Ancient Septimus Fraternal Order had spent millennia manipulating people and events to maintain a certain level of chaos to pave the way for the Change. Ernst's own father had been instrumental in fomenting much of the turmoil of the first half of the twentieth century. Of all living brothers, certainly no one had provided the One more personal service toward bringing the Change than Ernst Drexler. He'd been the One's go-to guy, as Americans liked to put it.

Ernst hadn't done it out of the goodness of his heart. He and the upper echelons of the Order expected to be rewarded in the world that followed the Change.

If they go our *way . . .*

Our way . . .

Yet not one word from the One since that night. He certainly hadn't been shy about contacting Ernst before that. Oh, they'd had a minor falling out, but that fence had been mended. He'd—

A bird buzzed past his ear.

Buzzed? Since when do birds buzz? It was sailing down the street toward the Lodge, and he got a better look at it as it slowed and banked around a streetlight. Not a bird. Something else, something insectoid, with four diaphanous wings and a pendulous translucent sack for a body.

When it completed its turn he realized it was coming back his way, heading straight for his face. Ernst ducked to the right and swung his cane as it passed. He might be well into his seventh decade, but he'd remained trim and agile. The silver head made a direct hit on the middle of the thing's back, damaging two of its wings with a satisfying *crunch*.

It caromed off a nearby car and dropped to the sidewalk where its remaining wings buzzed in a furious attempt to fly again but succeeded only in propelling it off the curb. Ernst stepped closer but couldn't make out more details in the shadowed gutter.

Nasty, aggressive thing. He stabbed it with the end of his cane, puncturing its sack. Clear fluid oozed from the wound. Ernst was about to stab it again when another buzzed past.

Deciding he might be better off inside, he hurried the rest of the way to the Lodge. As he neared he was surprised to see the front steps deserted. Ever since the Order had allowed Hank Thompson to use it as a headquarters for his Kicker movement, the front steps had become the smoking area for his followers, giving the stately, granite-block building the appearance of some sort of halfway house for paroled felons rather than a branch of the world's oldest fraternal order. Ernst didn't like Thompson, loathed his scruffy retinue, and had been opposed to allowing them use of the downtown Lodge.

He had to admit that the group had come in handy at times, but still . . .

When he reached the steps he glanced up at the second floor and noticed that the hurricane shutters Thompson had installed a couple of months ago on the windows of his quarters had been lowered. Another reason to dislike Thompson: He'd defaced this historic building.

As Ernst hurried up the steps he noticed a splash of fresh blood on the stone balustrade. And below that, among the cigarette butts littering the steps, a trail of blood leading to the heavy front doors. He pushed through them into the marble foyer.

"Close it!" said a familiar voice. The man himself, Hank Thompson, stood to his right, peering through one of the doorway's narrow sidelights. "Close it right now!"

Ernst ignored him, of course. Instead he strode a few steps farther into the lobby. The trail of blood led to a dreadlocked Kicker sitting on the floor against the far wall while a couple of his fellows ministered to him.

An entry door slammed behind him. He turned to see Thompson staring at him. Tall, lean, and shaggy-haired as usual, but his customary insouciance had vanished. He stood there tense, pale-faced, and wide-eyed.

"What's it like out there?" he said, pointing to the doors.

"Whatever are you talking about?"

"The birds! They're attacking!"

Ernst assumed he was referring to that thing that had come at him. A bit unsettling, yes, but Thompson looked nearly unhinged.

"Well, I saw some strange-looking—"

Thompson stepped closer. "You weren't attacked? Kewan was out there on a cigarette break, minding his own business, when this thing swoops down and takes a chunk out of his shoulder."

Ernst had had to deal with Kewan from time to time, and had found him brighter than he looked, despite his ridiculous hair.

Thompson leaned even closer and lowered his voice. "You think this is how it starts, with the birds turning on us?"

"Are you referring to that du Maurier story?"

Thompson made a face. "Who's that?" He shook his head. "Whatever. You think this is it? I mean, first that hole, now—"

Ernst nodded. "Yes, I believe the Change has begun."

Thompson kept his voice low but was speaking through his teeth. "Then what's the idea of attacking *us*? We're on his side! We helped him get here!"

Yes, Thompson and his Kickers had been useful in bringing down the Internet, but the end result had fallen short of everyone's expectations. Especially the One's.

"You didn't really believe your followers would get a pass, did you?"

"Well . . ."

"Only you and I and a few others will be exalted. The rest . . ." He shrugged.

Ernst doubted that Hank Thompson himself would be spared, but didn't say that. He still might have his uses.

"It's just like that dream I've been having. But I'm prepared. I'm protected. Ain't no birds getting to me."

With that he turned and hurried up the stairway to the upper floors. To his quarters, no doubt, to huddle behind his storm shutters and steel door.

They won't save you, Ernst thought.

Only those selected by the One to assist in his domination of the post-Change world would avoid the coming horrors. Ernst would be in that number. He had to be. How many people in this world did the One know by name? Barely a handful. And Ernst was one of them.

He glanced down and noticed something different about the distal end of his cane. He raised it for a closer look. The black rhinoceros hide that wrapped the shaft was missing near the tip—right where it had been splattered by fluid from the ruptured sack of that strange insect. It appeared to be eaten away, as if by acid. How odd.

He headed toward his office to call his car. The One might know his name, but Ernst did not want to venture unprotected into this night.

The party was over.

The area around the Sheep Meadow looked virtually deserted. Only a few workers and security people about.

Maybe it was the smell.

Jack caught his first whiff as he passed the Plaza. Something rotten, putrid. He wasn't the only one. The hotel guests emerging from their cabs and limos, or strolling down the steps from the entrances, wrinkled their noses as it struck them. He'd thought maybe a nearby sewer had backed up, but the odor had grown stronger as he entered the park.

It lay thick in the air of the Sheep Meadow.

Banks of floodlights lit the hole and the surrounding area like home plate at Yankee Stadium. As he watched he thought he saw something like a pigeon fly up from the hole, darting through the light and into the darkness beyond. But it moved awfully fast for a pigeon.

Jack spotted a middle-aged woman crossing the grassy buffer zone that had been cordoned off to separate officialdom and the hoi polloi; he moved laterally to intercept her.

"Is that stink coming from the hole?" he said as she ducked under the barricade. The answer was obvious but it was a good opener.

She wore a plastic badge that flopped around as she walked. Her first name looked like "Margaret"; he couldn't make out her last but he caught the words "Health" and "Department" above it. Her tan slacks and blue blazer had a distinctly masculine cut.

"It's not coming from me."

Ooh, a friendly one.

"I hope not. Smells like something crawled into my nose and died."

She smiled. "That pretty well captures it."

"Seriously." Jack matched her stride as she headed toward the street. "When did it start? There was a downdraft into the hole last night."

She glanced sideways at him. "How'd you know about that?"

"I was here when it opened."

"We already have plenty of witnesses. If you want to make a statement—"

"I'm just curious about the stink."

"Oh. Well, the downdraft became an updraft shortly after sunset. We started noticing the odor about an hour later. It's almost unbearable at the edge."

"I thought I saw something fly out of there a few moments ago."

Margaret nodded. "There've been a few. We're toying with the idea of trying to net one. We think they might be birds that flew in during the day. Maybe the smell is driving them out. But don't worry. It's not toxic."

"That's hard to believe."

"Believe it. We've checked it out eight ways from—"

Screams and shouts rose from behind them. They both turned. Jack saw a flock of birdlike things swarming in the air over the hole. No . . . not just swarming—swooping and diving at the people working along the perimeter.

"Oh, my God!" Margaret said and started running back toward the hole.

Jack kept pace. He wanted to get a closer look—but not too close. Those birds appeared to be going crazy, like something out of the Hitchcock movie.

When they got to within fifty yards of the hole Jack realized they weren't birds.

"Whoa!" He grabbed Margaret's arm. "I don't like the looks of this."

She pulled away.

"My reports! All my test data! They'll be ruined!"

Jack slowed his pace and hung back as she ran off toward one of the control tents. His gut crawled as he remembered another hole, in the Everglades, and what had flown out of it.

So he stood in the shadows and tried to identify these things filling the air . . . more like insects than birds. They must have come out of the hole. He sure as hell hadn't seen anything like them around New York.

Two kinds darting around on dragonfly wings. Both had strips of neonlike dots along their flanks. They looked like those weird deep-sea fish that show up every so often in *National Geographic*, the ones from miles down where the sun never shines. Only these were right here in Central Park.

One sort looked like a balloon filled with clear Jell-O, and appeared too heavy and ungainly for flight, the other—

"Oh, Christ!"

The things from the Florida cenote . . . that young girl Semelee had called them chew wasps—mostly mouth, little more than giant, fanged jaws attached to lobster-sized, wasp-waisted bodies.

Screams of pain and terror snatched his attention from the air to ground level. Suddenly everything looked red in the false daylight of the lamps. Jack dropped to a frozen crouch when he saw what was happening along the periphery of the hole. The things weren't just buzzing the folks stationed there, they were on the attack. People scattered in all directions, swatting at the air like picnickers who'd disturbed a hornets' nest.

But hornets would have been a blessing. The jawed things were like airborne piranhas, swooping in, sinking their teeth into an arm, a leg, a neck, an abdomen, ripping a mouthful of flesh free, and then darting away. Blood spurted from a hundred wounds.

Amid the melee Jack saw a bald-headed man go down kicking and screaming under a dozen chew wasps; a second dozen joined the first, and then more until they covered him like ants on a piece of candy.

Instinctively, Jack pulled his Glock and stepped forward to help, then stepped back. He'd seen those things in action before—nothing he could do. He watched helplessly as the man's screaming and kicking stopped, but the feeding went on.

He turned, ready to head for the street, when he noticed a bloated, distorted, vaguely human shape stumbling through the shadows in his direction. It gave off hoarse, high-pitched, muffled noises as it approached, its arms outstretched, reaching for him. At first Jack thought it was another sort of monstrosity from the hole, but as it drew nearer he noticed something familiar about the swatches of tan fabric visible on its legs.

Shock slammed him like a truck. Margaret—from the Health Department. But what—?

The other things from the hole, the ones with the Jell-O sacks—she was covered with them. Wings humming, sacks pulsating, a good thirty or forty of the creatures clung to every part of her body. Jack leapt to her side. The Glock was useless—might do as much damage to her as the things stuck to her—so he holstered it and began tearing at the things, grabbing them by their wings and ripping them off, starting with the pair that clung to her face.

Her scream of agony tore through the night and he stared in horror at the bloody ruin of her face. What was left looked melted, or corroded by acid. Her cheeks were eaten away, so deeply on the right that he spotted the exposed white of a tooth poking through.

He stepped back and looked at the two creatures squirming and writhing in his grasp, raking at his hands with their tiny claws. Their sacks were no longer clear, but red—with Margaret's blood.

He hurled them to the ground and stomped on them, rupturing their sacks. Crimson mucus exploded, smoking where it splattered his pants and sneakers, eating through the fabric and bubbling the rubber. Jack danced away from the mess and turned back to Margaret.

She was gone. He looked around. She couldn't have got far. Then he saw her, a still form facedown on the grass. He crouched beside her. As he reached toward her, one of the sack things lifted off her back, leaving a bloody patch of exposed ribs, denuded of flesh and muscle, and fluttered toward Jack. He tried to bat it away but it latched onto his forearm like a lump of epoxy glue. And the *pain*! Scalding—like boiling acid poured on his skin. It took Jack by surprise and he shouted with the sudden agony. He ripped it off his arm and as it came free he felt a layer of his skin peel away.

The pain drove him nearly to his knees, but he straightened up when he saw one of the chew wasps winging toward him. He swung the sack thing at it, right into its jagged-toothed maw. The pair left a trail of steaming red as they went down in a tangle and rolled along the grass.

Jack glanced back at the perimeter of the hole. Nothing moving there but flocks of chew wasps and jelly sacks swarming in the air. Many of the sacks were bloodred. As he watched, a new drove rose from the hole and circled for a moment, then massed into a rough V-formation and took off toward the East Side like a flying arrowhead.

East! Gia and Vicky were on the East Side.

As the remaining creatures spread out, some heading Jack's way, he took one last look at Margaret. The sack things were still massed on her. What he could see of her looked deflated, like a scarecrow with the stuffing pulled out.

He headed for the trees, removing his shirt and wrapping it around the raw patch on his left forearm. He spotted the lights of the Tavern on the Green visitor center and veered in that direction. When he reached the driveway, he saw a cab pulling away from the entrance. He flagged it down and hopped in the back.

"Sutton Square—quick! And roll up your windows!"

The driver turned in his seat and stared at Jack's arm. He was a thin black man with dreads and a thick island accent.

"Wha' hoppen to you arm, mon? If you in trouble—"

Jack rolled up the window on his right and began to work furiously on the one to his left.

"Roll up your goddamn windows!"

"Look, mon. You don't come into my cab and tell me—hey!"

Just then one of the chew wasps caromed off the taxi's hood and slammed against the windshield. Its crystalline teeth worked furiously against the glass, scoring it in a dozen places. A windshield wiper got caught in its maw and was ripped off its base.

It took the driver only a second or two to roll up his window.

"In the name of God, what is *that*?"

"They came out of the hole," Jack said, slumping against the seat back and allowing himself a few seconds to regroup. "They're *still* coming out of the hole. The park's loaded with them."

The chew wasp continued its ferocious, mindless gnawing at the windshield, trying to get through it. The driver stared at it in mute shock.

Jack slapped the back of the front seat.

"Come on! Let's get out of here. It'll only get worse. Sutton Square."

"Yes . . . yes, of course."

He threw the cab into gear and hit the gas. The chew wasp's wings fluttered in the sudden rush of air. It slid off the hood but became airborne, pacing the cab for about fifty yards, butting against the side windows a few times before it gave up.

"Persistent bugger," Jack said as it finally flew off.

"But what *was* that, mon? It looked like a creature from hell!"

"It just might be." He didn't want to get into explaining the Otherness. "Who knows how far down that hole in the Sheep Meadow goes? Maybe it popped through the roof of hell."

The driver glanced over his shoulder, real fear in his eyes.

"Don't say that, mon. Don't joke about something like that."

"Who's joking?"

They raced east on Central Park South. The things from the hole were there ahead of them. People running, screaming, bleeding, dying, cabs careening out of control. Jack's taxi ran the gauntlet, dodging people and vehicles, screeching to a halt as a driverless Central Park hansom cab bolted in front of them, its horse galloping madly, eyes bulging in pain and terror, a sack-thing attached to its neck. And then they were into the calm and relative darkness of 58th Street.

The driver started sobbing.

"It's the end of the world, mon! Oh, I know it is! God's finally had enough. He's going to punish us all!"

"Easy there. We're safe for the moment."

"Yes! But only for the moment! Judgment Day is here!"

He stopped at a red light and fumbled with something on the seat next to him. When his hand reappeared it held a joint the size of a burrito. He struck a wooden match and puffed furiously. As the cab filled with pungent smoke, he passed it back toward Jack.

"Here. Partake."

Jack waved him off. "No thanks. Gave that up in high school."

"It's a sacrament, mon. Partake."

The last thing Jack needed now was to get mellow. He wanted every reflex at the ready. And he wanted to beat those things to Gia's place.

"The light's green. Let's go."

Two minutes later he was flipping the driver a ten and leaping to the front door of the town house. He rang the bell and slammed the brass knocker. Gia pulled the door open.

"Jack! What—?"

"No time!" He brushed by her. "Get the windows! Close and lock them, all of them! Vicky! Help us out!"

After a flurry of running and slamming, all floors were sealed up tight. Jack checked and rechecked each window personally. Then he gathered Gia and Vicky in the library.

"Jack!" Gia said, clutching a very frightened Vicky against her. "You've got to explain this!"

Over dinner he'd wanted to tell her what Glaeken had said, but had kept mum because of Vicky. He gave them a sanitized rundown of what had happened since he'd left here a short while ago, editing out the more horrific details for Vicky's sake.

Gia pulled Vicky even closer. "What does it mean?"

He thought of what Glaeken had said about hundreds, thousands of these holes opening up all over the world.

. . . *the end of life as we know it* . . .

But he couldn't say too much in front of Vicky.

"The guy I've been telling you about—"

"The Adversary?"

Jack nodded. "He's making his move."

"Oh, dear God!"

"What is it, Mommy?" Vicky said.

As Gia tried to soothe her, Jack remembered how that flock of hole crea-tures had zoomed off so purposefully eastward. They hadn't come to Sutton

Square. Must have continued farther on. Where were they headed? Queens? Long Island?

Monroe, Long Island

"Mommy! Look at this bug!"

Sylvia heard Jeffy calling her from somewhere in the house. She tamped down the fresh soil around the roots of one of her *bankan* bonsai—the one with the quadruple-curved trunk—and followed the sound of his voice from the greenhouse to the kitchen, wiping the dirt from her hands as she moved. Bugs in the kitchen? She didn't like the sound of that. She noticed an unsettling odor as she approached.

She found a plate of cookies half eaten on the butcher-block kitchen table. Gladys, the cook and housekeeper, always left Jeffy a snack before she went home. The boy was standing at the back door, pointing up at the screen.

"See it, Mom? It looks like a giant booger!"

As much as Sylvia hated to admit it, Jeffy was right. What appeared to be a big glob of mucus with legs and buzzing wings was clinging to the outside of the screen.

She heard a growl. Old Phemus, their one-eyed mongrel, was crouched by the dishwasher, ears back, tail tucked under him, snarling at the thing on the screen.

"I know what you mean, old boy," she said, patting his head. "I've never seen anything like that either."

As bizarre as the thing was, Sylvia was almost glad to see it. This was one of the few times since yesterday morning that Jeffy had shown interest in something besides that Mr. Veilleur. He'd talked about the man incessantly since his visit. He seemed infatuated with him, repeatedly asking when he was coming back or when Sylvia could take him to see the old man. Sylvia kept putting him off, saying "We'll see" instead of "No," hoping the boy's fixation would pass. In the meantime, any distraction was welcome.

Sylvia wrinkled her nose. Whatever this creature was, it *stunk*. A part of her immediately loathed the thing, but curiosity edged her forward. Some of its mucus appeared to be oozing through the mesh of the screen. She leaned closer and heard Phemus whine.

"It's all right, boy."

She reached out a finger to—

A hand grabbed her by the shoulder and pulled her back. She whirled and saw Ba. Sylvia stared in shock at the giant Vietnamese. He never touched her, not even to help her out of the car. He looked paler than usual, and he was sweating.

"Ba? What's wrong?"

"Please, Missus, no. Terrible sorry, but mustn't touch."

"I wasn't going to touch it, just get a better look."

"Please—let me close the door."

"What is it, Ba? I've never seen anything like it before. Have you?"

"No, Missus, but is an evil thing. You can tell by the smell."

The smell was bad, that was for sure, but if odor were a worthy criterion, Limburger cheese would be evil too. Ba was obviously concerned, though, almost frightened. Sylvia had to respect that. Any overt sign of emotion from this man was an extraordinary event, not to be taken lightly. And for him to show fear . . . almost unthinkable. Sylvia was suddenly a little afraid herself.

"Very well, Ba," she said, stepping back. "We'll lock up if you think it best."

He smiled with relief. But as he reached for the door to swing it closed, something crashed into the screen. Another bug, but this one was different. A vicious-looking thing that seemed to be all mouth, its jaws lined with hundreds of transparent teeth that looked like tiny glass daggers. Some of those teeth had thrust through the screen on impact. The creature gripped the metal mesh with its tiny claws and began chewing, ripping an ever larger hole.

Ba slammed the door shut just as the head poked through.

"My God! What *are* those things?"

"What are what?" Alan said as he rolled his wheelchair into the kitchen.

"Tooth bugs and booger bugs!" Jeffy whimpered.

Sylvia felt him press against her leg, clinging to it. He seemed afraid now. She smoothed his blond hair and offered him what she hoped was a reassuring smile.

"Don't be afraid, Jeffy. They can't get in here."

"Yes, they can! They want to eat me!"

Just then another of the toothed insects buzzed against the screen of the casement window over the sink as Alan was passing. He stopped his chair and stared.

"What the—?"

As it began to chew at the screen, Ba stepped past Alan and tried to bat it away, but his efforts only seemed to enrage the thing. It buzzed more loudly, attracting another of its kind.

"Close the window!" Jeffy wailed as he trembled against Sylvia's leg. "Don't let them get me!"

Alan sat calmly in his wheelchair, staring at the creatures. He had to know he was directly in harm's way should those things get through, but nothing seemed to frighten him since his recovery from the coma last year. The only concession he made to the things was to pull a dish towel from under the sink and slowly wrap it around his right hand.

Sylvia saw the problem. The casement windows angled outward. If they wound them closed, the two things would be trapped between the glass and the screen and literally pushed into the kitchen. But if more were coming, it might be better to shut them.

Apparently Ba came to the same conclusion. He wound the windows closed on the things. And none too soon—seconds later a third bounced off the glass. The confined space trapped their wings and stopped their buzzing, but not their chewing. What was he going to do with—?

She saw Ba pull open the knife drawer.

"Come on, Jeffy," she said, turning him away. "Those things haven't got a chance against Ba and Alan, so why don't we go upstairs and—"

"I'm scared, Mommy," Jeffy said. "I don't want to go upstairs. What if they come in those windows too?"

The upstairs windows—she'd left them open. Such a beautiful day, she'd wanted to air out the house. God, she had to get up there and close them!

"How about the basement?" she said. "No windows down there. Want to wait in the basement for a few minutes while I check upstairs?"

He nodded eagerly. The playroom down there stocked lots of his toys. He'd be safe, and what was more, he'd *feel* safe.

"Want Phemus to come along?"

"Yes! That way he'll be safe too."

Sylvia ushered Jeffy and the dog down the hall to the basement door. When she flipped on the lights, Jeffy pointed down the steps.

"Look, Mommy. Mess is here too!"

She looked and saw the family cat huddled at the bottom of the staircase, its pupils wide, fur standing out in all directions. It looked spooked. Phemus ran down the steps and waited next to Mess.

"Great. Both of your friends will be with you."

She waited for him to go down but he stopped on the first step and sat on the little landing beyond the door.

"Aren't you going down?"

He looked up at her with frightened blue eyes. "Close the door and I'll wait right here."

"You're sure?"

He nodded solemnly.

"Okay. But I'll be right back. And don't you worry about a thing."

Feeling like some sort of abusive mother locking her child in a closet, she pushed the door closed. The click of the latch echoed in her heart like the clang of a jail cell door. But it was what Jeffy wanted. She'd never seen him so frightened. Granted, those things were vicious looking, ready to grind up anything that got in their way, but what made him think they were after him? A carryover from his years of autism?

She didn't want to think about that, didn't even want to entertain the possibility that he might slide back into his former impenetrable state.

She hurried back to the kitchen where she found Alan in his chair by the sink, towel-wrapped fist held before him, and Ba leaning toward the window with a raised meat clever. One of the things broke through the screen just as she arrived. Faster than her eyes could follow, it launched itself into the kitchen with a furious buzz. Alan batted at it with his fist. The thing sank its teeth into the towel and bit. Alan yelped with pain but held his hand steady while Ba's cleaver whizzed down and sliced through the creature just behind its head. The winged body dropped into the sink, then rose and flapped about the room, dripping orange fluid as it caromed off the walls and ceiling, leaving wet splotches wherever it impacted. Finally it flopped to the floor, twitched a couple of times, then lay still.

The head didn't relax its grip on Alan's hand, however. It clung there, its jaws weakly chewing, even in death. Finally it stopped.

Alan leaned in for a closer look. "Where the hell did you come from?"

He pried the head off and dropped it into the sink. It left behind a shredded section of towel. Crimson fluid began to seep through from within.

Sylvia found her mouth parched but she managed to speak.

"Alan? Are you all right?"

He winked at her and smiled. "Sharp teeth on those buggers. Only a scratch, though." He glanced at the second thing still caught between the screen and the window. "Better take cover before this one breaks through."

He wrapped a second towel around the first as he and Ba took their positions and waited.

"I'm going upstairs to close the windows," she told them.

"No, Missus," Ba said without taking his eyes from the window.

Alan glanced at her. "Don't risk it alone. Wait till we get this one, then we'll all go up together."

She headed for the stairs. "I'll only be a minute."

"Sylvia!"

She ignored Alan's call as she hurried through the front foyer and ran up the curved staircase. The lights were on in the master bedroom where she and Alan slept. She dashed from one window to the next, checking the screens for holes, then slamming them closed. No holes, no booger bugs.

One room down, five more to go.

She hurried down the hall to Jeffy's room. The door was closed. When she opened it and flipped the switch, nothing happened. The floor lamp in the corner was supposed to come on. Sylvia hovered on the threshold, afraid to enter. She held her breath and listened.

Silence. No . . . a faint telltale buzzing from the window near the corner. Silhouetted in the moonlight was a translucent globule clinging to the screen. Another booger bug. The one downstairs had seemed harmless enough. And anyway, it was outside.

Telling herself it was safe, Sylvia gritted her teeth and hurried across the darkened room. She was almost to the window when her foot caught on something. She went down on both knees with a bruising thud. She reached back and felt the beveled post of the floor lamp. It had been knocked over somehow. A breeze, or . . . ?

Suddenly afraid, Sylvia scrambled to her feet and fumbled for the lamp on Jeffy's end table, found the switch, twisted it.

Light. Blessed light.

She peered over at the window. The booger bug was still there alone on the screen, trying to strain itself through the mesh. It looked like it was making some headway too. Part of it seemed to have seeped through—

Her stomach dropped when she saw the jagged edges of the screen. The bug wasn't seeping through the mesh, it was bulging through a hole. She lunged for the window and slammed down the sash. Then she ran around the bed and closed the window on the other side.

But the question remained: Had anything got in?

She stood and listened again. No buzzing now. She let herself relax. She'd got here in time—*just* in time. But she had other rooms to secure. Before heading farther down the hall, she picked up the fallen floor lamp—

—and stopped, staring. The lampshade was shredded, as if a teething puppy had been working at it for an hour. She dropped it and spun, her skin rippling with fear. No movement, no sound. But the door was open, and if something had got in, it could get loose in the house if she didn't close it.

Moving slowly, smoothly, as casually as she could, she stepped toward the door. Her heart thumped madly. If one of those chewer bugs came after her she knew she'd fall apart and run screaming for the hall.

Almost there. Half a dozen feet or so and she'd be home free. She just had to stay calm and—

Sylvia heard it before she saw it. A ferocious buzz from the other side of the bed, a machine-gun rattle of hundred-toothed jaws banging against each other as they chewed the air, then a blur hurtling over the bed toward her face. She ducked but not quickly enough. It caught her hair, twisting her head around with an incendiary blaze of pain from her scalp. She felt a patch of hair rip from its follicles as the thing yanked free and swooped around the room. As she crouched, watching it, she heard another sudden buzz from behind her and instinctively threw herself to the side. A second chewer bug darted past her ear, jaws clicking dangerously close.

Two of them!

She stumbled in a circle, turned, felt something soft press against her calves, and then she was dropping backward onto the bed, landing on her butt. The mad clicking accelerated and the dissonant harmony of the buzzes rose in pitch as they homed in together. Sylvia grabbed Jeffy's pillow and held it before her. The impact of the two creatures knocked her onto her back amid a squall of feathers. She could feel them wriggling, chewing their way into the pillow. She turned it over, trapping them against Jeffy's bedspread.

"Got you!" Her cry was an awful sound, tinged with hysteria.

She glanced at the open door. With these things immobilized for the moment, she could make it. But just as she was about to ease her grip on the pillow, a pair of tooth-encrusted jaws burst through the case and snapped at her. She screamed and ran for the door, slipping on the feathers, scrabbling along on her hands and knees until she reached it. She rolled through, stretched up and grabbed the knob, and was just pulling the door closed when the two chewer bugs hurtled through the air above her and dove toward the first floor.

"No!"

And even before they were out of sight she heard an angry shout from Alan in the kitchen. She got to her feet and ran downstairs where she met him and Ba in the foyer. Ba, cleaver in hand, looked like a mad Asian chef.

Alan's eyes widened when he saw her.

"Sylvia! What happened?" He was staring at her head.

"Why?" She touched the sore spot on her scalp. Her fingers came away wet and red. Some of her skin must have ripped away with her hair. "Two of those things upstairs—in Jeffy's room. They got away and came down here. Did you see them?"

"No. The second one in the kitchen window got past us. We were just looking for it."

"Listen, please," Ba said, holding up his cleaver.

They quieted. A rasping sound . . . from down the hall . . . like chisels working wood.

"Where—?" Alan began.

"Oh, God, I think I know!"

She turned and led them toward the cellar door. As she rounded the corner she skidded to a halt and bit back a scream. All three chewers were there, nose-on to the cellar door, gnawing at the wood in blind determination to get through to what lay beyond it.

And from the other side she heard the wail of a child's small, frightened voice.

"Mommy? Are you out there, Mommy? What's that noise? What's happening, Mommy?"

"Get them!" she said in a controlled screech through her teeth. *"Get them!"*

Ba leapt forward, Alan rolling behind him. Ba cut one in half, then another. As their body parts flopped and flew around, Alan reached out with his towel-wrapped hand and grabbed the third by its tail. He swung it against the floor, smashing its head. Glasslike teeth flew in all directions. The last chewer lay still.

"Get the upstairs windows, Ba," he said. "I'll look after the ones down here."

As the two men hurried off in different directions, Sylvia opened the basement door just enough to slip through and step onto the landing, then quickly pulled it closed behind her.

Jeffy's face was ashen as he stared up at her.

"Don't let them get me, Mom!"

She took the boy in her arms and clutched him tight against her. Her mind raced. Jeffy had been right. Those things *were* after him. But why?

"It's okay. We've killed the bugs and as soon as the house is sealed up tight we'll get out of here."

A moment later she heard Alan's wheelchair on the other side of the door.

"Okay, gang," he said, pulling it open. "The coast is clear. All the windows are down. No holes in any of the other screens."

Sylvia stepped out into the hall, carrying Jeffy. Alan was smiling but she noticed that his eyes were apprehensive as he looked at the boy.

"Jeffy, why don't you and Ba go to the movie room while your mother and I get some hot chocolate. Then we'll all watch a movie."

The movie room? It was a converted oversize pantry where they'd set up the giant screen TV. Perfect for movies any time of day because it had no windows. Was that why Alan was suggesting it?

Jeffy let go of her and went with Ba. He no longer looked afraid. What could possibly harm you when Ba Thuy Nguyen was holding your hand?

As soon as Jeffy was out of earshot she turned to Alan.

"What's wrong?" Dumb question. "I mean, what *else* is wrong?"

"They're all over the place, Sylvia," he said in a low voice. "A huge flock of them swarmed in just as we finished closing up. They're at every window, trying to get in. Listen."

She did. And she heard it. A cadenceless tattoo, as if a thousand people were outside bouncing tennis balls off the windows. It congealed her blood to think of how many of those creatures it took to make that kind of noise.

"Who do we call? The police, the fire company, who?"

"All of the above." Alan grabbed the cordless phone from the counter, listened, then frowned as he put it down. "Phone's out. Try your cell."

Sylvia fished it from her pocket but found a two-word message on the display. "'No Service.' How can that be?"

He pointed to the dead creatures on the floor. "How can *they* be?"

"Then we're trapped."

"I think we're safe for now. We'll see what the morning brings. But until then, let's keep Jeffy as calm as we can."

"They're after him, aren't they?"

Alan nodded gravely. "Sure looks that way."

She bit back a sob as she dropped into Alan's lap and flung her arms around his neck. So afraid for Jeffy. If anything happened to him . . .

It took everything to keep from crying.

"Why, Alan?"

"I think Mr. Veilleur might know."

Sylvia said nothing. Mr. Veilleur . . . she'd thought of him too. But she didn't trust him. He was hiding too much. Besides, what could a feeble old man do against these hideous things?

She pulled away from Alan and stood. She took his hand.

"We'll handle this ourselves. Let's make that cocoa."

Ecstasy!

The horror, the pain, the bloodshed, the ravenous, screaming FEAR soaks through from above, filtering down the tissues of the earth, through the living granite into the conduits of Rasalom's changed being.

His raw flesh has healed now, hardened into a tough new covering. His limbs remain fused to the walls of the granite pocket, reaching deeper and deeper into the rock, sending intangible feeder roots through the surrounding earth, searching for more nourishment. More.

And as he feeds, Rasalom gains mass, grows larger, thicker. The granite walls of the pocket flake away to accommodate his increasing size. The chips slide to the bottom and collect there like shattered bones.

SATURDAY

Daybreak

Monroe, Long Island

It took Sylvia a moment or two to appreciate the silence, but shortly before sunup she realized the incessant beating on the windows had stopped.

She was the first to know because she hadn't slept a wink all night. Jeffy had dozed off halfway through his umpteenth viewing of *The Incredibles*. Alan had succumbed a short while later in his wheelchair. Ba had spent much of the night working on some sort of weapon—carving tiny niches into the wood of one of his billy clubs and fixing chew-bug teeth into them with Krazy Glue. But even he dozed now and then. Sylvia had sat by the door of the movie room, keeping it open an inch or two, listening at the gap.

Silence. She was almost afraid to believe it could be true. As she rose from her chair, Ba sprang up, instantly alert.

"Missus?"

"It's all right, Ba," she whispered. "I'm just going to take a look outside."

"I will come."

"That's okay. I'll just be—"

But he was already by her side, peering into the hall. When he was satisfied it was safe, he stepped out and held the door for her. Sylvia sighed, smiled her thanks, and followed him.

She wondered if she'd ever get used to having someone around who was ready at any moment to lay down his life for her. It had all started sometime when her father had recognized Ba in a TV news story about the boat people crossing the South China Sea with nothing but the clothes on their backs. He'd stood out because he towered above his fellow Vietnamese. Dad had dug out a photo and told her about this huge South Vietnamese kid his Special Forces group had trained as a guerrilla, how they'd become friends. The man in the photo and on the tube were the same.

He'd rushed to Manila, brought Ba and his wife, Nhung Thi, back to the States, and found them jobs in the Vietnamese community on the Lower East Side.

Shortly after that, her father died in his sleep. Years later, when Sylvia learned that Nhung Thi had lung cancer, she'd brought her to Toad Hall and paid her medical expenses until her death. Afterward, Ba stayed on as driver, groundskeeper, and one-man security force. Sylvia had told him a thousand times that he didn't owe her a thing, but Ba didn't see it that way.

Now, as he glided ahead of her, as silent and fluid as a shadow in the pale light filtering down the hall, his newly customized billy club poised at the ready, she was glad he'd never listened to her.

They entered the dining room and went directly to the windows. Sylvia pulled back the sheers and gasped. The screens hung in tatters, the panes were smeared and fouled, the mullions gouged and splintered.

But no bugs. Not a single chewer or booger bug in sight. As if they'd evaporated in the morning light—or gone back to where they came from.

"Let's take a look outside."

He led the way to the front door, motioned for her to stay back, opened it, then slipped outside. A moment later he returned.

"It is safe, Missus, but . . ."

"But what?"

"It is not nice."

Sylvia strode to the door and stepped outside. Down the steps, into the driveway, then she turned and faced the house.

"Oh . . . my . . . God!"

Toad Hall looked like a disaster area—as if it had sat empty for a decade, then been struck by a hurricane, a hailstorm, a horde of carpenter ants, and a plague of locusts all at once. Besides the shredded screens and splintered mullions on the windows, all the wooden siding looked *gnawed*. The chewers had left hundreds, thousands of their sharp, crystalline teeth in the wood. They gleamed like diamonds in the morning sun. And the trees—her beautiful willows! Half the branches, the ones facing the house, had been denuded of their leaves, as if the creatures had been so frustrated by their inability to get into the house that they'd attacked the trees in retaliation.

"Why, Ba? Why'd this happen? What's going on?"

Ba said nothing. He never offered opinions, even when asked. He stood beside her in silence, his tooth-studded club at the ready as he scanned the grounds, his head swiveling in a smooth, continuous motion, like a radar dish.

"Stay here," she told him. "I want to take a look next door."

Ba didn't stay, of course. He fell in behind her.

The stone wall that ran three sides of Toad Hall's perimeter lay a good fifty yards away. When Sylvia reached it she fitted her foot into a crevice and pulled herself up to where she could see over. She peered through the shrubs at the house next door, a contemporary that had fallen into disrepair for a while after its previous owner, a golden oldies DJ and entrepreneur named Lenny Winter, disappeared. But the new owners had done a complete overhaul. She pushed a branch aside for a better look.

Her stomach turned. The house was untouched. Well, not completely. She noticed a few ripped screens flapping in the breeze, and a wet smear or two on the cedar siding, but nothing near what had happened to Toad Hall. The owners might not be aware of the damage yet.

Weak and shaky, she dropped back to the ground. As she stared again at the violated exterior of her home, Jeffy's voice echoed in her brain.

They want to eat me!

He was right. They'd concentrated their attack on the house where he lived and they'd come after him when they broke in.

Why? Did it have anything to do with the *Dat-tay-vao?*

She couldn't let them hurt Jeffy. She'd risk anything to protect him. Even . . .

"Ba, do you remember that older man who was here the other day? He left a card on the foyer table. I told Gladys to throw it away. Do you know if she did?"

"No, Missus."

"Oh. Then I guess I'll have to wait until she arrives. I may just have to—"

She noticed that Ba was holding out a piece of paper.

"Gladys did not throw it away."

She took the card. *G. Veilleur* was embossed at its center.

She looked at Ba and saw only devotion and fierce loyalty in his eyes. But she remembered the fear there last night when he'd pulled her away from that mucus creature. Alan wanted her to contact the old man, and Ba obviously agreed.

Now it was unanimous.

"Thank you, Ba."

With her heart weighing heavy in her chest, she headed back to the house, hoping her cell phone was working again by now.

WNYW-TV

Hello, I'm Alice Gray, and we interrupt our usual Saturday morning programming to bring you this special news report. Sunrise was late again for the fourth morning in a row. But it never rose at all for many of our fellow New Yorkers. As most of you are no doubt already aware, chaos reigned in Manhattan last night as the midtown area became the set of the world's goriest horror movie. Except these horrors were real. Real people died, hundreds of them, perhaps as many as a thousand. The police and emergency services are still counting at this time. And these are the killers.

<cue dead insects>

From what we can gather, these creatures flew out of the hole in Central Park and attacked everyone in sight, leaving the streets littered with corpses. They were indiscriminate in their choice of targets, attacking men, women, children, even dogs and cats, creating a reign of bloody terror. But shortly before dawn they fled, forming swarms that streamed along the streets back to here . . .

<cue Sheep Meadow hole>

Witnesses described the smaller swarms gathering and mingling above the mysterious Central Park hole, swelling to a huge swirling mass before plummeting again into the depths of the earth where they originated.

<back to dead insects>

But what are these things? No live specimens are available, but dead ones abound. It appears that the ones that didn't make it back to the hole before dawn died in the daylight. People have already begun referring to them as "vampire bugs." Scientists from a variety of fields—biology, chemistry, even paleontology (that's the study of fossils)—are working at identifying the creatures and devising ways to combat them. State and federal authorities have already arrived and are conducting studies to find a way to prevent them from getting loose again. Talk of placing a huge metal mesh over the hole is circulating.

<back to Alice>

But that may prove futile. Chilling news just in from Long Island and New Jersey of other bottomless holes, identical to the one in our own Central Park, opening up in a Bayside cemetery, Glen Cove, Hackensack, and other places. These reports are unconfirmed as yet, but we have a team racing to St. Ann's Cemetery in Bayside at this very moment and will bring you live coverage from Queens as soon as they arrive and set up. . . .

Gatherings

Manhattan

Glaeken handed the drawings of the necklaces to Jack and watched the younger man study them. These were Xeroxes. He had the parchment originals safely tucked away in a vault.

"Good," Jack said, nodding appreciatively. "Great detail. Just what I need. Where'd you get them?"

"I've kept them in a series of safe places over the years on the outside chance that I'd need them someday. That day is here."

"Yeah," Jack said glumly. He rubbed his gauze-wrapped forearm. "I guess it is."

He rose from the chair and began pacing the living room, folding the drawings into a neat square as he roamed. Glaeken sensed the tension coiled within the man, the frustration boiling just under the skin. Jack was used to solving problems, usually other people's problems. Now he himself was faced with a problem for which he had no solution.

"It's like a butcher shop out there. I saw those things come out of that hole last night. And now there's rumors of other holes opening up all over the place."

"They're not rumors. I believe I told you—"

"I know." Jack slowed and stopped as he passed the window. "I know you told me." He pointed out toward the park. "Thousands of those holes? Really? *Thousands* of them?"

"I'm afraid so."

"What's going to keep one from opening up right under your building and swallowing it up?"

"I doubt very much that will happen. That would be too quick—mercifully quick. Rasalom wants me to witness the death throes of civilization before he comes for me. Besides, those holes cannot open just anywhere. They must locate at specific points in order to connect with the . . . other place. You've seen the map."

"On the Lady's back, yeah."

"Wherever a pair of the crisscrossing lines intersect—"

"But with swarms of those things pouring out through thousands of holes, the whole planet will be overrun. I'm sure we can find ways to exterminate the bugs, but—".

"The belly flies and chew wasps are just the first wave. Worse things are on the way."

Jack was slowly shaking his head as he stared out the window. "What could be worse than those little horrors last night?"

"*Bigger* horrors. But only during the hours of darkness. They must return to the holes before sunrise."

"Swell. I mean, that's a big comfort, isn't it, what with the sunlit hours shrinking day by day." Jack held up the folded drawings. "You're telling me these necklaces will help close up the holes?"

"They'll give us a chance. Without them we might as well quit right now."

"All right." Jack shoved them into the back pocket of his jeans. "Sounds crazy to me, but crazy seems to be in charge."

"Very true. But don't go yet. There are some people I want you to meet."

"I already know Bill."

"Not Bill. He's still with a hospitalized friend. I don't think he'll be back today."

He'd called last night to explain his absence and to relate what had befallen Nick. Glaeken had told him to do whatever he thought best for his friend.

But another call had come this morning—from Sylvia Nash. She told him what had transpired at her house last night. Glaeken had been shaken by the news. He had expected Rasalom's forces to home in on the *Dat-tay-vao* eventually, but not so soon. Certainly not on the first night. The news increased the sense of urgency boiling within him.

Mrs. Nash had wanted him to come out to Monroe and see the damage, but Glaeken had refused. He wanted her—no, not her, the boy—*here* where he could watch over and protect him and the *Dat-tay-vao* residing within. With obvious reluctance, she had agreed to meet him here today.

"I must tend to my wife for a few moments," he told Jack. "If the doorman announces a Mrs. Nash or a Mrs. Treece, tell him to send them up."

Jack tore his gaze away from the window. "What? Oh, sure. Why are they coming?"

"I must explain the situation to them."

"About the Conflict—the Ally and the Otherness?"

Glaeken nodded. "They need to know."

"Tough sell." He glanced out the window. "But after last night, maybe not so tough."

"That's what I'm hoping."

Jack jerked a thumb toward the rear rooms. "Go do what you have to. I'll take care of things here."

Glaeken headed for Magda's room. He knew Repairman Jack was very good at taking care of things.

WFPW-FM

JO: We've had a lot of requests for this next record here on F-Rock's All-Request Weekend. It's loads older than the stuff we usually play, but I guess it's got something to do with what happened last night.
                    <cue "The Night Has a Thousand Eyes">

Jack wasn't sure how long he'd been standing at the window, mesmerized by all the furious activity in the Sheep Meadow, when the doorbell rang. He glanced down the hall where Glaeken had gone but saw no sign of him.

Well, he'd said to answer the door, so that was what he'd do.

Jack found the Odd Couple standing in the hall. He didn't recognize Bill Ryan at first—the Roman collar and priest garb threw him off—as did the funny-looking younger guy with unfocused eyes, a stitched lip, and a dazed look on his puss. And was that drool in the corner of his mouth?

"Jack?" Ryan said. "I didn't expect you."

"I didn't expect to be here." Jack stepped out of the way.

Bill Ryan was taller than Jack, lots older, but looked fit. His face was battered and haggard and his blue eyes had the haunted look of a guy who'd seen too much of a bad thing.

Jack figured he might have the same look.

He led his shell-shocked companion into the living room and sat him on the sofa. He almost had to bend the guy's knees to get him to sit. Then he turned to Jack.

"Where's Glaeken?"

"Back with Magda." Although he'd met Ryan a few times, he didn't know much about him. He pointed to the Roman collar. "Is Halloween early or are you really—?"

"The *ex* kind. You know, I don't recall ever catching your last name." He seemed anxious to steer talk away from the priest thing.

"Jack'll do." Jack wanted to steer the talk away from names, so he nodded toward the guy on the sofa, and yeah, that was drool on his chin. "What happened to him?"

"That's Doctor Nick Quinn. He's one of the scientists who went down into the hole yesterday—the one who survived."

Jack stared at the man with new respect. "I saw what came out of there last night . . ."

Ryan put his hand on Quinn's shoulder. "I'm afraid Nick saw something much worse."

"Yeah." Jack watched the poor bastard stare blindly into space. Went down a rocket scientist, came back a geranium. "I guess he did. Where'd you come from this morning?"

"Washington Heights."

"How do things look up there?"

"Not too bad. Mostly you'd never know anything happened until you get to Harlem. And even there, you could convince yourself they had nothing more than a bad storm. But from the Nineties down it looks like we had a riot or something. And around here . . ." He shook his head in dismay. "There's still blood on the pavement."

Jack nodded. "It was worse when I walked over from the East Side."

His gut squirmed at the memory. He hadn't slept much last night. Spent most of the time standing anxious guard over Gia and Vicky and watching the tube for word from Central Park. The cable news channels talked all night, but without visuals. Camera teams sent to the area were never heard from again. Shortly after sunrise he'd ventured out into the streets. Sutton Square was quiet, and the usual early morning traffic was rolling uptown and down on Sutton Place. No flying monsters anywhere about, so he'd jogged up the incline toward midtown.

Between Madison and Park he came upon police barricades. He slipped past and continued west. Fifty-ninth Street became a nightmare. Deflated, sunken-cheeked, desiccated corpses littered the pavements, body parts were everywhere—a limbless, headless torso on the sidewalk, a leg in a gutter, a gnawed finger atop a mailbox. The closer he got to the park, the thicker the carnage.

Central Park South was the worst yet—dead people, dead horses still harnessed to their carriages, overturned cars, a taxi halfway through the side doors of the Plaza. Every emergency vehicle and meat wagon in the city seemed to have converged on the area to remove the bodies.

Live people were about too. All on their way out. The cops weren't allowing cabs or civilian vehicles into the area, so the surviving members of the Armani and Prada set were lugging their own suitcases out of the Plaza, the Park Lane, the St. Regis, and the rest and rolling them down the avenues to where they could flag a ride to the nearest airport.

Jack had picked his way through the area and hurried here.

The intercom buzzed then and Ryan answered it. He seemed pretty much at home. The doorman said that a Mrs. Nash had arrived. Ryan looked at Jack questioningly.

"It's okay," Jack said. "Glaeken said she'd be coming."

Ryan said to send her up, then turned and looked back toward the bedrooms.

"Wonder what changed her mind," he said to no one in particular. Then he shrugged and led Quinn to the kitchen. "I'm going to fix Nick something to eat. Want anything?"

"No, thanks."

Actually, Jack was hungry but too edgy, too unsettled to eat. Maybe later, at Julio's, over a pint of brew. A *gallon* of brew.

The doorbell rang. He opened it. The Addams family stood outside.

At least they reminded him of the Addams family: a slinky brunette in a dark dress, a Pugsley, and an Asian Lurch. But no Wednesday, and that wasn't Gomez in the wheelchair.

A knot tightened in his chest as he remembered calling Weezy and Eddie Wednesday and Pugsley when they were kids.

Weezy . . . jeez. Something squeezed inside his chest, then released.

"Is he here?" said the blond kid, his blue eyes wide and bright. He poked his head through the doorway and looked up and down the hall. "He's here! I know he's here!"

"Please, Jeffy," the woman said, placing a hand on his shoulder. She looked at Jack. "I'm Sylvia Nash."

Jack liked her voice. You could fall in love with that voice. But he was already in love.

"Hi." He stepped back and made way. "He's expecting you." A thought struck. "There's a sculptress named Sylvia Nash . . ."

She inclined her head. "That would be me."

He was impressed. "No kidding. I have one of your pieces. The Chrysler Building bonsai."

"You do?" She looked surprised. "I'm so pleased."

"Where's Mr. Veilleur?" said the guy in the wheelchair as he rolled forward.

Jack pointed toward the living room. "He's around. Come on in. Have a seat." Jack wanted to bite his tongue on that one. The guy already had a seat.

And he was staring at him.

"My name's Alan Bulmer," he said, extending his hand. "You look familiar."

Jack shook the hand. Bulmer . . . the name had a vaguely familiar ring, but not the face.

"Name's Jack and—no offense—you don't."

"I was a physician in Monroe until last summer. Were you ever a patient?"

Jack wondered about that. He'd been admitted unconscious to Monroe Community Hospital as a John Doe a couple of years ago but decided not to mention that. He'd left via a second-floor window to avoid the cop stationed outside his door.

"Don't get out to Long Island much."

Jack stood back and watched them as they all trooped toward the living room—all except the big Asian whose eyes never stopped moving. He stayed with the group as far as the end of the hall but halted at the threshold of the bigger room. He gave the living room the once-over, then stepped to the side and stood with his back against the wall, his big hands folded in front of him. The drawstring of a plastic Lord & Taylor's bag hung from one of his fingers. Out on the street he might have passed as a tourist who'd been shopping, but Jack had spied the billy club handle protruding from the bag.

Jack admired the way he moved—smooth, silent, *graceful* for a guy his age and size. Everything about him said he'd been trained for hand-to-hand combat and security. As he studied the big guy, he realized the big guy was studying him.

Jack wandered over to where he stood. He put out his hand.

"Name's Jack."

The big guy bobbed a quick bow and gave Jack's hand a brief shake.

"Ba," he said in a deep voice.

While Jack tried to figure if that was a personal assessment or a name, he noticed that the big guy's eyes did not stray from the living room for more than a heartbeat.

"It's safe here," Jack said. "You can relax."

Another bob from Ba and a fleeting, yellow-toothed smile. "Yes. I see. Thank you so very much."

Jack noted with approval that Ba did not relax one bit.

"Where'd you train?"

"In my homeland—Vietnam."

Jack wondered if he'd been a Cong.

"Army?"

His dark eyes never left the living room. "Help from Special Forces."

Knew it.

"What's in the bag besides the billy?"

Ba glanced at him, his eyes searching his face for a moment, then he handed the bag to Jack.

Jack took it and loosened the drawstrings. From its weight he guessed there wasn't much more inside but checked anyway. He pulled out the club and stared dumbfounded at the hundreds of tiny, gleaming, glasslike teeth protruding from the final ten inches of its business end.

"Jesus. These are chew-wasp teeth."

Ba said nothing.

Jack gave the club a few short test swings. He'd seen what those little teeth could do. A club studded with them made one *hell* of a weapon.

"How many did you kill?"

"A few."

"How about the glob things? Get any of those?"

Ba shook his head.

"Watch out for them." Jack lifted his partially eaten-away sneaker for Ba to see. "The glop in their bellies does this to rubber. It's even worse on skin."

Ba's eyes flicked to Jack's bandaged arm, then away.

Jack slipped the club back into the sack and held it out to him.

"Think you could make me one of those?"

Ba pushed the sack toward Jack. "You may have this."

Reflexively, Jack began to refuse. He didn't accept gifts from strangers. He didn't like to be indebted to anyone, especially someone he'd just met. But he caught himself. They'd met only a few moments ago, had spoken only a few words—Ba hardly any at all—yet he sensed a kinship with this man. Something like this had happened only a few times in his life. A good feeling. Ba must have sensed it too. The big guy was making a gesture. Jack could not refuse.

"What about you? Won't you be needing it?"

"I will make myself another. Many, many teeth where I live."

"All right. I accept." Jack hefted the bag and tucked it under his arm. "Thank you, Ba. I have a feeling this might come in very handy."

Ba nodded silently and watched the living room.

Alan glanced over at where Ba was standing with the dark-haired, quick-eyed man who looked familiar. Something going on between those two, communication on a level he was not privy to. Odd . . . Ba related to almost no one outside the household.

Alan hauled his attention away from the pair and directed it toward Sylvia and Jeffy.

"He's here, isn't he, Mommy?" Jeffy was saying. He was bouncing on the seat cushion, his head swiveling this way and that. "Isn't he?"

"Yes," Sylvia said patiently. "That's what we were told."

"I bet he's in one of those rooms back there. Can I go back and see?"

"Jeffy, please sit still. It's very bad manners to go wandering around someone's house."

"But I want to *see* him!"

She put an arm around the boy's shoulders and hugged him against her.

"I know you do, sweetie. So do I. That's why I'm here."

Poor Sylvia. She'd been having such a hard time with Jeffy since Veilleur had shown up two days ago. And now that he was here in the old man's home, the boy was like an overwound spring.

Alan could understand it. He too felt wired. Maybe it was the stress of last night, maybe it was all the coffee he'd poured down his throat this morning. But he had a feeling those were just a small part of it.

Veilleur was the major factor. For no good reason, something within Alan responded positively—no, *enthusiastically*—to the man. It had to have something to do with the months Alan had played host to the *Dat-tay-vao*. After reducing him to a comatose vegetable, the power—entity, elemental force, whatever it was—had deserted him. But it must have left some sort of residue, whether clinging to his peritoneum, coating his meninges, or riding the neural currents along his axons, he couldn't say. All he knew was that he was drawn to that old man, trusted him; he still remembered the warm glow he'd felt at first sight of him.

And if that's how I feel, what must Jeffy feel?

For Alan had no doubt that the *Dat-tay-vao* had chosen Jeffy for its new residence.

He saw the priest from yesterday, Father Ryan, walk from the rear of the apartment. Mr. Veilleur followed, wiping his hands on a towel as he entered. At the sight of him Alan felt that warmth again, glowing at his center, seeping through his torso and into his limbs.

And Jeffy . . . Jeffy was on his feet. He ran to the old man and clasped his leg in a bear hug. Veilleur stopped and smiled down at him as he smoothed the boy's hair.

"Hello, Jeffy. It's good to see you again."

The boy said nothing, merely looked up at Veilleur with glowing eyes.

Alan glanced over at the sofa where Sylvia, alone now, sat with a rigid spine and a tight, tense expression, chewing her lower lip as she watched the scene. Her eyes flashed with hurt—and anger. Alan knew the core of anger that coiled within Sylvia like a living thing. It had been quiescent the past few months, but he vividly remembered how it used to bare its fangs and strike out at the unwary. He sensed it waking and stirring within her now.

His heart went out to her. She had taken Jeffy in when he'd been abandoned at age three by unknown parents defeated by his autism. She had slaved over him with psychotherapy, physiotherapy, nutritional therapy, occupational therapy, butting her head and heart against the unyielding barricades of his autism without ever once entertaining the thought of giving up. And then, a miracle: The *Dat-tay-vao* smashed through his autistic shell and released the child trapped within. Sylvia at last had the little boy she had been seeking.

But now all that little boy seemed to care about was the mysterious old man who had appeared on her doorstep two days ago.

Alan felt her hurt as if it were his own. He wanted to go to her side and put an arm around her to let her know he understood and was with her all the way, but he couldn't reach her with his hand, and his wheelchair couldn't squeeze by the coffee table to where she sat, and these damn legs wouldn't carry him the lousy half-dozen feet to her side.

His legs. They infuriated him at times. Yes, they were getting stronger— slowly, steadily, he'd progressed to the point where he could stand unsupported for a few seconds. But that wouldn't help him now when Sylvia needed him. So he had to sit here, trapped in this ungainly wheeled contraption and watch the woman he loved suffer. At times like this he—

A harsh voice broke through his thoughts.

"You!"

Alan twisted in his chair, searching for the source. He saw a tall, stoop-shouldered man with unruly dark hair covering a misshapen skull standing in the hallway that led to the kitchen. His head was in constant motion, twisting back and forth, up and down.

Frozen silence all around. Even Jeffy fell quiet. The room had become a tableau. Finally the newcomer steadied his gaze and fixed it on the man called Jack.

"He *hates* you!"

Jack didn't look too worried. "Who?"

"You took his hand!"

"Oh, him." He shrugged. "It's mutual. *More* than mutual."

Father Ryan came up behind the man and gently took his arm, saying, "It's all right, Nick. Come back here with—"

"No." The man snatched his arm out of the priest's grasp and turned on him. "He hates you too! You almost killed him!"

"Nick—"

He turned again and pointed a trembling finger at Veilleur. "But he hates *you* most of all! He hates you *so*! He wants everyone to suffer, but he wants *you* to suffer the most!" He pointed to his head. "Here!" Then to his heart. "And here! And then he plans to make you suffer the tortures of the damned!"

Alan glanced at Veilleur and saw no sign of shock or fear in his wrinkled features. He looked like a man who was hearing exactly what he'd expected to hear. But his clear blue eyes narrowed ever so slightly.

"Come, Nick," Father Ryan was saying, trying to turn the man back toward the kitchen. "You're making a scene."

"Let him stay a moment," Veilleur said, stepping closer to Nick. Jeffy trailed along, clutching his leg. "This is your friend? The one who went into the hole yesterday?"

The priest nodded sadly. "What's left of him."

Into the hole? Alan had heard the news reports about yesterday's tragic expedition. A physicist and a geologist had been lowered into the depths, and the geologist had died in transit. Here was the survivor. What had happened to him down there?

"I've seen this before," Veilleur said to the priest. "On occasion, in the old days, one of the rare persons who survived a trek into a chaos hole returned sensitized." He turned to the man called Nick. "Tell me, my friend, do you know where Rasalom is?"

Nick stepped over to the picture window and pointed to the park. Alan had wanted to take a look through that window to see the hole from above but it had seemed like such a hassle to wheel his chair around all the furniture.

"He's down there," Nick said. "Way down there. I saw him. He opened his heart to me. I . . . I . . ." His mouth worked but he seemed incapable of describing what he had seen.

"Why?" Veilleur said. "Why is he down there?"

"He's changing."

For the first time, Mr. Veilleur appeared disturbed, and something deep inside Alan quailed at the thought of that man being afraid.

"He's started his change already?"

"Yes!" Nick's eyes were wilder than ever. "And when it's complete, he's going to come for you!"

"I know," Veilleur said in a low voice. "I know."

The light suddenly died in Nick's eyes. His gaze drifted and his shoulders slumped.

Father Ryan gripped his shoulder. "Nick? Nick?"

But Nick didn't answer.

"What's wrong with him?" Alan said.

He hadn't practiced medicine in over a year but he could almost hear the associations clicking into place. The man had lapsed into an almost catatonic state. Alan wondered if his behavior had anything to do with the cranial deformities he'd noticed. But that was unlikely. And they certainly wouldn't have sent a schizophrenic down into that hole.

"He's been like this since yesterday—since he came up from below."

"Has he been examined by a doctor?"

The priest nodded. "Scads of them. They're not sure what to do for him."

"Why isn't he in a hospital? He should be closely monitored until they work out an appropriate course of therapy."

Father Ryan looked at him a moment and Alan was jolted by the depth of the pain in his eyes. Then the priest looked away.

"Sorry, Doctor Bulmer, but it's . . . it's been my experience that modern medicine isn't equipped to deal with Nick's sort of problem."

He took Nick's arm and the younger man docilely followed him into the kitchen, leaving Alan to wonder what sort of hell that priest had been through.

"Well," Mr. Veilleur said, facing Sylvia and Alan. Jeffy still hung on his leg. "I'm expecting one more person any minute now; then our company will be complete." He pried the boy loose from his leg. "There now, Jeffy. Be a good boy and sit with your mother."

Reluctantly, Jeffy complied, seating himself next to Sylvia, but barely glancing at her. His eyes remained fixed on Veilleur.

"I'm glad you decided to come," Glaeken told Sylvia.

"You didn't leave us much choice," she said. "Not after what happened last night." She frowned. "Strange . . . you show up at our house Thursday, I kick you out, and on Friday all hell breaks loose."

"No connection, I assure you, Mrs. Nash. I'm not responsible for the hole or for the chew wasps and belly flies."

"So you say. But the area around your apartment building this morning looks like a slaughterhouse. And out on Long Island, way out in Nassau County, in the village of Monroe, the same little monstrosities that did all the damage around here swarmed in and attacked one house. Ours. Why is that, Mr. Veilleur?"

"Call me Glaeken," the old man said. "And I believe you know the answer to your own question."

Alan caught the slightest tremor along Sylvia's lips; he noticed her eyes were suddenly moist. He ached for her. What she must be feeling to let even this much through. In all the years he'd known her, Sylvia had never once let her feelings show in public. Around the house she'd let her hair down with the best of them, but in public she was pretty much like Ba.

"Why would anyone want to hurt him?" she said in a small voice.

Alan noted how she avoided saying Jeffy's name.

The man who wanted to be called Glaeken smiled sadly and ruffled the boy's hair.

"He's not the target. It's what resides within him."

Sylvia leaned back and closed her eyes. Her voice was a whisper. "The *Dat-tay-vao*."

Alan sagged with relief in his chair. Finally, after all these months, she'd admitted it. Now maybe they could get on with the problem of dealing with it.

"Yes," Glaeken said. "There's an instinctive enmity between the things from the hole and something like the *Dat-tay-vao*. That's why I'd like you to move into this building with me."

Sylvia looked at him as if he'd just propositioned her. Before she could answer, the doorbell rang.

"Will you get that, Bill?" Glaeken called toward the kitchen. "I believe it's Mr. and Mrs. Treece."

Father Ryan came out of the kitchen and headed for the door, tossing Glaeken a baffled look along the way.

An older woman entered, a slender, attractive ash blonde who had an immediate, bright smile for Father Ryan. The woman and the priest seemed to know each other. Alan sensed that they might be more than simply friends.

The priest asked her something but she shook her head. He introduced her around as Carol Treece, then she seated herself on the other section of the angled sofa. The priest stood behind her, but kept an eye on the entrance to the kitchen.

"I was hoping your husband would come," Glaeken said.

Carol looked flustered as she shook her head. "He was delayed on business . . . in Denver."

"Too bad," Glaeken said. "Well, at least everyone else is here. But before you can fully grasp *why* you are here, I must give you some background. It's a long story. Eons long. It begins—"

Suddenly there came screaming outside the window. Glaeken turned and Alan looked with the rest of them.

A woman floated there—portly, middle-aged, dressed in a white blouse and a polyester pantsuit—rising through the air a dozen feet beyond the glass, twisting, turning, kicking, writhing, futilely reaching for something, anything that would halt her helpless ascent. Her face was a study in panic. Her terrified screams penetrated the double-paned windows.

We're twelve stories up! Alan thought, as everyone but he, Ba, and Nick ran to the windows.

As quickly as she had appeared, she was gone, rising above the glass and tumbling out of sight like a lost balloon.

Sylvia's face was white, her lips tight; Mrs. Treece's hands were pressed over her mouth. The one named Jack turned to Glaeken with an uncertain smile.

"It's a gag, right?"

The old man shook his head. "I'm afraid not. That woman is a victim of another kind of hole that will begin appearing at random intervals and locations—a gravity hole."

"Can't we do anything for her?" the priest said.

"No. She's beyond our reach. Perhaps a helicopter . . ." He sighed. "But please, all of you, sit down and let me finish. Perhaps it's a good thing this happened now. It's no accident that it occurred outside my windows. But even so, what I'm about to tell you will strain your credulity. I had little hope of any of you believing me before now. However, the events of the past two days—the bottomless hole in Central Park, the depredations of the first wave of night creatures, this unfortunate woman outside—I hope they have put you all in a more receptive frame of mind. It is important that you believe me, because our survival, the survival of most of the human race, will depend on the course of action we take from this day forward. And for you to act intelligently and get the job done, you must know what you are up against."

Alan glanced around the room. At the rear, Ba was listening intently, but the man named Jack looked like he'd heard all this before. Nearby on his right, Sylvia wore her this-had-better-be-good expression. Father Ryan hovered behind the sofa with a faraway look in his eyes; Alan got the impression that he too had already heard what Glaeken had to say. On the far side of the sofa, Carol's expression mirrored the priest's.

Then Glaeken began to speak. He told of two warring forces existing beyond the veil of human reality—ageless, deathless, implacable, nebulous, huge beyond comprehension. One inimical to humanity, feeding on fear and depravity; the other an ally—not a friend, not a protector or guardian, an ally simply by circumstance, simply because it opposed the other force. He told of the endless war between these two forces, raging across the galaxies, across the dimensions, across all time itself; of the human named Rasalom who in ancient times aligned himself with the malign force, and of another man, equally ancient, who'd had thrust upon him the burden of bearing the standard of the opposing force. And now the ages-long battle was coming to a close with only one army on the field. The outcome depended on this small group of people collected in this room. Unless they acted to muster an opposing force, all was lost.

Emotionally, Alan believed Glaeken—deep within he *felt* the truth of what he was saying. Perhaps that too was the result of his entanglement with the *Dat-tay-vao*.

But intellectually he rebelled.

This was it? Humanity depended on this group gathered here?

He hoped the old man was crazy. Because if not, they were all doomed.

"Why are we so important to these . . . forces?" he blurted.

Glaeken shrugged. "It's almost impossible to divine the motives of such entities, but long experience has led me to conclude that we have not the slightest strategic value to either side. We are fought over because we exist. We are a piece on their game board. To win the game, you must have the most pieces—perhaps all the pieces."

"Then why—?"

"I think we are needed by the side that's come to be known as the Otherness. It is inimical to everything that gives our lives meaning, that makes life worth living. It thrives on what's worst in us, feeds on the misery and pain we cause each other. Perhaps it gathers strength from our negative emotions. Or maybe we're only a potential snack. Whatever, it is here to *feed*."

"And this other power," Sylvia said, leaning forward. "It wants to protect us?"

"Not *us*, as humans, per se. The Ally power cares not a whit for our welfare. It laid claim to us in prehistory and simply wants to keep us in its collection. Or did. The Otherness *needs* us, and so is a little more aggressive."

"Where was this Ally last night?" Alan said.

Glaeken looked away. "Gone."

"Dead?"

"No. Just . . . gone. Turned its attention elsewhere. Back in 1941 it thought it had won the little skirmish and pulled back."

"That's it?" Alan said. "This Ally or whatever battles for eons, thinks it's won, then goes 'elsewhere'? Didn't it want to hang around and show off the prize, or maybe just gloat a little?"

Glaeken fixed him with his blue eyes and Alan felt the power behind them.

"Tell me, Doctor: In chess, do you really *want* the other player's pieces for their intrinsic value? Do you have any plans for those pieces? After you've taken an opponent's knight in a match, do you give it another thought?"

The room was dead quiet for a long, breathless moment.

Glaeken glanced at Mrs. Treece. "You may wonder why Carol is here. In ancient times a man named Rasalom sided with the Otherness and became its agent. In so doing he became something more than human. Eventually, in the fifteenth century, he was imprisoned in Eastern Europe. He should have remained so forever, but the German Army inadvertently released him in 1941. Before he could escape, however, he was destroyed. Or at least appeared to have been destroyed."

Alan wondered at Carol's stricken expression, how she wouldn't look at anyone, as if she feared what Glaeken was about to say next.

"Through luck and unique circumstances, Rasalom was able to incorporate himself into the unborn body of an embryo who would grow to be James Stevens. But Rasalom was powerless within Jim Stevens. He could only watch the world pass by from within Jim's body . . . until Jim married Carol and they conceived a child."

Dear God, Alan thought.

He noticed Sylvia stiffen, saw her suppress a gasp.

Poor Carol.

Glaeken pushed on. "He moved into that child—*became* that child.. For decades after his rebirth he lay low while his new body matured, soaking up power from the world around him, from the wars and genocide in Southeast Asia, from the slaughters in Africa and the endless hatred and bloodshed in the Middle East, and from the countless spites, acrimonies, antipathies, rancors, and casual brutalities of everyday life as well. He has been preparing to make his move, setting the stage by deceiving the Ally into believing our world is dead. A few months ago he discovered he was unopposed here and succeeded in extinguishing the beacon that proclaimed our sentience to the multiverse. Since only sentient worlds have value in the game, the Ally has turned away from us and shifted what little of its attention it focused on us to other realities. Rasalom's first overt move was delaying the sunrise on Wednesday morning. He has been steadily escalating since then."

From the back of the room, Jack said, "What he's telling you is that in the old days we had some heavy backup, but now we're on our own. This is the Little Big Horn and we're not the Indians."

Glaeken's lips twisted. "You could put it that way. But we might have a chance of calling in reinforcements, so to speak."

"The necklaces," Jack said.

Necklaces? Alan thought. What necklaces?

Glaeken nodded. "The necklaces, plus the right smithies, and . . ." He gestured toward Jeffy. "This little boy."

"Would you mind being just a little more specific?" Sylvia said. She was speaking through her teeth. "Just what the hell are you talking about?"

Alan's sentiments exactly.

Glaeken seemed unfazed by Sylvia's outburst. He smiled her way.

"To put it in a nutshell, Mrs. Nash: We need to let the Ally know that this is not a dead world and that the battle here is not over; that we are still sentient, and that the Adversary is still active and about to take complete control of this sphere. We need to send the Ally a signal."

"And just how do we do that?" Sylvia said.

"We need to reconstruct an ancient artifact."

"A weapon?"

"In a way, but what I'm talking about is as much a weapon as an antenna, a focal point."

"Where is it?" Alan asked.

"It was deactivated more than a half century ago when it supposedly destroyed Rasalom in a Romanian mountain pass outside a place called the keep."

Alan's mind continued to rebel against Glaeken's words, more intensely now than ever, but his heart, his emotions insisted that he believe.

"All right. Suppose we accept all this at face value." That earned him a sharp look from Sylvia. "How do we go about reactivating the focus deactivated in Romania?"

"We don't," Glaeken said. "All the essences that made it a focus were drained off by the act of destroying Rasalom—or what appeared to be Rasalom's destruction. The remnant of that instrument was reduced to dust when Rasalom started on the path toward rebirth."

"If it's gone and we can't get it back," Alan said, "why are we talking about it?"

"Because there were two. The other was stolen in ancient times and dismantled—melted down into other things."

"Oh, jeez," Jack said. "The necklaces."

Glaeken smiled. "Correct."

"What are you two talking about?" Sylvia said. Alan sensed her anger edging closer to the surface.

"The other instrument—the other focus—was stolen and melted down. The melting process dislodged a powerful elemental force within the focus, releasing it to wander free. But a residue of that force remained in the molten metal. The metal was fashioned into a pair of necklaces which have been used for ages by the high priests and priestesses of an ancient cult to keep them well and to prolong their lives."

"And the elemental force?" Sylvia said, leaning forward, her face pale, her expression tight, tense.

The answer flashed into Alan's mind. He suspected Sylvia had guessed it as well.

"It wandered the globe for ages," Glaeken said. "It's been called many things in its time, but eventually it became known as the *Dat-tay-vao*."

Alan thought he heard a faint groan escape Sylvia as she closed her eyes and slipped an arm around Jeffy.

Just then a voice broke through from somewhere in the apartment.

"Glenn? Glenn!" It rose in pitch, edging toward panic. "Glenn, I'm all alone in here! Where are you?"

As Glaeken glanced toward the rear rooms, Alan saw genuine concern and dismay mix in his eyes. This was the first time he had shown a hint of uncertainty. He took a hesitant step in the direction of the cries.

"Let me go," Father Ryan said, moving from his spot behind the sofa. "She knows me by now. Maybe I can reassure her."

"Thank you, Bill." Glaeken turned back to his audience. "My wife is ill."

"Anything I can do?" Alan said.

"I'm afraid not, Doctor Bulmer, but I thank you for offering." Alan saw no hope in the man's eyes as he spoke. "She has Alzheimer's disease."

Alan could only say, "I'm sorry."

But Sylvia shot to her feet. "*Now* I get it!"

"Get what, Mrs. Nash?" Glaeken appeared confused.

Sylvia was leaning forward, jabbing her finger toward him over the coffee table. Her core of anger had fully uncoiled, baring its fangs, lashing out.

"I should have known! Do you think I'm an idiot? You want Jeffy here so you can use him—or rather use the power you think is in him—to cure your wife!"

"Not at all, Mrs. Nash," he said softly with a slow, sad shake of his head. "The *Dat-tay-vao* will not work against a degenerative process like Alzheimer's. It can cure disease, but it can't turn back the clock."

"So you say."

Then Jeffy tugged at Sylvia's sleeve. "Don't yell at him, Mom. He's my friend."

That did it. Alan saw Sylvia wince as if she'd been jabbed by a needle.

"We're leaving," she said, taking Jeffy by the hand and guiding him away from the sofa.

"But Mrs. Nash," Glaeken said, "we need Jeffy to reactivate the focus. We need to reunite the *Dat-tay-vao* and the metal from the instrument."

"But you don't have the metal, do you."

"Not yet, but—"

"Then I see no point in discussing this further. When you've located this magic metal, call me. You have my number. Then we'll talk. Not before."

"But where are you going?"

"Back home. Where else?"

"No, you mustn't. It's too dangerous. It's better that you stay here. I own the building. You can have your choice of the empty apartments. You'll be safe here."

"*Here?*" She stopped at the door. "This place is practically on top of that hole out there—all but falling into it. I'll take my chances in Monroe."

"This place is protected, in a way. It will be preserved until the end. You and Jeffy and your friends can share that protection."

"Why? What's so special about this place?"

"I'm here. I'm to be saved until the last."

. . . and then he plans to make you suffer the tortures of the damned!

Alan remembered Nick's words and wondered why the old man didn't look more frightened.

"Toad Hall will be protected too. Alan and I have already seen to that."

Alan turned his chair and wheeled it toward Sylvia and Jeffy. He'd been on the phone first thing this morning and called around until he found a contractor who could immediately start installing steel storm shutters. He'd offered a substantial bonus if the job was completed by sundown. Now he wondered if shutters would be enough.

Why not stay here? It might be a good move. Alan felt at home with this group, had a feeling they'd find safety here among this disparate, unlikely crew.

Something going on here. A subtle chemistry, a subliminal bond.

But Sylvia seemed oblivious to all that. When her anger-core broke free and took the helm, she'd dig in her heels and refuse to budge. Alan knew he couldn't talk to her when she got like this. Nobody could. He'd learned to recognize the signs and—when the storm came—to sit back and let it have its way with her. When the clouds and winds had blown past and she was cooler, calmer, she'd be a different Sylvia, and able to discuss it.

He might be able to change her mind later.

Sylvia's anger could be inconvenient, frustrating, even infuriating at times, but the anger was part of what made Sylvia who she was. And Alan loved who Sylvia was.

Jeffy, though, clearly wanted to stay.

"I don't want to go, Mom."

"Please don't argue with me, Jeffy," Sylvia said in a low voice. "It's time to go home."

He tried to pull away from her. "No!"

"Please obey your mother, Jeffy," Glaeken said softly.

The boy abruptly stopped struggling. The look Sylvia threw Glaeken was anything but grateful.

"There's something you should realize, Mrs. Nash," Glaeken said. "The creatures that attacked your house last night are active only in the hours between sunset and sunrise. They must hide from the sun during the day. However, as I'm sure you are all aware, the daylight hours are shrinking."

"But that can't go on forever," Alan said. "Can it?"

Glaeken nodded. "The pattern will continue. And accelerate. Sunrise was late again today. Tomorrow it will be even later. Sunset will keep coming earlier and earlier."

"But if that keeps up . . ." He looked at Sylvia.

"You see the pattern?" Glaeken said. "Shrinking daylight hours, lengthening periods of darkness. The hole creatures will have progressively longer time for their feedings, and shorter periods when they must be in hiding. And when daylight is gone completely . . ."

"They'll never stop," Jack said in a hushed voice.

Alan knew from looking at him that no matter what terrors he and Sylvia and Ba had experienced last night, Jack had seen far worse.

Glaeken nodded. "Correct. We are headed for a world without light, without law, without reason, sanity, or logic. A nightworld from which there will be no dawn. *Unless* we do something."

"Call me when you get the metal," Sylvia said.

Alan reached out and shook hands with Glaeken as he wheeled past, then guided himself to where Ba stood holding the door.

"Don't leave," said a strained voice.

Alan turned at the door and saw that Nick had stepped out of the kitchen. His eyes were bright again, and alive with concern as he stared at Alan.

"Why not?"

"If the four of you leave here today, only three will live to return."

A chill swept over Alan. He glanced out into the atrium and saw Sylvia, Ba, and Jeffy standing before the elevator. As he watched, the bell dinged and the doors slid open. Sylvia and Jeffy stepped inside. Ba stood waiting, restraining the doors with one of his big hands.

Alan was paralyzed for a moment. The three outside were waiting for him; the four people in the apartment were staring at him. He wanted to stay, but wouldn't—couldn't—without Sylvia. And no way was Sylvia moving. Not yet, at least.

He shrugged and flashed what he knew was a weak grin.

"We'll see about that."

Then he headed toward the elevator, feeling as if he were rolling himself toward an abyss as deep and dark as the one in the Sheep Meadow outside.

As the door closed behind Dr. Bulmer, Carol said, "I should go too."

So soon? Bill thought, returning from Magda's room.

"Why don't you hang out for a while?"

She shook her head. "I'd better get home. Nelson will be back soon."

She waved and let herself out. Something going on there. Bill would have followed, but he had Nick.

He guided Nick back into the kitchen. Carol's behavior disturbed him, but Nick's even more. He was acting like some sort of Delphic oracle, transmitting threats and predictions from beyond. Was it madness or had his brush with the abyss left him connected, as Glaeken had said, to the chaos encroaching on all their lives?

"Are you trying to frighten people, Nick?"

"No," he said as he resumed his seat at the kitchen table. His eyes were tortured. "They're in danger. One of them's going to die."

"Who, Nick? Which one?"

If Nick was actually tapped in, maybe Bill could get something concrete out of him before he went catatonic again. Those four people from Long Island—the woman, Sylvia, was a bit of a bitch, but he didn't want to see harm come to any of them, especially the boy.

"Who's going to die, Nick? Who's in danger? Is it Jeffy, the boy?"

But Nick was gone again, his face empty, his eyes blank.

"Damn it, Nick!" Bill said softly. He gave the slumped shoulders a gentle squeeze. "Couldn't you have held on a few minutes longer?"

No reply, of course.

He felt a surge of anger, but not at Nick. That Nash woman—talking to Glaeken like that. He was only trying to help, and all he was asking was her cooperation to save their own hides. But Bill had to keep reminding himself that the truth was so difficult to accept. He remembered how he'd fought it for years—decades. And Sylvia Nash was afraid of something. He didn't know what, but was sure he'd seen fear in her eyes as she walked past on her way out.

He heard an amused voice rising in the living room. He went to see what was up.

"Do you hire out?" Jack was saying as he clapped the old man on the back. "I mean, if I ever have guests who won't leave, will you come over and get rid of them for me?"

Glaeken smiled, and as concerned as Bill was about Carol and Nick and the whole situation, he had to laugh. It felt good, especially since he wasn't sure when he'd have cause to laugh again.

Preparations

Manhattan

"Well, what do you think?" Thompson said as Ernst accompanied him along Central Park West.

He'd called this morning and asked Ernst to join him to discuss "matters of mutual interest." Having little else to do, now that the Change had begun, Ernst agreed.

Thompson seemed more composed this morning. Perhaps because the "birds" were gone. But they'd certainly left their mark on this part of the city.

"About what?"

Thompson gestured toward the park. "About this. About everything that's happening."

The police weren't letting anybody into the lower end of the park, and they'd closed off the streets adjacent to it. He and Thompson were able to walk down the center of CPW. But yesterday's carnival atmosphere was gone. Fewer street vendors cluttered the curbs, and far fewer sightseers milled about. Plenty of curious standing outside the yellow tape, yes, but less noisy and jocular than yesterday.

The hole had been an event. What had issued from the hole had been a horror.

The deadly depredations of what were described as new breeds of insects had been all over the news this morning. The fatalities had been carted away but the damage to the buildings overlooking the park remained in evidence— hundreds, perhaps thousands of torn window screens and even some broken glass. All except one building. Ernst noted the number: *34.* It appeared to have suffered not one iota of damage during the night. He wondered why.

The sun was high and warm. His three-piece suit was white, as usual, and reflected some of the heat, but still he wished he'd worn a lighter-weight model.

"We couldn't have discussed this—whatever it is—in my office at the Lodge?"

Thompson shrugged. "Maybe. But the sun rose even later this morning, and I figure I might as well snag a few rays while I still can."

Not a bad idea, Ernst supposed.

They passed the barricades and began to see traffic again.

"Well, what's on your mind?"

Screeching tires and cries of terror brought them up short. Up ahead, a yellow cab began rising off the street, trunk first. The driver opened his door, hung by the seat belt, then dropped to the pavement. A woman and child leaned out the rear window and screamed for help.

"My God!" a nearby woman cried out. "Can't somebody do something?"

Thompson's face was a study in vulpine fascination as he watched the cab continue to rise, beginning a slow rotation as it cleared the tops of the surrounding buildings and kept on falling up.

"What the fuck?"

"The laws are changing," Ernst said, trying to sound calm and composed despite his suddenly dry tongue. "That's why it's called 'the Change.'"

The Order's lore was skimpy and vague about what exactly would happen during the Change.

Thompson looked at him. "The laws? But—"

"The laws of physics among them."

Finally the car drifted out of sight past the building tops. Good. Ernst had felt rather ghoulish watching it.

"Stay close to the buildings," he said as they began to move again. "That way we'll have something to grab on to if it happens to us."

Ernst stepped gingerly, wondering if a gravity hole lay in wait a few steps ahead.

Thompson glanced at him as they crossed the sidewalk. "You know what? I don't care what this One guy promised you, I think he's gonna fuck us over."

He had just verbalized Ernst's greatest unspoken fear.

"He owes us." He owes *me*. "He couldn't have done this without us."

"Yeah, well, maybe, but even if you get an invitation to the party, I got a bad feeling he's gonna leave me out in the cold. So I gotta consider all possibilities. If he brings me along, cool. But if not, I need a backup plan."

Thompson wasn't educated—high school dropout was probably an overestimation of his level of formal education—but Ernst had come to appreciate his native intelligence, and his particularly well-developed survival instinct. He would probably last longer than most in the post-Change world, but eventually he would succumb, no matter how elaborate his strategy.

Ernst had a simpler strategy if he found himself left behind: a hefty dose of cyanide waited at home.

At Eightieth Street they hurriedly entered the park and walked along the traverse past the budding Shakespeare Garden, keeping close to the trees. The sun shone, birds sang, bees hummed . . . just another spring day in Central Park. Nothing hinted at the changes Ernst knew were coming.

"Any ideas yet?"

Thompson nodded. "Yeah. Been thinking. If the Change works, things'll be a mess. But even if it fizzles out halfway through—"

Ernst doubted that. "I don't think—"

He stopped and jabbed a finger at Ernst. "It ain't over till it's over, and I don't hear a fat lady singing yet. Your One fella's got people and things working against him, right?"

"I suppose, but they haven't a chance."

"So you say, but shit happens on both sides of the fence." He started walking again. "Here's my point: Even if the Change stops half done, the world's gonna be messed up. Whether completely messed up or only half messed up, either way I'm gonna need an edge. Part of that edge is someone taking your back. I got a lotta someones."

"Your followers . . . of course."

"Right. Kickerdom'll do what I say. But that's not enough. *We'll* need an edge."

He stopped again, but this time he looked at the sky through the trees.

"What are you getting at?"

Ernst sensed a strange new intensity about Thompson. His eyes had taken on an almost feverish glow.

"Sunlight, Drexie. What needs sunlight—regular, measured doses of sunlight—more than anything else?"

As much as he loathed the insulting nickname, he wondered where this was going.

"I suppose I would have to say plants."

"Exactly! And right now, in the spring, they need sunlight for sprouting and seedling growth." He glanced at Ernst. "I worked a farm with my mother when I was little. So, if the daily dose of sunlight gets smaller and smaller over the next few weeks, we're gonna see huge crop failures all across the globe."

"When the Change is over, crop failures will be the least of the world's problems."

"But even if the Change fizzles, we'll still be seeing worldwide food shortages, maybe even famine. You agree?"

"Why . . . yes."

The realization startled Ernst. He hadn't bothered to think that far ahead or consider that contingency. Yes . . . if the One failed, and the Change—to use Thompson's term—*fizzled,* billions would starve in the aftermath. Even if the Enemy managed to stop the One, it would be a Pyrrhic victory.

He had to smile through the bitterness: *Otherness über alles.*

"Damn right, yes. So I figure I'd better start making plans for that. Those who can suss out the future can profit from it."

"I hope you're not thinking of the futures market or anything like that."

"Shit, no. We lose much sunlight for any length of time, I don't see there even *being* a stock market. Futures will go through the roof, but what are you going to pay with?"

Ernst saw it all: In the face of worldwide crop failures, money—currency— wouldn't be worth anything.

"Certainly not money."

"Damn right. Money's just paper, and you can't eat paper. When the crops fail and the grocery shelves are empty, we're going to see food riots in this city—in every city. The only thing that'll be worth anything is food. And the guy who's got the food—and the manpower to protect it—will rule the roost. That'll be me."

"That's your plan?"

He nodded. "Yep. Stock up—canned and bottled stuff, and things that'll keep a long time, like pasta. Nothing that needs refrigeration. We'll clean out every store in town."

"Do you have enough money for that?"

He gave a derisive snort. "Don't need money. We'll get a bunch of charge cards and max them out. Buy everything on credit." He grinned. "Odds are the credit card companies won't be around to collect." He glanced at his watch. "Gotta get my people to start stocking up." He grinned again and winked. "Before the hoarding starts."

CNN

—same in country after country around the globe: gigantic holes, seemingly bottomless, averaging two hundred feet across, opening one after the other throughout the day. The governments of Iran, North Korea, and China deny the existence of any such holes within their borders, but aerial reconnaissance says otherwise. And the question on everyone's mind: Is each of these holes going to release a horde of vicious creatures like those that were loosed on Manhattan last night? And if so, what can be done to stop them?

In Manhattan, preparations are under way for—

Wait. This just in from the White House: The President has declared a national state of emergency. Repeat: a national state of emergency. Reserve units of the Army are being activated. Congress has called an emergency session.

Jack sat at the counter of the Isher Sports Shop—one of the few places left on the Upper West Side that spelled shop with one P—and watched the people passing by outside. Amsterdam Avenue was sunny and only slightly less crowded than usual for a Saturday afternoon.

Like nothing's changed.

But everything had changed. They just didn't realize it yet. Jack had an urge to run out there and start grabbing people by the collar, to shout in their faces that last night wasn't an isolated incident or bizarre aberration. It was going to happen again. And worse. Tonight.

Abe Grossman, the owner, bustled from the pantry/storage area behind the counter carrying two cups of coffee. He handed one to Jack and perched himself on the stool behind the cash register. Jack sipped and winced.

"Jeez, Abe. When did you make this?"

"This morning. Why?"

"It's not like wine, you know. It doesn't get better with age."

"I should waste it? With a microwave in the back, I should throw out perfectly good coffee because Mr. Repairman Jack suddenly has a delicate palate?"

The stool creaked as he adjusted the two-hundred-plus pounds he packed into a Humpty Dumpty frame. He had receding gray hair and wore his usual black pleated-front pants, white shirt, and black tie. A bit of egg yolk from breakfast yellowed the breast pocket of his shirt; a red spot that looked like strawberry jelly clung to his tie; he had just finished sprinkling his entire shirt-front with bits of finely chopped onion from the fresh bialys Jack had brought.

"*Nu?*" he said when he was settled on his perch. "What have I been saying for so many years to the accompaniment of your derisive laughter? And now it's finally happening. The Collapse of Civilization. It's all going to fall apart, right before our eyes, just as I've been saying."

Jack had expected this. He'd known when he told Abe what Glaeken had said that he'd be in for an I-told-you-so lecture. But he had to let Abe know. He'd been Jack's friend, confidant, and arms supplier for most of his time in New York City. In fact Abe was the one who'd started calling him Repairman Jack, something Jack wished he hadn't. He'd come to hate the name.

"No offense, Abe, but you've been predicting an *economic* holocaust. You know, bank failures, runaway inflation, and so on. Remember?"

"And I pretty much got that already when—"

"This is different."

Abe stared at him over the rim of his coffee cup. "I checked the sun. It doesn't look like it's traveling any faster."

Jack shook his head. "The sun doesn't move, *we* do."

"I know that. But *something* has to be moving faster. I mean, Earth's tilt on its axis—that's what determines the varying duration of daylight through the year. Shorter days would mean we're either rotating faster or the Earth's shifted on its axis."

"All the scientific types say neither has happened."

"Yet the days *are* shortening. A paradox already. The impossible is happening. If that's true, then the impossible—or the impossible-sounding things Glaeken told you—could be true as well." He looked at Jack. "You really think this could be our last stand? The 'nightworld'? A real possibility?"

Jack nodded. "But not an inevitability if he can get some cooperation."

Abe was silent a moment, then, "For some reason, I believe it too. Maybe because I've been preparing for this eventuality most of my adult life. Maybe because I'd feel like such a *schlemiel* if I'd been preparing for such a thing for so long and it never happened. But you know what, Jack? Now that the time has come, it's not such a vindication. Happy I'm not."

"You still have that hideaway?"

"Of course."

Abe, the world's dourest pessimist, had been preparing for the Collapse of Civilization for as long as Jack had known him. He'd confided in Jack about his refuge in rural Pennsylvania, an overgrown farm with an underground bunker and deep stocks of water, weapons, and freeze-dried food. He'd said Jack was welcome there when the Big Crash came. He'd even told Jack where it was—something he'd never revealed to anyone else, even his own daughter.

"Go there, Abe. Get out of the city and hole yourself up. Today, if possible."

"Today? Today I can't go. Tomorrow maybe."

"Not 'maybe,' Abe. If not today, then tomorrow for sure. For *sure.*"

"You're really worried, aren't you. How bad we talking, Jack?"

"Bad like you've never dreamed." Jack stopped and grinned. "Jeez, Abe. I've been around you so much I'm starting to sound like you."

"That's because you're part chameleon. But how bad is bad like I never dreamed? I dream pretty bad."

"Whatever you've dreamed, trust me: This'll be worse."

Scenes from the bloody carnage around the Sheep Meadow hole flashed before his eyes. And now, more holes. Even if the predators remained limited to the two species he'd seen last night, the city would devolve into a nightmare. But Glaeken was saying the things would get progressively bigger and more vicious.

Jack's mind shied away from envisioning the holocaust.

"But I'd like to ask a favor."

"Don't even ask," Abe said. "You show up here first thing tomorrow morning with Gia and darling Vicky and we'll all head for the hills together."

"Thanks, man," he said, feeling a burst of warmth for this dumpy gunrunner. "That means a lot. But I won't be coming along."

"I should go and you should stay?"

"There's a chance I can do something about the situation."

"Ah. The necklaces you mentioned. I remember the one you had. With the pre-Vedic inscriptions."

"Right. I need to get copies made. I was thinking about Walt Duran. What do you think?"

"Walt's as good as you could ask. A *shtarker* in the world of engraving. And he could use the work."

"Really? What happened?"

"Computers and the new bills are what happened. Putting honest counterfeiters out of business."

Walt was a stand-up guy, a hard worker. If he'd put his talents to work in the jewelry industry, he'd probably have made more money in the long run and wouldn't have had to do that stretch in the joint. But even so, Jack wasn't unhappy to hear he'd fallen on hard times. That meant he could be goosed into high gear by the lure of a bonus for early delivery.

Because Walt was as slow as he was good.

"Okay," Abe said. "What's the plan?"

Jack choked down the rest of his coffee and stood.

"You gas up that van of yours and garage it for the night. Pack up your stuff this afternoon and get back here before nightfall. Spend the night in your basement here. No matter what you hear upstairs, don't come up to have a look. *Stay down there.* I'll have Gia and Vicky here right after sunrise. Sound okay?"

Abe frowned. "Sounds like you think things will be going downhill fast."

"Downhill?" Jack said as he headed for the door. "I think they're going to run off a cliff."

Okay, Jack thought as he drove his black Crown Vic from the Lower East Side. Walt Duran is on the job.

Now all he had to do was convince Gia that she had to leave town.

Walt had been glad for the work. Ecstatic, actually. He'd been reduced to living in a tiny overpriced studio. Jack had shown him the drawings, told him he wanted two copies on a one-to-one scale, and given him a down payment so he could go out and get the raw materials. Delivery time was a problem, though. Walt had said no way could he get it done by Monday morning. But when Jack promised a ten-thousand-dollar bonus, Walt reconsidered. *Maybe* he could have them by then.

Jack drummed his fingers on the steering wheel as he cruised along. Getting those necklaces out of Walt by Monday morning would be a breeze compared to getting Gia into Abe's van tomorrow. And he didn't have all that much time to persuade her. The afternoon was already on the wane. But if Glaeken was right about tonight being worse than last, maybe he wouldn't have to convince her. He could let the things from the hole do it.

He swung up toward the park to see how the cleanup was going and was amazed at the transformation. The barricades were still up to keep cars off Central Park South, but the corpses were gone, the wrecked vehicles had been cleared, the pavements washed clean. Cars were restricted, but not pedestrians. A *lot* of people were about on the sidewalks and the fringe of the park, the curious of all ages, come to see the notorious Sheep Meadow hole and check out the stories of bloody carnage they'd heard on the news.

Jack checked his watch. He had a little time to spare so he double-parked and jogged across the matted grass to get another look at the hole.

The crowd was thick there. Everyone seemed to be watching something going on down by the edge. Over their heads he could see cranes dipping up and down. He wove through the press until he got to a decent-sized tree. He shimmied up the trunk to where he could see the hole.

Its southern half was covered with some sort of steel mesh. Work crews were in the process of screening over the rest of the opening. Jack watched for a moment, then slid back to the ground.

"How's it going?" someone said.

Jack turned and saw a well-dressed young couple standing nearby with a baby carriage. The guy was smiling warily.

"Better than half done," Jack said.

The woman sighed and squeezed her husband's biceps with both hands and looked at Jack with uneasy doe eyes.

"Do you think those things will come back?"

"You can count on it."

"Will the net work?"

Jack shrugged. "Maybe. But this isn't the only hole."

"I know," the guy said, nodding. "But this is the one that counts for us." He put an arm around his wife's shoulders. "I'm sure we'll be all right," he told her.

Jack looked down at the baby in the stroller. Eighteen months at the most, all in pink, sandy-haired, grinning up at him.

"You got a cellar where you live?" he said, staring into those two innocent blue eyes. "Someplace with no windows?"

"Uh, yes we do. There's a storage area down by the boiler room where—"

"Move in there before sunset. Bring everything you'll need until morning. Don't go upstairs until sunrise."

He tore his eyes away from the child and hurried off.

Gia and Vicky. Dammit, even if he had to sling Gia over his shoulder and dump her in the back of Abe's van, he'd see them on their way out of town tomorrow morning.

Manhattan

"Yo, let's get behind granny, here. She's got next to nothin'."

Carol turned and saw four scruffy men line up behind her in the checkout lane. All looked to be in their thirties or late twenties and each had a shopping cart stacked high with food. Not individual cans and such, but cases of food. She glanced at her own purchases: a container of blueberries and three nonfat yogurts. With Nelson's return delayed yet another day, she saw no need in stocking up.

And then the man's comment struck home.

Granny?

Well, she did have a lot of years on them, but she stayed in shape, exercising regularly, watching her diet. She might be well into her sixties, but her body was trimmer, better toned, and younger looking than a lot of bodies in their thirties. But she *was* old enough to be their grandmother . . .

Grandmother . . . the word expanded in her chest, building a pressure, almost painful. She'd never be a grandmother. She'd been a mother . . . of sorts. Did she truly deserve to call herself a mother? She'd borne a child, but the child was not hers. Genetically, yes . . . she'd contributed half of his DNA, but the consciousness within that body had preexisted it—preexisted herself.

"What're you starin' at, granny?"

The words startled her. The man directly behind her had spoken. He wore a work shirt with the sleeves cut off at the shoulders, no doubt to show off all the tattoos on his muscular arms. She noticed a familiar one in the web between his thumb and forefinger.

She'd seen that around town a lot. Everyone knew it: the Kicker Man.

She hadn't realized she'd been staring,

"Sorry. And I wish you wouldn't call me that."

"You mean 'granny'? What? You ain't?"

"No, I'm not."

She'd almost said "unfortunately," but bit it back. God knew what kind of child that man, that creature Rasalom would father.

"But you could be, right?"

"Yes," she sighed. "I could be."

"Hey," said the second in line in a low voice. "She ain't bad lookin'. I guess that makes her a G-MILF."

They all had a good laugh at that. Carol didn't get it.

"Anyway," she said, "I wasn't staring, just thinking."

But now she was staring. The man's cart was stacked with five cases of spaghetti sauce. And the two carts behind him were overflowing with pasta of all shapes, sizes, and brands. Gristede's carried a lot of pasta, but there couldn't be much left.

"Italian night?" she said.

The guy laughed. "Not exactly."

"Did you leave any?"

The second in line—he had the little Kicker tattoo as well—said, "We ain't leavin' nothin' nowhere no how."

Carol began to count the negatives in that single sentence, but then the cashier began ringing her up. It took only seconds. She swiped her debit card and tapped in her PIN, careful to angle her body so those behind her couldn't see it.

They seemed friendly enough, but they had a bad reputation. She sensed violence percolating just below the surface.

"Your card was rejected, ma'am," said the cashier.

Carol heard the Kicker behind her mutter, "Aw, shit."

"It must have misread it," she told the cashier. "Clear it and I'll run it again."

She did, with the same result: rejected.

The cashier frowned. "'Insufficient funds.'"

The two words stabbed her. "But that's impossible! It's not even ten dollars. There must be—"

"Put it on our charge," the man behind her told the cashier as he held up a green American Express card.

Carol was not about to let someone pay for her.

"No. It's all right. I have cash—"

"Sure you do, granny, but the light's fading and we're on a tight schedule. You're holding us up."

"I can't allow—"

"You'll be doing us a big favor by getting the hell out of the way."

He gathered her blueberries and yogurt and thrust them into the shopping bag dangling from her arm. Then he was pushing her out of the aisle and moving into her place.

"But—"

He waved her off. "Go-go-go. You're starting to piss me off."

Carol hesitated, then moved off. The cashier had already turned his attention to the case of tomato sauce being lifted onto his conveyor belt.

As she exited the store, her thoughts turned to the debit card. *Insufficient funds?* Impossible. Nelson always kept at least a thousand in that particular account—never much more in case someone got hold of the card and PIN and emptied it—but never much less. He'd never let it go empty. Nelson's numbers always added up. There had to be a mistake. Unless . . .

She hurried home through the dying light and went directly to her computer, where she logged onto their CitiBank account. When she checked the balance in the debit account it registered $2.27.

She gasped. Someone must have gained access and raided it. And if they breached one account . . .

A growing sense of dread bloomed to horror as she accessed their other accounts. One after another they showed negligible balances—even Nelson's IRA. Every one of them cleaned out.

She grabbed the phone and speed-dialed Nelson's number. He was stuck in Denver. He didn't answer—probably in a meeting or something—so she left him a frantic message, then searched for the CitiBank customer service number. She'd start there. How could this have happened?

Monroe, Long Island

Sylvia stood in the driveway and watched the workmen swarming along the scaffolding they'd set up against Toad Hall's west wall.

"I think we're gonna make it," said Rudy Snyder as he stood by her side.

Sylvia looked at the sinking sun, the long shadows. The day was ending too quickly, as if winter were approaching instead of summer.

"You promised me, Rudy." She and Alan had called all along the North Shore this morning and finally had coaxed Rudy out of Glen Cove. "You guaranteed me you'd have every window shuttered before sunset. I hope I'm not hearing the sound of someone beginning to hedge."

She tightened her fists to hide her anxiety. She didn't think she could stand another ordeal like last night.

"No way, Mrs. Nash." Rudy wore a peaked cap with *Giants* across the front; he was tall and fat, with red hair and a veiny, bulbous nose. When he aided the work crew, he did so at ground level only. "We'll have them all in, just like I said. But they won't all be wired."

"I don't care about the wiring. You can do that tomorrow. Just get those shutters in good and tight, then pull them down and leave them down."

"You really think all this is necessary?"

She glanced at him, then away. He thought she was a nut, overreacting to some wild stories out of the city.

"You've seen all those little teeth in the siding?"

"Hey, I'm not saying you didn't have a problem last night, but do you really think they'll come back again?"

"I *know* they will. Especially since they don't have to come all the way from Central Park this time."

"You mean because of that hole that opened up in Oyster Bay this morning? Whatta y'think's goin' on?"

"Don't you know? It's the end of the world." My world, at least.

Rudy's smile was wary. "No . . . really."

"Please finish the job." She didn't feel like talking about it. "Seal the house up tight. That will earn you the bonus I promised."

"You got it."

He bustled off and began shouting at his workers to get their asses moving.

Sylvia sighed as she stared at Toad Hall. The old place's carefully maintained look of faded elegance was gone, destroyed by the rolling storm shutters. But they were good, tight, with heavy-duty slats of solid steel. The best. During the day they could be rolled up into the cylinders bolted above the windows; at sunset they'd slide down along tracks fastened to the window frames. They'd be cranked down by hand tonight, but after they were fully wired up tomorrow, Sylvia would be able to roll them all up and down with the flick of a single switch. This particular model was designed to withstand storms of hurricane force.

Tonight they were going to have to withstand a storm of a different sort. She prayed they'd be enough.

"The back's done," Alan said, rolling toward her. "They're moving around here to help finish up this side." His gaze followed Sylvia's to the anachronisms being attached to Toad Hall. "A shame, isn't it?"

Sylvia smiled, glad to know their thoughts were still in synch, even after the uncomfortable silence of the ride back from the city. Especially when Alan had told her what that nut had said as they were leaving.

Only three will live to return.

What an awful thing to say.

"I feel like I'm witnessing the end of an era."

"It might be the end of a lot more than that," Alan said.

Sylvia felt all her muscles tighten. She said nothing. She knew where Alan was leading and didn't want to go there. She'd been dreading this conversation since they left Glaeken's apartment.

"Talk to me, Sylvia. Why are you so angry?"

"I'm not angry."

"You're coiled like a steel spring."

Again she said nothing. *I'm coiled, all right,* she thought, *but it's not anger. I wish it were. I can deal with anger.*

"What do you think, Syl?" Alan said finally.

Why couldn't he let it drop?

"About what?"

"About Glaeken. About what he said this morning."

"I haven't had time to think much about anything, least of all that old crank's ravings."

"I believe him," Alan said. "And so do you. I saw it in your eyes when you were listening. I know your expression when you think you're being bullshitted. You weren't wearing it back in Glaeken's apartment. So why don't you admit it?"

"All right," she said through tight lips. "I believe him too. Does that make you happy?"

She regretted that last sentence as soon as she said it, but it seemed to roll right off Alan.

"Good. Now we're getting somewhere. So I've got to ask you: If you believe him, why did you walk out?"

"Because I don't trust him. Don't misunderstand me on that," she added quickly. "I don't think he's lying to us. I think he's sincere, I . . . just . . . don't think he's as much in control of his end of things as he thinks he is . . . or wants us to believe he is."

"Maybe not. He was trying to sell us—you, especially—on something none of us is prepared to accept. The only reason we *can* accept it is that we've already had our lives turned upside down by something that ninety-nine percent of rational humanity would swear is impossible."

Sylvia sighed. "The *Dat-tay-vao*."

"Yeah. And if he says he needs the *Dat-tay-vao* to try to close up those holes and keep the days from shrinking to nothing and the world being overrun by those monstrosities from last night, why would you hold Jeffy away from him? Jeffy doesn't need the *Dat-tay-vao*."

"How do you know that?"

"Has it ever treated its carrier well? Look at Walter Erskine. Look at me. Remember the lines from the old song about the one who carries the Touch? '. . . He bears the weight of the balance that must be struck.'"

"But the *Dat-tay-vao* hasn't harmed Jeffy."

"Only because he hasn't used it—yet. He hasn't had an opportunity—yet. But what if he does find out, and does begin using it?"

Here it comes. She felt the pressure building up in her, edging past the point of control until she had to say it.

"And what if the *Dat-tay-vao*'s relationship with Jeffy is different? Special?"

Alan's puzzled gaze searched her face.

"I don't—"

"What if the *Dat-tay-vao*'s presence is keeping Jeffy like he is?" She tried to hold the tremor out of her voice but it grew, lending the words a jittery vibrato. "What if it's the reason he's been alert, responsive, laughing, singing, reading, playing with other kids—a normal boy—for the past year? Alan, what if that old man takes the *Dat-tay-vao* away for his focus or whatever he was talking about and Jeffy goes back to the way he was when I adopted him?" The tremor spread from her voice to her body now. She couldn't control the shaking in her hands and knees. "What if he becomes autistic again, Alan?"

Sylvia pressed her hands against her face, as much to hide as to catch the tears springing into her eyes.

"God, Alan, I'm so ashamed!"

Suddenly someone was standing beside her. She felt a pair of arms slip around her and hold her close.

"Alan! You're standing!"

"Not very well, I'm afraid. But that's not the point. Watching you all morning, trying to figure out what's going on inside you, and never seeing how frightened you are. Christ, what a jerk."

"But you're standing!"

"You've seen me do it before."

"But not without the parallel bars."

"You're my parallel bars at the moment. I couldn't just sit there and watch you go to pieces and spout that nonsense about being ashamed."

"But I *am* ashamed." She twisted in his arms and clung to him. "If Glaeken's right, the whole world is threatened, billions of people in danger, and here I'm only worried about one little boy. I'm ready to let the whole world take a flying leap rather than jeopardize him."

"But that's not just any little boy. That's Jeffy—*your* little boy, the most important little boy in your world. Don't be ashamed of putting him first. That's where he should be. That's where he belongs."

"But the whole *world*, Alan! How can I say no?" The panic welled up again. "How can I say *yes*?"

"I can't answer that for you, Syl. I wish I could. You've got to weigh everything. Got to figure that if Glaeken's right, and he can't get the *Dat-tay-vao* for the focus he was talking about, then Jeffy's a goner along with everybody else. There's nothing to say that he can't lure the *Dat-tay-vao* from Jeffy without harming him. If Glaeken can then turn all these horrors around, Jeffy will have a safer world to live in."

"But if Jeffy is left in autistic limbo again . . ."

"That branches into two possibilities. Glaeken succeeds and Jeffy's back to where he was a year ago and we deal with it and hope for a medical breakthrough in autism. Or Glaeken fails despite Jeffy's sacrifice."

"Then it's all been for nothing."

"Not necessarily. If nothing else, Jeffy's relapse into autism will shield him from the living hell Glaeken's predicting. That might be a blessing."

She clung more tightly to Alan. "I wish this weren't up to me."

"I know. Too bad he's not old enough to be brought in on the decision."

Sylvia felt a vibration begin to shimmer through Alan's lean body. She looked down and saw that his left leg had begun to tremble. As she watched, it began to jitter and shake. Alan reached a hand down to steady it, but as soon as he let go, the tremors started again.

Alan smiled. "I feel like Robert Klein doing his old I-can't-stop-my-leg routine."

"What's wrong?"

"Spasm. Happens when I'm on it too long. Used to be in both legs, now it's just my left. Maybe I could try an Elvis imitation."

"Stop it. Nobody listens to Elvis anymore."

"I do. But only his Sun stuff, and pre-Army RCA."

Sylvia smiled. Alan and his oldies. Part of his therapy after the coma had been to rebuild his doo-wop collection. It had worked miracles with his memory linkages.

"Here. Sit down."

He eased himself back into the wheelchair. The leg stopped its jittering as soon as he took his weight off it.

"Uh-oh," Alan said, slapping the still leg. "There goes my new career."

Sylvia bent and hugged him around the neck.

"Have I told you that I love you?"

"Not today."

"I love you, Alan. And thanks."

"For what?"

"For standing up and holding me when I needed it. And for making things clear. I think I know what I'm going to do now."

"Missus?"

Sylvia started at the sound of Ba's voice. She wished he'd learn to make a little more noise when he moved about. He was like a cat.

He stood behind her holding the new club he'd been working on most of the afternoon to replace the one he'd given to that Jack fellow. Like its predecessor it was studded with diamond-like chew-wasp teeth.

"Yes, Ba?"

"Where is the Boy?"

Fingers of unease brushed her throat.

"I thought he was with you."

"He was in the garage with me. He wished to go outside. I knew the Missus and the Doctor were here so . . ."

Ba's voice trailed off as he did a slow turn, scanning the perimeter of the grounds.

Sylvia started toward the backyard. She never let Jeffy out alone by the water. Nightmares of dragging the Long Island Sound for his body . . .

"Maybe he's—"

"No, Missus. I watched him run around house to front."

"Maybe he's inside, then."

"He is not, Missus."

The long shadows seemed to be reaching for her. The sun had become a red glow behind the willows along the west wall. The fingers of unease at her throat stretched, reaching toward panic, encircling and squeezing.

Rudy came toward her across the lawn. "We're done!" he said, grinning.

"Have you seen Jeffy?" she asked. "My little boy?"

"The blond-haired kid? Not for a while. Not for a few hours. But we've been kinda occupied with getting those shutters up on time. Now, about that bonus—"

"I'll pay you everything later—tomorrow. Right now we've got to find Jeffy!"

Alan said, "I'll check the waterfront. Ba, you beat the bushes along the wall. Sylvia, why don't you check the road?"

As Alan and Ba went their separate ways, Sylvia hurried down the drive-way toward the front gate. When she reached the street she stopped, looking both ways, straining to see in the waning light.

Which way?

Shore Drive followed the curve of the sound, running east toward the center of town and west toward Lattingtown and Glen Cove. Instinctively, she started east, toward the pale moon rising full and translucent in the fading light. Jeffy loved the toy shops and video arcades along the harbor front. If he was traveling Shore Drive, that was the way he'd go. She took a few steps, then stopped, suddenly unsure.

If I were Jeffy, she thought, which way would I go?

Slowly she turned and faced the other way, where the sun perched on the horizon, sinking behind Manhattan.

Manhattan . . . where Glaeken was . . . where Jeffy and the power within him wanted to be . . .

She began running west. Her heart was a claustrophobic prisoner, trapped in her chest, pounding frantically on the bars of her ribs. Her eyes roved left and right, scanning the yards along the road. All oversize lots here, with as much frontage along the street as the shoreline. Unlike Toad Hall, most of the other yards were open, their manicured grounds studded with trees and shrubs and free-form plantings. Jeffy could have followed a squirrel or a bird into any one of them.

He might be anywhere.

She slowed but kept moving. She didn't want to miss him. To her left a bat-tered red pickup truck squealed to a halt on the street. Rudy leaned out the window as the rest of his work crew sped by him in their own cars and trucks.

"Any sign of your boy?"

Sylvia shook her head. "No. Look, we call him Jeffy. If you see him on your way—"

"I'll send him back. Good luck."

He sped off and Sylvia, with increasingly frequent glances at the disappearing sun, resumed her search. Before she'd traveled a block—the blocks were long out here—the sun was gone.

My God, my God, she thought, the sun's down and those horrible insects are probably rising out of that new hole and heading this way right now.

If she didn't get Jeffy back to the house soon those things would rip him to pieces. And if she stayed out here much longer, *she* would be ripped to pieces.

What am I going to do?

WFPW-FM

> FREDDY: All right, everybody. It's official—the sun's gone down early again. It sank outta sight at 6:44. One hour and thirty-nine minutes early. If I were you I'd get off the streets. *Now.* Get indoors and keep it tuned here. We'll keep you updated between the greatest songs ever recorded.
> <cue: "Frantic Desolation">

Hank thumbed the DOWN button on the remote and watched his steel hurricane shutters slide down their steel tracks outside his two windows. Then he stepped to his steel door and locked it.

Safe.

The Lodge was built like a fortress with an exterior of thick granite block and stone walls within. Steel and stone—what could be safer?

He owed much of that to the Kicker Man—or rather his more recent Kicker Man dreams. These had come to him months ago, showing the Kicker Man being attacked by birds—or at least what he'd assumed at the time to be birds. Now he knew they were big bugs from hell. Same difference. The dreams had inspired the shutters and the steel door, and they'd keep him safe from any goddamn bugs.

The good old Kicker Man. He'd inspired the book and he'd returned whenever anything heavy was going down. Hadn't let Hank down yet.

But the food . . . that was all Hank's idea.

He sat on his bed and looked around the room. One hell of a busy day. Running in and out with five-gallon jugs of spring water, boxes of batteries, a propane stove, and food, food, food. Cartons of canned goods—*stacks* of cartons leaned against the walls. It looked more like a warehouse than a bedroom.

After he'd sent his guys out to the grocery stores, he had a better idea. Why think small? Why not go to the source? So he rented a van, looked up a distributor, and really stocked up. Drove it around back of the Lodge and had some of the hangers-on bring it all up here.

Tomorrow he'd send the guys out in an army of trucks and they'd fill the Lodge's cellar.

But he'd had a second coup today.

He reached under his bed and dragged out a pair of canvas bags. Heavy suckers—almost fifty pounds each. They clinked as they settled on the floor. He pulled one open, reached inside, and pulled out a fistful of quarters.

Yeah. Two whole bags of pre-1964 quarters. Four thousand of them, all solid silver. He'd bought them from a coin dealer on Fifty-sixth. And *charged* them. He couldn't believe it. The clueless jerk took Visa for them!

Didn't anyone get it? If daylight shrank to nothing and things really started falling apart, these coins were going to be like gold, like diamonds. Each of these quarters could be worth fifty dollars apiece in buying power. Precious metals would be what mattered. Gold, silver, gems would replace government paper.

He looked up at the cases of food around him. But food would be more valuable than any metal. Can't eat gold or silver. In a world without sunlight, where nothing but mushrooms can grow, nothing was going to be more valuable than food. The man with the full larder would be king.

Nightwings

"There they are!"

Bill Ryan focused the binoculars on the hole in the Sheep Meadow. They brought the people below into sharp focus, seemingly within reach, but the people weren't what interested him.

"Right on time," Glaeken said from behind his right shoulder.

Bill watched the fluttering things begin to collect under the barrier stretched over the hole, watched them straining upward against the steel mesh. Arrayed against them under the banks of lights was an army of exterminators sheathed in heavy protective gear and masks, wielding hoses attached to tank trucks equipped with high-pressure pumps. At a signal from somewhere, all the nozzles came to life, spewing golden fluid.

"What are they spraying?" Glaeken said.

"Looks like some sort of insecticide."

Glaeken grunted and turned away. "No toxins are going to hurt those things. They'd do far better with gasoline and a match." He turned on the TV. "Here. It's being broadcast. You'll get a better angle here."

Bill stepped to his side and watched the scene below in living color. Apparently Glaeken was right: In the telephoto close-up on the screen, the insecticide was having no effect on the steadily increasing number of creatures massed under the mesh, wetting them down and little else. He looked at Nick, sitting on the sofa, staring at the wall, then turned back to Glaeken.

"Think the net will hold through the night?"

"It doesn't matter," Glaeken said with his predictable pessimism.

Bill shook his head. Perhaps being pessimistic was being realistic, but he couldn't suppress the thrill of hope that shot through him when he saw all those monstrosities trapped under the steel mesh.

"Why not? It shows we can contain them."

"Even as we speak, the holes in Queens, on Staten Island, and out on Long Island are spewing out the very creatures they think they've defeated here."

"Then we'll cap those too."

"Bigger things are coming. The speedy little flying things arrive first because they're the quickest. Then come the slower flying things. Then come the crawlers."

Crawlers . . . the very word made Bill's skin ripple with revulsion.

"Then we've bought only a little time here," Bill said, his spirits palpably sagging.

"They haven't bought even that. For somewhere along the way . . . the leviathans will come."

Bill was about to ask for some elaboration on that when he heard a whining howl from the park, loud enough to be audible through the locked and sealed windows. On the screen he noticed the exterminators and observers start to back away from the hole. The streams from the hoses seemed to be blowing back in their faces.

"Something's happening."

He returned to the window with the binocs. Down in the Sheep Meadow, a gale-force wind was roaring from the hole, bulging the heavy steel mesh upward as it crushed the insects against it.

"Looks like the hole is trying to blow the lid off!"

Glaeken came up beside him. "No," he said softly. "Something's coming. Something big."

Bill squinted through the binoculars as the wind howl grew louder. The exterminators had turned off their hoses and were still backing away. As he watched, a number of the steel girders anchoring the mesh at the south side tore from the ground. That end of the mesh began to flap free, releasing a horde of the killer insects. Panic took charge of the Sheep Meadow.

"Big?" Bill said. "How—?"

And then it happened. Something burst from the hole. Something beyond big. Something gargantuan, filling the two-hundred-foot diameter, something dark as the deepest cavern at the bottom of the Mariana Trench at midnight. It rammed through the steel mesh like a night train through a spider's web and kept hurtling upward, a monstrous, glistening, rough-hewn piling thrusting its seemingly endless length into the darkening sky.

Bill tore the glasses from his eyes and watched as it came free of the hole and continued upward. Awed, he pressed his face against the windowpane and followed its course, wondering how far it could go before it lost momentum and fell back to earth, his mind reeling at the thought of the damage from something the size of a small skyscraper crashing down on the city.

Its rate of rise slowed, then stopped. For an instant it paused, a cyclopean column of black hanging vertically in the air. Then it began to tilt and fall. But as it fell it changed. Huge wings unfolded, unfurling like flags, and spread, stretching across the sky, obscuring the emerging stars. The thing leveled itself and began to glide. It swooped over the park, then banked to the east and was gone.

Thoroughly shaken, Bill turned to Glaeken.

"The leviathan you mentioned?"

Glaeken nodded. "One of them. There'll be more."

"But how's that thing going to get back into the hole at sunrise?"

"They don't have to. They can keep to the nightside and stay ahead of sunrise as they roam the skies." He looked up at the stars. "Do you know the constellations?"

"Not really. The Big Dipper, maybe, but—"

"I do. And they've changed. Those aren't the same stars up there as last night."

Outside, another whining howl began to issue from the hole.

"Here comes another," Glaeken said.

Part of Bill wanted to pull the curtains, shut off the TV, and crawl under the couch. But another part had to watch. He dragged a chair up to the window and waited in horrid fascination to see what would happen next.

WFPW-FM

Reports are filtering in from around the globe, especially from Europe where night-fall occurs hours ahead of ours. All the new holes that opened during the day are spewing forth swarms of creatures tonight, just like the ones that caused such devastation in our town last night. The reports also describe four species now—two more than we saw around here. Some of the local reports say the infestation is particularly heavy on Long Island . . .

Monroe, Long Island

Trembling, Sylvia hurried through the growing darkness, crying out, *screaming* Jeffy's name. But only the faint echo of her own voice answered. She was panting from the unaccustomed exertion.

Suddenly a red pickup roared around the curve ahead. Rudy—and God, could that be a little blond head peering through the windshield from the passenger seat? Sylvia ran into the street and narrowly missed being hit as the pickup swerved into the curb.

Rudy grinned as he hopped out of the cab and came around the front of his truck. "I hope this is him, Mrs. Nash. 'Cause if he ain't, somebody's gonna have me up on kidnappin' charges sure."

Sylvia, weak-kneed with relief and fighting tears, said, "No, that's him." She pulled open the passenger door and reached for Jeffy. "I don't know how to thank you."

"Found him *way* down the road there, truckin' along like he had some-place real important to go."

She hugged the child against her. "Oh, Jeffy, Jeffy, you had me so worried!"

"I want to go see Glaeken."

"You can't right now, honey. We've got to get back to the house so those"—what had the old man called them?—"so those chew wasps don't get us."

"But Glaeken needs me."

Sylvia held him tighter. Something unholy about this child's attraction to that old man.

Rudy laughed. "Kids. Aren't they somethin'? Who's Glaeken? A little friend of his? Must really want to see him bad. I damn near had to drag your little guy into my truck to get him back here. I guess you've drilled it into him not to—"

Something *whizzed* between them. Rudy jerked his head back.

"What the hell was that?"

Sylvia cringed and wrapped her arms around Jeffy.

"It's a chewer bug, Mom!"

Another of the things sailed by. Rudy ducked but not quite fast enough. The creature knocked his Giants cap askew. He took it off and gawked at the piece bitten out of the beak.

"Christ!"

"Run, Jeffy!" Sylvia cried. "We've got to get home!"

Rudy grabbed her arm before they could get moving.

"Into the truck! I'll drive you back!"

Sylvia pushed Jeffy ahead of her into the cab, slammed the door behind her, and rolled up the window. Rudy hopped into the driver seat and yanked on the gearshift. The pickup lurched forward.

"Close your window, Rudy!"

He flashed her a lopsided smile. "It don't go up."

"Then I think you'd better plan on staying at our place tonight."

"Nah! Ain't no buncha bugs gonna keep me from goin' home. I don't care how big they are. They're only—what the fuck?"

He downshifted and the pickup lurched to a slower speed. They were almost to Toad Hall, but up ahead something was floating across the road—a group of somethings. They reminded Sylvia of the belly flies from last night, only these things were much bigger. Football-sized sacs sat atop their bodies like transparent balloons. Double dragonfly wings jutted from their sides, and long gray tendrils dangled below. They looked like a school of airborne Portuguese men-of-war.

Rudy swerved to try to go around the floating phalanx, but the balloonlike creatures banked toward the pickup. The front tire on the passenger side caromed off the Belgian block curb, violently bouncing Sylvia and Jeffy in the seat, and veering the truck toward the hovering men-of-war.

The pickup slammed into them, splattering the hood and windshield with ruptured sacs, broken wings, and gray fluid.

"Yeah!" Rudy shouted. "That'll show 'em!"

He hit the windshield wiper switch but the blades were jammed under the debris.

"Damn! Can't see."

He slowed the truck to a crawl, stuck his head out the window, and reached around to the windshield.

"No!" Sylvia cried. "Rudy, don't—!"

His scream cut her off. He jerked his head and arm back but a mass of gray tendrils came with him. They were alive, writhing, twisting, curling, crawling along Rudy's arm to his shoulder, reaching for his face. Close up like this Sylvia could see the tendrils were lined with tiny suckers, like octopus tentacles, except these were rimmed with tiny teeth, and in the center of each was a pale, curling tongue. The teeth were drawing blood as they moved, and the tongues were lapping it up.

Rudy looked at her, his eyes wide with pain and terror. He opened his mouth, whether to say something or scream again, Sylvia never knew, for another mass of tentacles swept through the open window and engulfed his head, the tips plunging into his mouth and worming into his nostrils. She had one last glimpse of his bulging eyes, and then he was pulled kicking and flailing through the side window.

As Jeffy's scream mingled with her own, the pickup stalled and jerked dead. Sylvia pulled the handle at her side and kicked the door. As it opened a mass of tentacles and broken wings slid off the roof. The tentacles reached for her as they fell past but she pulled back in time to avoid them. Then, grabbing Jeffy, she leapt out and they crouched beside the front wheel.

The darkening air was alive with flying things and thrummed with the low-pitched hum of their wings as they darted and swooped about the pickup.

Sylvia rose warily and looked about for Rudy. She froze at the sight of a huge, ungainly, twisting shape rising slowly on the far side of the hood—a cluster of a dozen or so men-of-war, their float sacs bumping one another, their tentacles a writhing gorgonian mass, slithering about on—

Sylvia groaned as she recognized Rudy's boots and denimed legs protruding from the lower end of the mass, his toes dangling three or four feet above the pavement. His head and torso were engulfed in the hungry tangle of squirming, feeding tentacles. As she watched, the legs kicked feebly once, twice, then shuddered and hung limp in the air.

Rudy! Oh, dear God, poor Rudy!

Prompted by the breeze, the floating, feeding mass began a slow drift down the twilit street.

Sylvia swiveled, frantically looking for a hiding place, wondering if they might not be better off in the cab of the truck. Across the street she spotted a corner of the wall that surrounded Toad Hall. Farther down the sidewalk the wrought-iron gate stood open.

Jeffy was still crouched by the tire. She pulled him to his feet and pushed him around the front of the truck ahead of her.

"Run, Jeffy! Run for the wall!"

Crouching over him as a shield, she propelled him ahead of her across the street toward the wall; when they reached its base, they raced for the gate, hugging the stones as they ran. Belly flies and chew wasps circled about with another new species, similar to the chewers in size but equipped with a spear-shaped head. Most were winging toward Toad Hall. Apparently the bugs hadn't spotted them in the shadows. But that would change once they got through the gate. She and Jeffy would be completely exposed in the open stretch along the driveway between the gate and the willows. But she forced that out of her mind for the moment. She'd worry about it when the time came. First they had to reach the gate.

Something moved in her peripheral vision and she glanced right. Men-of-war, three of them, in the middle of the street opposite the gate, their long trailing tendrils curling and uncurling with hungry anticipation as they glided her way with graceful, deadly purpose.

They've spotted us!

Stifling a scream, she caught Jeffy under the arms and lifted him, carrying him ahead of her as she threw every ounce of strength and will into her pumping legs. She had to reach the gate before those things cut her off. Suddenly a belly fly was swooping toward her face. She ducked, stumbled, regained her balance and kept running.

But the men-of-war were closer. They were slow but they had the angle on her. Sylvia moaned softly as she realized she wasn't going to beat them to the gate.

Only three will live to return.

The words crawled across her mind. Were they going to prove true? Was she the one who wasn't going to make it? Or would it be Jeffy?

Her limbs responded to the horror of seeing Jeffy end like Rudy and she picked up speed. Her arms were throbbing, her lungs burned with the unaccustomed exertion, her legs wanted to fold under her, but she pushed it.

Almost there!

But so were the men-of-war. Seeing them closing, Sylvia pushed her speed up a final desperate notch. They were so close she could smell their foul carrion odor. The tendrils swept forward through the air, reaching for her. She screamed in horror and despair of making it as she ducked and rounded the gatepost corner with only inches to spare.

A sob of relief was bursting free in her throat when something tangled in her hair and yanked her back. She pushed Jeffy ahead of her.

"Run home, Jeffy!"

He started to obey her, but when he glanced over his shoulder he stopped and screamed.

"Mommy! It's got you!"

"Jeffy! Run for the house! Please!"

But he stood rooted to the spot, transfixed with horror.

Sylvia reached back and felt a clump of slimy tentacles tangled in her hair, worming toward her scalp. A few wrapped around her fingers and she felt the sharp bite of the suckers, the rasping licks of the tiny tongues before she snatched her hand free. To her right and left she saw other men-of-war sailing her way, their hungry, questing tendrils extended toward her face. She had a sudden vision of herself as a floating corpse like Rudy.

It's me! she thought. I'm the one who's not going to make it!

She ducked as they closed in on her, her scalp blazing with pain as the thing in her hair tried to hold her back. The tentacles of the others were only inches away now, reaching for her face. She put her hands up to swat them away but they became entangled and trapped. Frantically she yanked and twisted but couldn't pull free. She felt the bites, felt her blood flow, felt the tiny tongues begin to lap. But she bottled her screams. She wouldn't let those tentacles reach into her mouth like they did Rudy's. As they climbed up her arm, her vision swam, darkened. The earth seemed to tilt under her—

She heard a *crunch* and suddenly the tentacles sheathing her right hand and forearm loosened their grip. She yanked free and stared.

The creature was sagging toward the driveway, its float sac ruptured, its wings broken and fluttering futilely. And then she realized she was not alone.

"Ba!"

He towered over her in the dimness, his clothes torn and bloody, swinging his razor-toothed billy club. Another *crunch* and the tentacles clutching her left hand spasmed and loosened their grip enough for her to pull free.

"Hold still, Missus," he said, and he swung his club at her head.

Sylvia winced instinctively, heard a third crunch behind her, and then her hair was free. Ba pulled her forward. She needed no further encouragement. She picked up Jeffy and started to run.

The air was alive with buzzing, soaring, biting *things*. Fully alerted to their presence now, the bugs were all around her and Jeffy. Wings brushed her

face and hair, jaws clicked on empty air as they narrowly missed her. They'd
have had no hope without Ba. He took the lead, running tall, daring the creatures to attack him as he slashed left and right with his club. Sylvia clung to
the back of his coat, awed by his reflexes, by the length of his reach, and by his
seeming ability to see in the dark. Maybe he struck at the sound of the things.
Whatever his method, he was clearing a path for them through the winged horrors.

Almost to the house. Another twenty feet and they'd be at the door. The
closed door. What if it was locked?

Where was Alan? Good God, if he was still outside he was a goner, a sitting duck in that wheelchair.

Just then one of the chew wasps whizzed past her cheek and buried its
teeth into Ba's shoulder. He grunted with pain but kept running, kept swinging
his club ahead of him and clearing the path. Fighting her rising gorge, Sylvia
shifted Jeffy's weight to one arm and reached up with her free hand; she forced
her fingers around the chewer's body and gave it a violent twist. The body
cracked and the teeth came free of Ba's back as cold fluid ran down her arm.

Ba turned and nodded his thanks, and at that instant, a writhing mass of
tentacles dropped onto the back of his neck. He stumbled but managed to hold
his balance and keep moving. And then they were at the door, Sylvia pulling
whatever tentacles she could reach free of Ba's neck as he groped for the door-
knob. If the door was locked they were doomed. They'd die right here on Toad
Hall's front steps.

But the door opened before Ba reached it. Light flooded out. She had a
glimpse of Alan looking up from his wheelchair as he held it open. They tumbled through to the foyer and the door slammed shut behind them. Ba dropped
his billy and sank to his knees, clawing at the tentacled monstrosity wrapping
itself around his throat. Sylvia put Jeffy down and went to help him but Alan
suddenly rolled between them and reached toward the floor.

"Drop your hands a second, Ba."

As Ba obeyed, Alan lifted the spiked club. He swung at the man-of-war,
ripping its air sac and tearing open its body. The tentacles loosened their grip
and Ba ripped it free, hurling it to the floor. As it tried to flutter-crawl toward
Jeffy across the marble floor, Alan ran it over with the big wheel of his chair.
Twice. Finally the thing lay still.

Behind her, Jeffy was sobbing. From somewhere in the basement, Phemus
barked wildly.

Ba staggered to his feet. His neck was a mass of blood, his clothing shredded and bloody. He faced her, panting, ragged, swaying.

"You and the Boy are all right, Missus?"

"Yes, Ba. Thanks to you. But you need a doctor."

"I will go wash myself." He turned and headed for the guest bathroom.

Sylvia looked at Alan. Tears streaked his face. His lips were trembling.

"I thought you were dead! I knew you were out there and needed help and I couldn't go to you." He pounded his thighs. "God *damn* these useless things!"

Sylvia lifted Jeffy and carried him to Alan. She seated herself on Alan's lap and adjusted Jeffy on hers. Alan's arms encircled them both. Jeffy began to cry. Sylvia understood perfectly. For the first time today she felt safe. And that feeling of safety opened the floodgates. She began to sob as she had never sobbed in her life. The three of them cried together.

The Horror Channel's Drive-In Theatre

Night of Bloody Horror (1969) Howco International

Cataclysm

Maui

The *moana puka* appeared around dusk.

Kolabati and Moki had been standing on the lanai watching the sun sink into the Pacific—earlier than ever. Barely a quarter to seven. They were also watching the airport far below. Kolabati couldn't remember ever seeing it so busy.

"Look at them," Moki said, grinning as he slipped an arm around her waist. "The shrinking daylight's got them all spooked. See how they run."

"It's got me spooked too."

"Don't let it. If it sends all the Jap *malahinis* scurrying west back to their own islands, and all the *haoles* back to the mainland—preferably back to New York, where they can fall into that hole in Central Park—it's all for the good. It will leave the islands to the Hawaiians."

She'd been fascinated by the news of the mysterious hole in the Sheep

Meadow. She knew the area well. Her brother Kusum had once owned an apartment overlooking Central Park.

"*I'm* not Hawaiian."

He tightened his grip on her waist. "As long as you're with me, you are."

Somehow his encircling arm was not as comforting as she would have wished. They watched the airport in silence awhile longer, then Moki released her and leaned on the railing, staring out at the valley, the sky.

"Something's going to happen soon. Do you feel it?"

Kolabati nodded. "Yes. I've felt it for days."

"Something wonderful."

"Wonderful?" She stared at him. Could he mean it? She'd been plagued by an almost overwhelming sense of dread since the trade winds had reversed themselves. "No. Not wonderful at all. Something terrible."

His grin became fierce. "Terrible for other people, maybe. But wonderful for us. You wait and see."

Kolabati didn't know what to make of Moki lately. His behavior had remained bizarre since Wednesday when the gash on his hand had healed so quickly. At least once a day he'd cut himself to see if the healing power was still with him. Each time he healed more quickly than the day before. And with each healing the wild light in his eyes had grown.

As the daylight began to fade, Kolabati turned toward the door, but Moki grabbed her arm.

"Wait. What is that?"

He was staring east, toward Kahului and beyond. She followed his gaze and saw it. Something in the water. White water, bubbling, roiling. A gigantic disturbance. With foreboding ballooning within her, Kolabati grabbed the binoculars from their hook and focused on the disturbance.

At first all she saw was turbulent white water, giant chop, a chaos of sloshing and swirling. But as she watched, the turbulence became ordered, took shape. The white water began to swirl in a uniform direction, counterclockwise, around a central point. She identified the center in time to see it sink below the surface and become a dark, spinning, sucking maw.

"Moki, look!" She handed him the glasses.

"I see!" he said, but took them anyway.

She watched his expression as he adjusted the lenses. His smile grew.

"A whirlpool! It's too close to shore to be from converging currents. It's got to be a crack in the ocean floor. No, wait!" He lowered the glasses and stared at her, his face flushed with excitement. "A hole! It has to be a hole in the ocean floor, just like the one in New York! We've got our own hole here!"

Together—Moki with undisguised glee, Kolabati with growing, gnawing unease—they watched the whirlpool organize and expand. The troubles from the outer world, from the mainland, were intruding on her paradise. That could bring only misfortune. They watched together until it was too dark to see, then went inside and turned on the TV to catch what the news had to say about it. The scientists all agreed—the ocean floor had opened in a fashion similar to the phenomenon in Manhattan's Central Park. Already the locals had a name for it: *moana puka*—ocean hole.

Moki could barely contain his excitement. He wandered the great room, talking a blue streak, gesticulating wildly.

"You know what's going to happen, Bati? The water's going to be sucked down into whatever abyss those holes lead to, and it's going to keep on disappearing into nowhere. And eventually the ocean level is going to drop. And if it drops far enough, do you know what will happen?"

Kolabati shook her head. She had an inescapable feeling that she was witnessing the beginning of the end—of everything.

"Greater Maui will be reborn." He went to the doorway that opened onto the lanai and gestured into the darkness. "Molokai, Lanai, Kahoolawe, even little Molokini—all of them were part of Maui before the Ice Age, connected to our island by valleys rather than cut off by channels of sea water. I see it happening, Bati. I see them all joined again, reunited after ages of separation. A single island, as big as the Big Island. Maybe bigger. And I'll play a part in the future of Greater Maui."

"What future?" Kolabati said, joining him at the door. "If the Pacific Ocean drops that far we'll be looking at the end of the world!"

"No, Bati. Not the end. The beginning. The beginning of a new world."

And then the sky caught fire. All around them, like a sustained flash of sheet lightning, the night ignited. At the far end of the island she saw the Lahaina coast and the Iao Valley of West Maui light up like day. The same with the island of Lanai across the channel. Then a blast of superheated air, choked with flaming debris, roared overhead and to the sides, withering west Maui, searing Lanai, yet she and Moki remained in cool shadow, shielded by the enormous bulk of Haleakala.

"Shiva!" she cried in the Bengali dialect of her childhood. "What are you doing?"

And then came the sound. The floor shook and seemed to fall away beneath her as the night exploded with a rumbling, booming, deep-throated roar that shuddered through her flesh, shook every cell of her body, and rattled the very core of her being.

As she tumbled to the floor she heard Moki's voice faintly above the din. "Earthquake!"

He crawled to where she lay and rolled on top of her, using his body to shield her from the shelves and lamps and sculptures crashing down about them.

It went on forever. Kolabati didn't know how the house's cantilever supports managed to hold. Any moment now they were going to give way and send the house tumbling down the slope. Only once before in her life—when Jack had borrowed her necklace for a number of hours and all of her years had begun to assert their weight upon her—had Kolabati felt so close to death.

The earth tremors and shudders persisted but became quieter, muffled. Moki lifted himself off her and she struggled to her feet.

"Pehea oe?"

"All right . . . I think," she said, not bothering to reply in Hawaiian.

They clung to each other like sailors on a heaving deck. Kolabati looked around. The great room was a shambles. Moki's sculptures lay all about in pieces, their carved wood cracked and splintered, their lava bases shattered.

"Oh, Moki. Your work!"

"The sculptures don't matter," he said, clutching her tight against him. "They're the past. I would have had to smash them myself. Don't you see, Bati? This is it! The new beginning I told you about. It's here!"

He drew her to the trembling lanai where they leaned over the railing and stared up at the dark mass of Haleakala, toward her summit, rimmed now with fiery light.

"Look, Bati!" he said, pointing up the slope. "Haleakala is alive! After hundreds of years of dormancy, she's come back to life! For me! For us!"

Kolabati pulled away and fled back inside. She flipped one light switch after another but the room remained dark. She picked her way through the debris to the television but could not get it to work. The electricity was gone. At least they had a generator. She hoped it still worked.

"Bati!" Moki called. *"Hele mai.* Stand with me and watch Haleakala. The House of the Sun has rekindled her fires. She's calling us home!"

Kolabati stood amid the shambles of their house—their *life*—and knew that her time of peace had ended, that things would never be the same. She was afraid.

"That wasn't just Haleakala erupting, Moki," she said, her voice trembling like the floor beneath her. "Something else happened. Something far more violent and cataclysmic than an old volcano coming to life."

It's the end of the world, she thought.

She could feel it in her bones and in the way the ancient necklace pulsed against her skin. The air about her screamed with tortured *atman,* released in sudden, violent death.

Haleakala had awakened, but what else had happened?

The pain is gone. Only the ecstasy remains. And it grows. The night things run rampant in the dark sectors above. Rasalom senses the delirium of fear and pain and grief and misery they leave in their wake.

And then came the convulsion of death and horror when the Pacific volcanoes roared back to life. The surge was almost unbearable.

As a result, the pace of the Change has picked up. He is so much larger now, and his granite womb has grown to accommodate him. The chips of sloughed stone have disappeared down the hole that opened in the bottom of the chamber. Like the other holes that have opened around this globe, it, too, is bottomless. But it leads to a different place. A place of icy flame. Even now, a faint glow creeps up from the depths.

And the Change . . . his limbs have thickened, hardened to a stony consistency. His head has drawn into his trunk, concentrating his essence in a soft, bulbous core, a fleshy center in the hub of a four-spoked wheel.

He spreads his intangible feeders farther and farther afield, seeking more nourishment. He can never get enough.

SUNDAY

Sunday in New York

WNYW-TV

And now the news: The sun rose late at 7:10 A.M. this morning and found not only a devastated New York City but the entire world reeling from the events of last night . . .

Manhattan

What a night.

Jack stood yawning in the chilly dawn outside Gia's town house. He shivered and tugged the zipper on his jacket a little higher.

Almost June. Wasn't the weather supposed to be getting warmer?

Across the East River the sun was rising red and quick over Queens. He thought he could almost see it moving. Around him, Sutton Square had never looked so bad. The little half block of town houses hanging over the FDR Drive had been spared Friday, but last night more than made up for it. Shattered glass on the sidewalks, lacerated screens hanging in ribbons from the windows.

The chew wasps and belly flies had been back, but other things—bigger, heavier things—had come as well. Luckily, the louvered wooden shutters flanking the windows of Gia's town house hadn't been merely ornamental. They were hung on real hinges and able to swing closed over the windows. The night had been long and tense, filled with hungry, predatory noises, but they'd passed it in safety.

Other places hadn't been so lucky. Jack was wondering whether he should check out some of the neighboring town houses to see if anybody needed help when he noticed something hanging over the arm of the streetlamp on the corner. Something big and limp.

He took a few steps toward it and stopped when he realized it was a corpse. Female, maybe, but so torn up and desiccated it was hard to tell.

But how had it got there? Twenty feet up. Was there a hole creature big enough to fly off with someone?

Things were worsening faster than he'd imagined.

Jack checked the Glock at the small of his back and the extra magazines in his pockets, then went to check his car. The Vic's black paint had bubbled off in spots as if it had been splashed with acid, and the windshield was fouled with some putrid-smelling gunk that Jack wiped off with a rag from his trunk.

"Eeeeuuuu! What happened?"

Jack turned and saw Vicky standing in the town house doorway, dressed in bib-front overalls, a flannel shirt, a jacket, and her green-and-white Jets cap. With the little suitcase in her hand, she looked like a country cousin arriving in the big city for a visit. But her blue eyes were wide with shock as she stared at the car's ruined finish.

"The things from the hole," Jack said, waving her forward to distract her from the corpse on the lamppost. "That's why I want you and your mom to leave."

"Mom still doesn't want to go."

"I know that, Vicks."

Jeez, do I know.

Gia didn't want to leave the city, thought she and Vicky could weather the wolf just fine in their brick house here on Sutton Square. Jack wasn't having any of that. He was willing to let her have her way in most anything unless he thought she'd be in danger. He'd been relentless last night, wearing her down until she'd finally agreed to leave the city with Abe first thing this morning.

"Is that why you and Mom were yelling last night?"

"We weren't yelling. We just had a . . . difference of opinion."

"Oh. I thought it was a fight."

"Your mother and I? Disagree? Never! Now come on, Vicks. Let's get you settled in the car."

As Vicky stepped down onto the sidewalk, Gia emerged behind her. She was dressed in jeans and a navy-blue V-neck sweater over a white T-shirt. Her eyes, the same shade of blue as Vicky's, went as wide as her daughter's when she saw the street. She ran her fingers through her short blond hair.

"Oh, Jack!"

"I'll bet this is nothing compared to the rest of the city."

He put his index finger to his lips and pointed to the body on the lamp-post. Gia started and staggered back a step when she spotted it.

"Dear God!"

"Still think you'll be safe here?"

"We did okay last night."

Stubborn to the end.

"But it's going to get worse."

"So you've said—a thousand times."

"*Two* thousand times. I get paid to know these things."

"And you're sure Abe's place is better?"

He mimicked Abe's accent. "Like a fortress it's built."

She shrugged resignedly. "All right. I'm packed. Like I promised. But I still think this trip is overkill."

Jack ducked past her into the house to grab the suitcases before she changed her mind. Everything fit in the trunk with plenty of room to spare. He wondered about the toddler accessories he'd be packing if Emma were with them. A high chair probably. And what else? Toys. Yeah, toys. Toys in a survival bunker.

He swallowed the lump in his throat and climbed behind the wheel. He zigzagged down to 57th Street and started up the long incline toward Fifth Avenue.

Bad, but not as bad as yesterday. Most people—the sane ones, at least—had stayed in last night. Early Sunday morning was about the only time mid-town Manhattan could be called quiet, but even fewer cars than usual roamed the streets today. Most of those were either police or emergency vehicles of one sort or another. All the streets were littered with sparkling glass fragments. Here and there along the way he spotted an occasional shrunken husk that had once been a human body. One or two dangled from high places, as if they'd been dropped or thrown there after being sucked dry. Jack kept glancing back at Vicky but she was slumped down in the backseat, engrossed in one of her *Nocturnia* books, oblivious to her surroundings.

Good. He kept an eye on Gia, as well, watching her expression grow tighter, her face grow paler with each passing block. By Madison Avenue she was ashen. As he pulled to a stop at a red light, Gia looked at him with eyes even wider than before. Her voice was barely audible.

"Jack . . . I'm . . . what . . . ?"

She closed her mouth and stared ahead in silence.

Jack said nothing, but he was sure he wouldn't have any more resistance to the idea of getting out of town.

From the right came a sudden explosion of glass as a display case crashed through a corner jewelry store's only unbroken window to land on the sidewalk.

A guy with glazed eyes and lank, oily brown hair, sporting a stained black T-shirt and torn jeans, followed it through the hole, laughing as he landed and rolled on the pavement. He was white but wore enough tats and gold chains to qualify as a charter member of the Lil Wayne wannabe club. His fingers were stacked with so many rings he couldn't bend them. Another guy, heavier but dressed identically and sporting an equal amount of gold, made a more traditional exit through the door. They gave each other a metallic high five. Then they spotted the Vic.

"Hey, man!" the first one said, smiling as he approached the car. Jack spotted the Kicker Man tattoo on his right hand. "It's a ride!"

The heavier one followed him. "Yeah! Want some gold? We'll give you some gold for a ride downtown. We got plenty!"

Jack couldn't help laughing.

"Yeah, right. And like maybe I'll let you hold my wallet while I drive you around."

As the looters' disarming grins twisted into rage, he gunned the car and pulled away through the red light.

Trouble was, Vicky was now sitting up and alert to her surroundings.

"Why didn't you give that man a ride, Jack?"

"Because he's one of the bad guys, Vicks. What's called a looter."

"But he just wanted a ride."

"I don't think so, Vicks. You know those silverfish we find crawling in the bathroom every so often?"

Vicky made a face. "Yuck."

"Yeah, well, looters are lower than silverfish. When the good folks are occupied fighting fires or helping earthquake or storm victims, looters sneak in and carry off anything that's not nailed down. Those guys didn't want a ride; they wanted our car."

"That's not fair!"

"Fair's not a word they care about, Vicks."

"Look!" she said, pointing to her left as they crossed Fifth Avenue. "More looters!"

She was right. Knots of people were jumping in and out of the broken windows all along Fifth, scampering off through the dim dawn light with jewelry, leather, anything they could carry. Someone had pulled a panel truck up on the sidewalk in front of Bergdorf's and was loading it with dresses. As Jack was pulling away, he saw a bearded, professorial type step through the open space that had once been the big front window of a bookstore balancing a two-foot stack of books against the front of his tweed jacket.

"Everybody's getting into the act," he said.

Gia looked around. "Where are the police?"

"Stretched pretty thin, I'd guess. At least when the sun's all the way up these cockroaches will crawl back under the floorboards."

"It's been only two days. I never dreamed . . ." Her voice trailed off.

"What? That things could fall apart this fast? This city's become a sewer, Gia. During the past year all the garbage wandering around this half of the country seems to have got themselves a Kicker tattoo and ended up here. Its veneer of civilization is now about as thick as the layer of gold on the jewelry they hawk on the streets. A couple of good rubs against your jeans and the base metal shows through."

"What about neighborliness and hanging together in times of trouble?"

"Maybe they'll have some of that out in Iowa where you grew up, and maybe there'll be pockets of it around here, but not enough to matter. The good folks will be driven into hiding and the slime will be free to do whatever they damn well please."

"I don't believe that. I don't *want* to believe that. And it disturbs me to know you believe that."

Jack shrugged. "In my work, you get to spend a lot of time hip-deep in slime. You—"

"Oh, my God!" Gia cried, craning her neck and staring up through the windshield.

Jack slowed and glanced up. Something bright in the sky. He stuck his head out the window—and stopped the car to stare.

Vicky popped her head out behind him. "Ooooh neeeeat!"

"Jack! What's happening? What *is* that?"

"Looks like an apartment building," Vicky said.

Half a mile up, probably over the West Side Highway or the midtown piers, a building floated in the air. It hung as if suspended on an invisible wire, rotating slowly, its roof canted slightly eastward, its torn underside westward. Light from the rising sun flashed off the few intact windows. Broken-away masonry floated around it. Tiny figures leaned out the windows, waving shirts and towels in panicked attempts to attract the attention of the police helicopters that circled it like flies around a corpse.

"Jeez!" Jack said as he stared upward at the slowly dwindling shape. "It's still rising."

Those poor bastards trapped up there were doomed unless they could find a way of transferring to one of the helicopters.

At least now he knew where a lot of the cops were.

"Let's keep moving," Gia said, looking around.

Jack hit the gas and they continued west. He refrained from saying *I told you so* as he ran red lights all the way to Amsterdam Avenue, then raced uptown to the Isher Sports Shop.

Abe stood outside, waiting by his panel truck in front of his store's smashed windows. So fixated was he on the flying building that he barely noticed their arrival. Jack screeched to a halt a half dozen feet in front of him.

That got his attention.

He cringed. "*Gevalt!* You're trying to squish me already?"

He was wearing a black suit jacket; his white shirt and black tie were clean. Obviously he hadn't had breakfast yet.

"Ready to go?" Jack said, pulling Vicky from the backseat.

"Yes, of course." Abe gave Gia a hug and Vicky a kiss on the top of her head. "I should want to keep two such beautiful young ladies waiting? Come with me. I've got Parabellum, coffee, juice, and not-so-fresh bagels in the front seat."

He opened the rear doors of the panel truck, then ushered Gia and Vicky around to the front. He returned as Jack was loading the last suitcase into the rear compartment. He pointed a trembling finger at the building in the sky.

"It's happening like you said, isn't it?" Abe's accent was gone. "All rules—man's and God's—*pffft!*"

Jack looked and saw that the building was considerably higher than before. When would it stop rising? *Would* it stop rising?

"Double-*pffft!*" Jack nodded toward the shattered storefront windows. "Looters?"

Abe shrugged. "Nothing's missing. Must have been those flying things. Haven't seen any looting."

"Plenty of it going on in the high-rent district. They just haven't got this far yet."

Abe thrust a set of keys into Jack's hand. "Here. These are for the basement. A cannon it'll take to get in without them. You need anything, help yourself."

Jack pointed toward the small armory inside the truck.

"You mean there's something left?"

Jack hefted the keys and stuffed them in a front pocket. "The basement of the Isher Sports Shop was where Abe stocked his weapons—the illegal ones, plus the legal ones he sold illegally. He carried everything from black-jacks to Claymore land mines. Might be handy to have access to that sort of variety.

"I might move in."

"Be my guest. You have the wavelength written down?"

"Yeah. Got the shortwave set on it. If I don't hear from you on the cell, I'll be listening at seven A.M. and seven P.M. Don't forget to call in."

Communications were getting iffy, so they'd decided to resort to shortwave radios.

"Don't worry."

"Which way you heading out? The Lincoln?"

Abe nodded. "It's closest. And from what you say, the quicker we get out, the better."

"You know it. You carrying?"

Abe patted the heavy lump in the right-side pocket of his jacket. "Of course."

"Good. But maybe I'll tail you through the tunnel anyway—just in case."

Abe huffed. "You don't think I can protect your women?"

"I wouldn't be sending them off with you if I wasn't sure of that."

They stared at each other in silence a few seconds.

"Seems like we should say something here," Abe said. "I mean, two old friends at the end of the world. One of us should be able to come up with some-thing meaningful."

"You're the guy with all the education. You do the honors."

Abe looked down, then smiled and thrust out his hand.

"See you soon, Jack."

Jack smiled as they shook hands. That just about said it all.

"Enough of this stuff. Get behind the wheel and I'll say my good-byes to the ladies."

After a big hug from Vicky, Jack held Gia in his arms.

"Be careful, Jack," she whispered in his ear. "And thanks."

"For what?"

"For making us get out of town. You're right. The city's turning ugly. But *you* watch out."

He grinned. "Hell, I'm uglier than any city you can name."

"I'm not talking about that. I'm talking about *her*."

"Oh."

He'd told Gia last night about how he was going to try to find Kolabati and snag her necklaces for Glaeken. Gia knew a few things about Kolabati, but

Jack had never quite got around to telling her that they'd been lovers for a brief—*very* brief—time.

"Don't give me 'oh.' You got involved with her before and it almost killed you."

"That was my choice."

"She left you to die, Jack. This time she might finish the job."

"This time is different. I know what she is. I'll be careful. I've got a lot to come back for."

She kissed him one last time, long and deep, then she got back into the front seat of the idling truck. Jack hurried back to his Crown Vic.

He followed Abe over to West End and then downtown. Along the way, the lights were against them. They'd gone out of synch for some reason and Abe stopped at every red. Jack knew why. He probably had enough weaponry in the back to overthrow a banana republic. He didn't want to get stopped and searched.

It happened at about where West End starts calling itself Eleventh Avenue. As Abe pulled to a stop at yet another red light, three guys leapt from a doorway and charged the truck, two running around to the driver side, one leaping up and reaching in the passenger window.

One of the guys on the left had a big hunting knife and the other carried a lead pipe. As Abe tried to pull away, the second guy began beating on Abe's window. Jack was already accelerating when the glass shattered and the guy started swinging the pipe at Abe.

The guy with the knife spotted Jack coming. He leapt out of the way as Jack sideswiped the truck, catching the pipe swinger hard on the backs of both legs. As he was spun and twisted between the two vehicles and tumbled to the pavement, screaming with the agony of two broken legs, Jack swerved at the guy with the knife and caught him head-on with the Vic's nose. But the car wasn't moving fast enough then to knock him sprawling. Instead he rolled up and over the hood and windshield and landed on the roof. He had to be hurt but he wasn't out of action yet. He blindly stabbed his blade through the open window, narrowly missing Jack's face. Jack ducked and grabbed the swinging wrist, wrenched the knife free, and paused, wondering what to do. Then he heard Vicky scream.

Jack raised his window, trapping the arm below the elbow, then turned the wrist and rammed the blade—honed side down—through the belly of the forearm, between the two bones and out the other side. Above on the roof the guy howled and flopped about and tried to pull his arm free. But the protruding edges of the point and grip caught on the sides of the opening, forcing the cutting edge of the blade to slice farther down his arm. The guy screamed now.

Jack jumped out the passenger side and saw Abe holding his bloody scalp with his left hand, a .45 automatic in his right. Vicky was next to him, crying, but Gia was nowhere in sight.

Jack charged around to the far side and found another guy with a knife, the point against Gia's throat.

"All we want is the truck," he said, breathing hard. He wore a clean plaid short-sleeved shirt and beige slacks, white socks and running shoes; he looked almost preppy except for the tattoos on his arms. "Give us the truck and no one gets hurt."

"*We?*" Jack said, pulling the Glock from its holster and slowly, methodically working the slide for effect, even though he already had a round chambered. He'd have to play this very carefully. "*Us?* We and Us are already down. They're out of the picture. You're on your own."

He paused to allow the guy to appreciate the wails and moans from his buddies on the far side of the truck and get a good look at the 9mm semiautomatic in Jack's hand. He slid farther behind Gia.

"You think you can get away with this?" Jack said softly.

"Yeah. I can get away with *anything*, man! All the rules are off! Don't you see that?" He stared for a moment into the sky over Jack's left shoulder. "We got buildings and people flyin' off into space during the day and monsters chewin' up everything in sight all night. I been through detox twice, man, and I ain't never seen shit like this, even when I·was strung out like bubble gum. Anything goes, man. School is *out!*"

"Not my class," Jack said. "Let her go."

The guy pressed the knife blade against Gia's throat. She winced at the sharp pressure.

"The truck or I'll cut her, man! I swear t'Christ I'll cut her fucking throat!"

Jack felt his heart begin to hammer. Gia's panicked eyes pleaded with him. He gave her a little nod of encouragement as he controlled himself. Had to be cool here. Had to go slow.

But if this bastard so much as broke her skin . . .

Jack settled the Glock into a two-handed grip and raised it until it was sighted at the guy's right eye where he peeked out from behind Gia's ear.

"You've been watching too many movies, turkey. This kind of thing doesn't work in real life. I've got a gun and you've got a knife. You cut her, you've lost your shield." Jack took a step closer. "Now, so far today you and your buddies have hurt a very good friend, deeply frightened a little girl I couldn't care for more if she were my own flesh and blood, and manhandled the woman I love."

Another small step closer. "So I'm royally pissed. But I'm willing to work a deal. Drop the knife and you live. I'll let you walk."

The guy's laugh was flat and tremulous as he peeked out from behind Gia's head to speak.

"Don't try to bullshit me. I got your bitch here. I've got a knife at her neck. *I'm* callin' the shots!"

A car came by, slowed for a look, then sped away. Jack slipped forward another step.

"Maybe I didn't make it clear. Listen again. Drop it, you live. Spill one drop of her blood, you die—slowly. First I shoot off your right kneecap, then your left, then your right elbow, then your left. Then a gut shot. Then I take your knife and start cutting off pieces I decide you don't need anymore and feed them to you."

"Jack . . . please!" Gia said.

"Sorry. Just want to let this guy know what he's in for."

"You think that scares me?" the guy said, peeking out again. "I'll show you how scared I—"

Jack shot him in the eye. His head snapped back, a red mist blooming behind him; his arms flung outward as he lurched back and collapsed on the pavement.

Jack leapt forward and encircled Gia with his arms.

"Don't look," he said, watching over her shoulder as a red puddle grew under the guy's head.

But Gia turned for a quick glance, and just as quickly turned away. Jack led her back to the truck and they spent a few minutes calming Vicky. When mother and daughter were tightly wound in each other's arms, Jack looked past them to Abe.

"You okay to drive?"

Abe nodded. "Only a scratch. But that guy on your car—what's his problem?"

"Oh, yeah," Jack said. "Almost forgot about him."

He went back to his car and found the other knifer lying on the roof, pale, sweaty, looking sick.

"Don't hurt me," he said in a weak voice. "I give up."

Jack wondered how the guy would respond if situations were reversed. How much mercy could he expect from him and his buddies? He decided it didn't merit much consideration.

He ducked inside the Vic. The driver window and door were smeared with blood.

"You bled all over my car!" Jack shouted.

On the roof he heard a blubbering whimper. Disgusted, Jack yanked the knife blade from the guy's forearm and lowered the window. A muffled scream from above as he jerked his arm free and rolled off the roof to the street. A couple more cars passed as Jack went to the corner and dropped the knife through a sewer grate, then returned to the truck.

He gave Gia and Vicky one last hug, then slammed the door.

"Better get going, Abe. Traffic's picking up."

"Jack," Gia said as he started back to his car. Her face was pale and tear-streaked as she stared at him through the window. "Would you have let him go if he dropped the knife? You had that look in your eyes, Jack. I've seen that look before. I know what it means. Would you have kept your word?"

"Doesn't make much difference now."

"I just want to know."

"Yeah. Sure."

He hoped he was convincing. Because he was anything but sure.

Pulling away from the scene, Jack glanced in the rearview mirror. One of the attackers lay dead in a pool of blood, staring skyward with his remaining eye, another squatted on the pavement, moaning and cradling a bloody arm, while a third crawled toward the curb, dragging his broken legs behind him. Gia's question echoed in his head then and followed him the rest of the way to the Lincoln Tunnel.

She knew him too well. Why'd she have to ask that question? He didn't like to think about that sort of thing. It wasn't necessary. The guy was dead. A part of Jack had taken immense pleasure in blowing his brains out the back of his head. But he'd learned to wall off that part of himself, to refrain from joining the joyous partying in the dark corner behind the wall.

Would he have let the guy go? Abe bloodied, Vicky terrified, a knifepoint jabbed against Gia's throat—how could he forgive that? Turn his back as the guy who'd caused it all sauntered off unscathed? Jack wasn't sure. Allowing someone who'd done damage to his friends to walk the streets with no pain or scars to remind him never even to think about doing something like that again . . . That might be too much to ask.

But if he'd said he'd let the guy go in exchange for dropping the knife, he'd have to do it. Or would he?

All the rules are off, man!

No. Not all of them. Some rules—at least the ones he had some say about—had to stay in effect.

He yawned. He hadn't had much sleep last night, and he found introspection tough work.

He followed Abe's truck the rest of the way to the Lincoln Tunnel, watched and waved as it rolled down the ramp into the tiled gullet, then headed crosstown to Walt Duran's place. He hoped he'd made it through the night okay. And he hoped he was on schedule with his engraving. If not, Jack was going to have to induce him into a higher gear.

WNYW-TV

Ladies and gentlemen, we are interrupting our special report from Central Park with catastrophic news from the Central Pacific. The Big Island of Hawaii is gone. Shortly after sunset, the chain of eight islands that make up our fiftieth state was shaken by a cataclysmic explosion. At that instant, all communications with Hawaii, or the Big Island as it is called, were cut off. The mystery was quickly solved.

<run file footage of Hawaii>

This is how the Big Island looked. A lush volcanic island supporting four thousand square miles of paradise, including the world's longest steadily active volcano. But now . . .

<run feed from Honolulu>

. . . as we see here in a live aerial transmission from our affiliate in Honolulu, the Big Island is no more. Hawaii's active crater, Kilauea, along with supposedly extinct volcanoes Mauna Loa and Mauna Kea, simply blew up, taking the entire island with them. It is just dawn in the Central Pacific, but even so you can see that nothing remains of the island of Hawaii but a flaming, steaming cauldron of bubbling lava. We can only show you the site of the Big Island's grave from the west. The plume of smoke, steam, ash, and debris that stretches far into the sky is drifting east. Meteorologists are presently calculating when the ash cloud will hit the West Coast. It is sure to affect weather around the globe.

You can't see it now but there are reports of a giant whirlpool situated off Maui, north of where the Big Island used to be. The whirlpool is believed to be the result of a hole similar to the one in our own Central Park, opening in the ocean bottom some nineteen thousand feet below the surface. Whether this has any relationship to the Big Island disaster is still a matter of conjecture at this time.

Those flames you see now on the left of your screen are from another volcano. It's been confirmed that Haleakala, a formerly extinct volcano just seven miles away on the island of Maui, is active again. Although most of its lava flow has been down its eastern flank, away from the heavily populated areas, we've been told that the

lovely town of Hana is no more. It was completely submerged in an avalanche of lava during the night.

<cut to Alice>
Meanwhile, in Manhattan, the situation is rapidly deteriorating. . . .

Glaeken stared at the TV screen in dismay, barely aware of the picture. But he was listening intently, hoping for fresh news from Maui. As a geologist came on, spouting his theory of how the hole in the channel between Hawaii and Maui had destabilized the Pacific "hot spot" that had formed the Hawaiian Islands over the ages, Glaeken hit the mute button on his remote.

Apparently the doorman had rung while he'd been intent on the TV—he saw Bill leading a familiar figure into the room.

"Jack! I see you made it through the night. Did you take care of that 'business' you mentioned?"

Jack nodded, a bit glumly, Glaeken thought.

"Yeah. All taken care of."

As Bill returned to the kitchen to finish helping Nick eat breakfast, Jack dropped into a chair.

"Anything I can do?" Glaeken said.

He shook his head. "I sent some people off into the hinterlands. I'm just hoping they get where they're going without any trouble. The city's already starting to fall apart."

"So I've heard. I understand the National Guard is on alert but that fewer than half of the Guardsmen are reporting in."

"Not surprised. Probably want to stay home and protect their own. Who can blame them?"

"You should have had your people stay here. They're welcome."

"I thought about that after they left, but I think far from the city might be better for them. However, I've got some other friends who could use this place. Good people. You got room?"

"The building's practically empty."

"How come? It looks like a prime spot."

"I'm very choosy about my neighbors. You've heard about Maui, I presume?"

"No. What?"

Glaeken capsulized the news reports for him.

"You think she's still alive?"

Glaeken nodded. "There's a good chance. She lives on the northwest slope. If she was home . . ." He asked the question that was uppermost in his mind. "When can you leave, Jack?"

"Tomorrow."

"No. You must leave today. Every moment counts."

"No way. I just checked with the engraver. The bogus necklaces won't be ready till tomorrow morning at the earliest. And I'm not going without them. They're my ace in the hole."

Glaeken considered that for a moment. At the rate the situation was deteriorating, tomorrow might be too late. But he didn't see that he had much choice. He had no way of forcing Jack to leave today.

"I promise—I'll catch a flight out there first thing tomorrow—soon as those necklaces are ready."

"That may not be so easy. A number of airlines have grounded all flights."

"Why? Pilots not showing up?"

"Partly that. But a number of flights have disappeared. I should say, a *lot* of flights have disappeared. They take off but never land."

"Swell. What've we got now—holes in the sky?"

"No. Leviathans in the air, snatching the planes, pulverizing them."

"How about the Air Force?"

"According to the reports, surface-to-air and air-to-air missiles are ineffective and interceptor jets are disappearing as well."

Jack said nothing, simply sat and stared at Glaeken with a skeptical look.

"I've seen them," Bill said, leading Nick in from the kitchen. He sat him in a chair that caught the morning sun. Nick stared emptily at the wall.

"The leviathans?"

Bill nodded. "Big. Big as towns, gliding through the night."

"At least we've got the days," Jack said. "The daylight time may be shrinking, but maybe Rasalom made a mistake giving us some slack like this."

"Not at all. The days give us time to be at our worst. A constant onslaught might drive us together, bring out the best in us. But the respite offered by the daylight gives the terrors of the night before and the anticipated terrors of the night to come a chance to work on us. It allows fear to demoralize us. Fear is the key to Rasalom's power. Fear is the great divider. From war and racism to the mundane vices of greed and gluttony—they're all rooted in fear. What is religion, after all, but a ritualized response to fear—fear of death, fear of the perversities of luck and happenstance that afflict every life at one time or another?" He pointed out the window. "Fear is rampant out there now. It's dividing us, hurting us, bringing out the worst in too many of us. It will be the end of us." He turned to Jack. "That's why you've got to get to Maui and retrieve those necklaces."

"I'll find a way," Jack said softly. "There's always a way."

Glaeken wondered even if Jack did find a way to retrieve the necklaces, then what?

Tension rolled out from his chest along his limbs. He flexed his arthritic fingers to disperse it. What indeed? Knowing the source of the metal from which they'd been fashioned, he was almost afraid to be in the same room with those necklaces. What would happen if he touched them? Or even got near? Nothing, he hoped. But he couldn't risk it. He'd have to keep his distance when and if Jack brought them back.

Jack said, "You know, with the way things are going, I think I'm going to need some backup on the trip."

Bill said, "I could come along if you wish."

At first, Glaeken was startled by Bill's offer. He glanced at the ex-priest and caught a desperate look in his eyes. Desperate for what? And then he understood. Bill felt lost, adrift, already a resident of the land to which most of humanity would soon be emigrating. Poor man. The New York City police records still listed him as a fugitive suspect in a capital crime, he had broken with his church, his family was dead, his last friend was sitting there lapsing in and out of catatonia, and Glaeken suspected that his feelings for Carol Treece ran deeper than he dared admit.

Small wonder he was feeling reckless.

Glaeken hoped Jack had the good sense not to take him up on the offer.

"Uh, nothing personal, Bill," Jack said after a long pause, "but I'm looking for someone with maybe a little experience in hand-to-hand work."

"If I were younger . . ." Glaeken said wistfully.

He remembered times when he had cursed the ages he'd spent in a body in its mid thirties. Now, with the burden of eternity off him, he had moments when he would have relished tight muscles, mobile joints, and a supple back.

"Yeah," Jack said, smiling. "We'd have made a helluva pair, I think. But I was wondering about Ho Chi Minhzilla. Think he'd be up for it?"

"Ba? I don't know. I doubt he'd be willing to leave Mrs. Nash unprotected, but it wouldn't hurt to ask. I'll call if you like."

"Might be better I go in person. Maybe I can sway him with my magnetic charm."

Bill laughed aloud. Jack gave him a sidelong look.

"Something funny, guy?"

Bill grinned. "I didn't know what to make of you at first, but I think you're all right."

"Which says loads about your character judgment. None of it good."

Glaeken gave Jack directions to Toad Hall and said he'd call ahead to let them know he was coming.

When he was gone, Glaeken reached for the TV remote control. Before he could resume the audio, Nick spoke.

"They won't be enough," he said in his monotone.

Bill squatted before him and looked into his eyes.

"What, Nick? What won't be enough?"

"The necklaces. They won't do the job. You'll need more to make it work. Pieces of something else. Pieces of the rest of it."

"What does that mean, Nick? Pieces of what?"

But he was gone again. Bill turned to Glaeken.

"Any idea what he's talking about?"

Glaeken sat numb and cold and sick as he stared at Nick.

"Yes, I'm afraid I do."

WFPW-FM

JO: Well, the news keeps getting worse, folks. Reports from the Midwest and the Plains States say that the nation's cattle herds were decimated by the bugs last night. Measures are being taken now to protect them but no one knows how successful they'll be. Our advice: Enjoy your Big Macs and Whoppers today, man, because pretty soon you won't be able to afford them.

FREDDY: And now, continuing with our F-Rock All-Request Weekend, we've got Marvin Gaye asking the question that's on everybody's lips.

<cue "What's Goin' On?">

"There!" Thompson said, pointing to the radio. "Am I brilliant or what? Food! Food is going to be the new gold."

Ernst didn't come here to listen to Thompson pat himself on the back. He needed help.

"I want to know where you got your storm shutters."

Thompson grinned. "Why? Want some?"

He hated to admit it, but . . .

"Yes."

"After all the stink you made about defacing this wonderful old historic building, now you want them for your office?"

"No . . . my apartment."

The grin broadened. "Why? Rough night?"

"You might say that."

A *very* rough night.

When buying into his building, he'd opted for one of the lower floors. For safety reasons, he wanted quick access to the outside in case of fire or another emergency. Conversely, if a blackout occurred and the elevators were shut down, he didn't want a long walk up.

But most of the lower floors had taken a beating last night. The bugs broke through his windows and chased him through the apartment. He had to spend all night in the hall closet with those things right outside the door, clawing, chewing, scratching, trying to get in at him.

Horrifying.

With the dawn—the *late* dawn—they'd scurried back to their holes, leaving Ernst with a trashed apartment and severely frazzled nerves.

The first thing he'd done was call the head of the Order's High Council of Seven to see if he'd had any contact with the One. He hadn't. And he'd sounded as frightened as Ernst felt.

The conclusion was unmistakable: The One was excluding them from the Change. Which meant they would have to fend for themselves, just like the Great Unwashed.

Unfortunately, certain members of the Great Unwashed, like Hank Thompson, seemed better prepared. When Ernst had arrived at the Lodge this morning he'd noticed its smashed windows and torn screens. Every window but two showed damage: the pair that had been protected by hurricane shutters during the night.

"You want the name of my guy?" Thompson jerked a thumb at his own windows. "The one who did these?"

"I would appreciate it."

"No good. Had a run on them and he's outta stock." He grinned. "Which means you're outta luck."

"Well, I'm sure if the price was right—"

"Don't count on it. Pretty much everybody in the place was chased down to the basement last night. Luckily, there's no windows down there, so they were safe. But come the dawn, those boys were on the phone and could hardly find anyone even willing to talk to them. Everybody's got the same idea."

"I'll find someone," Ernst said, with more confidence than he felt.

He *had* to find someone. He could not endure another ordeal like last night. He glanced at his watch. Still early. He had all day. But a day wasn't what it used to be.

Monroe, Long Island

Sylvia recognized the old man's voice immediately. A wave of resentment surged through her.

"I hope this isn't about moving in with you in the city," she said, controlling her tone. "Pressure tactics won't work, Mr. Veilleur. I don't wear down very easily."

"I'm quite well aware of that, Mrs. Nash. And please call me Glaeken. That's my real name."

Sylvia didn't want to do that. She didn't wish to be on a first-name basis with this man. So she said nothing.

"I didn't call to pressure you into anything," he said after a pause. "I merely wished to inquire as to how you and your household fared last night."

"We did just fine, thank you." No thanks to you.

She repressed the urge to tell him that the strange attraction Jeffy had developed for him had nearly cost the boy his life—and Ba's and her own as well; that if Jeffy hadn't become so fixated on Glaeken he wouldn't have wandered off last night. But in the back of her mind she knew Glaeken could crush her with the simple admonishment that a good mother should know the whereabouts of her child. She'd spent most of the night telling herself the same thing, berating herself for letting Jeffy wander off. If only she'd kept an eye on him, Rudy might still be alive and Ba wouldn't have dozens of ugly wounds on the back of his neck.

"This is a tough old house," she said. "And with the metal storm shutters we installed yesterday, it's like a fortress."

The racket last night had been horrendous. Those things from the hole had pounded incessantly against the shutters until sunrise. Sealed in as they were, the silence from outside had been their only clue that daylight had arrived. She'd greeted the dawn with relief and exhaustion.

"Good," Glaeken said. "I'm very glad to hear that. I hope your defenses remain as effective against future assaults. But I called for two reasons. The other is to let you know that Jack, the fellow who let you in yesterday, will be stopping by later for a visit."

"I warned you about pressuring me."

"Have no fear, Mrs. Nash. He's not coming to see you. He wishes to speak to Ba."

"Ba? What does he want with Ba?"

She vaguely remembered the wiry, brown-eyed man Glaeken had mentioned—a rather ordinary-looking sort. She had an impression of him and Ba standing at the back of the living room, speaking together in low tones. So unusual for Ba to speak at all to a stranger that she remembered wondering if they'd met before.

"Perhaps I'd better let Jack explain that himself. Good day, Mrs. Nash."

WFAN-AM

DAVE: And now our next caller on the FAN sports radio is Rick from Brooklyn. What's on your mind, Rick?

RICK: Yeah, hi, Dave. I just want to say that I really love your show, and I'd like to talk about the commissioner's canceling all games indefinitely.

DAVE: What's wrong with that, Rick?

RICK: It's not fair to the Mets. They've got one of their best teams ever. They was headin' for the Pennant for sure. I think it's a dirty trick. And you know what else . . . ?

Monroe, Long Island

Jack arrived in the early afternoon. Sylvia heard him drive up and watched as he got out of a big black car with a damaged paint job and odd reddish stains on the roof and driver door. Since Ba was outside, reinforcing whatever weak points he could find in the house's defenses, and Alan was in the back tossing a football to Jeffy, Sylvia went downstairs to let him in. He didn't come to the door, however. Instead, he walked around to the side of the house to where Ba was working.

What on earth could those two have in common? She resisted the temptation to tiptoe to one of the windows and eavesdrop. She'd know soon.

And sure enough, a few minutes later Ba was leading Jack through the back door. Alan rolled in behind them and Jeffy brought up the rear, flipping his football from hand to hand.

"Hi, Mrs. Nash," Jack said, extending his hand. "We met yesterday."

She shook it briefly. "I remember."

"Can we all talk?"

Alan looked at Sylvia and gave her a puzzled shrug. "Why don't we go into the den," he said.

Sylvia sent Jeffy upstairs to wash his hands and seated herself where she had a view of the stairway. If Jeffy came down, she'd see him. No wandering off this time. She was determined to know his whereabouts every minute of the day.

Jack seated himself across from her. Ba remained standing near Alan. She sensed his tightly coiled tension.

Jack said, "Do you remember Glaeken talking about a certain pair of necklaces yesterday?"

Sylvia nodded. "The ones supposedly made from the 'second focus.'"

"Right. Well, he's located them on Maui, and I'm going to head out there tomorrow to see if I can get them back."

"I see." Sylvia kept her tone noncommittal. "What does that have to do with Ba?"

"I'd like him to come along."

"And what did Ba say?" She suspected the answer but wanted to hear it for herself.

"He refused. Said he couldn't leave you here unprotected."

Sylvia turned to him. "Thank you, Ba."

Ba gave her one of his little bows.

"I respect that," Jack said, "but I think it's shortsighted. When the light goes altogether, you're not going to get a break like this. Those things'll be at you nonstop. You won't get a chance to go out and repair the damage and shore up the weak spots. And I don't care how well fortified you are, Mrs. Nash, sooner or later they're gonna break through."

She glanced at Alan, who was nodding silent agreement. And why not? The logic was unassailable.

"You can't do this alone?"

"I might be able to. I usually work alone, but this is different. Time is critical. I've been out in the dark with those things. And I see by Ba's neck that he has too."

"So have I," Sylvia said.

Jack's eyebrows lifted. "Really? Well then, you know what it means to have someone watching your back."

Sylvia remembered the tentacles entwined in her hair, pulling her backward . . .

Repressing a shudder, she said, "How long have you known this Glaeken fellow?"

"We met a little over a year ago. We've spent most of our time since then trying to prevent all this from happening."

"But you failed."

"I think that's obvious. But even if I'd known him only a few days, I'd be a believer."

Reluctantly, Sylvia admitted to herself that she too was becoming a believer.

"When would you be leaving?"

"Tomorrow morning. With any luck I'll have Ba back on your doorstep sometime Tuesday. Wednesday morning at the latest."

"Two days at the most. You're sure?"

"Pretty sure. Either I can get the necklaces back or I can't. I'll know fairly soon after I get there."

"Two nights," she said slowly. "Ba . . . maybe you should reconsider."

"No, Missus. It is too dangerous here for you to stay alone."

Out of the corner of her eye she saw Alan stiffen—a barely perceptible straightening of his spine that would have passed unnoticed by a stranger. But Sylvia knew him too well. Ba would be devastated if he even suspected that his words had stung Alan. He'd never forgive himself.

"Glaeken's offer still stands," Jack told her. "Come into the city. Stay in his building. He was right about his place being spared. He's practically hanging over that hole and he hasn't been bothered by a single bug."

Sylvia shook her head. "Out of the question. Alan and I are quite capable of handling the situation. We won't be driven from our home by these things." She turned to Ba. "We're safe in here, Ba. You saw that last night. Once we locked the doors and rolled down the shutters, we had no further problems. Tonight will be the same. And the night after that. And the night after that."

"Missus, I am not sure—"

"Neither am I, Ba. We can't be sure of anything anymore. Except perhaps that the situation will steadily deteriorate until we're all mad or dead."

"I vowed to protect you, Missus. Always."

"I know you did, Ba."

Sylvia's heart warmed at his unflagging devotion. But that devotion could be a burden as well as a benefit. She took great comfort in knowing she was protected, but she also had to *allow* herself to be protected. And that wasn't always easy.

Pulling away from the snug cocoon of that guardianship, even temporarily, was difficult—akin perhaps to leaving all the windows open in a storm. And knowing the distress it caused in Ba made the move all the more difficult.

She asked Jack, "What will the return of these necklaces do?"

He shrugged. "Only Glaeken knows. Set things right, I hope."

"If that's true, Ba . . . if acquiring these necklaces will help end this nightmare, perhaps you would be adhering closer to the spirit of your vow by going with this man."

Ba stood silent for a moment, the center of attention. His eyes were tortured. "Missus . . ."

"Let's do it this way," Sylvia said, lighting on an idea. "We'll see how tonight goes. If Alan and I need your help to get through, then I'll ask you to stay. But if it turns out we can handle things ourselves, then I think you should go with Jack."

"Very well, Missus. If that is what you wish."

I don't know what I wish, she thought. But I know we can't spend the rest of our lives sealed up in Toad Hall.

"That is what I wish."

"All right!" Jack said, clapping his hands once as he rose to his feet. "I'll be here first thing tomorrow morning—bright and early."

Alan said, "It probably won't be bright and it certainly won't be early."

Sylvia watched Jack go over to Ba and extend his hand.

"I respect where you're coming from, Big Guy, but believe me, this is our only chance to really *do* something about this—to maybe turn it around and stop it so we can all get back to our normal lives. That's worth risking a couple of days, isn't it?"

Ba shook his hand slowly. "I will go with you tomorrow."

Jack smiled. "Try to control your enthusiasm, okay?"

Then he waved and headed for the front door.

When he was gone, Ba turned to her. "Excuse me, Missus. I have work outside."

"Of course."

As Sylvia watched him go, she caught her breath as that recurring phrase slipped into her mind.

Only three will live to return.

"Something wrong?" Alan said.

They were alone now and his gentle brown eyes were fixed on her.

"Is something right?"

"You looked frightened."

"I was thinking about what that lunatic in Glaeken's apartment told you and wondering if I was sending Ba to his doom. What if he's killed on this trip? It will be my fault."

"I've never believed anyone could tell the future," he said. "And as for fault, that's a no-win game. If Ba goes off and gets killed, is it your fault? But if you *don't* convince him to go and he gets killed around here, then isn't that also your fault? Neither scenario is anybody's fault. It's nothing but a mental trap."

"I guess you're right. I'm treating some nut's rant as if it's really going to happen. I must be as crazy as he is." She leaned over and kissed him. "Thanks, Alan. You're good for me."

He gave her a kiss of his own. "And thank *you*."

"For what?"

"For saying, 'Alan and I are quite capable of handling the situation.' That meant a lot."

So . . . he *had* been stung by Ba's remark.

"Ba didn't mean anything."

"I know that."

"Ba admires you and respects you. He's forever in your debt for the care you gave Nhung Thi before she died. You're on his good-guy list."

"I'd hate to be on his bad-guy list."

"Ba doesn't really have one of those. All the people he considers bad guys seem to disappear. And he'd be crushed if he thought he'd offended you."

"I wasn't offended."

Sylvia stared into his eyes. "Truth, Alan."

"Okay," he said, glancing away. "That crack about not wanting to leave you 'alone' did get to me. I mean, what am I—a houseplant? I know I'm in a wheelchair, but I'm not helpless."

"Of course you're not. And Ba knows that too. It's just that he's been my self-appointed watchman for so many years, he thinks he's the only one who can do the job. If I had the Eighty-second Airborne camping in with me, he'd still consider me unprotected if he wasn't at my side."

"It's funny," Alan said, staring at the wall. "You hear women complaining about being labeled as 'the weaker sex' and not being given a chance to prove their competence and equality and maybe even superiority to men. They don't see the flip side of the coin. The guys are saddled with the macho ethic. We're expected to be tough, we're supposed to be able to handle anything, be cool in any situation, never back down, never surrender, never admit we're hurt, and for God's sake, never *ever* cry. It's not easy to handle even when you're at the top of your form; but when something happens to knock you off your feet, I tell you, Syl, it becomes a crushing burden. And sometimes . . . sometimes it's just plain murder."

Sylvia didn't know what to say to that. She simply reached over and held his hand. She hoped that said it all.

Carol was returning from the mailbox—empty. No delivery today, apparently.

The elevator doors opened to reveal a middle-aged couple, each weighted with a pair of suitcases. They looked pale, drawn, shaken. Carol recognized the woman—she'd seen her by the mailboxes a few times.

"Moving out?" she said, stepping aside to let them step out into the foyer with their luggage.

The woman nodded glumly. "My sister's got a place in the Catskills. We're going to move in with her until this mess gets straightened out."

"What happened?"

"We were invaded by the bugs. All the lower floors were."

"How awful!" Carol said.

She realized then how lucky they were to have an apartment on an upper floor. She'd been in and out of bed repeatedly, checking the windows. A few times she'd found one sort of monstrosity or another clinging to the screens, but for the most part she'd been spared last night. But what about tonight?

"Not as awful as what happened to the Honigs in two-twelve," her husband said. "Jerry lost his left hand and their little girl got carried off."

The woman's brave facade crumbled as she began to sob. "Poor Carrie!"

Carol's heart went out to the Honigs, whoever they were.

"If there's anything I can do for them—I mean . . ."

Her voice trailed off. What could she do? She wasn't sure how to handle her own problems.

She wished them luck as she stepped onto the elevator and pressed the *10* button. The door closed, leaving her alone with her fears. More like uncertainties. Still no word from Nelson despite dozens of calls. She'd filled his voice mail and now it wasn't accepting new messages.

The bank had been no help. They said all the transactions had been verified with the proper PINs and phone inquiries. They'd all originated from Atlantic City.

That last convinced Carol that something awful had happened to Nelson. He was—or had been—in Denver, and had never been a gambler. He'd always joked that it made more sense to take your money and simply hand it to a casino pit boss and save everyone a lot of time and effort. He must have been kidnapped or—

The phone rang. She checked the caller ID and knew the number. She snatched it up.

"Nelson!"

A croak: *"Carol."*

She barely recognized the voice, but was sure it was Nelson.

"Where are you? What happened?"

"I owe you an explanation. I—"

Her own voice seemed to have a will of its own. "Are you still in Denver? Did you get my messages? What—?"

"Can I get a word in here?"

"Yes, yes, of course."

"I got your messages. I'm in Atlantic City. I—"

"Atlantic—!"

"Yes, Atlantic City—and I'm not coming back."

Carol found herself speechless.

"All my 'business trips' to Denver have actually been down here to AC. I . . . I found someone and I'm going to stay with her. I've been a tight-ass all my life. Time to live a little. I emptied my accounts because I need the money."

"But you—"

"What? You're going to complain about that? It's my money. I earned it. And you've got plenty of your own. More than you can spend. So I don't understand all these frantic calls about the accounts."

She did have more than she could spend—forty million? Fifty? She didn't know. When he'd walked out at age fifteen, Jimmy—Rasalom—had taken half the fortune he'd amassed, and left the rest. It had kept growing. She'd given millions away to charities, but it kept growing, and growing.

She felt a surge of anger. "I wasn't worried about the money, I was worried about *you!*"

A long pause, then, *"Well, don't be. It's not you. I just don't want to be married anymore."*

"You could have been man enough to tell me in person!"

He sighed. *"I'm sorry about that, but I thought this was just a temporary thing. After all, I'm seventy freaking years old. But when I saw that Central Park hole on the tube, something inside told me it was all over."*

"Oh, give me a break!"

"It's true, Carol. It's the end times. I'll spend my last days down here, you spend yours up there with your priest friend."

That last shocked her more than anything.

"Bill? Don't be—"

"Don't bullshit me, Carol. I've seen the looks passing between you two. Maybe you had something going on in the past, maybe something's going on now. I don't know. But if not, my advice is to get it on now. *There's not much time left."*

Were her feelings for Bill that obvious?

He said, *"That's it, Carol. Get out of the city. Get someplace safe. It's all going to fall apart. Sorry if I'm hurting you, but this is the way it has to be."*

And then he hung up.

Carol stood in her living room, the silent phone in her hand, and felt a cascade of disparate thoughts, feelings, and observations take shape.

Nelson . . . he'd been somewhat distant over the past few months but she hadn't paid all that much attention. Her own life had been turned upside down earlier in the year by revelations of what her child had become, the horrors he'd perpetrated. And then . . . the return of Bill Ryan.

Was she to blame? Had she helped send Nelson off the rails? Or was he simply giving in to the off-kilter zeitgeist? He hadn't had a midlife crisis, so now he was having a late-life crisis?

Whatever the reason, he was gone, off with someone new, leaving her alone.

No . . . not alone. She didn't have to face this alone.

WNYW-TV

CAMERON: But Dr. Sapir, how exactly did you arrive at these figures?

SAPIR: I simply charted the times of sunrise and sunset and the resultant hours of daylight since Wednesday on a graph. Those figures yielded the curve you see here. I have merely continued that curve.

CAMERON: And that shows . . . ?

SAPIR: All you have to do is follow it. We'll have approximately eleven hours of sunlight today; slightly less than ten hours tomorrow, Monday; about eight hours and forty minutes of daylight on Tuesday, about seven hours on Wednesday, and—you see how steep the curve is becoming—four hours and forty-two minutes of light on Thursday.

CAMERON: And on Friday?

SAPIR: On Friday, nothing.

CAMERON: Nothing?

SAPIR: Correct. If the curve holds true, the sun will set at 3:01 P.M. on Thursday and will not rise again. There will be no sunrise on Friday.

CAMERON: But how is that possible?

SAPIR: It's not.

CAMERON: Then how—?

SAPIR: It is what it is. <sobbing> It just . . . is.

Manhattan

Bill Ryan sat stunned before the TV in Glaeken's study. He'd turned on the Sapir interview to see if the sight of Nick's old colleague would shock him back into the real world. Instead it was Bill who had received the shock.

No sunrise on Friday? It seemed impossible, but Dr. Harvey Sapir was world renowned. And to see him break down and cry . . .

"Nick," Bill said, turning to the younger man. "What's going to happen? You've been coming on with all sorts of predictions lately. How's all this going to turn out?"

Nick didn't answer. His vacant gaze remained fixed on one of the curlicues in the wallpaper design.

Bill closed his eyes and tried to keep from shouting in frustration. Nothing was right. Especially Nick. Because every time he looked at Nick he was reminded of all the people who had suffered because they were close to him, because he'd cared for them. His parents, little Danny Gordon, Lisl, and now Nick. All of them either dead or mad. And to what end? To isolate him? To make him doubt himself? To make him afraid to get close to anyone, or care for anyone again?

Hello, down there! he thought, looking out the study window at the Sheep Meadow hole, a dark splotch in the afternoon light. Guess what? It's working.

What the hell good was he? Of what use was he to Glaeken? If anything, he was a Jonah. Why did the old man keep him around?

Answerless questions. Glaeken wasn't even home. He was somewhere in the building readying the deserted apartments for refugees people would be bringing in. Bill would have liked to help—the physical activity might do something to dispel this lethargy weighing upon him—but someone had to stay with Nick. And Bill felt responsible for him.

The doorbell rang.

Strange, he thought as he headed for the door. You needed a key to get up here. Who'd come this far and then ring the bell?

He was startled when he saw the woman standing in the atrium.

"Carol! I didn't know you were coming."

The sight of her swept away his lethargy.

"Neither did I. Glaeken sent me up."

Immediately he knew something was wrong. He looked at her more closely and saw how prominent were the lines in her face. Carol had always looked younger than her years, but today she showed every birthday.

"Come in." He glanced out into the atrium as she passed. "Nelson back yet?"

"No. And he's not coming back." Her eyes filled with tears. "He's left me."

"What?"

She sat on the couch and told him about the agony of worry she'd been weathering, and then the phone call she'd just received.

The bastard! He dumped her over the phone? The *phone*?

"You should have come to me when you learned about the accounts," he heard himself say. "You didn't have to go through that alone."

Without realizing it, he had slipped into his old priestly, family-counselor role. He pulled back from it. This wasn't some parishioner, this was Carol. Someone he knew. No, not just knew, but—he could admit it now—loved since he was a teenager. Silly to try for emotional distance where she was concerned. He'd never make it.

"I didn't want to get you involved." She glanced at the vacant-eyed Nick. "You have your own problems."

"Do you love him, Carol?"

The words slipped out and immediately he wanted to call them back. He went to tell her she didn't have to answer, then realized she knew that. So he let it hang. The question had plagued him since his return to the city a few months ago. He wanted to know, damn it.

"Yes. In a way. Not like I loved Jim. Nothing like that. This relationship had a much lower ambient temperature."

"Why did you marry him?"

He couldn't believe he was asking these questions. But here in the darkening room, with Carol becoming a silhouette against the dying light, he felt
he could. Should. He didn't reach for a lamp. That would break the mood set
by the half light.

"I guess I was lonely. When I came back to New York, I knew no one.
Mostly, I wanted it that way. I wanted a fresh start. I didn't want to go back to
Monroe and look up old friends. Too much time had passed. They'd just remind me of Jim and the life we had there. And they'd want to know where I'd
been all these years, they'd want to know why I left, and they'd want to know
about . . . the baby. I didn't want to talk about any of it. It would be too much
like reliving everything. I wanted to create a new Carol."

"I can understand that. Perfectly."

"Can you?"

"Sure. I did it myself in North Carolina. Even changed my name to Will
Ryerson. But for different reasons. Strange, isn't it? We were a thousand miles
apart but we were both trying to remodel ourselves, and at just about the same
time."

"Well then, maybe you understand how lonely it can be. At least you have
your religious beliefs—"

Bill shook his head slowly. "Had. Had my beliefs. They're gone now." Like
just about everyone or everything else in my life I've cared about. "But go on.
Please."

"This isn't an easy city to build relationships in. Not if you're my age and
unconnected. You get hit on by men who think because you've got some miles
on you you're an easy mark who'll be so grateful for the attention you'll hop
into bed with them right off, or you're pursued by ones who've already got a
couple broken marriages behind them and think nothing of trying a third, or
others who are simply looking for someone to take care of them. That's why
Nelson was so refreshing."

"What was he looking for?"

"Nothing. He was self-sufficient—a lifelong bachelor who knew how to
take care of himself. He wasn't on the make, and neither was I. So we wound
up feeling very comfortable with each other. No pressure. Just companionship—
real companionship."

Bill made no comment. He'd heard far worse reasons for marriage.

"Companionship led to a . . . um . . . closer relationship, which led to us
moving in together. We seemed a good fit, made a good couple, caring and attuned to each other's needs. After a while we decided to make it legal." A soft

laugh in the growing darkness. "Not the stuff that makes for a hot romance novel, but it worked for us. Until now."

Bill racked his brain for some brilliant words of advice while fighting the conflicting feelings roiling through him. Carol had been hurt, dealt an emotional slap in the face, and yet he was . . . glad.

"Carol—"

"You're still here?" Glaeken said.

They both looked up. He'd entered silently, as he tended to do.

Carol stiffened and turned to look out the window. "My God, it's almost dark! I'd better get going."

She shot to her feet and Bill rose with her. It seemed like the day had just begun. He opened his mouth to object but Glaeken beat him to it.

"It's sunset. You can't go out now. You'd never make it to the other side of the park, let alone to your apartment. You'll spend the night here. We've plenty of apartments."

Bill repressed a fist pump. Try as he might, he could not douse the gleeful elation sparking at the prospect of having her near all night.

The Bunker

"I don't like this place, Mom."

Gia gave Vicky's shoulder a gentle squeeze and thought, Neither do I. But she didn't voice it.

"We'll be safe here. That's the important thing."

"Safe doesn't come close," Abe said, panting as he strung a curtain across the back third of the bunker. "Like a fortress it's built. Four feet of steel-reinforced concrete above, below, and around, all nestled ten feet underground. We've got freeze-dried food, running water, a microwave, lights, beds, DirecTV, a DVD and VCR player, a toilet even. What's not to like?"

How about a window? Gia thought.

They'd made good time along Route 80 through Jersey and into the rolling farmlands of Pennsylvania. She had no idea where she was, and what good would knowing do? As long as trouble stayed far away from Vicky, wherever she was was fine.

They'd spent much of the latter part of the day moving in. Carrying their belongings down through a narrow tube on a vertical ladder—nothing more than rungs set in the concrete—had been an experience. But they were about as settled as they were going to be. Good thing too. Night was falling.

She rubbed her upper arms. Chilly down here. And damp.

And close.

Good thing neither she nor Vicky were claustrophobic. Not yet, at least. She could imagine herself becoming that way if she stayed cooped up within these blank concrete walls too long.

"Anyway," Abe was saying, "we'll only have to be down here during the dark hours."

"Which are getting longer and longer," Gia said.

"When it's light we can eat and hang out in the farmhouse. Lots of fun things we can do on the farm."

"Can I milk a cow?" Vicky said.

Abe laughed. "No cows in that barn. Maybe a few feral chickens left over from the original owner. Fresh eggs instead of powdered would be nice once in a while."

"So what kind of fun stuff?"

"How about learning to shoot?" He gave one of Vicky's braids a gentle tug. "How does that sound?"

Gia stared at him. The thought of Vicky with a gun left her momentarily speechless.

"Abe, you're not . . . you can't be serious."

"I should joke about such a thing?"

"I hate guns."

He shook his head. "A woman who loves Jack but hates guns. This I'll never understand. Gun hate was a dubious luxury before the bugs. Now . . . if what's been going on keeps up, a gun might be all that stands between you and your daughter and being eaten."

"You're the gun expert. I'll leave the guns to you."

Abe's gaze bored into her. "And if something, God forbid, should happen to me?"

Gia gestured around at all the enveloping concrete. "What could happen to us here inside the Berlin Wall?"

"Think about it, okay? Please? For your own sake."

"Okay. I'll think about it."

And I know just what I'll think: No way.

She fumbled a slip of paper out of her pocket. Jack had written a wavelength on it.

"It's almost time to contact Jack. What you *can* teach me is how to use your shortwave radio."

"Topside I've got a cell repeater up on the barn with the dish and the shortwave antenna. Try the cell first."

She shook her head. "We agreed that the shortwave would be the most reliable if things got worse. I want to get used to that."

She needed to hear Jack's voice. He knew he'd be worried about her, even though she was here. But Gia was twice as worried about him. He'd stayed in the belly of the beast.

"Hey, Mom," Vicky said. "Where's Parabellum?"

Gia turned and saw the empty cage.

"He's gone!" Abe cried. "We've got to find him! He'll never survive!"

WFPW-FM

This just in: The New York City Department of Corrections has reported a massive jailbreak from Riker's Island less than an hour ago. After approximately eighty-five percent of guards on the third shift called in sick, the second shift refused overtime pay and walked off.

The police commissioner reports similar third-shift problems in most of the city's precincts.

Hank braced the thick wood-and-steel bar across his door, then checked his window shutters to make sure they were locked down good and tight. Now—

A knock at the door.

Who the hell?

He stepped closer but made no move to lift the bar.

"Yeah?"

"Mister Thompson," said a familiar voice on the other side. "Ernst Drexler here. May we have a word?"

"Sure. Shoot."

"I'd prefer not to shout through the door."

"Well, that's the way it's gonna be. New rule: My door doesn't open after sundown."

"Please, Mister Thompson—"

"Speak your piece or move on."

A pause, a sigh, then, "I find myself in an awkward position."

"Meaning?"

"I have no accommodations for the night."

Hank knew what was coming, but no way he was letting the white-suited twit off easy.

"I guess that means you couldn't find anyone to put up storm shutters."

"Unfortunately, yes."

"Too bad."

"I was wondering . . ."

"Yeah?"

Another sigh. "I was wondering if I might share your quarters for the night."

Hank paused, as if considering it—which he wasn't.

After a lengthy silence, he said, "Nah."

"Hank, please. I have no place to stay."

So it was "Hank" now? And had he ever heard Drexler say "please"?

"Sorry, Drexie. Not keen on roommates."

"Need I remind you that you are here at the leave of the Ancient Septimus Fraternal Order, of which I am a member and you are not?"

"You've reminded me of that more times than I can count. But you're still not getting in here tonight. You can stay in the basement with the guys. No windows there so you'll be safe enough."

"Now listen here—"

"No, *you* listen: You and your Order can do what you want—try to evict us, whatever. But no matter what, I'm spending the night alone and not opening this door till sunrise. That's all I'll say on the matter."

As Drexler began pounding on the door, Hank turned away and flopped onto his bed. Pretty soon the pounding stopped. He closed his eyes and searched for sleep.

Carol stood beside Bill at Glaeken's picture window. He watched the park but she watched the living room instead. Jack and Glaeken stood in huddled conversation on the far side. Jack had arrived earlier, jubilant that he'd heard from someone named Gia over the shortwave. Now, as he and Glaeken conversed, they'd occasionally glance her way, but she realized they were really looking at Bill, and that made her uneasy.

She turned to the window and saw lights and bustling figures below.

"What's going on?"

"I'm not sure," Bill said. He lifted a pair of binoculars from a nearby table and peered through them. "They were dropping some sort of depth charges in it earlier today. Looks like they're going to try spraying them with insecticide again." He passed the glasses to her. "Take a look."

The Sheep Meadow swam into focus through the lenses. Carol remembered watching a similar scene on TV last night, a scene that had ended in bloody horror.

"I can't believe they're going to try this again," she said. "Those men down there must be either very brave or very crazy."

"I'd venture they're neither. They're doing a job. Everybody else can go nuts, throw up their hands and say nothing matters anymore, the world's coming to an end so screw everything and let's party, let's go wild, let's do all the things we never allowed ourselves to do when we knew there'd be a price to pay. Let's get drunk, get stoned, rape, pillage, kill, destroy, burn everything to the ground just because we feel like it. But we'll always have a certain small percentage who'll go on doing their jobs, people with an overriding sense of duty, of responsibility, of obligation to try to keep things running, to ignore the end-of-the-world zeitgeist and simply keep going. People who know that to let yourself go crazy is to say that your day-to-day life has been a sham, that you've been a hypocrite, that your lifestyle has been little more than playacting; like saying, 'Hey, you know everything I've said and done up till now? It's all been a lie. *This* is the real me.' No matter what Rasalom throws at that small percentage of humans, they're not going to back down. Some of them are around that goddamn hole right now."

Carol found herself staring at Bill, a lump in her throat, tears in her eyes. She knew she was standing next to one of those people. The sound of applause made her turn. Behind them, Jack and Glaeken were clapping.

"I bet you used to give some wicked sermons," Jack said.

Bill looked sheepish. "Sorry. Preaching to the choir. I got a little carried away."

"No," Jack said softly. "It was cool."

Glaeken was smiling. "You've just demonstrated one of the reasons Rasalom hates you so. The type of person you describe is the only threat to his supremacy.

Unfortunately, there aren't enough of them. If the percentages were reversed, however—if there were as many people sticking to their posts, holding on and refusing to allow fear to rob them of everything they believe in, everything they've lived for, as there now are people falling victim to their fears—Rasalom wouldn't have a chance. But the opposite is true. The violent anarchy growing outside feeds his power, helps him shorten the days even further, which increases the fear and irrationality, which in turn makes him stronger, and around and around it goes until he is the victor."

A flash of light from below caught Carol's attention. She turned and stared out at the park.

"Oh, look!"

The others joined her at the window as she raised the glasses and watched as the men around the Sheep Meadow hole sprayed fire at the things winging up from the depths.

"I'll be damned!" Jack said from over her left shoulder. "Flamethrowers! King Kong flamethrowers!"

"I think it's working!" Bill said.

And sure enough, the fire did seem to be working. The things flying out of the hole were caught in the crossfire. Arcs of flame streamed inward from all sides. Powered by the pumps on the trucks around the rim, they crisscrossed over the opening, waving back and forth, catching the winged things as they tried to escape into the night. Doused with gasoline, or whatever the hoses were spraying, they caught fire and hurtled out of control into the darkness, twisting, turning, tumbling, fluttering up and down and about like windswept embers from a fresh-lit campfire.

A thrill ran through Carol. The things were dying! They could be contained! Here was the spark of hope they'd all been looking for!

"Do you know what this means?" she said, lowering the glasses and turning to the others. "If they can set up flamethrowers around all the holes—"

"Hey, what's going on down there?" Jack said.

Carol peered through the glasses again. The arcs of flame were wavering, faltering, some dropping, falling, pouring straight down into the hole; others were backing away from the edge, spraying the ground along the rim with liquid fire. And then Carol saw why.

"Oh, no!"

The flying things weren't the only creatures leaving the pit tonight. Through the lenses she saw other shapes—bulbous creatures with hard, shiny, black bodies; sinuous, multi-legged crawlers as long as a man and as thick around as a muscular thigh, and more—moving along the rim, crawling over the edge, worming their way onto the grass. They leapt upon the men directing the flamethrowers, began tearing them to pieces.

Carol snatched the glasses from her eyes and held them away from her. Jack took them, watched for a moment in silence, then handed them to Bill.

Bill's voice sounded dry, quavering. "Every night some new horror is added to the others."

"And each night is longer than the last," Glaeken said. "But come away from the window for now. We have something to discuss."

Carol was glad to retreat to the lighted space of the living room. She huddled next to Bill. Despite the warmth of the apartment she felt cold. She almost wished he'd put an arm around her and hug her close. She'd spent the last few nights alone, but tonight she *felt* alone.

Jack sat across from them. Glaeken remained standing.

"Jack is leaving for the Central Pacific tomorrow. The object of his mission is crucial to our survival. However, even if he's successful in retrieving the necklaces, I fear they won't be enough. We need something else. One more component. And to obtain that, someone must travel in the opposite direction. Jack can't do both—there's not enough time. I need a volunteer to go the other way."

A sick feeling grew in the pit of Carol's stomach as she noticed both men staring at Bill.

He said, "How . . . how far in this other direction?"

"Romania."

Carol grabbed Bill's hand and squeezed. *No!*

"How can I get there? The airlines—"

He's already decided! Carol thought. They didn't even ask him and he's already making travel plans.

"I know some pilots," Jack said. "A couple of brothers. They run an executive jet service out on Long Island."

"They're still flying?"

Jack smiled. "You know the kind of people you were talking about before— the ones who keep on keepin' on, no matter what? Frank and Joe Ashe are two of those. They don't back down—I don't think they know how."

"Frank and Joe," Bill said. "They sound like the Hardy Boys. Will they fly me?"

Jack nodded. "For a price. I just spoke to them. They're not crazy about heading into Eastern Europe, but for the right price—in gold—they'll do it."

"Gold?" Bill said. "I don't ha—"

"I have plenty," Glaeken said. "Are you willing to make the trip?"

"Of course."

"Bill!" Carol gave his hand a hard squeeze. "Maybe you should think about this."

"What's to think about?" His clear and untroubled blue eyes stared into hers. "Somebody's got to do it. Might as well be me. I want to be useful, Carol. I'm tired of feeling like a fifth wheel. I need to *do* something. Hell, I'm not needed for anything else around here."

I need you!

The intensity of the emotion behind that thought startled her.

"You could be killed."

"We'll all be dead if we don't do what we can now." He looked at Glaeken. "When do I leave and what am I supposed to get?"

"You leave tomorrow morning—"

"Oh, no!" Carol couldn't help it.

"—and you'll be searching a rocky ravine for scraps of metal, shards from a sword blade that shattered there in 1941."

Bill looked shocked. "Do I have to get them all?"

"Just a few. Just a sampling is all we need. You must—"

An explosion rattled the apartment windows. Carol followed Glaeken, Bill, and Jack to the picture window.

Below, in the Sheep Meadow, flames billowed high into the night air. One of the tank trucks supplying the fuel for the flamethrowers had exploded. In the flickering light, even without the binoculars, Carol could see that the entire Sheep Meadow was now acrawl with the new horrors from the hole. They were on the move, spreading out into the city streets in a glistening, wriggling, undulating carpet.

She wondered if something similar was happening in Atlantic City . . . to Nelson and his new woman. No reason she should worry about the man who'd abandoned her, but she did. All those years together . . .

She glanced up and saw the moon rising huge and orange over the rooftops of the city. But something was . . . different about it tonight.

"What's wrong with the moon?"

The others stared along with her. Jack spotted it first.

"The face—the man in the moon face is gone. Jeez—even the moon's been changed!"

"Not changed," said a flat voice by her shoulder.

A small cry of surprise escaped Carol as she turned and saw Nick standing directly behind her. But he wasn't looking at her. His attention was focused on the moon.

"It's the same moon. It's just been turned. You're looking at what people called the dark side of the moon."

Carol turned back and stared up at the vaguely threatening orb that had been a symbol of romance for ages.

Even the man in the moon has turned his back on us.

"Take me with you tomorrow," Nick said to Bill. "You won't find anything without me."

Carol watched Bill stare at Nick, then look questioningly at Glaeken.

After a pause, Glaeken nodded. "He's right, I think. He may help shorten your trip. And right now anything that saves time is worth a try."

Feeling colder than ever, Carol turned back to the window and leaned against Bill. As she stared at the pale, unfamiliar ridges of the moon's new face, she gasped. Something dark, hideous, and mind-numbingly huge was sweeping across the sky, blotting out the light. It passed slowly, like a floating shroud, casting a chill over everything in its enormous shadow, and then it moved on, leaving the moon visible again.

She shuddered and felt Bill's arm slip around her shoulders. But even that could not dispel the chill of foreboding that had insinuated its way into her bones.

Ernst huddled under a blanket in the Lodge basement, counting the hours till dawn. Surrounded by snoring Kicker louts, with cases of Hunt's canned baked beans for his bed, comfort was an impossibility, sleep a forlorn hope.

What had become of his life?

Last summer he had been on top of the world. The *Fhinntmanchca* had been gestating in the subcellar directly beneath where he now lay, he was the One's right-hand man, and the future was his to command.

Now, less than a year later, he saw no future except suffering and death along with the hoi polloi.

At least he was safe for tonight. Both his apartment and his office right upstairs had been invaded last night, but the cellar was secure: windowless foundation walls of thick stone, with a single bolted door the only access to the outside world. Running water, a couple of hot plates, a microwave oven, a kerosene stove.

He could survive as long as the door held up and the food held out. And then . . . what? If only—

He felt the floor vibrate and sat up.

What was that? Another hole opening in this end of the city?

More vibrations. They seemed to be coming from the subcellar. But the only thing down there was the remains of the Orsa. It had started out made of stone but had become organic, and after completing its task of creating the *Fhinntmanchca,* it had begun to decay. Back in the fall of 2001, the subcellar wall had been breached to bring it in, and then repaired. To dispose of it would require a similar excavation, and the High Council had not got around to allocating the funds.

Was the onset of the Change affecting the Orsa? Reviving it? Perhaps Ernst could find a way to turn this to his advantage.

More vibrations, but no one else seemed to notice. He rose and stole across the littered floor to a small room off the main area. He opened a door to a closet, and inside pulled up a trapdoor in the floor. All the Order's lodges had been built with subcellars and escape routes, but this building had been sealed off with the arrival of the Orsa.

He stood over the rickety wrought-iron spiral staircase and listened to the vague, unidentifiable sound that echoed from the dark, dank space below. He started down. The staircase had been damaged by the *Fhinntmanchca,* and wobbled under his weight. When he reached bottom, he found the light switch in the wall and flipped it.

He repressed a scream as the space lit up to reveal a horde of beetlelike creatures with shiny black bodies four to five feet long pouring through a break in the subcellar wall—the very spot that had been breached to bring in the Orsa.

They must have been attracted to the subcellar by the Orsa, for they seemed too intent on devouring it to notice him.

Ernst watched for only a single heartbeat, then he turned and started back up the staircase. His hands shook and his sweaty palms slid on the steel railing as he moved as silently as possible. He did not look back—did not *dare* look back until he reached the top.

As he closed the trapdoor he peeked below and saw two of the beetles starting up the staircase. Frantic, he let the door drop and looked around for something to weigh it down. Food! Cases of canned goods in the main room, but he'd never get to them in time.

He had to get away, but where? Thompson's room. He'd break the door down if he had to.

So he ran. As he passed through the main room he opened his mouth to shout a warning, then thought better of it. When running from a bear, one needn't run faster than the bear, only faster than the slowest of those with you. And if those with you weren't running at all . . .

He kept mum as he hurried to the exit door, unlocked it, and stepped out into the stairwell to the main floor. Deserting all caution, he ran up to the front vestibule. A few of the globular flies clung to the marble walls there, but otherwise it seemed quiet. No victims readily available, he supposed.

Without pausing, Ernst darted for the stairway to the second floor. He heard wings buzz behind him and increased his speed. His aging heart beat a terrified rhythm and the air seemed thin, lacking oxygen. He wasn't used to physical exertion and his muscles screamed in protest.

He ran to Thompson's door and began pounding on it.

"Hank! You must let me in! The bugs have breached the cellar and I have nowhere else to go!"

No answer. He pounded harder.

"I am begging you. For the love of whatever god you believe in, let me in!"

Buzzing to his right—the globular bugs floated out of the stairwell and veered toward him.

"PLEASE!"

Silence from within.

This was it, then. He pulled the ampoule of cyanide from his pocket and raised it to his lips. One bite and—

A furious buzz to his right and something tore at his arm, blasting a blaze of pain into his elbow and sending the ampoule flying.

"No!"

He couldn't—wouldn't die like this!

He dove for the floor, for the cyanide, and then they were upon him.

Ernst Drexler screamed in agony.

Hank snapped awake.

He'd been roused before by sounds from the security shutters. Bugs—spearheads most likely—ramming themselves against them. They'd have swarmed in and eaten him alive if not for the warning from the Kicker Man. He'd listened for a while as they battered futilely against the steel, then fluttered off, heading for redder pastures.

It used to be the nights were never long enough for Hank. His head would hit the pillow and before he knew it, he'd have to rise. At various times during the night he'd heard screams from outside on the street, but was never tempted to peek.

But this was different. Someone pounding on his door.

Drexler.

He sounded hysterical, crying about bugs in the cellar, in the hallway, begging to be let in.

As if.

Hank turned the light on and watched the door, but didn't move from the bed. He pressed his hands over his ears to shut out the noise.

Never liked Drexler, never liked his stupid white suit, never liked the way he always looked down his nose at Hank and the Kickers with his Euro sophistication and aristocratic 'tude. But even if it had been his brother Jerry out there, no fucking way Hank was opening that door. Who knew what else would invite itself into the room?

A sudden agonized scream broke through the seal of his palms and he snatched them away to listen. No further screams came, but he heard violent thrashing just beyond the door, accompanied by muffled, gurgling sobs that were awful to hear, even if it was Drexler.

Then silence.

Yeah, hard to feel sorry for Drexler. He and his Order had paved the way for all the shit that was coming down outside.

As Hank reached for the light switch he noticed something dark and gleaming on the floor. He looked closer and realized that blood was leaking under the door and pooling by the threshold.

So much for Ernst Drexler.

The Horror Channel's Drive-In Theatre—Special All-Nite Edition
Up from the Depths (1969) New World
The Fly (1958) 20th Century Fox
Return of the Fly (1959) 20th Century Fox
The Curse of the Fly (1965) Lippert/20th Century Fox
Night Creatures (1962) Hammer/Universal
Not of This Earth (1956) Allied Artists

Ceremonies

Maui

"It's a gift, Bati! A sign from Pele herself!"

Moki's voice was barely audible over the blast-furnace roar of the volcano. Dressed only in his *malo,* he stood near the ruins of the visitor center on the rim of the newly awakened Haleakala. Perspiration coated his skin, giving it a glossy sheen as red and orange light from the fires below flickered off the planes and curves of his taut, muscular body, making it glow against the inky night sky.

The two yellow stones in his necklace seemed to glow with internal fires of their own. And why not? The necklace had been working overtime on Moki. Only moments ago he had emerged from the crater with second-degree burns blistering most of his body. But the blisters had shriveled and the damaged skin had peeled and sloughed away to reveal fresh, unmarred flesh beneath.

Kolabati backed away from the heat and worried about Moki. He'd changed so drastically. He was no longer the man she'd loved and lived with. He was a stranger, a deranged interloper fashioning his own delusions out of the madness around him.

Yesterday she had been afraid for him. But now she was afraid *of* him. The cataclysm that had destroyed the Big Island and reawakened Haleakala seemed to have pushed him over the edge.

And tingeing Kolabati's fear, coloring it a deep, dull red, was anger. Why? Why now? Why did all of nature choose this time to go mad? Coincidence, or fate? Was her enormous karmic burden—and she knew too well the extent to which the deeds of her many, many years had polluted her karma—finally catching up to her?

"What does it mean, Moki?" she called back, humoring him. "What kind of sign would the fire goddess be sending you?"

"She didn't want me leaving Maui to gather lava from Kileau, so she destroyed Kileau and brought her fires to my backyard."

Kolabati shook her head in silent dismay. Didn't Moki's mania admit any limits? How many hundreds of thousands had died on the Big Island when it had exploded? How many more here on Maui in those areas not shielded from the blast by Haleakala? But Haleakala herself had gathered her share of lives. Hana was gone, as were the Seven Sacred Pools, buried under the tons of ash and dirt from Haleakala's explosive awakening, then sealed over by the initial gush of lava that had filled the Kipahulu Valley and burst through into the Waihoi, running down to the sea. According to the news gleaned from their radio, the whole southeast corner of the island, from the Kaupo Gap to Nanu-alele Point, was a seething bed of molten lava.

All so Moki wouldn't have to leave Maui on day trips?

Fortunately the lava had flowed along its old paths. If Haleakala had erupted through its northern wall, the heavily populated central valley would have become a graveyard. Moki even had an explanation for that: Pele wished to spare Moki and his *wahine*.

So Moki had changed, and with his transformation Kolabati recognized unwelcome changes within herself. The inner tranquillity had been shattered, the peace broken, and she found her thoughts traveling along old familiar ways, the cold, calculating paths of the past.

She shivered in the chill wind. Shielded as she was from the heat of the crater, it was cold nearly two miles above the ocean. She wanted to flee, but where to? The news from the mainland was frightening. It might be safer here on the islands, but not with Moki. He was an explosive charge, ready to deto-nate at any moment and destroy everything and anyone nearby. Yet she could not leave him. Not while he wore the other necklace. That belonged to her, and she would not leave without it.

Yet how to retrieve it? How to unbell the cat?

She had considered removing it while he slept but had not yet dared to try. Since the madness had come upon him, Moki hardly slept. And if he awoke from one of his short naps to find the necklace gone, he would track her down, and then only Kali knew what he might do to her. He might even rip her own necklace from her throat and watch as a century and a half caught up with her. He of course would not age noticeably without his necklace, for he had worn it only a few years. But Kolabati would grow old and crumble into dying ashes before his eyes.

So she kept quiet, acted supportive, and waited for her chance.

With a start Kolabati realized that they were not alone on the crater rim. A group of perhaps sixty men of varying ages in traditional Hawaiian dress had joined them. Led by their *alii*, an elderly man in a chieftain's feather robe and headdress, they were approaching Moki where he stood watching the fires. The *alii* called to him and he turned. She caught snatches of traditional Hawaiian chattered back and forth but had difficulty grasping the gist of what was being said.

Finally, Moki turned and walked down the slope toward her. The others remained up near the rim, waiting.

"Bati!" he said in a low voice, his grin wide and wild, his eyes dancing with excitement. "Do you see them? They're the last of the traditional Hawaiians. They sailed all the way from Niihau looking for Maui."

"They found it," Kolabati said. "What's left of it."

"Not the island—Maui the god. You know the story."

"Of course."

Before dawn one day long ago, Maui, the mischievous Polynesian demigod, crept to the summit of Haleakala, the House of the Sun, on a mission of filial love. His mother had complained that the days were not long enough to allow her to finish her tasks of cooking, cleaning, and drying tapa cloth, so Maui decided to do something about it. When the first ray of the sun appeared over the summit, Maui snared it with his lasso, thus trapping the sun. The sun pleaded for freedom but Maui would not release it until it promised to lengthen the days by slowing its trek across the heavens.

"The Niihauans say the shorter days show that the sun has broken its promise and so they've come to aid Maui when he returns to recapture the sun. They want to know if I've seen him! Can you believe it?"

Kolabati looked past Moki at the grown men dressed in feathers and carrying spears, and pitied them.

"What did you tell them?"

"I temporized. I wasn't sure what to say. But now I do."

Kolabati didn't like the look in his eyes.

"I'm almost afraid to ask."

His grin widened. "I'm going to tell them *I'm* Maui."

"Oh, Moki, don't toy with them. Aren't things bad enough already?"

"Who's toying? I sense a strange power in me. I have a feeling I just might *be* Maui, or at least his avatar. I tell you, Bati, I'm here in this place at this time for a reason. Perhaps this is a sign as to why."

Kolabati grabbed his hand and tried to lead him down the slope.

"Moki, no. Come back to the house. Work on that new sculpture you started."

He pulled free. "Later. After I've told them who I am."

She watched him stride back up to the rim and face the Niihauans, saw him pound his chest and gesture to the fires below and then to the night sky above. The traditional Hawaiians stepped back from him and whispered among themselves. Then the *alii* gestured to one of the younger men, who stepped forward and drove his spear into Moki's chest.

Kolabati screamed.

His consciousness is fuzzy, but he still has control, even though his being is in solution.

Such a strange feeling to have all his tissues—bones, brain, organs, nerves, intestines—distilled to liquid. All that he was resides now in a sack suspended from the hub of the four-spoked wheel that was once his body. The spokes have grown thicker, longer, and the stony womb has enlarged to accommodate his increased size. A cavern now, stretching downward into the infinity where the cold fire burns. The icy glow from below chills the sack where he grows, where his components reorganize into his new form. The petrous columns that arch across the cavern act as conduits for the fear, the violence, the pain, the misery they siphon from the surface, feeding him, shaping him.

His new form shall be ready by the undawn on Friday.

But now it is time for the next step—to deny them sight of the sun.

PART TWO

TWILIGHT

MONDAY

Fellow Travelers

WFPW-FM

And in business news, we are witnessing a global collapse of the world's stock markets. The Nikkei Exchange has crashed. All stocks from Hong Kong, throughout Europe, and in London are in free-fall. There is no reason to expect the U.S. exchanges to fare any better when they open in New York this morning. We are witnessing the greatest financial cataclysm in history.

Precious metals, however, are a different story. Gold opened in Hong Kong at twenty-four hundred fifty-one dollars an ounce and went through the roof from there. Silver opened at an astounding fifty-seven dollars an ounce and hasn't stopped rising. No price seems too high to bid on these metals.

Manhattan

Hank thought of his bags of silver coins as he watched his TV. He'd called that right. And he knew he was just as right about the food. The picture flickered now and again, but he never totally lost power. He had a battery-powered portable ready if needed. About the only things on were preachers, movies, and news—disastrous news.

The president had proclaimed a state of national emergency but the armed forces were proving ineffective against an enemy of such overwhelming numbers and so intimately mixed with the population they were meant to protect. Soldiers with wives, husbands, children, parents were staying home to protect their own. The remainder were vastly outnumbered. For every hole they plugged with explosives—in the instances where they could safely use explosives—two more opened up elsewhere. People were quickly losing confidence in the government's ability to manage the situation. The social contract—if such a thing had ever existed—was dissolving.

He listened at the door. Quiet out there. He wondered if any of the Kickers had left the basement yet. Probably waiting for sunrise. But why wait till dawn?

He raised one of the window shutters a couple of inches and peeked out. The sky was getting lighter now. The night things should be on their way back to the holes already if they wanted to make it before sunrise. Should he risk stepping outside his little cocoon? Might be good for the Kickers to see their Fearless Leader out and about before anyone else.

Hank lifted the bar off the door and opened it an inch or so for a quick peek. Dim out there. All the lights either out or broken. The only illumination came from broken windows at the ends of the hallway.

Someone out there. Down the hall to his left a still form lay curled on its side. A long trail of smeared blood ran from his doorway to the body. No one else in sight. No *things* either. Who was that? Looked vaguely male. Drexler?

He stepped outside, twisted the knob to make sure it wouldn't lock, and closed the door behind him. He'd just started along the blood trail when he heard an angry buzz from far down the hall behind him. He whirled. He couldn't see anything, but he knew that buzz. He'd heard it enough these past nights. Wings. Big, double dragonfly wings. And then he heard another sound—the gnashing teeth of a chew wasp.

Terror rammed a fist down hard on his bladder. Too early! He'd left the room *too damn early*.

The buzz grew louder, angrier, closer. And then he saw it, hurtling down the hall at a level of about five feet, directly at him. The grinding of the teeth picked up tempo. With a scream building in his throat, Hank leaped back to his door, pushed through and slammed it closed—

—right on the chew wasp's head. Its crystalline teeth gnashed in fury as it struggled to squeeze into the room. Hank kept pressure on the door, not daring to let up for an instant. If it got through, no telling what it would do to him. Worse, it might be attracting others. Had to do something—*now*.

He spotted the door bar a few feet away. He stretched for it, got a grip, then swung it with all he had, once, twice, three times, crushing the creature's head.

When its jaws stopped working, he eased his pressure on the door and let it slip to the floor. He quick-kicked it into the hall and then slammed the door. He leaned against it, gasping, waiting for his heart to slow.

He decided he didn't need to be the first out and about.

He gave it another ten minutes, then stepped out into the hall again. But this time he stayed by the door, squinting left and right, listening for the sound of wings. A bit brighter now. And still quiet.

Taking a deep breath, he once again approached the corpse. As he neared he recognized Drexler. Well, sort of. If not for the white suit—now 90 percent red—he'd never have been able to tell. His body was shrunken, wizened, all his exposed skin shredded, chewed up but strangely bloodless. His eyes had been eaten out, leaving red, raw sockets.

How did you die, Drexie?

As if in answer, he heard a sound, something between a cluck and a gurgle. It seemed to come from the corpse. As he stared, he saw the throat work, the jaw move. But he couldn't be alive!

And then Drexler's mouth opened and Hank saw something moving inside. No, not inside anymore, slithering out. A flat, wide, pincered head, dark brown where it wasn't bloody red, followed by a sinuous six-foot body as big around as a beer can, powered by countless fine, rubbery legs, all dripping red.

Some sort of giant millipede, squeezing out Drexler's gullet and coming right for him. And it was *fast*.

Hank yelped and backpedaled until his back slammed against the wall. He turned and tried to climb it.

But the thing wasn't interested in him. It veered toward the doorway and raced down toward the lobby. Heading for the street and nearest hole, no doubt.

He'd never seen anything like that before. It had to be the latest addition to the bug horde.

Leaving Drexler's remains behind, he slipped downstairs to the front lobby area. The big double doors stood open, the left half off its hinges. He eased through and stood on the front steps.

Monday morning. The sky looked funny. Not quite sunrise yet. Ordinarily the streets would have been jumping by now, clogged with cabs and cars and delivery trucks. But nothing moved. No, wait. Up the street he spotted a garbage-can-size beetle with a wicked set of mandibles spread wide before it, scuttling by at the corner, heading uptown; an occasional flying thing whizzed through the air, also in the general direction of Central Park. Except for those, the streets were empty. Where had the giant millipede gone? How could it have got around the corner so fast?

He went back inside. Where the hell was everyone? And then he re-membered Drexler screaming through the door something about bugs in the cellar.

He hurried to the stairwell to the basement, and when he saw the smashed door, he knew what he'd find beyond it.

His in-house Kicker crew had been wiped out.

In that instant he saw his next move with perfect clarity: He had to get out of town. And he knew just where to go. During the summer he'd taken a few jaunts down to the Jersey Shore, to places like Asbury Park and Seaside Heights. Even rented a bungalow for a week in an oceanfront town called Chad-wick Beach. Most of the houses there were little more than plywood boxes, but he remembered a couple of places that looked fairly sturdy, equipped with storm shutters and heat. They'd be empty now, the beaches and boardwalks all but deserted, waiting for the summer renters—renters who wouldn't be coming. A perfect hideaway.

Had to get moving. The guys had left a couple of hand trucks in the lobby, and a van out back. He could fill that with cases of food and haul ass out of here. It would take a bunch of trips with the hand truck, but if he didn't waste time, he could be on the road in less than an hour.

WFPW-FM

JO: Hi, this is Jo and Freddy. Yeah, I know we're early but we're the only ones left at the station. No one knows where the other guys are.

FREDDY: Headed for the hills, if they're smart.

JO: Yeah. But we're not smart. We're sticking this out. In fact, we're moving into the station. We're living here, man, and we're staying on the air as long as they let us. And since nobody else is around, that could be a long time.

FREDDY: Yeah. Jo and Freddy all day and all night.

JO: Right. So let's get this started. It's Monday morning, May twenty-second. The sun rose at 7:40 A.M. According to the Sapir curve, it will set at 5:35 this afternoon, leaving us with a measly nine hours and fifty-five minutes of sunlight today.

FREDDY: So do what you have to do quick and get home soon. And be careful out there, folks. Be good to each other. We're all we've got left.

JO: Hate to interrupt the Youngbloods, man, but you're not gonna believe this: The Pentagon is . . . gone. I mean, gone, man. One of those holes opened under it during the night and it just ain't there no more.

"Isn't the sun coming up?" Bill said, looking out the window. The sky was brightening but no sun, just a strange yellow light.

Jack came up beside him. "Looks overcast."

"But those aren't clouds up there, or even haze. It's like . . . I don't know what it's like. Looks like a yellow scum of some sort's been poured over the sky."

"Whatever," Jack said. "We've waited long enough. The boogie beasts have called it a night and it's time to roll. You ready?"

"Soon as I get back from Carol's place. She needs to pick up some things."

"All right. I've got a couple of stops to make myself. When I get back, you and I and the Amazing Criswell will all head out to the Ashe brothers' airfield."

"Okay. I'll be ready."

"Don't get lost. There's not a lot of time to spare." He turned to go, then turned back. "How you getting there?"

"Car."

Jack reached into his belt and pulled out a pistol. He held it out to Bill, grip first.

"Better take this."

Bill stared at the thing. Its dark surface gleamed dully in the diffuse light from the window. It seemed as if some sort of alien creature had invaded the apartment.

"A gun? I wouldn't know what to do with it."

"I'll show you. First you—"

"I couldn't use it, Jack. Really."

"It's ugly out there, Bill. People were calling this city a jungle last week. They thought it was bad before the first hole opened up. They had no idea how bad it could get. Not much trouble right around here—the creeps are no more anxious to get near that hole than anyone else—but you get too far up- or downtown and you'll run into spots that would make a jungle look like a Sunday afternoon drive. Take the gun. Just for show if nothing else."

"All right." Bill took the pistol and was surprised at its weight. "But what about you?"

Jack smiled. "Plenty more where that came from. Besides, I never carry just one."

As Jack hurried off, Bill slipped the pistol under his belt and pulled his sweater down over it. Then he took the stairs down to the apartment where Carol had spent the night.

Jack found Julio's open but damn near deserted. Half of the front windows were smashed, most of the dead plants had been ripped from their hangers. And worst of all, something had gnawed on the *Free Beer Tomorrow* . . . sign.

"Where is everybody?"

Julio paused in his sweeping up the glass fragments and shrugged. "Some hiding, some gone. You hear from Gia?"

"Yeah. Spoke to her during the night and this morning. They're doing okay. No bugs out their way."

Not yet, at least.

Gia had sounded on edge, but he'd expected that—ripped from her home, living in a bunker. He kept telling her it was all for the best. And he believed it.

"You planning on staying open?"

Another shrug. "Don' know. Hate to give in to the bugs, but we spent last night in the cellar and it was scary. The power's been off and on. If I got no power, I gotta serve warm beer. And that's no good."

"Close up and get some stuff together. I got a safe place for you—at least temporarily safe. We've got room. Whattaya say?"

He watched the muscular little man as he looked around the place that was his life, his livelihood. He knew how stubborn Julio could be. They'd been friends forever. Jack wanted to see him safe.

Finally Julio nodded. "Yeah, why not? But just at night. I stay open in the day. Every day."

At least that's something, Jack thought.

And who knew how many more days there'd be?

In the strange, shadowless yellow half-light that was passing for day, Bill skirted the park to the south and headed east across town in a borrowed Volvo. No roadblocks and no traffic to speak of. No police, either, and that concerned him. As he readied to turn uptown he glanced at the Queensboro Bridge.

"Carol!" he said as he screeched to a halt. "Look!"

"Oh, my God!"

A section of the span had broken up and now floated in the air, tethered to the rest of the bridge by twisted pieces of steel that groaned in the breeze.

"A gravity hole," Carol said. "And it was such a beautiful bridge."

"The engineers have been saying for years what poor shape the bridges were in. Now we know how right they were."

Aiming for the Upper East Side, he drove along the middle of the street. With the exception of Glaeken's building, it seemed as if almost every window in the city had been broken.

He eased to the left and upped their speed when he spotted a mob clustered around the front of a grocery store.

"Nelson and I used to grocery shop there."

Nobody was shopping now. Pillaging was more like it. People were jumping in and out of the broken door and windows, looking for anything remotely edible. But with nothing left to pillage, the enraged mob was tearing out the empty shelves and hurling them into the street. Three men were brawling over what looked like a can of tuna fish.

Farther on, groups of tight-faced people hung about on the glass-bejeweled sidewalks, clustered in tense circles, glancing nervously over their shoulders this way and that with fear-haunted eyes. He saw three women standing around a doorway sobbing as a sheet-covered body was carried out. The people on the streets looked like ghosts.

"It's falling apart." Carol had her arms crossed in front of her chest as if to ward off a chill. "Just like Nelson said it would."

As Bill was slowing for a red light at 63rd—habit, pure habit—somebody shot at them. The bullet punched through the rear window and smashed the right rear side pane on its way out. Bill floored the gas and sped uptown, ignoring traffic lights the rest of the way.

He double-parked in front of Carol's apartment building and led her toward the shattered front door. Inside, she gasped when she saw a body on the floor. Someone had covered it with a drape from one of the ruined windows.

The elevator ride was slow and rough, as if the motors weren't getting enough juice. As soon as the doors opened on her floor, Carol bolted from the car and ran down the hall. Bill noticed some drying brown stains on the carpet and what looked like a trail of the same leading past her apartment but said nothing. She had her door open by the time he caught up with her. He stayed close behind as she entered.

He bumped up against her back when she stopped dead inside the threshold.

"It's a wreck!"

The windows were broken, the furniture gnawed and gouged.

"Good thing you weren't here."

If Nelson hadn't run off, they might have stayed here last night, and might have ended up like that corpse in the lobby.

So damn it all, Bill was glad he'd taken off. Because it meant one less barrier between him and Carol. He loathed himself for that. But he wanted her. God, how he wanted her.

He forced himself to pull back and take her arm.

"Let's move it."

She led him to a storage closet where they each grabbed a suitcase, then to the master bedroom. She pulled clothing out of drawers, handed it to him, and he stuffed it in a suitcase. Then she opened a closet. She stopped and touched one of Nelson's suits.

"I still can't believe . . ."

"Do you hate him?"

She shook her head. "I don't think much of him now, but I can't bring myself to hate him."

"I don't think you're capable of hate, so I'll hate him for both of us."

She turned and looked at him. "I'm the one he ran out on."

"No, he ran out on *us*."

Carol stared. "Us?"

"All of us. Now's the time when we have to stick together, help each other through this catastrophe. Doing what Nelson did, that just makes Rasalom stronger. It's another brick in the walls going up between people. Don't you see what's happening? All the intangibles that link us are being destroyed. Love, trust, brotherhood, community, camaraderie, neighborliness. The simple everyday things that make us human, that make us more than just a pile of organisms, that make us larger than ourselves—they're all going up in smoke."

"It's fear, Bill. Everyone's afraid. Death is everywhere. Up is down, down is up—nothing's sure anymore."

"That's *outside*. Rasalom's wrecking everything outside. He's calling all the shots out there. But inside"—he pounded on his chest—"inside you've got who you are, and you've got the bonds you've formed with other people. That's where those bonds are anchored. Rasalom can't get inside unless he's allowed in. You let that fear in and it will destroy those bonds. And that's the beginning of the end. For without them we divide into small, suspicious enclaves, which soon deteriorate into warring packs, which finally degenerate into a bunch of backstabbing lone wolves."

"Nelson would never—"

"Excuse me, Carol, but I believe you've got a knife in your back. One with Nelson's fingerprints all over it. As far as I'm concerned, running off like this is aiding and abetting the enemy."

Carol didn't argue.

They finished packing what they could, then headed for the elevators. They descended in silence and didn't talk much as they started the ride back. More traffic about now, but scattered and fitful. Bill headed west toward the park on 72nd. As he slowed for a passing truck on Madison, three tough-looking Hispanics, either high or drunk or both, stepped in front of the car.

"A car," the biggest of them said, slurring his words. "I could use me some wheels."

Bill pulled out the pistol and pointed it through the windshield at one of the men, hoping the bluff would work. He knew he couldn't pull the trigger. The big man smiled sheepishly, held up his hands, and the three of them staggered away. Bill glanced at Carol and found her staring at him.

"A pistol, Bill? You?"

"Jack's idea. I don't even know how to fire it."

Carol held out her hand. "I do. I spent fifteen years roaming around the South with Jonah and . . . that boy."

She took the gun, pulled the slide back maybe an inch, and looked inside. "One in the chamber. All set."

She flicked a little switch on its side, then held the pistol up in plain view next to her window.

Speechless, Bill drove on. They had no trouble the rest of the trip back.

Jack pulled into a no-parking zone on Seventh Avenue in front of a battered hospital and hopped out of his car. The West Village had taken a beating last night and he was pretty sure an illegally parked car would be low on the police priority list. He wasn't staying long anyway.

He saw a slim brunette using a cordless drill to screw sheets of plywood over broken windows. Something familiar about her. A second look and he recognized her.

"Alicia?"

She turned, squinted at him with her blue-gray eyes. Her black hair was pinned up, making her look younger than her thirty-something years.

"Jack? What are you doing here?"

Alicia Clayton, M.D., pulled off a work glove and extended her hand.

"Came by to see if you needed a safer place to stay."

She shrugged. "Don't we all. But I'm bunking here. The kids, you know."

Yeah, the kids. Alicia was a pediatric infectious disease specialist. She ran the Center for Children with AIDS.

"Listen, the place I'm talking about has lots of space—empty apartments galore. You could move the kids—"

She shook her head. "No way. Some of them are too sick to be moved anywhere without a full hospital setup. This place of yours have that?"

"Well, no. But . . . it's going to get uglier, Alicia."

Her mouth twisted. "I don't see how—"

"Trust me, it will. You need to get to a safe place." She was good people. Jack was one of the few who knew the hell she'd lived through growing up. Yet she'd overcome all that. Most of it anyway. "We're going to need doctors."

"I appreciate the offer, Jack, but these kids are stuck here, and that means I am too."

Jack hadn't expected any less, but he'd felt compelled to offer.

Just then a dapper fellow in green scrubs stepped through the entrance carrying a toolbox.

"Raymond," Alicia said. "You remember Jack."

"Of course," he said and shook hands, but Jack knew the guy had no clue who he was.

"How come two of the medical staff are out here boarding up windows?"

Raymond fluttered a hand in the air. "Because the maintenance people didn't show up this morning. Somebody's got to do it."

Alicia smiled. "But this is the last board. After this we'll be sealed in safe and sound."

Jack doubted that, but said nothing. He knew Alicia's type. No way she'd walk away from a responsibility—and those sick kids were a responsibility she lived for. And would die for.

He said his good-byes and headed for his next stop, knowing he'd likely never see her again.

New Jersey Turnpike

Clear sailing on the blacktop. Hardly any other cars. Hank had most of the six southbound lanes to himself.

He wondered why more people weren't on the move, then realized that gas was probably in short supply—all the service areas he'd passed so far had been deserted. And where was there to go? According to the news reports, hell was everywhere. It might be a horror show where you were, but you could be fleeing into something far worse. And what if dark fell before you made it to where you were going? Better to stay where you were, hunker down, and try to hold on to what you had.

He saw the sign for exit 11—the Garden State Parkway. That was his. The Parkway would take him down the coast to the shore towns. Just past the sign was another for the Thomas A. Edison Service Area. Under that, on the shoulder, sat a sheet of plywood, hand painted:

WE HAVE GAS
DEISEL TOO

Yeah, but can you spell?

Hank checked his gas gauge: half a tank. They were probably charging an arm and a leg per gallon, but who knew when he'd get another chance—if ever?

Ahead he saw a beat-up station wagon turn off the road onto the service area approach. Hank decided to follow.

As he approached the gas lanes he saw one of the two overalled attendants leaning in the passenger window of the station wagon. He straightened up and waved the wagon on.

Probably doesn't have enough money, Hank thought.

He smiled and clinked his heel against the canvas bags stowed under the front seat. He had something they couldn't refuse: silver coins. Precious metal. Always worth something, but more in bad times. The TV had said silver was going for eighty dollars an ounce. And the worse things got, the more it would be worth.

He slowed, reached down, and pulled out a handful of coins; he shoved them into his pocket, checked that both door locks were down, then headed for the gas lanes.

The two attendants were clean-cut and clean-shaven, one blond, one dark, both well built, each about thirty. The blond one came around to Hank's side.

"You've got gas?" Hank said, rolling his window down a couple of inches.

The fellow nodded. "What've you got for it besides plastic or paper?"

Hank pulled out his quarters. "These should do. They're all pre-1964—solid silver."

The blond stared at the coins, then called to the dark-haired one.

"Hey, Chuck. He's got silver. We want silver?"

Chuck came up to the passenger window. "I dunno," he said through the glass. "What else you got?"

"This is it."

"What you got in the back?" the blond one said.

A trapped feeling had begun to steal over Hank. He grabbed for the gearshift. "Never mind."

His hand never reached it. Both side windows exploded inward, peppering him with glass; a club came in from his left and smashed against his cheek, showering cascades of flashing lights through his vision. He heard the door open, felt fingers clutch his hair and his shoulder, then he was dragged from the van and dumped onto his back on the pavement.

Pain shot up and down Hank's spine as he writhed, trying to catch the wind that had been knocked out of him. Above he was dimly aware of one of the attendants reaching into the van's cab and turning off the engine, then taking the keys around to the rear. He heard the doors swing open.

"Holy shit!" said Chuck's voice. "Gary! Take a look! This guy's loaded!"

Terrified, Hank struggled to his feet. A part of him wanted to run, but where? For what? To be caught out in the open when dark came? Or to starve to death if he did find shelter? No! He had to get his supplies back.

He staggered to the rear of his van and tried to slam the nearest door closed.

"That's mine!"

The fair one, Gary, turned on him in red-faced fury and lashed out with his fists so fast, so hard, so many times in rapid succession that Hank barely knew what hit him. One moment he was on his feet, the next his head and abdomen were exploding with pain and his face was slamming onto the asphalt drive.

He used to be pretty tough, able to hold his own against anyone, but this guy was tough and fast, and the good life Hank had been living the last year had left him soft and slow.

He raised his head and spat blood. As his vision cleared, he saw a white car speeding toward them from the highway. He blinked. Something on top of the car—a red-and-blue flasher bar. And the state seal on the door. A Jersey State Trooper.

He'd never liked cops, but he was glad to see this one.

Groaning, he forced himself up to his knees and began waving with both arms.

"Help! Over here! Help! Robbery!"

The police unit screeched to a halt behind Hank's van and a tall, graying, bareheaded trooper, resplendent in his gray uniform and shiny Sam Brown belt, hopped out and approached the two thieves still leaning inside the back doors.

"Yo, Captain," Chuck said. "Look what we found."

"Fucking supermarket on wheels," Gary said.

The trooper stared at the stacks of cartons. "Very impressive. Looks like we caught us a live one."

"Officer," Hank said, not quite believing his ears, "these men tried to rob me!"

The trooper swiveled and looked down at Hank, fixing him with a withering glare.

"We're commandeering your hoard."

"You're *with* them?"

"No. They're with me. I'm their superior officer. I set up this little sting operation to catch hoarder scum and looters on the run. You have the honor of being our first of the day."

"I *bought* all that stuff!" Hank struggled to his feet and stood swaying like a sapling in a gale. "You have no right!"

"Wrong," the trooper said calmly. "I have every right. *Hoarders* have no rights."

"I'll report you!"

His smile was white ice. "Move away, little man. I'm the court of last resort around here. Be thankful I don't have you shot on the spot. Your hoard is about to be divided up among those who'll make the best use of it. It'll see us through until the time comes to restore order."

Hank couldn't believe this was happening. There had to be something he could do, someone he could turn to. He shouldn't have come alone, should have brought a few Kickers for backup, but he didn't trust—

And then he saw the tattoo in the thumb web of the officer's hand and relief flooded through him.

"You're a Kicker!"

"We all are. So?"

"I'm Hank Thompson!"

"That supposed to mean something?"

"I wrote *Kick!* I created that symbol. I created Kickerdom!"

The officer sneered. "Yeah, right."

He reached for his wallet. "I can prove it!"

The cop kicked him in the gut. "You ain't nobody."

As Hank gagged with the pain, he saw Gary rip open a carton and pull out a cellophane envelope.

"Hey, look! Oodles of Noodles. My favorite!"

Something snapped inside him. Ignoring the pain, he rolled to his feet. Screaming, waving his fists, he charged at Gary.

"That's mine! Get your hands off it!"

He never made it. The captain stepped in front of him and rammed his forearm into Hank's face. Hank reeled back, clutching his shattered nose.

"Get running, little man," he said in a tight, cold voice. "Run while you still can."

"You can't do this to me! I'm your leader!"

"Git!"

Mortally afraid now, Hank said, "I can't! There's no place to go! We're in the middle of nowhere! I've got two bags of silver coins under the front seat. You can have them. Just give me back my van!"

The captain reached for the revolver in his holster. He didn't pause or hesitate an instant. In one smooth, swift motion he pulled it free, ratcheted the hammer back with his thumb, and pointed it at Hank's face.

"You just don't get it, do you?"

Hank saw nothing in his eyes as the captain pulled the trigger. He tried to duck but was too late. He felt a blast of pain in his skull as the world exploded into unbearable light, then collapsed into fathomless darkness.

Manhattan

Jack spotted a few people sitting on the park benches in Union Square as he passed. Didn't notice any movement, so he couldn't be sure if they were alive or dead.

He parked on 17th Street before a storefront diabetes clinic—or at least a place that had once been a clinic. The Laundromat next door was equally demolished, but at least the wrecked equipment still resembled washers and dryers. The clinic . . . nothing but smashed furniture.

He stepped through the front room to the office and treatment areas in the rear. Just as deserted as the rest of the place. In the office he spotted the remnants of a Mr. Coffee. He shook his head. That brought back memories. W. C. Fields had his fatal glass of beer; here was where Jack had drunk a near-fatal cup of coffee.

Which, now that he thought of it, might have led to his first encounter with Dr. Bulmer.

He heard glass crunch behind him and whirled. A stocky young woman with straight dark hair stood in the doorway, staring at him. She wore a turtleneck sweater, a short plaid skirt, and dark tights.

"Jack? What are you doing here?"

Nadia Radzminsky, M.D., had let her hair grow, but otherwise looked pretty much the same as the last time he'd seen her.

"Looking for you. Don't have your home address, so I thought I'd give this place a try."

He told her about Glaeken's building and the invitation to stay there.

With a dazed expression, she looked around at the destruction. "But my patients . . ."

"Are gone."

Her head snapped around. "You don't know that."

"Nadia, you treat the poor, the homeless, the marginal folks." He kept his tone gentle. "Lots of people who live behind thick walls with sturdy doors and double locks didn't make it through the night. What do you think happened to your people?"

Her eyes glistened with tears. "Some of them must have survived."

"Then they'd be here, wouldn't they."

She didn't reply, just stood there and chewed her lip.

"The one thing we're going to need when this is over—if it's ever over—are doctors. You want to do the most good, you'll keep yourself safe."

She was looking around again. "I don't know . . ."

"And doesn't your mother live in the city? She's welcome too."

That seemed to tip her Jack's way.

"Okay. Where is this place?"

Jack gave her the address, then added, "You'll bring Doug too, of course."

She nodded. "Of course."

"Okay. See you there. And don't waste time. There's not much of it."

Good. He had a doctor for the building. Next stop, finish up a little business with an engraver. And after that, a visit to a ghost and his brother.

WFPW-FM

JO: Stay out of the water, everybody. In fact, stay *away* from the water. There are things in the rivers and apparently they don't go into hiding during the day. We've just received a confirmed report of a fisherman being pulled off a dock in Coney Island and eaten alive right in front of his kids.

FREDDY: Don't go near the water, man.

<cue: "Fishin' Blues">

"W'happen t'yer car, buddy?"

Jack had seen the drunk staggering along the glass-littered sidewalk; he'd veered toward Jack's car as it pulled into the curb in front of Walt Duran's apartment building.

"Ran into some bugs," Jack said as he got out.

The drunk stared at the ruined paint. He was fiftyish, overweight, and needed a shave; he wore a gray wool suit of decent quality, but filthy. A liter of

Bacardi Light dangled from his hand. His complexion was ghastly in the yellow light.

"Tried to dissolve her, didn't they," he said, then his face screwed up and he began to sob. "Just like they dissolved my Jane!"

Jack didn't know what to do. What do you say to a crying drunk? He put a hand on the guy's quaking shoulder.

"Hang around. Maybe I can find you a place to stay."

The guy shook his head and stumbled away along the sidewalk, still sobbing.

Jack hurried up the building's front steps. He pressed the button for Walt's room but got no answering buzz. The glass panel in the front door was broken. Maybe the buzzer was too. He reached through the shattered pane and let himself in, then hurried up to the third floor.

Despite repeated knocks, Walt didn't answer his door.

Concerned now, Jack pulled the piece of clear, flexible plastic he kept in his back pocket, slipped it between the door and the jamb, and jimmied the latch. The door swung open.

"Oh, shit," he said when he saw the carnage within.

The front room was a shambles of shattered glass, torn upholstery, and broken furniture. Jack dodged through the wreckage and hurried to the bathroom where he'd installed Walt last night.

Empty, damn it. He went to the one remaining place to look, the tiny bedroom.

Blood. Blood on the sheets, on the floor, on the glass daggers remaining in the frame of the smashed bedroom window.

"Walt," Jack said softly, staring at the dry brown streaks on the glass. "Why didn't you come back with me last night? Why didn't you stay locked up like I told you?"

Angry and sad, and not sure which to give in to, he wandered back to the bathroom. Walt's metalworking tools were set up across the rust-stained tub.

But where were the necklaces? Probably hadn't finished them, but Jack knew he'd started them.

And what was Jack going to do without them?

Then he spotted something silvery and serpentine in the tub, under the work board. He dropped to his knees and reached in.

Out came a necklace.

Jack cupped it in his hands and inspected it. The sculpted, crescent-shaped links, the weird engraved inscriptions, the pair of topazes with dark centers. The look of it, weight of it . . . perfect.

A deluge of memories, most of them bad, engulfed him. He especially re-membered the night he had worn the genuine article, how it had kept him alive when he should have died, how removing it had damn near killed him.

He shook off the past and felt a lump form in his throat for the man who had made this.

"Walt. You were the best."

He reached into the tub and found the second necklace, but groaned when he got a good look at it. Only half done. The links on the left side were blank. Walt hadn't got around to engraving them before . . . well, before whatever had happened to him.

One and a half necklaces wasn't going to cut it. Jack's plan required two phonies to get the real ones.

He got to his feet and stuffed the completed copy into his pocket. He'd have to come up with a new plan.

Out on the street again he looked around for the drunk and spotted him sitting on the curb at the corner. He called to him, but the guy was absorbed in staring down at the sewer grate beneath his feet. Jack walked toward him.

"Hey, fella! I'll get you to a safe place where you can sober up."

The guy looked up. "Somebod's downair," he said, pointing into the sewer. "Can't see'm but I hear'm movin' 'round."

Jack wondered if people were hiding in the sewers.

"Swell. But I don't think you'll fit through that opening, so—"

"Prolly c'use a drink."

The guy reached down to pour a taste of his rum through the grate.

Something flashed up from the sewer, something long and thick and brown whipped out and grabbed the drunk by his neck and yanked him down face-first onto the grate. Then it began tugging him into the opening in the curb face. Not slowly, smoothly, inexorably, but with violent heaves, accompanied by sprays of blood and frantic but futilely flailing arms and legs. Three heaves did it.

Before Jack could recover from his shock and take a single step forward to help, the man was gone. All he'd left behind were splashes of blood and a bottle of rum on its side, slowly emptying into the sewer after its owner.

No people hiding in the sewers from the night things . . . night things—big night things—were down there hiding from the day.

Jack backed up a few steps, then turned and hurried for his car. He had one last stop before heading for Monroe: Astoria.

WFPW-FM

FREDDY: —and at sea, the QE2 appears to be missing, man. She was last heard from Sunday evening and since then, nada. If she hit one of the gravity holes she'd have radioed for help. The single air-sea rescue plane that was sent out has found no survivors. Bummer, man.

<cue: "Beyond the Sea">

Astoria, Queens

With the Queensboro Bridge out of commission, Jack had to take the Triboro, which was jammed. Not like it had been during the Internet crash, but slow, slow going.

When he finally reached Menelaus Manor in Astoria he was struck by its condition: The neighbors up and down the block showed extensive bug damage, but the old stone house remained intact, almost . . . pristine.

Jack knocked on the front door. Lyle Kenton answered. He looked awful—eyes sunken, skin a dull black, his usually neat dreads in disarray.

"Jack?" He stepped back and opened the door wider. "You're just about the last person I expected to see."

Jack stepped inside. "Hey, you're the psychic. Should've seen me coming."

Lyle didn't smile. "Charlie's gone."

"What do you mean, gone?"

Lyle's brother had died a couple of years ago, but part of him—his ghost, his spirit, his personality, whatever—had hung around.

"As in not here anymore. As in I can't contact him. As in he doesn't answer when I call his name."

"Since when?"

Lyle ran a hand over his face. "Last Wednesday. He woke me up early—still-dark-out early—and said something was wrong. No, wait. He said *everything* was wrong. Said he'd hit the wall."

"What wall?"

"You know how he can see some of the future."

"Yeah. Up to a point, and then he couldn't see any further."

"Right. He said everything was darkness after that certain point. He called it 'the wall' that he couldn't see over. Well, early Wednesday morning he said he'd hit it. I was beat so I told him we'd talk about it in the morning. But in the morning he was gone. Haven't heard from him since." Lyle's eyes puddled up. "He's gone, Jack. Charlie's gone."

Jack didn't know what to say. He laid a hand on Lyle's shoulder.

"He'll be back." Lame . . . so lame. Then a thought. "Look, Wednesday was the first day the sun rose late. That's got to have something to do with it. When this mess is straightened out, he'll be back."

Lyle looked at him. "Straightened out? How's it going to get straightened out? Maybe there's a reason Charlie couldn't see the future past a certain point. Maybe because there isn't one."

Jack didn't like the sound of that. It struck a little too close to home.

"It's not over yet. There's a guy who might have a way out. He's got a place that's temporarily safe. I came over to invite you to stay."

Lyle shook his head. "Can't leave. What if Charlie comes back and can't find me?"

"He'll know you're safe—and he'll be glad."

"No. Got to stay here. Got to be here if he comes back. Besides, the bugs seem to avoid the house."

"Yeah, I noticed. Because of Charlie, you think?"

Another head shake. "The stones in the cellar—the ones Dmitri Menelaus moved in. Don't know where he got them, but I think they scare off the bugs. I'm probably safer here than in your place." A wan smile. "Want to move in?"

Am I going to lose you too? Carol thought as she stood next to Bill in his bedroom and helped him pack a small duffel bag with some extra clothes for the trip.

Why was it always she who was left behind? Jim had died and left her— although that certainly hadn't been his choosing. And her son—at least at the time she had thought of him as her son—had left her. Nelson had run off like a thief in the night, and now Bill was preparing to fly to Romania.

"What are your chances of getting back?"

"I don't know. Not great, I think."

"Oh." Carol couldn't manage any more than that.

Bill straightened and looked at her. "Do I sound brave? I hope so. Because I sure as hell don't feel it. I mean, I want to do this, but I don't want to die or even get hurt. But I've got to do something."

"Can I go with you?"

Anything would be better than being left behind again, especially now when she had nothing else to do but sit around and wait.

"To Romania?" Bill said, staring at her. "It's too dangerous."

"Is anyplace safe anymore?"

Even the daytime was no longer safe. Jack had returned a short while ago with a story of horrors hiding in the sewers and storm drains.

"You're safe here. And Glaeken seems to want you around."

"But why? What can I do besides help him take care of Magda? Not that I mind, but what else?"

"I don't know. Maybe you're part of the equation. I don't pretend to understand why he's doing what he's doing. Sometimes I wonder if he knows. But he's all we've got. And if he says we need these bits of metal from Romania, and I'm the only one left who can get them, then I'll give it my best shot. And if he says you're important to the solution to what's happening to the world, then I'll go along with him. He hasn't let us down yet."

"'Part of the equation.'" Her throat constricted around the words. "I've been part of some sort of equation since I got pregnant and provided the body that allowed this . . . this monster back into the world." Her voice cracked. "He took my baby, Bill! He kicked out whoever my real baby might have been and took over his unformed body. And now he's going to take you!"

She felt Bill's arms go around her shoulders and pull her tight against him. His flannel shirt smelled lightly of detergent, and as its rough surface pressed against her cheek, the thought that he really should use fabric softener wafted inanely across her mind. She slipped her arms around his waist and pulled herself closer. If she could just hold him here like this it soon would be too late for him to leave, and then she wouldn't lose him.

She realized then how much she wanted him. Not like the last time, not like back in '68 when the beast that had usurped her womb twisted her into trying to seduce Bill from his vows. That had been lust, induced lust. This was something else. This was love. An old love, following a long and winding road from the puppy love when they'd dated in their teens, to something deep and real. In a way, perhaps she'd always loved Bill. And now that he'd turned away from his church and his old beliefs, now that the cocoon of his priesthood had unraveled, he seemed real again, flesh and blood. She wanted to tell him how she felt but the decades-old memories of that degrading scene of attempted seduction still echoed around her and held her back.

And yet, if she didn't tell him now, would she ever get the chance again?

Jack's voice shattered the moment: "Time's a-wastin', Bill. We've got to make a stop in Monroe on the way."

Monroe . . . her hometown. Bill's too. Where Rasalom had usurped her child's body at conception. The torrent of memories was cut off as Bill pulled free of her arms.

"Got to go, Carol."

He went to kiss her on the forehead. Impulsively, Carol lifted her face and kissed him on the lips. From the way he pulled back and the way he looked at her, she knew that he hadn't forgotten 1968 either.

"Come back to me, Bill," she said softly. "I don't want to lose you too."

He swallowed, nodded. "Okay. Yeah." His voice was sandpaper dry. "I'll be back. We can talk more about this then." He picked up his duffel and started for the door, then stopped and turned. "I love you, Carol. I can't think of a moment when I didn't."

And then he was gone. But his final words lingered after him, filling Carol with a bewildering mix of emotions. She wanted to laugh with joy; instead she sat on the edge of the bed and cried.

Long Island

It took Jack longer than he'd planned to reach Monroe. A lot of traffic outbound on the LIE. Maybe they thought it would be better out on the Island. He'd talked to Doc Bulmer on the phone this morning, and from what he'd said, things didn't seem a whole hell of a lot quieter out here.

So he did the best speed he could. Nick sat in the backseat, his zombie stare fixed straight ahead. Bill wasn't much better company. He sat in the passenger seat and said nothing, just gazed out the window, lost in a world of his own.

Jack wondered what was going on between him and that Mrs. Treece. Her husband had run off and left her. Was Bill moving in? He'd been a priest for most of his life. Had a lot of lost time to make up for. Jack couldn't blame him. She was attractive, even if she could have been Jack's mother. But he sensed more to it than opportunity knocking. Those two seemed to go back a long way.

So Jack thought about his conversation with Gia—his last for a while. She hadn't liked the idea of him taking to the air in all this, but seemed to realize that he was the only one for the job. The good news was that everything was fine in and around Abe's bunker. That was a load off his mind. His ladies were safe—he couldn't have made this trip if he'd had the slightest doubt about that.

He tried the radio. A lot of stations were gone, nothing but static in their slots on the band, but a few DJs and newsfolk were hanging in there, still playing music, still broadcasting the news, keeping their listeners informed to the best of their ability as to what was fact and what was merely rumor. He had to hand it to them. They had more guts than he would have given them credit for.

He clicked it off. Not in the mood for music.

"So, Bill," he said, jerking his thumb toward the backseat. "How are you going to handle Renfield back there?"

Bill turned from the window and fixed Jack with a stare.

"Don't make fun of him. He's an old friend and he's a victim, just like a lot of other people these days."

Jack instinctively bristled at the sound of someone telling him what to do, then realized that Bill was right.

"Sorry. I didn't know him before he . . . before he went down into the hole."

"He was brilliant. Hopefully he'll be brilliant again. A mind like a computer, but a good heart too."

"Bit of a spread in age between the two of you. How'd you meet?"

"I was his father for a few years."

When Jack shot him a questioning look, Bill went on to explain about his stint as director of a Jesuit orphanage in Queens, and how a certain little boy had died and how he'd spent years on the run as a result.

Jack was shocked to realize he was sharing the car with the kidnapper priest who'd been all over the news years ago, the object of a nationwide manhunt—still hunted.

The story fascinated him. He'd been seeing this guy every day lately and never guessed what kind of a man he was, or the hell he'd been through. How could he? Bill seemed to have built a wall around himself, as if he were practicing being a nobody.

But now that Jack had got a peek over that wall, he decided he liked Bill Ryan.

And besides, the story made the trip pass faster. Here they were in Monroe, on Shore Drive.

Ba must have been watching from one of the windows. He stepped out the front door as they pulled in the driveway. He approached the car with only a Macy's shopping bag dangling from his hand. The Nash lady, Doc Bulmer, and the kid, Jeffy, were all clustered at the front door to see him off, like the Cleavers sending an Asian Wally off to war.

Jack got out, waved Ba toward the car, then trotted to the front door.

"Glaeken wants me to *urge* you folks—his word—to come stay with him in the city. He says it's going to get a lot worse out here."

"We'll be okay," the doc said. "We've got our own protection."

Jack glanced around at all the steel storm shades. The place looked like a fortress.

"Maybe you do," he said, nodding. "But I promised him I'd ask."

"You've kept your promise to Glaeken," the Nash lady said softly, and Jack thought he saw tears in her eyes. "Now keep one to me: You bring Ba back, okay?" Her voice sounded like it was going to break. "You bring him back just the way he left, you hear?"

"I hear you, Mrs. Nash."

Jack was touched by her show of emotion. No doubt about it, she genuinely cared about the guy. Maybe he'd misjudged her. Maybe she wasn't quite the hard case she pretended to be.

"Either we both come back," he added, "or neither of us comes back. You've got my word on that."

"I'll hold you to it," she said, her eyes steely blue.

As Jack hurried to the car he figured he'd damn well better get Ba back safe and sound.

The sign atop the hangar read *TWIN AIRWAYS* in bold red letters. Tension coiled around Bill's gut as they bumped toward it along a rutted dirt road. Where were they? Somewhere off Jericho Turnpike was all Bill knew.

And the Ashe brothers. Who were they? He'd never heard of them and didn't know a thing about them and yet he was going to get into a jet and let one of them fly him across the Atlantic. And why? Because this fellow named Jack—who had maybe a dozen last names and an immediate avoidance response to anything labeled *Police,* who carried two or three pistols and God knew how many other weapons at all times—had said the Ashe brothers were "good guys."

Glaeken, old boy, he thought as they skidded to a halt beside the hangar, I hope this trip is worth it.

Two reed-thin, blue-eyed men with fair, shoulder-length hair came out to meet them. They might have been mirror images had not one of them sported a stubbly beard and the other a long, droopy mustache. Both wore beat-up jeans so low on their hips they looked ready to fall off; the bearded one wore a purple paisley shirt tucked in behind a Jack Daniel's belt buckle. The one with the mustache had on a fringed buckskin jacket over a Gov't Mule T-shirt.

"They look like holdovers from the sixties or seventies," Bill said softly out of the corner of his mouth.

"It's okay. They sort of think they're the Allman Brothers. Not really, of course. I mean, Duane being dead and all. But Allman soul mates, so to speak. They *are* from Georgia and they do like the blues, but trust me: You're looking at two of the best damn pilots going. Not a place in the world with an airport they haven't been."

Jack introduced them as Frank and Joe. Joe had the beard and the JD buckle and he was going to be Bill's pilot. But Bill's flight was of secondary importance. The big concern seemed to be getting Jack and Ba into the air as soon as possible. After payment was made—a sack of gold coins transferred from the Crown Vic's trunk to the Ashe brothers' office safe—Joe left Bill and Nick in the tiny office while he went out to help install the high-power short-wave radio Jack had insisted on bringing along.

Twenty minutes later, Bill heard the Gulfstream's jet engines whine, then roar off into the western sky.

"Shouldn't we be hurrying too?" Bill said when Joe returned to the office.

"I reckon," he said with a heavy drawl. "But it ain't as critical for us as them. If Frank hustles his ass he's got a damn good chance of staying in daylight a lot of the way to Hawaii. Not us. We're heading east—right into the dark. It's 'bout six P.M. in Romania now. Already past sunset."

His expression showed how little he relished the trip.

"How did you wind up with us?" Bill said.

"We flipped a coin."

"And you lost."

Joe Ashe shrugged. "Six o' one, half dozen t'other. We're talking round trips here. Frank'll have to fly east on the way home while we're flying west." He frowned. "Maybe I should say it's four o' one and half dozen t'other. We'll have a shorter daylight window on the way back." He grunted. "Shit. I *did* get the short end of this stick. That Frank's always trickin' me. Boy's my evil twin, he is."

Great, Bill thought. I've got the slow one.

"You want to back out?" Bill almost hoped he'd say yes.

Joe Ashe grinned. "Nah. Said I'd do it and so it's a done deal. Unless o' course you've changed *your* mind."

Bill shook his head. "I'm afraid we're stuck with each other."

"Guess so. But what about your friend there? He's lookin' right poorly, I'd say."

"He's . . . he hasn't been well lately."

"Bummer. Maybe you oughta leave him behind. Things could get a mite hairy on this little jaunt."

"I know. I wish I could, but I need him along."

"Y'don't say." Joe studied Nick's blank face a moment, then turned to Bill. "What the hell for?"

"I don't know yet." But Glaeken assures me I will.

Joe let out a soft, low whistle through his teeth.

"Okay, pal. You're the boss. Let's roll. I've got the flight plan all worked out. Got a ten, eleven-hour trip ahead of us, and a seven-hour time difference between here and Ploiesti."

"Ploiesti? I thought we were going to Bucharest."

"Ploiesti's a little further north, closer to the Alps where this pass you're headed for is supposed to be—couldn't find it on any of my maps."

Bill handed Joe the packet Glaeken had given him.

"You'll find it on these."

Joe took the packet. "Good. I'll check them out on the way. Get your friend there moving now. Time to rock 'n' roll."

The Horror Channel's Drive-In Theatre—Special All-Day Edition
Beginning of the End (1957) Republic
The Last Days of Man on Earth (1974) New World
The Monsters Are Loose (1965) Hollywood Star
Fear in the Night (1947) Paramount
Horror of the Blood Monsters (1970) IIP
Destroy All Monsters (1968) Toho/AIP
I Drink Your Blood (1971) Cinemation
Jaws of Death (1976) Selected
Night of the Blood Beast (1958) AIP
The Day the Fish Came Out (1967) International Classics
Target Earth (1954) Allied Artists
The Blood Suckers (1971) Chevron

Over the Atlantic

Flying east, night came especially early. As darkness engulfed them, the sky cleared, became an onyx dome set with the foreign face of the moon amid alien constellations.

Bill left Nick sleeping back in the passenger compartment and headed forward to take the copilot's seat next to Joe. As he gazed out at the night, he was glad for the lack of clouds and excellent visibility in the moonlight. He could find no sign of the air leviathans he'd seen swooping from the Central Park hole Saturday night. No sign of anything in the air, but the water below seemed *alive*. It churned with shadows and swirled with phosphorescent flashes.

He turned back to the stars, studying them, trying to make sense of them, or find a familiar pattern.

"Where are we?" he said, wondering aloud as he glanced at the dead GPS screen.

"Over the Atlantic," Joe replied from his left.

"Thanks. I mean where in space? The sun's fading away, the moon's been turned around, and the stars have been shifted into new formations."

"Not just new formations," Joe said, stroking his beard as he craned his neck to see the sky. "Notice there's *fewer* stars up there? And ever' night there's even less than the night before. I wonder if some night soon I'll take a peek and find there ain't no stars at all."

The stars did look kind of sparse.

"Almost as if the planet's been moved to a different part of the universe."

Joe's eyes widened. "Cosmic, man. Maybe it has."

"No. That would be too logical an explanation, and easier to accept than what we're going through."

"Magnetic north's changed too," Joe said. "Compasses been pointing anywheres they damn well please the past couple days."

"Really? I hadn't heard that." And then something occurred to him. "If the stars are changed and compasses no longer point north, and the GPS satellites are out, how do you know where you're going?"

"Radio beacon. I'm homing in on a signal from the English coast. We're not headed for England, but it's on the way."

"Where are we—good God!"

Bill had glanced off to his right at what had looked like a lone cloud in an empty sky. It wasn't the cloud that had startled him, but what was under it.

Joe was leaning over his shoulder, squinting into the darkness.

"Shee-it! What the hell is that?"

Far to the south, a huge pillar had risen from the sea. It was made of some grayish substance that gleamed dully in the moonlight and streamed with lightninglike flickers of phosphorescence. Bill guessed it was hundreds of feet across and thousands of feet—maybe *miles*—high. Its top disappeared into the dark cloud growing above it.

So alien, so Cyclopean in size, the sight gave him a crawling feeling in his gut.

Joe must have felt it too. His voice was hushed.

"Almost looks like it's holding up the sky."

"Do we have enough fuel to maybe—?"

"No way, José!" Joe straightened in his seat and checked his instruments. "Even if we had plenty to spare, I wouldn't get a foot closer to that thing than I absolutely had to. And I don't gotta get no closer than I am now, thank-you-very-much."

As they continued east, Bill's eyes remained fixed on the giant column. The dark gray cloud above it continued to grow, and as it grew it began to sink around the column, eventually obscuring it from view.

"I'll be damned!" Joe said. Bill turned in his seat and found him pointing north. "There's another one!"

Bill wished the moon were brighter so he could get a better look at it.

And then the moon went out for a second.

"What was that?" Joe said.

Bill's mouth was suddenly dry. "Something big."

"Yeah? How big?"

"Very big. A body two hundred feet across and square miles of wing."

Joe glanced at him with raised eyebrows, then scanned the night.

"I see it," he said after a moment. "Or rather I don't see the stars where it's cruising. It's—shee-*it*! It's coming this way!"

Joe threw the Gulfstream into a screaming dive that jammed Bill back into his seat. And then the world got darker as something swooped through the air where they had been only seconds before. The jet bucked and rocked in the backwash from the monstrous wings. Bill craned his neck back and forth looking for the behemoth as Joe continued the dive. He saw it, off to the south, banking around, coming back to make another run at them.

"Never seen nothin' so goddamned big in my life!"

And still he held the jet into the dive. The black water was looming terrifyingly close.

"Joe, aren't you getting kind of low?"

"Not near low enough yet."

And still they dove. Not till Bill was ready to shout with terror and hold his breath for a plunge into the sea did Joe level off. They raced along at fifty feet above the surface.

"You see it?"

Bill twisted around. "Yeah. I can see its right wing. It's on our tail, coming up fast. Oh, *God* it's coming fast!"

"Tell me when it's almost on us. Don't tell me too soon—and f'God's sake don't tell me too late. Just wait'll you think its about to chomp us, then give a shout."

It didn't take long. The thing was moving faster than the Gulfstream. Bill barely had time to wonder how something so big could move so fast when suddenly it was upon them.

"Now, Joe! Now! NOW!"

Abruptly the Gulfstream banked a sharp left, rocking Bill against his safety belt. And suddenly the ocean exploded with white.

The leviathan was gone.

"Wh-what happened?"

"It hit the water," Joe said, grinning. "Simple aerodynamics, boy. You want to make a sharp turn in flight, you've gotta bank. You bank at this altitude with wings that size, the downside one's gonna catch the surface. And then it's cartwheel time. Fuck you, Rodan."

Bill figured that thing could have eaten Rodan for breakfast. He leaned back in the seat and wanted to vomit. But he swallowed hard and held out his hand to Joe.

"You are one hell of a pilot."

Joe slapped his palm. "I don't argue that."

"When's day?"

Joe glanced at his watch. "Not for a long while. Still some daylight left back home, I'd guess. Though not much."

WFPW-FM

FREDDY: It's 5:15, folks. Twenty minutes to sundown.
  JO: Yeah. Everybody inside. Get inside NOW.

New Jersey Turnpike

Hank didn't know how long he'd been phasing in and out of consciousness, but eventually he felt strong enough to move. His head felt three times its normal size and throbbed viciously, but he forced it off the pavement to look around. The movement triggered an explosion of pain through the left side of his skull as the world spun around him. He choked back the bile that surged into his throat, squeezed his eyes shut, and held still. And while he held still, he tried to remember what had happened.

He recalled loading the van, driving down the turnpike, turning in for gas—
Oh, Lord. The Kicker State Trooper. The pistol. The shot.

Hank reached up and gingerly touched the left side of his head. A deep wet gash above his ear there, clots and soft crusts all up and down the side of his head and neck.

But he was alive. The bullet had glanced off his skull and plowed a deep furrow through his scalp. He was weak, sick, dizzy, hurting like he'd never hurt before, but he was alive.

Hank opened his eyes again. He was looking down. A puddle of coagulated blood had pooled on the pavement a few inches below his nose. He pushed himself farther up, pulled his knees under him, then straightened. The vertigo took him for another twirling ride, but when it stopped he took his bearings.

Green metal bins on either side—garbage Dumpsters. Framed between them he could see the rest stop gas pumps a hundred or so feet away. Deserted now. No phony attendants waving cars forward. To his left was the stuccoed side of a building. The restaurants: Bob's Big Boy, Roy Rogers, TCBY.

They must have dragged him over here out of sight and left him for dead while waiting for the next hapless traveler.

Clenching his teeth against the pain and nausea, he pulled himself to his feet and peered over the Dumpsters. The whole rest stop was deserted. Beyond the pumps the turnpike stood quiet and empty. The cars he'd seen parked over here earlier were gone now.

So was his van.

Hank wanted to scream. Robbed. By Kicker cops, no less. What the fuck? His own followers out during the day were as bad as the inhuman ones that ruled the night.

Night! He glanced at the sky, at the horizon. Shit, it was getting dark. In a few minutes those horrors would start flying and crawling from their holes. He couldn't be caught out in the open.

He hobbled to the door on the near flank of the restaurants. Locked. He made his way around to the front entrance. The glass double doors were chained shut from the inside. He peered through. A shambles within. It looked as if the place had been ransacked and looted before it had been locked up. No matter. He wasn't worried about food now. All he wanted was shelter.

He looked around in the failing light for something to break the glass—a rock, a garbage can, anything. He found a heavy, stuccoed trash receptacle nearby but no way could he lift it.

Near panic now, he circled the rest stop, desperate to find a way in. He was halfway around the back when something whizzed by his head, its jaws grinding as it passed. Then another. He couldn't see them in the dusky light but he didn't have to. Chew wasps. Here already. Must be a hole nearby.

In a low crouch he ran for the Dumpsters on the far side of the building. Maybe he could hide in one of them—crawl inside and pull the top down over him. Maybe he'd even find some scraps of food among the refuse.

When he reached the Dumpsters he hoisted himself up the side of the first but found its hinged top gone. Same with the other. Now what?

As he eased himself back down his toe caught in a slot in the pavement. A storm drain. His foot rested on a rusty grate, square, a couple of feet on each side. No problem getting through if he could pull it free.

Try it! he thought, bending and yanking on the grate.

Another bug whistled by—close enough to ruffle his hair. A spearhead.

Ignoring the throbbing in his skull that crescendoed toward agony with the effort, he poured all of what little strength he had left into the task. The metal squeaked and moved a quarter inch, then half an inch, then screeched free of its seat. Hank pushed it aside and slid through the opening into the darkness below. Four feet down, his feet landed in a puddle. No problem. Not even an inch deep. He reached up and slid the grate back over the opening. When it clanked into its seat, he slumped into a crouch and looked up at the sky.

Dark up there, but still lighter than down here. As he watched a lonely star break through the dispersing haze, a huge belly fly plopped onto the grate directly over him and tried to squeeze through. Its acid sack strained against the openings, bulged into the slots, but it was too wide. Buzzing angrily, it lifted off and flew away.

He should have been relieved, happy he'd found a safe haven. Instead he found himself sobbing. Why not? None of his Kickers around to see. He was alone, hurt—still bleeding a little—cold, tired, hungry, no food, no money, no ride, and now he was hiding in a storm drain with dirty, stagnant water soaking through his sneakers. He'd gone from King of the World to bottom.

He forced a laugh that echoed eerily up and down the length of the drain. If nothing else, he could soothe himself with the knowledge that things couldn't get worse.

Something splashed off to his right.

Hank froze and listened. What was that, oh shit, what was that? A rat? Or something worse—something much, much worse?

He eased his feet out of the water and inched them up the far side of the pipe until he spanned its diameter. If anything was moving through the water, it would pass under him. He peered into the darkness to his right, straining ears and eyes for some sign of life.

Nothing there.

But from his left came a furtive scurrying, moving closer . . . countless tiny clicks and scratches as something—no, some*things*!—with thousands of feet slithered toward him along the concrete wall of the drain.

More splashing from the right, bolder now, *lots* of splashes, hurried, anxious, eager, avid, frantic splashes coming faster, racing toward him. The storm drain was suddenly *alive* with sound and movement, all converging on him.

Hank whimpered with terror and dropped his feet back into the water as he slammed his palms against the grate above and levered it up from its seat. But before it came free a pair of tonglike pincers vised around his right ankle. He shouted his terror and agony but kept pushing. Another set lanced into his left calf. His feet were pulled from under him and he tumbled to his knees in the stagnant water.

And then in the faint light through the grate he saw them. Huge, pincer-mouthed millipede creatures, like the one he'd seen wriggling from Drexler's throat in the lobby. The pipe was acrawl with them, five, six, eight, ten feet long. The nearest ones raised their heads toward him, their pincers clicking. Hank slapped at them, trying to bat them away, but they darted past his defenses and latched onto him, digging the ice-pick points of their mandibles into his arms and shoulders. The pain and horror were too much. His scream echoed up and down the hungry pipe as he was dragged onto his back. His arms were pulled above his head and his legs yanked straight as he was positioned along the length of the pipe. Cold water soaked his clothes and ran along his spine. And then more of the things leapt upon him, all over him, their countless clawed feet scratching him, their pincers ripping at his clothing, tearing through the protective layers like so much tissue paper until every last shred had been stripped away and he lay cold and wet and naked, stretched out like a heretic on the rack.

And then they backed off, all but the ones pinning him there in the water. The drain grew quiet. The sloshing and splashing, the scraping of the myriad feet died away until the only noise in the pipe was the sound of his own ragged breathing.

What did they want? What were they—?

Then came another sound, a heavy, chitinous slithering from the impenetrable darkness beyond his feet. As it grew louder, Hank began to whimper in fear. He thrashed in the water, struggling desperately to pull free, but the pincers in his arms and legs tightened their grip, digging deeper into his already bleeding flesh.

And then in the growing shaft of light from the rising moon he saw it. A millipede like all the rest, but so much larger. Its head was the size of Hank's torso, its body a good two feet across, half filling the drainpipe.

Hank screamed as understanding exploded within him. These other, smaller horrors were workers or drones of some sort; they'd captured him and were holding him here for their queen! He renewed his struggles, ignoring the tearing pain in his limbs. He had to get free!

But he couldn't. Sliding over the bodies of her obedient subjects the queen crawled between Hank's squirming legs until she held her head poised over his chest, staring at him with her huge, black, multifaceted eyes. As Hank watched in mute horror, a drill-like proboscis extruded from between her huge mandibles. Slowly, she raised her head and angled it down over Hank's abdomen. Hank found his voice and screamed again as she plunged the proboscis deep into his belly.

Liquid fire exploded at his center and spread into his chest, ran down his legs and his arms, draining the strength from them.

Poison! He opened his mouth to scream again but the neurotoxin reached his throat first and allowed him to voice little more than a breathy exhalation. His hands were the last things to go dead, and then he was floating. He still lay in the water but could not feel its wetness. The last thing he saw before tumbling into a void of blessed darkness was the queen horror with her snout still buried in his flesh.

WNYW-TV

News from NASA: We have lost contact with most of our higher orbiting satellites. The communication satellites are still operational—otherwise you would not be watching this broadcast—but the rest are simply . . . gone.

Over the Pacific

They got in and out of Bakersfield in record time. Or so Frank said. Jack would have to take his word about the record part, but it sure as hell had been fast. The main reason was that Frank's plane was one of only a half dozen scheduled there today.

It hadn't been Bakersfield, actually, but a small airstrip just outside it. Frank seemed to know everybody in sight; not very many of those, but they all seemed impressed that he was still on the job. Especially impressed that he was making arrangements to get refueled here on his return flight.

"Yer gonna be flyin' inna dark comin' back, y'know," the old guy who ran the place had said as the wing tanks were filling.

Wrinkled and grizzled and looking old enough to have been Eddie Rickenbacker's wingman in the Lafayette Escadrille, he was the one who'd pocketed a stack of Glaeken's gold coins for the fuel.

"I know," Frank said from the pilot seat. He had his iPod earphones slung around his neck and was playing with one of the drooping ends of his mustache.

Jack sat beside him in the pilot's cabin—he'd called it the "cockpit" earlier and had been corrected—while Ba sat in the passenger compartment, adding more teeth to his billy clubs.

"Lotsa planes disappearin' inna dark these days, Frankie. Go up, neva come down."

"So I've heard."

"Some are even disappearin' inna *day*. Inna *day*! So nobody's flyin'— nobody with any sense, that is. Scared to get off the ground. 'Fraid they won't come back. Don't want you t'be one a thems that don't come back, Frankie."

"Thanks, Pops. Neither do I."

"Where's Joe?"

"On his way to Bucharest."

"Hungary?"

"No. Romania."

"Same difference. Shit! What's the matter with you two? You need the money that bad? Hell, I can lend you—"

"Hey, Pops," Frank said. "It ain't the bread. I'm a pilot, man. I fly folks places. That's what I do. I ain't changin' that, okay? Not for anybody or any bugs. Besides, we once like promised this here dude that any time he really needed to get somewhere, we'd take him. You can dig that, can't you?"

"No, I can't dig nothin' of the sort. Where y'goin'?"

"He says he's got to get to Maui and back real bad."

Pops stared past Frank at Jack like he was looking at a lunatic. Jack smiled and gave him an Oliver Hardy wave.

"Got to see my girl. It's her birthday."

Pops rolled his eyes and started to turn away.

"Real weird kind of weather you got around here," Frank said, glancing up at the lid of gray overhead.

"All that shit from Hawaii." Pops wiped his finger along the fuselage and held it up to demonstrate the coating of gray ash. "Just like your last name, Frankie. And you're headed straight into it. Tops off at twenny thou, though. Watch yer intakes."

"Will do."

Pops went back to check on the refueling. A few minutes later they were airborne. Jack sniffed the air that leaked into the cabin at the lower altitude.

"Smells burnt."

"That it is," Frank said. "It's *vog*—a mixture of like water vapor, smoke, and fine, fine, super-fine volcanic ash. Under normal conditions it would give us awesome sunsets all over the world. But now? We don't seem to get real sunsets anymore."

Jack felt closed in, trapped by the formless grayness pressing against the windows. Wasn't even sure if they were headed up. He'd have to trust Frank on that.

Which was probably one of the reasons he didn't like to fly. He liked to be in control of a situation. Up here he was at Frank's mercy. He didn't know which way they were headed, and if something should happen to Frank, Jack didn't have the faintest idea of how to get them down safely. Scared the hell out of him when Frank had put the controls on autopilot over Denver and made a trip to the head. He'd returned soon, but nowhere near soon enough for Jack.

Suddenly the grayness darkened as if a curtain had been drawn, and the jet wobbled.

"What's up?" Jack said as calmly as he could.

"Don't rightly know."

"Those are three little words I do not want to hear from my pilot."

Jack held on to his seat's armrests and knew if he looked down at his hands he'd see two sets of white knuckles.

"We'll be okay."

"Good. I like those three words much better."

"Be cool, Jack. Gotta expect some weird voggish updrafts and down."

The grayness lightened as abruptly as it had darkened. Jack began to breathe easier. He was leaning against his window, staring out into the unrelieved grayness, when the plane passed through a brief break in the vog. His throat closed and his hands renewed their chokehold on his armrests. Directly below the wings he saw a broad flat surface, smooth and black as new asphalt, spanning off in all directions until it disappeared into the gray. He was about to shout to Frank that they were going to crash when he saw the eye: Far off to his right, perhaps a quarter-mile away, cathedral-sized, huge and yellow with a slit pupil, it sat embedded in the black surface, staring back at him like a lab tech eyeing a microbe.

Jack slammed back in his seat.

"My God, Frank!" he said, his voice a croak. "What *is* that?"

Frank glanced past him. "What's what?"

Jack took another look. The vog had closed in again. Nothing there now but gray.

"Never mind."

Jack remembered Glaeken mentioning winged leviathans big as towns cruising the skies, but he'd said they'd keep to the nightside. Looked like he was wrong. At least one of them had made itself at home in the dense vog. Maybe more than one.

His mouth felt dry. "How long till we get above this junk?"

"Any minute now."

Sure enough, two minutes later they broke into clear air. But no sign of the sun. The whole sky was now some sort of tinted filter, a ground-glass lens that wouldn't allow direct sunlight through. Right now, Jack didn't care. They were out of the vog, out of reach of that thing in the clouds.

He looked down. As far as he could see, nothing but a smooth dome of gray. Plenty of room for a gaggle of leviathans down there. Frank said they were over the Pacific; for all Jack knew they could be headed back toward New York.

The pilot's cabin suddenly seemed too small. Jack decided to head back and see what Ba was up to. He slapped Frank on the shoulder.

"Get you anything?"

"A hefty J would be super right about now. I've got a lid of bodacious—"

"Frank, don't even kid about that."

"Who's kidding, man? It's the only way to fly. Hell, I recall the time I jumped the Himalayas and coasted into Katmandu totally wrecked. It was—"

"Please, Frank. Not on this trip."

Six miles above the Central Pacific with a blitzed pilot. Not the kind of Friendly Skies Jack wanted.

Frank grinned. "Okay, man. Another coffee'd be good."

"Not getting sleepy, are you?"

"Not yet. I'll let you know when. Then you can take over the controls."

"*Two* coffees coming right up! An *urn*!"

Abe's Place

"What's wrong with the sky, Mom?"

Gia looked up for maybe the hundredth time. Nothing special about the few puffy clouds, but no blue behind them. Just a wan, diffuse yellow light that threw strange shadows across the verdant hills rolling away in all directions.

"I don't know, honey, but at least we're up here in the fresh air."

One night in that concrete coffin and she was already itching to flee back to the city. She'd pushed two of the folding beds together for Vicky and her. Vicky had slept straight through. Gia hadn't been so lucky. Between Abe's thunderous snoring on the other side of the curtain and worrying about Jack, sleep had proven hard to find.

Abe had snagged some eggs from the chickens in the barn and they'd had breakfast in the farmhouse. The property sat atop one of the taller hills in the area and offered peaceful, wide-angle views of the countryside. The leaning, peeling barn was showing its age, but the house was in pretty decent shape. Gia had cast longing glances at the airy bedrooms.

"Look!" Vicky said. "There's the cat again!"

She started after the barn cat. As in all their previous encounters, the cat took one look at Vicky and headed in the other direction.

"Be careful."

"She'll be all right," Abe said, waddling up behind her. "Nothing sharp or dangerous left in the barn. And no sign of Parabellum."

Gia figured here was a chance to float an idea that had been perking since breakfast.

"What do you think about sleeping in the house tonight?"

Abe shook his head. "Too risky. And besides, everything is below."

"We could bring up what we need. There don't seem to be any bugs in the area."

"I know. Not a single tooth mark I've seen. But still . . . I promised Jack I'd keep you safe and—"

A low rumble filled the air and shivered through the ground.

Abe did a quick turn. "What?"

After fifteen to twenty seconds it faded away.

"That felt like an earthquake."

Abe's expression was grim. "Something worse, I fear." He pointed to the rise on the far side of the house. "That way."

They hurried past the house to a stony outcropping that overlooked the valley. Abe was panting by the time they reached the crest and got a look at the landscape spread out below.

"*Gevalt!*"

Gia felt her stomach knot when she saw the huge, circular opening in the floor of the valley.

"Oh, no."

"Everywhere it's happening. Only a matter of time before it happened here." He glanced at Gia. "Still want to spend the night in the house?"

Gia didn't answer. She turned and looked for Vicky. She wanted her close. Didn't want her out of arm's reach as long as they were topside.

The breeze didn't seem so fresh, and the thought of another night in the bunker didn't seem so bad.

Over the Pacific

Jack was glad he'd brought the shortwave along. With the way those low-frequency signals bounced off the ionosphere, he could talk to Gia from anywhere in the world. Which he'd just done and almost wished he hadn't. A hole right under Abe's nose . . . didn't like that at all. At least everything was working in the bunker. They'd be safe from anything down there.

He tried to put it out of his mind by spending a few hours with Ba in an attempt to get to know him. Not easy. He did learn a few things about Sylvia Nash that cast her in a different light—about her dead husband, Greg—a Special Forces non-com who'd made it through the Gulf War in one piece only to go out one night for a pack of cigarettes and get killed by an armed robber when he stepped into the middle of a 7-Eleven heist.

He learned about Jeffy, the once autistic kid, and about the *Dat-tay-vao* that had inhabited Dr. Bulmer for a while, then left him a cripple, and now lay dormant in Jeffy, waiting. He learned about the powerful love between Sylvia and Doc Bulmer, how they were soul mates who locked horns and butted heads on a regular basis but whose karmas were so intertwined that one could not imagine life without the other.

A bit like Gia and me, Jack thought.

Jack learned all that, but he learned very little about Ba other than the fact that he grew up in a poor Vietnamese fishing village and was intensely devoted to Sylvia—referred to simply as "the Missus"—and how that devotion extended to anyone who mattered to her.

When Jack ran out of questions, they sat in silence, and Nick Quinn's words to Alan Bulmer came back to him. *Only three of you will return.* He brushed them away. Nick may have had a run-in with Rasalom's essence down in that hole, but he'd yet to prove that he had any powers of prediction. He talked in riddles anyway.

He noticed the plane banking to its left, so he headed up front to see what was going on. He found Frank chicken-necking to his iPod. The volume was so high Jack could recognize "Statesboro Blues" from where he stood. He sniffed the air. No trace of herbal-smelling smoke.

When he tapped Frank on the shoulder the headphones came off.

"Are we there yet?"

"You sound like my sister's kids. Yeah, we're there. Past it, in fact. Got to come around to make our approach from the west."

Jack strapped himself in the copilot's seat and peered out the window. The vog was gone. The air was clear all the way to the pristine blue of the Pacific below, but still no direct sunlight. Off the upturned tip of the right wing an irregular patch of lush green, spiked with mountains and rimmed with white sand and surf, floated amid the blue.

"Maui?" Jack said.

Frank shook his head. "Oahu. Pearl Harbor's down there in that notch. Hang on. We're coming around toward Maui now." A moment later the plane leveled off and three islands swung into view. "There. That's Molokai on the left, Lanai on the right, and Maui dead ahead."

Jack had been studying the maps Glaeken had given him. Molokai looked okay, and the resort hotels along Maui's Ka'anapali Bay seemed intact but looked deserted. Inland, the tops of the western mountains were tucked away within a wreath of rain clouds.

But as Frank banked southward, Jack found the old whaling town of Lahaina in ruins—everything burned, blackened, flattened. To their right the whole southern flank of Lanai was scorched and smoking. And then Jack's stomach lurched, not so much from the movement of the plane as from what he saw ahead of them. He felt as if he'd been thrown into any one of a dozen prehistoric island movies of the *Lost Continent / Land That Time Forgot* type.

Maui looked swaybacked from here, as green as Oahu but with mountains at each end and a broad flat valley between. But the big mountain that took up most of the eastern end, Haleakala, was belching fire and pouring gray-black smoke. The old volcano's sides, however—at least from Jack's vantage—were still lush and green.

And somewhere on the slope of that chimney flue to hell dwelt Kolabati with her necklaces.

Jack studied the scene, wondering what the hell he'd got himself into. Maui looked so fragile, like it could blow any minute. Just like Hawaii on its far side.

"Can we swing around the island? Like to get the lay of the land before we touch down."

"I dunno, Jack. Gettin' late. And we'd have to fly low to see anything. Air currents could be tricky on the far side. I mean, with the wide temperature variants between the ocean and the lava and the vog, we could hit some weird thermals. I don't like to do that when I'm straight."

"Okay," Jack said casually. "If you don't think you can hack it, I'll find somebody at the airport to take me up after we land."

Frank grinned. "You're a rotten, despicable, evil dude, Jack, and I hate you very, very much. May your karma turn black and fall into the void. Hang on."

Frank swung the jet out and banked around the western flank of the reactivated Haleakala toward the south end of the island. The scenery changed abruptly from lush green to scorched black, as if a giant flamethrower had been played over the terrain. The eastern slope was a scene from Dante's *Inferno*. Molten lava streamed down the broken-out side of the cone, cooling black crusts surfing the faces of crimson flame-waves, throwing up immense clouds of salty steam as they wiped out in the sea.

Frank skirted the turbulent clouds for a few miles. On the right lay the immense bubbling, boiling cauldron of ocean where the Big Island of Hawaii had once stood, the main source of the lid of vog that covered much of the Eastern Pacific.

Frank turned to Jack. "You sure you want to go all the way around?"

Jack nodded. "All the way."

"Okay. Strap in and don't say I didn't warn you."

He banked and gunned the jet into the roiling steam. Water sluiced off the windshields like rain as updrafts and downdrafts and mini-vortices buffeted the craft, but Frank guided her through with a clenched jaw and steely-eyed determination. When they broke free into the light again, he relaxed his grip on the controls and half-turned to Jack.

"Aw*right!* Far freaking out! Let's try that again. Maybe we can— Jesus H. Christ!"

Jack had already seen it. His stomach was fluttering in awe. The news reports had mentioned it and he'd seen photos, but nothing had prepared him for the reality of it.

A whirlpool. A maelstrom. A swirling, pinwheeling, ten-mile-wide mass of water spread out below him like the planet's navel. Its perimeter moved slowly where it edged into Kahului Bay, but quickly picked up speed as the water progressed inexorably toward the whirling center where it funneled down into a black hole somewhere far below in the ocean floor.

Both Jack and Frank stared dumbly through their windows on the first two passes, then Jack began noticing details.

"Frank!" Jack said, staring down on the third pass. "It looks like—"

He grabbed the binocs from the clamp in the ceiling panel and focused in on the colorful specs he'd spotted below, riding the rim of the maelstrom, then darting in toward its swirling heart and out again.

"What's doing?"

"Windsurfers! There's a bunch of nuts down there windsurfing along the edge of the whirlpool!"

"That's Ho'okipa Bay, windsurfing capital of the world. Those dudes live for that shit. I know where they're comin' from. So do you, I reckon."

"Yeah, I can dig it," Jack said, nodding slowly. Jeez, he was starting to sound like Frank. "But one little slip and you're gone."

"Yeah, but what a way to go!" Frank said dreamily. "If I've gotta go, I want it to be right here, strapped into my jet. Stoked to the eyeballs and Mach one straight down into the earth so's after we hit, me and the plane are so tangled and twisted up they can't tell Frank Ashe from Frank Ashe's plane and so they bury us together. Or better yet, straight down into one of those holes until I run into something or run out of fuel. Whatta trip that'd be! Might even try that one straight. Whatcha think?"

"Drop me off first. I think it's time to land."

Frank grinned. "Aw. And just when we was startin' to have some fun!"

He radioed down to Kahului airport for clearance; they told him the winds were out of the west and that they'd cleaned off the runway. All was clear and he'd better land fast because once it was dark, the hangars would be locked and wouldn't be opened for anyone.

"'Cleaned off the runway'?" Frank said to Jack as he started his approach. "What's that mean?"

They found out after they landed and opened the hatches. From off to the east came a dull roar, the low, gurgling rumble of uncountable tons of water being sucked down through the ocean depths. Looming behind them, Haleakala smoked and thundered. The steady breeze was warm and wet, and it stank.

"Sheesh!" Jack said as he stepped down onto the tarmac.

The ripe, putrid odor clogged his nose and throat. He shifted the strap of his duffel bag on his shoulder and glanced around at the deserted runways and empty buildings, searching for the source.

Frank made a face. "What *is* that, man?"

"Dead fish," said Ba, debarking behind him. "I know that smell from village where I grew."

"You get used to the *pilau* after a while," said the tractor driver who'd come out to tow their jet into a nearby hangar.

"Don't tell me Hawaii always smells like this."

"Hell, no. Didn't they tell you? It's been raining fish the past two nights."

"Fish?"

"Yeah. You name it: ahi, squid, crabs, blues, mahi-mahi, everything. Even a few dolphin. Raining out of the sky. And first thing every morning I've got to go out with the plow and clear them off the runways. Don't know why I bother. Nobody's flying much these days since all the tourists upped and went home."

"But raining fish?"

"It's the *puka moana*—the whirlpool. It backs up at night."

With that he jumped on his tractor and started towing the jet toward the hangar, leaving Jack wondering how a whirlpool could back up. It wasn't as if it were a toilet. Or was it?

Frank led them toward the terminal building.

"Let's see what we can do about getting you guys a car."

The main terminal building looked like an Atlantean relic raised from the sea. Its windows and skylights were smashed, rotting fish and seaweed draped its roof and walls. Inside was worse.

"Shee-it!" Frank said, waving his hand before his face. "Smells like a fish market that's run out of ice."

They trooped through the gloomy, deserted building, looking for someone, anyone. Finally they ran across a dark, middle-aged fat guy squeezing into a wrinkled sports jacket as he hurried toward them down a ramp. His badge read "Fred" and he looked part Hawaiian.

Jack waved him down. "Where are the car rentals?"

"There ain't. All closed up. Nobody to rent to."

"We need a car."

"You're outta luck, I'm afraid."

Jack looked at Ba. "Looks like we'll have to wait till morning, Ba. What do you say?"

Ba shook his head. "Too long away from the Missus."

Jack nodded. He knew Ba was feeling the time pressure as much as he; maybe more. He grabbed the guy's arm as he tried to squeeze by.

"You don't understand, Fred. We *really* need a car."

Fred tried to pull away but Jack tightened his grip on his flabby upper arm. Ba stepped closer and looked down at him.

"I can't help you, Mister," Fred said, wincing. "Now let me go. It'll be getting dark in half an hour. I've got to get home."

"Fine," Jack said. "But we're new around here and you're not. And since you seem to be the *only* one around here, we've elected you to find us a car. And if you can't help us out, we'll be forced to take yours. We'll pay you a generous rental price before we take it, but we *will* take it. So where do they keep the cars around here?"

Fred stared at Jack, then up at Ba, then at Frank who stood behind them. Jack felt a little sorry for the guy, but they had no time to play nice.

"Okay," Fred said. "I can do that. I can show you to the rental lot. But I don't know about keys or—"

"You let me worry about keys. You just get us there."

"All right." Fred glanced up through one of the broken skylights. "But we've got to hurry!"

Fred drove them to the rent-a-car lots, only a couple of hundred yards from the terminal. Jack used his Glock to shoot a link out of the chain locking the gate to the Avis area. Rotting fish littered the lot—on the cars, between the cars, in the lanes—and so the stench was especially vile here. Fred's tires squished through them, spraying rotting entrails left or right whenever he ran over a particularly ripe one. He drove them around the return area until they found a Jeep Laredo. Jack was ready to hot-wire it but didn't have to. The keys were in the ignition. It started easily. The fuel gauge read between half and three-quarters. That would be enough.

Jack returned to where Ba and Frank waited in Fred's car. He pulled out the Maui road map Glaeken had given him and pointed to the red *X* drawn above a town called Kula.

"What's the best way to get here—to Pali Drive?"

"You want to go upcountry? On Haleakala?" Fred said. "Now? With night coming? You've got to be kidding!"

"Fred," Jack said, staring at him, "we've only known each other for a few minutes, but look at this face, Fred. Is this face kidding?"

"All right, all right. I've never heard of Pali Drive but this spot you've got marked here is somewhere between the Crater Road and Waipoli Road."

He rattled off directions.

"But there's nobody up there . . . except for the *pupule kahuna* and his witch woman."

Jack grabbed Fred's wrist. "Witch woman? Dark, Indian looking?"

"That's the one. You know her?"

"Yeah. That's who we're going to see."

Fred shook his head. "Lots of strange stories coming downhill. Now I'm *real* glad you're not taking my car. Because you ain't coming back."

"We'll see about that."

After Fred rushed off to drop Frank at the hangar where he planned to spend the night in his plane, Jack pushed a half dozen dead fish off the Jeep's hood, unzipped his duffel bag, and began laying out its contents.

"Okay, Ba. Name your poison."

He laid out the chew-wasp-toothed club Ba had given him, plus a .45 1911 Colt, a pair of Glock .40s, two HK MP5s, and a pair of Spas12 semiautomatic twelve-gauge assault shotguns with pistol grip stocks and extended magazines.

Ba didn't hesitate. He picked out the 1911 and one of the shotguns. Jack nodded his approval. Good choices.

Ba turned the Spas12 over in his hands. "Semiautomatic?"

Jack nodded. "Yeah. Abe was fresh out of Benellis, but these'll do."

Jack already had his own Glock; he added the toothed billy, an MP5, and the remaining shotgun to his armament, then tossed a fifty-cartridge bandolier to Ba.

"You ride shotgun."

Ba pumped the Spas12, checked the breach, then handed it to Jack.

"No," he said, his face set in its usual mortician's dead pan. "I am much better driver."

"Oh, really?" Jack repressed a smile. This was the longest spontaneous comment he'd been able to elicit from Ba all day. "What makes you say that?"

"Driving to airport this morning."

Jack snatched the offered shotgun from his grasp.

"Fine. You drive. But try not to wear me out with all your empty chatter as we go. It distracts me."

They'd gone about half a dozen miles or so on Route 37—some of the signs called it "Haleakala Highway"—driving on stinking pavement slick with the crushed remains of countless dead fish. The outskirts of a town called Puka-lani were in sight when Jack glanced back at the lowlands behind them. Fairly dark below, lights few and scattered, the airport completely dark. He glanced beyond the coast to the strange-faced moon peeking huge and full above the edge of the sea, but when he saw the sea itself, his heart fumbled a beat and he squinted through the thickening dusk to confirm what he thought he saw.

"Whoa, Ba," he said, grabbing his shoulder. "Check out the whirlpool. Tell me if you see what I see."

Ba braked and looked over his shoulder.

"There is no whirlpool."

"Thank you. Then I'm not crazy."

He wished he'd thought to bring the binocs, but even from this distance in the poor light it was plain the huge pinwheel of white water was gone.

Had the hole in the ocean floor closed up?

"I don't understand any of this. But then, I'm not supposed to. That's the whole point."

He was about to tell Ba to drive on when he noticed a white area of water bubbling up where the center of the whirlpool had been. The bubbling grew, became more violent, and finally erupted into the night. Not volcanic fire, not steam, just water, a huge thick column of it, hundreds of feet across, geysering out of the ocean and lancing into the sky at an impossible speed. It roared upward, ever upward, ten thousand, fifteen thousand, twenty thousand feet into the air until it plumed into billowing cumulus clouds at its apex.

And it kept spewing, kept on pouring unmeasured thousands of tons of water into the sky.

"My . . . God!" was about all Jack could manage in the face of such a gargantuan surreal display.

"It is as the man said. Whirlpool back up at night."

Ba threw the Jeep back into gear and continued up the highway. They had the road to themselves.

They'd traveled three or four miles uphill from Pukalani when heavy drops of seawater began to splatter all around them. Jack rolled up his window as the shower evolved into a deluge, forcing Ba to cut his pace.

A few minutes later, a blue-and-green parrot fish bounced off the hood with a nerve-jarring *thunk.* Then a bright yellow butterfly fish, then they were being pelted with sea life, banging on the hood, thudding on the top, littering the road ahead of them. The ones that didn't burst open or die from the impact flopped and danced on the wet pavement in the glare of the headlights. A huge squid splatted against the windshield, momentarily blocking Ba's vision; when it slid off he had to swerve violently to the right to avoid a six-foot porpoise stretched dead across the road.

And then fish weren't the only things in the air. Chew wasps, spearheads, belly flies, men-of-war, and a couple of new species Jack hadn't seen before began darting about. Ba accelerated. Jack was uneasy about traveling at this pace through pelting rain and falling fish over an unfamiliar road slick with dead or dying sea life. But the headlights and speed seemed to confuse the winged predators, and Ba plowed into the ones that wouldn't or couldn't get out of the way.

After they passed through Kula, Jack spotted the turnoff. Ba slid the Jeep into the hairpin turn as smoothly as a movie stuntman, downshifted, and roared up the incline.

Jack had to admit—silently, and only to himself—that Ba was indeed the better driver.

The Waipoli Road turnoff came up so quickly they overshot it. But Ba had them around and back on track in seconds. And then the going got really rough. The pavement disappeared and devolved into an ungraded road that wound back and forth in sharp switchbacks up a steep incline. The slower pace allowed the night things to zero in on the Jeep. They began battering the windows.

But soon the headlights picked out a brightly painted hand-carved sign that read *Pali Drive.* Ba made the turn and the road narrowed to a pair of ruts. They bounced along its puddled length until it ended at the cantilevered underbelly of a cedar-sided house overlooking the valley. Ba stopped with the headlights trained on a narrow door in the concrete foundation.

Jack rechecked his map and notes by the dashboard light.

"This is it. Think anybody's home?"

Ba squinted through the windshield. "There are lights."

"So there are. I guess that means we've got to go in."

A spearhead rammed the tip of its spike through the roof then. Hungry little tongues wiggled through the openings behind the point and lapped at empty air. As it pulled back, seawater began to dribble in through the hole.

"Let's go," Jack said. "Shotguns and clubs?"

Ba nodded and picked up the other Spas-12.

"Okay. We meet at the front bumper and head for the house back-to-back. Use the shotgun only if you have to. Go!"

Jack kicked open his door, leapt into the downpour, and dashed-splashed toward the front of the Jeep. Something fluttered near his head; without looking he lashed out at it with the wasp-toothed billy. A crunch, a tear, and whatever it was tumbled away. He met Ba in the glow of the headlights and they slammed their backs together. A spearhead darted through the light, low, toward Jack's groin, while a belly fly sailed in toward his face. The wound where the first belly fly had caught him on the arm had healed, but he remembered the pain. He wasn't about to let this one in close. He swung the club at the spearhead and shredded its wings while ramming the muzzle of the shotgun into the belly fly's acid sac, rupturing it.

"Let's move!" Jack shouted. "I'll lead."

Like a pair of Siamese twins fused at the spine, they moved toward the door, Jack clearing a path with his billy and shotgun, Ba backpedaling, protecting the rear. When he reached the door, Jack began pounding on its hardwood surface, then decided he couldn't wait. He handed Ba his billy and pulled the plastic strip from his pocket, all the while congratulating himself for bringing Ba along. The big guy was faced into the headlights now, a club in each hand, batting the bugs away left and right. Fortunately, they weren't nearly as thick here as they'd been in New York, but even so, without Ba, Jack would have been eaten alive as he faced the door.

He quickly slipped the latch and they burst into a utility room. He spotted a sink and a washing machine before they slammed the door closed behind them and stood panting and dripping in the safe quiet darkness.

"You okay?"

"Yes," Ba said. "And you?"

"I'm just groovy. Let's go see who—"

Suddenly the overhead lights went on. A tall, dark-skinned man with reddish hair stood in the doorway. He was dressed in a loincloth and a feather headdress and Jack might have laughed except that he was pointing a Marlin 336 their way.

"Who are you?"

Jack put up his hands. "Just travelers seeking shelter from the storm."

"No shelter here for *malihini*." He stepped forward and raised the rifle. "Get out! *Hele aku oe!*"

"Easy there," Jack said. "We're looking for Miss Bahkti, Kolabati Bahkti. We were told she lived here."

"Never heard of her. Out!"

Even if the guy hadn't flinched at the sound of her name, the necklace around his neck, a perfect match to the copy Jack carried in his pocket, would have proved him a liar.

Then Jack heard a woman's voice call his name.

"Jack!"

Kolabati had followed Moki down to the lower level to see who was pounding on the door; she'd hung back in the dark hallway, watching the scene in the utility room over Moki's shoulder. Two wet and weary men there, one white, the other a tall Asian. Something about the smaller man, the brown-haired, brown-eyed Caucasian, had struck her immediately as familiar. But she didn't recognize him until he spoke her name. It couldn't be! But even with his hair plastered to his scalp and down over his forehead, he could be no one else. Her heart leapt at the sight of him.

She brushed past Moki and ran to him, arms outstretched. Never in her life had she been so glad to see someone.

"Oh, Jack, I thought you were dead!"

She threw her arms around his neck and clung to him. He returned the embrace, but without much enthusiasm.

"I am," he said coolly. "I just came back to see how you were doing."

She stepped back and stared at him. "But when I left you, you were—"

"I healed up—my own way."

Kolabati sensed Moki close behind her. She turned and was relieved to see that he had lowered his rifle. She manufactured a smile for him.

"Moki, this is Jack, a very old and dear friend."

"Jack?" His gaze flicked between her and the newcomer. "The Jack you said you once loved but who died in New York? That Jack?"

"Yes." A glance at Jack's face revealed a bewildered expression. "I . . . I guess I was wrong about his being dead. Isn't that wonderful? Jack, this is Moki."

Kolabati held her breath. No telling how Moki would react. He'd become so unpredictable—*unbalanced* was a better word—since the changes had begun.

Moki's jaw was set and his smile was fierce as he thrust his open hand toward Jack.

"*Aloha,* Jack. Welcome to my kingdom."

Kolabati watched the muscles in Moki's forearm bulge as he gripped Jack's hand, a wince flickered across Jack's features before he returned the smile and the grip.

"Thank you, Moki. And this is my good friend, Ba Thuy Nguyen."

This time it was Moki's turn to wince as he shook hands with the Asian.

"You're both just in time," Moki said. "We were about to leave for the ceremony."

"Maybe now that they're here we should stay home," Kolabati said.

"Nonsense! They can come along. In fact, I *insist* they come along!"

"You're not thinking of going outside, are you?" Jack said.

"Of course. We're heading uphill to the fires. The night things do not bother us. Besides, they seem to avoid the higher altitudes. You shall have the honor and privilege of witnessing the Ceremony of the Knife tonight."

Moki had told her about the ceremony he'd worked out with the Niihauans, a nightly replay of last night's bloody incident. She wanted no part of it, and Jack's arrival was a good excuse to stay away.

"Moki, why don't you go alone tonight. Our guests are cold and wet."

"Yeah," Jack said. "How about a rain check on that? We're kinda beat—"

"Nonsense! The awakened fires of Haleakala will dry your clothes and renew your strength."

"Go yourself, Moki," Kolabati told him. "After all, the ceremony can go on without us, but not without you."

Moki's glare spelled out his thoughts: *Leave you here with your reborn lover? Do you take me for a fool?* Then he faced Jack.

"I shall be insulted if you do not come."

"A guest must not insult a host," the tall Asian said.

Kolabati noticed a quick look pass between Jack and Ba, then Jack turned to Moki.

"How can we refuse such an honor? Lead the way."

Kolabati held on as Moki bounced their Isuzu Trooper up the rutted jeep trail toward Haleakala's fire-limned summit.

"What sort of a ceremony is this?" Jack said from behind her.

"You'll find out soon enough," Moki said.

"I mean, is it traditional, or what?"

"Not entirely. It has its traditional aspects, naturally—ancient Hawaiians often made sacrifices to Pele—but this variation is one of my own devising."

Jack and his silent Asian companion were two jouncing shadows in the rear as Kolabati turned from the front seat to face him.

"Pele?" said Jack's shadow.

"Hawaii's Goddess of Fire," Kolabati told him. "She rules the volcanoes."

"So what are we doing—throwing some pineapples and coconuts over the edge?"

Moki laughed as he turned onto Skyline Trail. "Pele has no use for fruits and nuts. She demands tribute that really matters. *Human* tribute."

Jack's laugh was low and uncertain.

Kolabati said, "He's not joking."

Jack said nothing then, but even in the dark Kolabati could feel the impact of his gaze. She heard his silent questions, asking her what she had come to, what had brought her to this. She wanted to explain, but couldn't. Not now. Not in front of Moki.

The quality of the road improved as they approached Red Hill and the observatory. Moki pulled to a stop a quarter mile from the summit and the four of them walked under the cold gaze of the unfamiliar moon to the crater's edge.

And there, half a mile below them, a sea of fire. The boiling center of the crater, the terminus of a delivery tube from the planet's molten core, was alive with motion. Bubbles rose on the storm-tossed surface and burst, splattering liquid rock in all directions. Geysers of molten lava shot like whale spume, hurling red-orange arcs a thousand feet into the air before joining the steady downward flow to the sea in a wide fan of fiery destruction.

Even here, thousands of feet above, with the reversed trade winds blowing cold against their backs, the fire stroked them with its heat. Kolabati watched Jack hold out his hands to warm them, then turn his wet back toward the fire. The wind had an icy bite at ten thousand feet. He must have been freezing. The Asian, too, rotated his wet clothing toward the heat.

"I've figured out why Pele is so *huhu*," Moki said, shouting above Haleakala's roar. "She's seen her people abandoning the old ways and becoming *malihini* to their own traditions. She's sent us all a message."

Jack was staring down into the fire. "I'd say she's one very touchy lady."

"Ah!" said Moki, glancing off to their right. "The other celebrants arrive. The ceremony can begin."

He strode away toward the approaching Niihauans. Their elderly *alii* raised his feathered staff and they all knelt before Moki.

Kolabati felt a cold hand grip her arm: Jack.

"He's just kidding about this human sacrifice stuff, isn't he? I mean, I keep expecting Bob Hope, Bing Crosby, and Dorothy Lamour to show up."

Kolabati could barely meet his eyes. "I wish he were, but he means it. The group over there, the ones wearing the feathers and such, they're the last of the purebred traditional Hawaiians from the forbidden island of Niihau. Moki confronted them last night and told them he was Maui."

Jack's eyes widened. "He thinks he's an island?"

"No. He's mad but not *that* mad. Maui was a god who came up here ages ago, right where we're standing, and trapped the sun and forced it to make the days longer. When Moki told them he was Maui, the Niihauans didn't believe him. One of them stabbed him in the chest with a spear."

Jack glanced over to where Moki stood talking with the Niihauan *alii*.

"You mean *tried* to stab him in the chest."

"No. The spearhead sank to its full length right here."

She reached out and touched a spot over Jack's heart.

He gave her a quick look, then stared again at Moki.

"The necklace?"

Kolabati nodded.

"It didn't work that way when I wore it."

"It's never worked that way. Something's happened to it. It's been activated, *stimulated* in some way that I don't understand."

"I do," Jack said, still staring at Moki.

"You do? How can you—?"

"That's why I'm here. I need that necklace. There's someone back in New York who might be able to set the world right again. But he needs the necklace to do it."

The thought of giving away the second necklace to a stranger jolted Kolabati. She turned to look at Moki and held her breath as she saw a middle-aged Niihauan rise and step toward him with a raised knife. Moki stood firm, showing no fear. In fact, he gestured the man forward. The Niihauan stepped closer, and in a blur of motion raised the knife and plunged it into Moki's chest.

Jack cried, "Jesus Christ!" while Ba stiffened and muttered something unintelligible.

Kolabati watched the rim with fatalistic distaste as Moki staggered back a step, then straightened. He grasped the knife handle with both hands, and slowly, deliberately, his body shaking convulsively, withdrew the bloody blade from his chest. The Niihauan looked on in openmouthed amazement, then raised his face and arms toward the sky. Moki gave him a moment, then rammed the dripping blade into his heart.

As the man screamed in agony, Jack turned away, cursing under his breath. Kolabati continued to watch. Human sacrifices had been part of her childhood. When you are born to a priest and priestess of a temple where humans were regularly thrown to rakoshi, it became a matter-of-fact event. In their case, a necessity—the rakoshi had to be fed. But this was different. This was obscene, serving no useful purpose other than feeding Moki's delusions.

As she watched Moki lift the Niihauan's corpse and hurl it into the fire, a sacrifice to the false goddess, Pele, Jack turned to her.

"How the *hell* did you get involved with this maniac?"

"A long, sad story, Jack. Believe me, he was nothing like this before the sun and the earth began to betray us."

Inside she mourned for the Moki who had been, the Moki she sensed was irretrievably lost to her.

"I'll have to take your word for that. But right now he's got to be stopped. And one way to stop him is to get that necklace from him."

"More easily said than done when you're talking about a man who heals like Moki."

"I might have a way." His eyes bored into hers. "Will you help?"

She nodded vigorously. "Of course."

But don't expect to walk out of here with Moki's necklace when we get it back.

TUESDAY

Passages

WFPW-FM

JO: Hey, we're back. You probably thought we jumped ship like most everybody else in town, didn't you. Not us, man. We lost our power for a bit there. As we're sure you already know, the whole city's dark.

FREDDY: Yeah, but we've got a generator going now so we're staying on the air, just like we promised.

JO: Trouble is, we won't be able to bring you much news. The Internet is shaky again and the wire services are shutting down. But we'll stay on and do the best we can.

FREDDY: Yeah. Semper fi, man.

<cue: "Life During Wartime">

Dinu Pass, Romania

"I think we're lost, Nick," Bill said.

They were tipping and grinding and scraping along what passed for a road in these parts as Bill fought the wheel of the Romanian equivalent of a Land Rover—rust-streaked, an odometer in kilometers, creaky, ratchety steering, failing brakes, and a leaky exhaust system. But it seemed damn near indestructible, and its thick glass so far had proven itself impervious to the bugs that had swarmed them in the Ploiesti area. Not too many bugs around here, though. Not many humans or animals around to feed on.

Bill squinted ahead. Sheer mountain walls towered on either side, closer on his left, but the formerly seamless blackness beyond the flickering, dancing headlights was showing some cracks. Morning was coming. Good. Although traveling east had made the night mercifully short, he was tired of the darkness. He had a blinding headache from the car's carbon monoxide–tainted air as well as the tension growing in his neck; his left leg and right arm burned from fighting the creaky clutch and stubborn gearshift; and he was sure they'd missed a crucial turn about ten kilometers back.

And he'd begun talking to Nick. Nick hadn't deigned to reply yet, but the sound of his own voice gave Bill the feeling that he wasn't completely alone out here in a remote mountain pass in the heart of a benighted country where he spoke not a word of the native language.

"We'll never find our way back home again. Unless it's in a pine box."

Joe Ashe had piloted them into Romania in great time, riding the jet stream all the way. The field at Ploiesti had been deserted except for one of Joe's East European pilot buddies—apparently the Ashe brothers had a global network of kindred spirits—who had this beat-up old land rover waiting for them.

They'd assumed Bill would wait until daylight before setting out. But dawn, such as it was these days, had been nearly three hours away. And three hours seemed like a lifetime. Sure, it was 6:02 A.M. local time, but the clock in Bill's body read only midnight. He was too wired to sleep, so why not put the time to good use? The Romanian rover looked sturdy enough—more like a converted half-track mini-tank than a car—so he'd loaded Nick into the passenger seat and headed out into the darkness.

A foolish mistake, Bill realized now. He glanced at his watch. Eight o'clock. According to the Sapir curve, the coming day would be about half an hour shorter than the shortest day of the year in the dead of all the Decembers that had preceded the celestial changes.

Bill shivered. A new kind of winter had come. A winter of the soul.

"I know what you're going to say, Nick. You're going to say, 'I told you so.' And maybe you did, but I guess I wasn't listening. Doesn't matter now, though. We're stuck out here in the middle of nowhere and we'll just have to wait until the light comes and hope to find somebody who can tell us how to get to this keep place."

Nick, ever polite, refrained from an I-told-you-so.

Bill scanned the terrain ahead for a level place to park and noticed the road widening. Great. He could pull to the side and wait for the light. Then he saw the white shapes ahead. As he got closer he realized they were houses. A cluster of them. A village.

"Maybe there is a God after all, Nick," but he knew Nick didn't believe that. Neither did he.

Bill almost wished again for the old days when he did believe. Because he'd be praying now for help, for direction, for the Lord to inspire his hands on the wheel to guide them to the right road and lead them to their destination.

But those days were gone. His god was dead. Mumbled words would not bring help from on high. He was going to have to do this just the way he'd always done things—by himself.

As he followed the road on its winding course among the houses, he felt no lessening of his sense of isolation. What had appeared to be a village was really no more than a collection of huts, and those huts looked beat up and run down. As the headlight beams raked them he saw how their white stucco walls were scarred and chipped, noted the gaps in the thatch and shakes covering their roofs. Hard times had come to this place. He didn't have to search the huts to know the village was deserted.

"Now we're really lost." Fatigue settled on him like a ratty blanket. "Lost in the middle of nowhere. If there is a God, he's forsaken this place."

Then he saw the flames. On the far side of the village, flickering fitfully in the fading darkness. It looked like a campfire. He drove toward it, steadily picking up speed.

A fire meant people and that meant he wasn't completely lost. Maybe he could still salvage this trip.

But suddenly he saw nothing ahead—no road, no grass, no earth, only emptiness. He stood on the brakes, tumbling Nick into the dashboard as the rover swerved and skidded to a stalling halt at the edge of a precipice. A hole, dammit! Another one of those bottomless holes!

No, wait. To his left, vague and dim, an ancient bridge of some sort, with stone supports plunging into the pit. It coursed across the emptiness—a rocky gorge, he saw now; not a hole—toward the campfire. And now that he was closer and the sky was lighter, Bill realized the campfire wasn't outside. It was *inside*, glowing through a tall open gate set within a massive stone wall that seemed to spring from the mountainside. He could make out human forms standing around it. Some of them might even be staring back at him. On the structure's leading edge, a thick, sturdy tower rose a good forty or fifty feet above the top of the wall. The whole thing looked like a small castle, a pocket fortress. He felt a smile spread over his face—how long since he'd really smiled?

He was here. He'd found it.

The keep.

Bill let out a whoop and pounded the steering wheel.

"We made it, Nick!"

He restarted the vehicle and headed for the causeway, intending to drive across. But when the headlights picked up the worn and ragged timbers, he stopped, unsure if he should risk it.

"What do you think, Nick?"

The question was rhetorical, but Bill noticed that Nick seemed more aware than he'd been a few moments ago. Had the impact with the dashboard jostled his mind? Or was it something else?

Maybe it was all the bugs swarming around the keep. He hadn't noticed them before, but he could see now that the air was thick with them. Perhaps because the only people in the pass were clustered around that fire inside. But why were the doors open? And why weren't the bugs running rampant through the place, chewing up the inhabitants?

One thing Bill did know was that walking across the causeway now was impossible. They'd be ground beef before they traveled twenty feet. Of course, they could wait. But Bill couldn't wait, not another minute. He hadn't come this far through the dark simply to sit here with his destination in sight and wait for dawn. Screw the bugs. He was going across. Now.

"All right, Nick. Here goes nothing."

He put the rover in first gear and edged forward, fixing his gaze on the timbers directly ahead. Not so easy with the bugs batting against the vehicle with increasing frequency. A bumpy ride, but smoother than the ridge road they'd been traveling. A glance ahead showed a group of figures clustered in the gateway of the keep, watching him.

"Stop."

Bill slammed on the brakes. Nick's face was pressed against the side window. His voice was as lifeless as ever, but Bill sensed real emotion hidden within it—almost excitement.

"What is it, Nick? What's wrong?"

"I see them. Down there. Little pieces of the sword."

He was pointing down to his right, below the base of the tower, down to where its rocky foundation melted into the gorge, fifty feet below. Bill could barely make out the bottom. How could Nick see little pieces of metal?

"I don't see a thing, Nick."

"Right there. They glow with bright blue fire. Are you blind?"

Bill strained to see but could find only darkness below.

"I guess so. But as long as one of us can see them, we're in business."

Bill was congratulating himself on how smoothly this mission was going when the rear window cracked and bellied inward as one of the bigger bugs hit

it like a cinder block. It held, but for how long? Because suddenly they were
under full-scale attack as the bugs launched a blitzkrieg on the rover, scraping, gnawing, pounding, and slapping against every square inch of the vehicle's surface, as if the approach of dawn had driven them into one final feeding
frenzy before they'd be forced to return to their hole.

Bill hesitated to release the clutch. He couldn't see. With all the chew
wasps, belly flies, spearheads, men-of-war, and other things clustered against
the windshield and the other windows, the outer world had become a squirming mass of gnashing jaws, writhing tentacles, and acid-filled sacs. He'd be
driving blind. No guardrail, and fifty feet of empty air awaiting them if the
rover strayed more than three feet left or right.

Then the rear window bulged farther inward with the weight of the onslaught and he knew he had no choice. Even going over the side was preferable
to sitting here and being eaten alive when that window gave way.

Taking a deep breath, Bill eased up on the clutch and they started to
move. He found that by looking down through the very bottom of his side window he could catch an occasional glimpse of the causeway's edge. He used
that as a guide.

As they rolled forward, he heard a noise, faint and indistinct at first, but
growing steadily in volume. It sounded almost like human voices—*cheering*
voices. It was. The sound reached into the rover and touched him, warmed
him. Using it as a beacon, he increased his speed, homing in on it.

And suddenly—like driving under an overpass in the heart of a
cloudburst—the bugs were gone. Swept away, every last one of them. Silence in
the rover. Except for the voices. Instead of bugs the vehicle was now surrounded
by cheering people. Men and women, middle aged and older with rugged peas-
ant faces, coarse clothing, sheepskin vests, woolly hats. They pulled open the
rover's door and helped him out, all the while shaking his hand and slapping
his back. Bill returned the smiles and the handshakes, then glanced back
along the causeway. The bugs crowded the air outside the arch of the gateway,
but not one ventured through.

He turned back to the people and saw children and goats wandering
around behind them. And beyond those, on the stone block walls, crosses.
Hundreds of crosses. *Thousands* of crosses.

What sort of place was this? And why did he feel as if somehow he'd returned home after a long journey?

With the coming of day the bugs fled back to the darkness where they lived and the peasants trooped out of the keep with their children and animals, crossing the causeway to what was left of the real world, leaving Bill and Nick and their vehicle behind with the ashes of the night fire.

He knew he and Nick should head down into the gorge to search for the shards of the shattered sword, but he could not leave this place. Not just yet. The keep took him in, wrapped him in the arms of its walls, and demanded his attention.

The crosses . . . how could he spend two thirds of his life in the priesthood and not be taken in by a place so thoroughly studded with crosses? Not dull, dreary, run-of-the-mill Latin crosses, but strange thick ones, with brass uprights and nickel crosspieces set high, almost at the top. Like a tau cross or what was called St. Anthony's cross.

Not all of the villagers had left. An ancient, white-bearded gent—eighty if he was a day—named Alexandru remained behind. He spoke as much English as Bill did Romanian, but they found common ground in German. Bill had studied the language in high school and college and had been fluent enough to read *Faust* in the original text. He found he'd retained enough to communicate with Alexandru.

The old man showed him around the structure. His father, also named Alexandru, had been the keep's last caretaker in the days before World War Two. It could have used a caretaker now—a whole crew of them. Snow, wind, rain, drought, heat, and cold had left their marks on the keep. All the upper floors within the tower had collapsed, leaving nothing but a giant, rubble-choked stone cylinder. Yet although crumbling and in sad disrepair, it still exuded a certain power.

"It used to be a bad place," Alexandru said. "Now it is a good place. The little monsters will not come here. All around they fly, but never in here."

He went to the gate and gestured off to the left. Bill's gaze followed the pointing arm to a black circular area, hundreds of feet across, marring the verdant floor of the pass.

A hole.

"That is where they come from, the little monsters."

"I know. The holes are everywhere."

Alexandru then led him to the keep's cellar and showed him the opening in the stone floor there. He told of how the Germans had camped in the keep in the spring of 1941 and nearly wrecked the place, of how something immeasurably evil had awakened and slaughtered all the soldiers, of how it had almost escaped before it was destroyed.

Alexandru looked at Bill with watery blue eyes.

"At least we *thought* it was destroyed. Now I am not so sure."

"How was it destroyed?"

"A redheaded stranger came and slew it with a magic sword—"

. . . a magic sword . . .

"—then he limped off with a Jewish woman from Bucharest and was never seen again. I wonder whatever happened to him."

"He's old and gray now like you," Bill said, wondering what Glaeken had looked like in his prime. He must have been magnificent. "And he and the woman are still together."

Alexandru nodded and smiled. "I am glad. He was a brave man, but terrible to see when he was angry."

With the aid of Alexandru's directions, Glaeken's notes, and a flashlight, Bill led Nick down through the utter blackness of the subcellar to the lower segment of the tower. A narrow stairway wound down to the base where some of the foundation had crumbled. Alexandru had said something about a strange American named Dmitri Menelaus who had carted off many of the loose stones years ago. Light seeped through the opening into the base of the tower.

"All right, Nick," he said, leading him outside. "Do your thing. Where are they?"

Nick stood blinking in the light. Thin, and paler than ever, he didn't look well. And he'd crawled back into himself.

Bill scanned the ground, looking for the shards Nick had said he'd seen. It was like river-bottom here, fist-sized stones jumbling down a gentle slope to a sluggish stream. He looked up to his right at the mountains soaring behind the keep. This gorge was probably all water in early spring when the snows melted. Half a century had passed since the sword blade had shattered here. How could anything be left? How could they hope to find the remnants even if any still existed?

"Well, Nick? Where are they?"

Nick said nothing, only stared ahead.

Desperate, Bill knelt and picked among the stones and gravel. This was impossible. He'd never find anything this way.

He straightened up and brushed off his hands. Earlier, in the dark, Nick had said he'd seen the pieces, glowing "with bright blue fire."

Maybe he could see them only at night.

"Damn!"

He'd risked their lives rushing to get here so he could return to Ploiesti as soon as possible and start their homeward journey in the light. Now he was going to have to wait until dark.

He turned and aimed a kick at the tower's granite-block hem. The keep, a dark, brooding, lithic presence looming over him, took no notice.

Bill led Nick back inside the tower to a gloom as deep and dark as his spirits. The delay meant it would be Wednesday before he got back to Carol. He wondered how she was doing.

The Horror Channel's Drive-In Theatre—Special All-Day Edition
Eaten Alive (1976) New World
Day of the Nightmare (1965) Herts-Lion
Nightwing (1979) Columbia
Raw Meat (1972) AIP
The Devils of Darkness (1965) 20th Century Fox
Tentacles (1977) AIP
Phase IV (1974) Paramount
It! The Terror from Beyond Space (1958) United Artists
They Came from Beyond Space (1967) Amicus
The Last Days of Planet Earth (1974) Toho
The Flesh Eaters (1964) CDA
They Came from Within (1975) TransAmerica
The Earth Dies Screaming (1964) Lippert/20th Century Fox

New Jersey Turnpike

Hank wasn't sure if he was awake or dreaming. He seemed to be awake. He was aware of noises around him, of a stale, sour odor, of growing light beyond his eyelids, but he could not get those eyelids to move. And he could *feel* nothing. For all he knew, he no longer had a body. Where was he? What—?

And then he remembered. The millipedes . . . their queen . . . a scream bubbled up in his throat but died stillborn. How can you scream when you can't open your mouth?

No. That had been a dream. It had all been a dream—the holes, the flying horrors, the rest stop, the trooper, the gun, the bullet, the millipedes—a long, horrible nightmare. But finally at an end. He was waking up now.

If he could just open his eyes he'd see the familiar ceiling of his bedroom. And then he'd be free of the nightmare. He'd be able to move then.

The eyes. They were the key. He concentrated on the lids, focusing all his will, all his energy into them. And slowly they began to move. He didn't feel the motion but saw a knife-slit streak appear, pale light, like the glow on the horizon at the approach of dawn.

Encouraged, he doubled his efforts. Light widened around the horizon as the edges of his lids stretched the gummy substance that bound them, then burst through as they broke apart. Not the blaze of the rising sun, but a wan, diffuse sort of light. He forced his lids to separate further and the light began to take form through the narrow opening, breaking down into shapes and color. Vague shapes. A paucity of color. Mostly grays. His pupils constricted, bringing the images into sharper focus.

He was looking down along a body. His own body, lying in bed, naked atop the sheets. Hazy, but he knew his own body. Thank God, it had all been a dream. He tried to turn his head to the left, toward the light, but it wouldn't move. Why couldn't he move? He was awake now. He should be able to move. He slid his eyeballs leftward. The bedroom window was over there somewhere. If he could just—

Wait . . . the walls—rounded. The ceiling—convex. Concrete. Concrete everywhere. And the light. It came from above. He forced his eyelids open another millimeter. No window—the light filtered through a grate in the concrete ceiling.

The stillborn scream from a moment ago came alive again and rammed up against his throat, pounding at his larynx, crying to be free.

This wasn't the bedroom. He was in the pipe—the drainage pipe! It hadn't been a dream. It was real. *Real!*

Hank fought the panic, beat it down, and tried to think. He was still alive. He had to remember that. Still alive and it was daytime. The things from the holes were quiet in the daylight hours. They hid from the light. He had to think, had to plan. He'd always been good at planning.

He shifted his eyes down to his body. His vision was clearer now. He saw the gentle tidal rise and fall of his hairy chest, and farther down, on his belly, he spotted the bloody wound where the queen millipede had spiked him and injected him with her poison. The neurotoxin was still in effect, obviously, paralyzing his voluntary muscles while it let his heart and lungs go on working. But it didn't have complete control. He'd managed to open his eyes, hadn't he? He could move his eyeballs, couldn't he? What else could he move?

He pulled his gaze away from his abdominal wound and searched for his hands. They lay flopped out on either side, palms up. He checked out his legs. They were intact, slightly spread with the toes angled outward. He could have been a sunbather. His body was the picture of relaxation . . . the relaxation of complete paralysis. He returned his gaze to his arm and followed it down to the hand. If he could move a finger—

And then he noticed the webbing—surrounding him, running in all directions, crisscrossed like gauze. It curved away from each arm and leg like heavy-duty spiderweb and ran out to the wall of the drainpipe where it melted into a glob of some sticky-looking gelatin smeared on the concrete. He looked down as much as his slit perspective would permit and realized that he wasn't lying in the pipe, he was *suspended* in it. From the horizontal lie of his body he guessed that he was resting on a hammock of web across the diameter.

Hank marveled at the coolness of his mind as it analyzed his position. He was trapped—not only paralyzed, but effectively and securely bound in position. The web hammock, however, was not entirely without its advantages. Long, uninterrupted contact with the cold concrete would have made it difficult for his body to maintain its temperature; the webbing also kept him out of the water, thereby preventing his flesh from breaking down in the constant moisture.

So in a very real sense he was high and dry, but also bound, gagged, and paralyzed.

Reminded him of his days as a slaughterhouse worker. Here he was, hung up like a side of—

Beef.

That last thought impacted with the force of a sledgehammer. That was it! He was food! They'd shot him full of preservatives and stored him away alive so he wouldn't decompose. So when pickings got slim above, they could come down here and devour him at their leisure.

He willed down the rising panic. Panic wouldn't help here. They'd already paralyzed his body. Allowing fear to paralyze his mind would only make matters worse. But that one cold hard fact battered relentlessly at his defenses.

I'm food!

But I'm alive. I came up from nothing, I wrote *Kick!* and I started the Kicker Evolution. I can beat these bugs.

He knew their pattern. They'd probably stay dormant all day and crawl up to the surface to hunt during the dark hours. That was when he'd get free.

But first he had to regain control of his body. He already controlled his eyeballs and eyelids. Next—his hands. If he was to get free he'd need them the most. A finger. He'd start with the pointer on his right hand, concentrate all his will and energy into that one digit until he got it to move. Then he'd proceed to the next, and the next, until he could make a fist. Then he'd switch to his left.

He glared at his index finger, narrowing his vision, his entire world to that single digit, channeling all his power into it.

And then it moved.

Or had it? The twitch had been almost imperceptible, so slight it might have been a trick of the light. Or wishful thinking.

But it *had* moved. He had to hold on to that thought. It *had* moved. He was regaining control. He was going to get out of here.

With climbing spirits, he redoubled his concentration on the reluctant digit.

WFAN-AM

<dead air>

Monroe Village, Long Island

Alan rolled his wheelchair along the network of cement paths that encircled Toad Hall, heading from the backyard to the front. Off to his left, to the west, he saw smoke rising over the trees. Not near smoke, not from the Shore Drive neighborhood, but farther away. From downtown Monroe, most likely. He'd heard stories of roving gangs, looting, burning, raping. They hadn't shown up out here, but perhaps that was simply a matter of time.

Strange how things had worked out. He'd always imagined that if the world ever descended into anarchic nihilism, the violence and chaos and mob madness would occur at night, screams and flames hurtling into a dark, unseeing sky. But given the current situation, human violence was confined to the daylight hours. The night was reserved for *un*human violence.

Alan turned from the smoke and inspected Toad Hall. The old mansion had absorbed another merciless pummeling last night, but like the valiant, indomitable champion she was, she remained on her feet.

Her injuries were accumulating at an alarming rate, however. Her flanks were cut and bruised and splintered, her scalp showed through where her shingles had been torn up. She could still open her eyes to the dwindling daylight, though. Most of them, at least.

Which was why Alan was out here now. A couple of the storm shutters had refused to roll up this morning. Even from the inside Alan could see they were deeply dented, more deeply than he'd have thought possible from a bug attack, at least from any of the bugs he'd seen so far.

Which meant there might be something new under the new moon, something bigger than its hellish predecessors and consequently more dangerous to the little fortress Toad Hall had become. He coasted to a halt and stared as he rounded to the front.

The damage to the steel shutters was worse than he'd realized. They'd been scored by something sharp and heavy, with the weight and density of a steel spike.

But the remains of the rhododendrons under the shuttered windows bothered him more.

They'd been trampled flat.

Alan rolled across the grass for a closer look. These were old rhodos, maybe fifty years or better, with heavy trunks and sturdy branches, thick with healthy deep-green leaves through Ba's magical ministrations. Tough wood. Alan remembered that from the times he'd cut back the rhodos around his old house before it had burned down.

These hadn't been cut, though. The trunks and branches had been crushed, and their splinters pressed into the ground. Something awfully big and heavy—or a number of big and heavy somethings—had attacked these windows last night, banging and scraping at the shutters.

But they hadn't gotten in. That was the important thing.

As Alan pushed his left wheel forward and pulled the right backward to turn and roll back to the path, he saw the depression in the lawn. His stomach lurched. He'd been too intent on the shutters and the ruined rhodos to notice before. But from this angle you couldn't miss it.

The fresh spring grass, overdue now for a trimming, had been crushed in a wide swath that angled in from the front gate, curved around the willows, and led directly to the house. Alan tried to imagine what sort of creature could leave such a trail but all he could come up with was a thirty-foot bowling ball. With teeth, most likely. Lots of them.

He shuddered and rolled back to the path. Each night got a little rougher. Eventually Toad Hall's defenses would fail. It was inevitable. Alan prayed he'd be able to persuade Sylvia to move out before that happened, or that Glaeken would be able to assemble the pieces he needed to call for help.

Alan could feel it in his bones: They were all going to *need* help. Lots of it. And soon. Otherwise, if the Sapir curve was correct, they had two more day-times left. Then the light would die for the last time at three o'clock on Thursday afternoon. And the endless night would begin.

Abe's Place

The bugs had done their dirty work—with a vengeance.

During the night, entombed in all that concrete and locked in behind the triple-hatched entry chimney, Gia hadn't had a clue. But now, topside . . .

All the farmhouse windows had been smashed, and everything inside had been torn up. Gia had no emotional connection to the place, but still the devastation got to her.

"We ate breakfast here yesterday," she said, staring at the mindless wreckage of the kitchen.

Abe stepped in through the ruined door.

"The barn is worse. No eggs, just scattered feathers where the chickens used to be. And still no sign of my poor Parabellum."

"What about the cat?" Vicky said.

Abe shook his head. "I didn't see him." As Vicky's lower lip trembled and her eyes filled, Abe hurriedly added, "But barn cats are tough. He probably found a good hiding place."

He glanced at Gia and she knew what he was thinking: Not likely.

He nodded toward the rear of the house. "Let's take a walk to the ridge. I want to show you something."

"The hole?"

"Something else."

The hole was the same, but the valley had changed. The ground was torn up, the trees partially denuded, and . . .

Gia pointed at the linear mounds radiating from the hole like spokes on a wheel.

"What are those?"

"I don't know from lawns, but those look like mole hills."

Gia's skin crawled as she looked at them.

· "But if those are moles, they're as big as humans."

"Bigger even. But I don't think they're moles. More like worms, I'll bet. And this I hate to mention, but a lot of them are pointed this way."

Maui

Even the coffee tasted like fish.

Jack knew the water was pure—he'd watched Kolabati draw it from the cooler—but it still tasted fishy. Maybe because everything *smelled* fishy. The air was so thick with the odor of dead sea life he swore he could taste it when he breathed.

He was standing on the lanai, forcing the coffee down, looking out at the valley below and the great whirlpool spinning off Kahului. It would have been heart-stoppingly beautiful if not for the stench. Behind him, sounds of chopping, chipping, sawing, and hammering drifted through the door from the house's great room.

He thought about Gia and Vicky, hoping they had a quiet night, wishing he had a way to check up on them.

Kolabati joined him then, coffee cup in hand, and leaned on the railing to his right. She wore a bright flowered muumuu that somehow enhanced her figure instead of hiding it. Jack's eyes locked on her necklace. He tried to be casual but it wasn't easy. Half the reason for this hairy trip dangled a couple of feet away. All he had to do was reach out and—

"My silverswords are all dead," she said, looking down at a wilted garden beneath the deck. "The salt water's killed them. I'd hoped to see them bloom."

"I'm sorry."

She gestured with her cup toward the giant maelstrom.

"There's no point to it. It sucks water and fish down all day, then shoots it all miles into the air at night."

"The point," Jack said, remembering the gist of Glaeken's explanations, "is not to have a point. Except to mess with our minds, make us feel weak, impotent, useless. Make us crazy with fear and uncertainty, fear of the unknown."

Jack noticed when he said "crazy" Kolabati stole a quick glance over her shoulder at the house.

"And speaking of points," he said, "what's the point of Moki? How'd you get involved with a guy like that? He's not your type, Bati."

As far as Jack could see, Moki was nobody's type. The guy was not only out to lunch, but out to breakfast, dinner, and the midnight snack as well. A homicidal megalomaniac who believed he was a god, or at least possessed by one: Maui, the Polynesian Prometheus who brought fire to humanity and hoisted the Hawaiian Islands from the bottom of the sea with his fishing pole.

After last night's ceremony the four of them had returned to the house where Ba and Jack spent the night in the garage, the only place in the house secure from the bugs. Moki and Bati were never bothered by the creatures—more proof of Moki's divinity. He'd kept them up most of the night elaborating on his future plans for "Greater Maui" and the rest of the remaining Hawaiian Islands.

Running under it all Jack sensed a current of hatred and jealousy—aimed at him. Moki seemed to see Jack as a threat, a rival suitor for Kolabati's affections. Jack hadn't planned on any of this. He'd spent the morning wondering how he could use that jealousy to get to the kook's necklace. But so far, short of putting a bullet through his skull, he'd come up blank.

"How do you know my type?" Kolabati said, eyes flashing and nostrils flaring. "What do you know of me?"

Jack studied her face. Kolabati had changed. He wasn't sure how. Her wide, dark, almond-shaped eyes, her high cheekbones, full lips, and flawless mocha skin were the same as he remembered. Maybe it was her hair. She'd let it grow since he'd last seen her. It trailed long over her near shoulder and rustled in the sour wind like an ebony mane. But it wasn't the hair. Something else, something inside.

Good question, he thought. What *do* I know about her?

"I know you don't hang out too long with people who don't see things your way."

She turned and stared down at the valley.

"This is not the real Moki—or at least not the Moki who shared my life until a week ago."

Shared her life? Jack was about to make a crack about the ability of this over 150-year-old woman to share anything when he saw a droplet of moisture form in the corner of her eye, grow, and spill over the lid to run down her cheek.

A tear. A tear from Kolabati.

Jack was speechless. He turned and stared through the doorway where Moki feverishly worked like the madman he was. But on what? And didn't he ever sleep? He'd harangued them for hours, then he'd rushed to the upper floor where he'd gone to work on the shattered pieces of sculpture littering the great room, recutting them, fashioning a new, single giant work from the remnants.

Ba was in there with him now, sitting in a corner, sipping tea and watching him in silent fascination.

"He was wonderful," Kolabati said.

Jack looked at her again. The tear remained. Others joined it.

"You love him?"

She nodded. "I love who he used to be." She turned toward Jack, wiping her cheeks. "Oh, Jack, you would have loved him too. I only wish you'd known him then. He was gentle, he was so alive and so much a part of his world, these islands. A genius, a true genius who couldn't flaunt his brilliance because he took it for granted. He never tried to impress anyone, never tried to be anyone but Moki. And he wanted to be with me. *Me.* Nobody else. I was happy, Jack. I was in love. I thought I'd found an earthly Nirvana and I wanted it to last forever. And it could have, Jack. You know it could have."

He shook his head. "Nothing lasts forever." He reached out and touched her necklace. "Even with that."

"But so soon? We'd just begun."

He searched her face. Here was the difference. The seemingly impossible had happened. Kolabati, the cool, aloof, self-absorbed, ruthless Kolabati who had sent him out to kill her own brother, who had walked out with her own necklace as well as Kusum's and left Jack bleeding in a chair because he had refused her offer of near immortality . . . Kolabati Bahkti had fallen in love and it had changed her. Maybe forever.

Amazingly, she began to sob—deep, wrenching gasps of emotional pain that tore at Jack. He'd come here expecting to find the old, cold, calculating Kolabati and had been fully ready to deal with her. He wasn't prepared for the new model.

He resisted the impulse to take her in his arms. No telling what Moki-the-Unkillable might do if he saw that. So he settled for touching her hand.

"What can I do? What will fix it?"

"If only I knew."

"Maybe it's the necklace. Maybe the necklace is part of the problem— maybe it *is* the problem. Maybe if you take it off him—"

"And replace it with a fake?" Her eyes flashed as she dug into the pocket of her muumuu. She pulled out a necklace exactly like her own. "This one, perhaps?"

Since Kolabati was wearing one of the genuine necklaces, and Moki the other, this had to be Jack's fake.

He swallowed. "Where'd you get that?"

"From your duffel bag." Her eyes hardened. "Was that your plan? Steal my brother's necklace and replace it with a fake? It never occurred to you that I might have given it to someone else, did it?"

Time to bite the bullet, Jack thought. Let her know the whole story.

"Kusum's necklace isn't enough," he said, meeting her gaze. "We need both."

She gasped and stepped back, her hand clutching at her throat.

"Mine? You'd steal *mine*?"

"It wouldn't be stealing, exactly. I'd just be returning it to its original owner."

"Don't joke with me about this, Jack. The people who carved the necklaces have been dead for ages."

"I know. I'm not working for them. I'm working for the guy they stole the original metal from. He's still around. And he wants it back. All of it."

Kolabati's eyes widened as she studied him. "You're not joking, are you."

"You think I could make up a story like that, even if I tried?"

"All those years will rush back upon me without it, Jack. I'd die. You know that."

"I intended to ask you for it."

"And if I refused?"

He shrugged. "I was going to be very convincing."

Actually he'd had no firm plan in mind when he'd come here. Good thing too. He hadn't counted on Moki. Not in his wildest dreams had he counted on the likes of Moki.

Kolabati's hand still hovered protectively over her necklace. She couldn't seem to drag it away.

"You frighten me, Jack. You frighten me more than Moki."

"I know it sounds corny as hell, but the fate of the whole world depends on this guy Glaeken getting those two necklaces back and restoring them to their original form."

Kolabati gestured to the stinking valley, to the whirlpool beyond. "He can change all this? He can make everything as it was?"

"No. But he can stop the force that's making it this way, that's working to destroy everything we see here. You don't have it too bad here, Bati. This is really pretty decent because there aren't many people around. But back on the mainland, in the cities and towns, people are at each other's throats. Everyone's frightened, scared half to death. The best are holed up, hiding from the monsters by night and their fellow humans by day. And the worst are doing what they've always done. But it's the average Joes and Janes who are really scary. The ones who aren't paralyzed with fear are running amok in the streets, looting and burning and killing with the worst of them. You can do something to stop it, turn it all around."

"I don't believe you. It can't be that bad. I've lived more than a century and a half. I saw my parents shot down by an English officer, I witnessed the Sepoy rebellion in the 1850s, two world wars, the Bolshevik revolution, and worst of all, the atrocities in the Punjab, Indian killing Indian during the partition. You have no idea what I've seen."

"This is worse. The whole world's involved. And after sundown Thursday it'll be night everywhere, forever. There'll be nowhere to run. Unless you do something."

"Me." The word was spoken in a very small, faraway voice.

"You."

Jack let that sink in awhile, let her stare down at the island she seemed to love so much, let her breathe the reek of its slow death. And then he put the question to her. He'd never have considered asking the old Kolabati, the one he'd known in New York. But this new version, someone who'd loved a man, who loved this island, maybe this Kolabati could be reached.

"What do you say, Bati? I'm not asking you to take it off and hand it to me. But I am asking you to come back to New York and talk to Glaeken. He's the only guy on earth who's older than you. Hell, you're a newborn compared to him. You sit down with him and you'll believe."

She turned and leaned against the railing, staring through the door into the great room of her house.

"Let me think about that."

"There's no time to think."

"All right," she said slowly. "I'll come see this man. But that's all I promise you."

"That's all I'm asking." He felt his fatigued muscles begin to uncoil with relief. It was a start. "Now, about Moki's . . ."

She looked at him sharply.

"He's not going to die," Jack added quickly, "or even age appreciably if someone should manage to replace his real necklace with a look-alike. Who knows? Get it off him and maybe he'll revert to his old self."

Before Kolabati could answer, Moki's voice boomed from within the house.

"Bati! *Hele mai!* And bring your ex-lover. See what your god has fashioned!"

Kolabati rolled her eyes and started forward. Jack grabbed her arm, gently.

"What do you say?"

"I'll think about it."

She pulled her arm away and dropped the dummy necklace back into her pocket. Jack followed her.

And stopped inside the door, staring.

The great room had been transformed. All the wood and lava from the broken sculptures had been reshaped, combined, coalesced into a single huge assembly that stretched from wall to wall. And where he'd run out of sculpture remnants, Moki had smashed furniture and added pieces to the mix. He'd arranged assorted stained and bleached fragments so they appeared to spring from the wood paneling of the walls, forming four spokes in a giant lopsided wheel, weaving crooked paths toward a common center. A lava center. Moki had somehow joined all the red and black lava fragments—the gleam of wire, the dewy moisture of still-drying epoxy were visible within the irregular mass—into a new whole, a jagged, haphazard aggregate that had no coherent shape, no symmetry, no discernible intelligence to it, yet somehow looked menacing and implacably predatory.

Moki stood near the center, hands on hips, grinning like a caricature of Burt Lancaster in *The Crimson Pirate*.

"What do you think of Maui's masterpiece?"

Ba squatted in the far corner, a gaunt Buddha, silent, watching.

"It's . . . disturbing," Kolabati said.

"Yes!" He clapped his hands. "Excellent! Exactly what it is supposed to be! Disturbing. True art *should* disturb, don't you think? It should challenge all your comfortable assumptions, tip them over so you can see what crawls around on their underbellies."

"But what is it?" Jack said.

Moki's smile faltered, and for the first time since he'd arrived, Jack detected a hint of uncertainty in the man's eyes.

He hasn't the faintest idea what he's done.

"Why . . . it's a vision," he said, recovering. "A recurring one. It's plagued me for days. It's . . ." His eyes brightened with sudden inspiration. "It's Maui! Greater Maui! Yes! The four separate islands—Molokai, Lanai, Kahoolawe, and Maui itself—drawing back to where they belong—together. Forming one seamless mass at the center!"

Jack stared at the construct. This was no island or regrouping of islands. Too bizarre, too menacing. It was something else, but even the artist hadn't a clue as to what.

Moki grabbed Kolabati's hand. "Come. Maui is tired. He needs to rest before the ceremony tonight. And he needs his woman by his side." He stared at Jack, challenging him. "The woman who once loved you now loves a god. She can never go back. She will never want to. Isn't that true, Bati?"

Kolabati smiled and nodded. "Very true, my love."

Jack watched her carefully. Kolabati was not the type to allow herself to be pushed around like this. No one told this woman what to do.

As Moki led her away by the hand, she glanced back at Jack and patted the pocket of her muumuu. The one that bulged with the fake necklace.

Jack nodded. *That* was the Kolabati he knew.

"You kids play nice, now," he called after them.

He watched until they disappeared into the bedroom, then went over to where Ba squatted. He leaned against the wall next to him.

"What do you think, Big Guy? You've been watching the whole process. What's it look like to you?"

"It is evil."

Jack waited for Ba to elaborate, but that was all he was going to say. So Jack walked around it, ducking under the spokes, crouching, stretching up on tiptoe, looking for a fresh perspective, an angle that would reveal the work's secret. But the more he looked, the more unsettled he became. Why? Nothing but an assemblage of wood and lava. One that looked like nothing in particular. If anything, it resembled Da Vinci's Vitruvian Man—except the man here was some sort of headless amoebic embryo.

He had an inescapable sense that more than Moki was at work here. Jack couldn't help but feel that the sculptor's madness had tapped into something outside himself, outside everything humans knew, and he'd built a crude model of it.

And Ba was right. Ba had said it all.

Whatever it was, it was evil.

Dinu Pass, Romania

"Look down, Nick. At the ground. Do you see anything?"

Night had come. So had the bugs. The air was dense with them. From the base of the keep's tower, Bill watched their bizarre and varied forms buzzing, darting, drifting in the air a mere half dozen feet away.

But though they stood in the opening, he and Nick were safe. The bugs kept their distance. As soon as darkness fell, Bill had guided Nick back into the stone depths to where they now stared into the hungry night.

"Come on, Nick. Take a good look. Do you see any of that glow you saw last night?"

He nodded and pointed straight ahead. "There."

A slow change had come over Nick during the day. He seemed more alert, more responsive to the world around him. Were the effects of his descent into the hole wearing off?

"All right, then." Bill's insides were coiled tight. "I guess this is it."

He turned to the baker's dozen of villagers armed with chairs and torches, waiting behind him in the tower base. The thirteenth was Alexandru, standing off to the side.

Through Alexandru, Bill had explained that the red-haired man who'd come here in 1941 was still alive and in America, that if he could recover some pieces of the "magic sword" that had shattered here on these stones, he might be able to close up the hole out there in the pass and bring back the sun. They'd helped him search around the base of the tower this afternoon but their efforts had been no more fruitful than his own in the morning. They'd have to go out at night.

Bill had expected to be laughed off as a madman, or rudely rebuffed at the very least. Instead the villagers had conferred, then agreed to help him. The women had begun wicker-weaving while the men set about making torches. Now they waited, dressed in multiple layers of clothing, wicker armor on their thighs and lower legs, heavy gloves, sheepskin hats and vests. They looked ready for an arctic blizzard, but they'd be facing a different sort of storm.

Bill nodded to the men. It was time. Their faces remained expressionless, but he noticed glances pass between them, saw them begin to breathe more heavily. They were scared, and rightly so. A perfect stranger had asked them to put their lives on the line, to perform the equivalent of wading into a piranha-infested river with only a crab net and a spear for protection. If they turned and headed back up the stone stairs now, he wouldn't blame them.

But they didn't. They filed out through the opening with their shields and torches raised, forming a shallow semicircle of protection into which Bill and Nick stepped. And then, just as they'd rehearsed it inside the keep, they advanced as a group, the end members closing the circle behind Bill and Nick as they moved away from the tower wall.

The bugs assaulted in a wave. The men in the circle around him began to cry out in fear and revulsion as they blocked the swooping creatures with the raised chairs and shields while thrusting at them with their torches. To the accompaniment of buzzing wings and sizzling bug flesh, they inched forward.

Bill crouched next to Nick, his arm over his shoulders, keeping his head down as they moved. He shouted in his left ear.

"Where, Nick? Show me *where!*"

Nick searched the rocky ground, saying nothing. Bill had a sudden, awful fear that Nick might not be able to see the glow because of the torches the circle of villagers carried. If daylight obscured it, would torchlight do the same?

As if in answer to Bill's unasked question, Nick said, "Here's one."

He was pointing at a spot two inches in front of his left shoe.

Bill shouted to the group to stop, pulled out his flashlight and began pawing through the stones with his free hand. He felt the circle constrict around him as the villagers were beaten back into a tighter knot by the bugs. But under the stones he found only dirt.

"There's nothing here, Nick!"

But Nick kept pointing. "There, there, there."

"Where, dammit?"

"The glow. There."

Nick sounded so sure. Out of sheer desperation, Bill began digging through the moist silt. It didn't seem likely, but maybe rains over the decades had buried some of the fragments and the glow was filtering up through the ground. The trip had been a bust so far and they didn't have much time out here, not with the increasing ferocity of the bug attack, so he was willing to try almost—

Bill's fingers scraped on something hard and slim with rough edges, something that felt nothing like sand or stone. He forced his fingers down into the silt, worked them around the object, under it, then pulled it free.

A rusty, dirty, jagged piece of metal lay in his palm. He held it up.

"Is this it, Nick?"

"Can't you see the glow?"

Bill turned the object over and over in his hands. No glow. Just a broken, pitted piece of metal.

"No. Are there more?"

"Of course." He pointed to Bill's left. "Right there."

Bill began to dig again. One of the men shouted something to him. Bill didn't know the language but the meaning was clear.

Hurry!

Bill placed his flashlight on the stones and used the first piece to help dig after the second, throwing dirt in all directions. He heard a faint clink of metal on metal and was reaching into the hole to feel for it when a chew wasp darted between the legs of one of the men and sank its needle teeth into his arm. Without thinking, Bill lashed at it with the metal fragment in his hand.

The flash nearly blinded him for an instant. He blinked, and when the purple afterimage faded, he saw the chew wasp flopping on the stones and gnashing its teeth in waning fury, a deep, blackened, smoking wound in its back.

Bill stared at the metal fragment in his hand. Whatever power this blade had once held was not completely gone, not by a long shot.

He threw himself into probing deeper into the bottom of the second hole. He found a second piece of metal almost immediately and held it up.

"How about this one, Nick? Quick! Does it glow?"

Nick nodded. "Yes."

"Great. All right now. Where's the—"

Then one of the villagers screamed and fell backward, landing across Bill's back and nearly knocking him flat. Bill thought the bugs might have broken through his defenses and latched onto him en masse, but he was wrong.

This was worse.

Something had the man by the ankle, something uncoiling out of the darkness like a long black rope, but alive, tapered, twisting, and powerful. His fall had broken the circle and now the bugs were inside, attacking from within as well as without. The men tried to regroup but wavered as the snakelike thing began to drag their friend from their midst. Some bent to grab his arms to pull him back but the bugs were immediately upon them and they had to let him go to protect themselves. Bill watched in horror as the man was dragged screaming into the darkness, the bugs swarming him, ripping at him.

Another inky snake darted through the night and snared a second villager. And as he was pulled crying to his doom, a third creature caught Nick and pulled him off his feet. Nick made no sound as he landed on the rocks. Bill wrapped an arm around his chest but the snake began to drag them both away. Bill sensed something huge and dark looming in the blackness beyond the reach of the torchlight and realized then that these weren't snakes but the long, smooth tentacles of a single monstrous creature. Glaeken's offhanded comment floated through his mind . . .

The bigger ones tend to be slow; it will take them a while to get here, but they'll get here.

Bill knew from the inexorable pull it exerted on Nick that he couldn't resist its strength.

In desperation he reached down to the tentacle and slashed at it with the sword fragments. Another blinding, sizzling flash and suddenly the tentacle had uncoiled and its severed tip was writhing and flopping furiously about like a beheaded snake.

The villagers were now in complete disarray, stumbling about, swinging their torches and shields wildly.

"Back!" Bill cried. "Back to the keep."

He pulled Nick to his feet and half carried him over the rocky ground toward the base of the tower, flailing about in the air with the metal shards, clearing a path through the bugs. Finally they made it, trailing some of the villagers, just ahead of a few others, stumbling through the opening into the blessedly empty air of the keep. Bitten, bleeding, burned, they collapsed into panting heaps on the granite floor; compared to the rough stones outside, its smooth surface felt almost soft. Only the elderly Alexandru stood, exactly where they had left him.

"Where are the others?" he said, his eyes ranging through their ranks. "What happened to Gheorghe? And Ion? And Michael and Nicolae?"

Bill lifted his head and counted. Only eight of the dozen villagers who'd gone out with him had made it back. He went to the door and looked out. Four torches burned on the stones of the gorge. The men who had carried them were nowhere in sight. Behind him, the survivors began to weep and he felt his own throat tighten. Four brave men had sacrificed themselves so a stranger could dig up some chunks of old metal.

Bill looked down at the fragments in his hand, then again at the four sputtering torches.

These had damn well better be worth it.

Outside he heard something huge dragging its enormous weight over the rubble of the gorge.

Manhattan

Carol watched the light fade from the sky over the darkened city and thought of how lucky they were to have generators here. She thought of Bill. He'd been an integral part of each thought since he'd left yesterday morning, but especially now, with dark coming.

"Where is he?" she said to Glaeken.

He was passing by, carrying an empty tray from Magda's room. He paused beside her.

"Still in Romania, I should think."

She glanced at her watch. Almost five here. That meant it was almost midnight over there. Almost Wednesday.

"But he should have been back by now."

"*Could* have been back, perhaps, but as for should . . ." He shook his head. "I don't think so." He reached out and gently laid a scarred hand on her shoulder. "Don't worry yet. Not until tomorrow. If he's not back by this time tomorrow, then worry. You'll have company then—I'll be worrying with you."

He left her and headed toward the kitchen.

Carol continued to stare at the darkening city, wondering if Bill was alive, on land, or in the air. If only she knew.

Dinu Pass, Romania

With the two metal shards settled deep in his pocket and Nick strapped into the passenger seat, Bill was ready to go. The villagers had nailed a board across the land rover's broken rear window. Bill hoped it blocked the bugs half as well as it blocked his view.

"I don't want to go."

Bill glanced at Nick and was shocked to see tears running down his cheeks. "Nick . . . ?"

"I like it here. I feel . . . better here. Please let me stay."

"Nick, I can't leave you. I've got to go back and we may need you there. But once this is all over, I'll bring you back."

He sobbed. "Do you promise, Father Bill?"

Bill felt a sob building in his own throat. He gripped Nick's hand.

"Yeah, Nicky. I promise."

He felt miserable but hid it as he waved to Alexandru and the others.

"Tell them I'll be back," he told the old man in German. "After this is all over, after the holes are closed and the monsters are gone, I'll be back. And I'll tell the world of the bravery of your people."

Alexandru waved but did not smile. Tears rimmed his eyes. Bill shared his grief, not only for the dead but for Alexandru's little community. A village atrophying and dying as was his could ill afford to lose four of its most vital men.

"I'll be back," he said again. "I won't forget you."

And he meant it. If he survived this, if he was alive to do so, he'd be back.

He threw the vehicle into first and started out the gate onto the causeway. The bugs swarmed him. He was halfway across when the headlights picked up the first tentacle. It lay stretched lengthwise along the planks and lifted its tapered tip at Bill's approach, as if watching him, or catching his scent.

Bill stopped and squinted into the darkness as other tentacles pushed forward to join the first. Soon the causeway was acrawl with them. He found the high-beam button on the floor to the left of the clutch and kicked it.

He gasped and instinctively pressed himself back in his seat when he saw what waited at the far end. The light from his high beams reflected off a huge, smooth, glistening, featureless black mass, thirty feet high and at least a hundred feet across. He looked for eyes or a mouth but could find none. Just slimy-looking blackness. A huge sluglike creature with tentacles.

And those tentacles were reaching for him, stretching closer.

Bill looked for a way out, a way to get around it, but its massive bulk blocked the end of the causeway. Even if he could run the land rover over the tentacles, he'd end up against the immovable wall of the thing's flank.

The tip of one of the tentacles suddenly appeared at the end of the hood. It coiled around the hood ornament and pulled. Bill shifted into reverse and backed up a dozen feet. The tentacles inched after him.

Trapped, dammit! Trapped until morning!

He pounded the steering wheel in impotent rage and undiluted frustration. He had the shards that he'd come for and he couldn't get them back to Glaeken, couldn't even set off for his return trip to Ploiesti until dawn.

More time wasted. And another night without seeing Carol. He wanted to be with her. Every moment was precious. How many did they have left?

Using the side mirror, he carefully backed the vehicle through the gates, then sat behind the wheel and swallowed the pressure that built in his chest as he stared out at the night. He felt like crying.

"We're back?" Nick said, smiling. "Oh, I'm so glad we're back."

WFPW-FM

FREDDY: Jo's catching some much-needed Zs, man, but I'm still here with you. The phones are down and our cable's out. And hey, it's time for you to get back inside. It's 4:48. Get your butts to safety right now. Ten minutes of light left.

<cue: "Baby, Please Don't Go">

New Jersey Turnpike

By nightfall Hank was exhausted, but he would allow himself no sleep.

How could he? With darkness the drainpipe had come alive. First the sibilant stirrings, echoing softly around him, ballooning to a cacophony of hard-pointed mandibles clicking a hungry counterpoint to countless chitinous feet scraping against the concrete; then the sinuous shapes, faint and vague in the rising moonlight slanting through the grate, undulating toward him from left and right, sloshing through the water below, crawling along the ceiling directly above, the thinnest of them as thick as his upper arm, the largest as big around as his thigh, ignoring him as they slid by, weaving over, under, and around each other with a hideous languid grace that seemed to defy gravity, blackening the pale gray of the concrete with Gordian masses of twisting bodies, blotting out the moon as they nosed against the closed grate.

He heard a metallic scrape, a screech, then a clank as the grate fell back onto the pavement above. A sudden change came over the millipedes. Their languor evaporated, replaced by a hungry urgency as they thrashed and clawed at each other in a mad frenzy to join the night-hunt on the surface.

Moments later, the last of them had squeezed through. Once again Hank was alone with the moonlight.

No . . . not alone. Something coming. Something big. He knew without looking what it was. A few minutes later he saw her huge pincered head rise and hover above him, swaying.

Not again! Shit-shit-shit! Not again!

He'd worked since dawn on regaining control of his limbs, and for most of the day it had seemed a hopeless task. No matter how he concentrated, how he strained, his body simply would not respond. But he'd kept at it, and as the light had started to fail, he'd begun to achieve some results. He'd noticed twitches in his arms and legs, in his abdominal muscles. Either the toxin was wearing off or he was overcoming it. It didn't matter which. He was regaining control—that was what mattered.

But all his efforts would be for nada if the queen dosed him again.

She made no move, simply hovered there with her head hanging over him. Did she suspect anything?

Get the fuck away!

He'd spent the entire day willing his muscles to move, now he was begging them to be still. One twitch, one tremor, one tiny tic, and she'd ram her proboscis into his gut again and put him back to square one.

She watched him for what seemed like forever, then she began to move—

No!

—her head lowering toward his belly—

NO!

—and past him. She arched over him, her hard little feet brushing across the skin of his abdomen. He could feel nothing but he saw his abdominal muscles twitch and roll with revulsion and prayed she wouldn't notice.

She didn't. Her near-endless length finally cleared him and she wound her way up through the drain opening and into the night.

At last—time for action.

He strained his arms and legs upward as if fighting against steel manacles. To his delight he saw the muscles bulge with the effort. His fingers didn't move, didn't close into the rebellious fists he willed for them, but he watched the veins in the undersides of his forearms swell as blood coursed into the resistant muscles, watched his abdominals ripple and swell around the wound as he tried to sit up.

But nothing was happening. His veins and arteries continued to surge, stretching against the envelope of skin, his abdomen rippled like the Atlantic in a hurricane, but no sign of voluntary movement, only chaos.

And then his eyes snapped to the wound below his navel. Something moved there. Something wriggled within it. This morning's scream built again in his unresponsive throat as two slim black pincers, each no more than an inch long, poked into the air. A multi-eyed head, deep brown and gleaming, followed. It paused, glanced around, fixed Hank with its cold black gaze, then dragged its long, many-legged length from the wound with a crinkling *slurp*. Another identical creature quickly followed. Then another.

Hank's once quiescent and unresponsive body was moving now with a will of its own, writhing, bucking, convulsing, rocking up and down, back and forth in its webbed hammock as his veins and arteries bulged past the limits of their tensile strength and ruptured, freeing more wriggling, pincered, millipedic forms.

Something snapped within Hank's mind then. He could almost hear the foundations of his sanity crack and give way. And that was good. He welcomed the collapse.

For it brought a whole new perspective. Everyone aboveground was dying. Dying and decomposing. Not Hank. No way. Hank was alive and would stay alive through these, his children.

Parenthood.

If only I could cry!

He'd never wanted children, but now it had happened. His children. He'd considered the Kickers his children—after all, hadn't he fathered the movement? But these were true offspring. They'd grown within him. Fed off him. Made him part of them. He'd go on living through them while everybody else—including the Kicker cop captain and his two renegade underlings—died.

If only I could laugh!

He watched with pride as dozens more of his children broke from the cramped confines of his body to swarm and crawl with wild abandon over his skin. So good to see them free and moving about, stretching their slender, foot-long bodies, gaining strength before heading to the surface and joining the great hunt.

If only I could cheer!

Some of them tangled and began to rake and spear each other with their pincers.

No fighting, children. Save it for topside.

Just then two more broke from the sides of his throat, glistening with blood from the vessels through which they'd been traveling. They reared up and faced him, swaying back and forth like cobras before a snake charmer.

Yes, my children, he wanted to tell them, I am your daddy and I'm terribly proud of you. I want you to—

They darted forward without warning, each burying a pincered head hungrily into his eyes.

No! he wanted to say. I'm your daddy! Don't blind Daddy! How can he watch you grow if you eat his eyes?

But they were naughty children and didn't listen. They kept burrowing inward, deeper and deeper.

If only I could scream!

Maui

Night was falling.

Jack stood in the great room and stared again at Moki's giant sculpture. The closer darkness came, the more repellent he found it. The stench of rotting fish from outside made it worse. Its foulness urged him to smash it back into its component fragments.

He'd driven down to the airfield earlier. Frank and his plane had survived the night. Jack had called Gia on the shortwave. She'd said everything was okay but he'd sensed a new tension in her voice. She denied any problems but during the grisly ride back he couldn't get it out of his head that she was worried about something.

He turned now at a sound behind him and saw Kolabati emerging from the bedroom. Alone. Finally. Her dark eyes flashed with excitement as she strolled toward Jack. And as she passed she pressed something into his hand—warm, heavy, metallic. He glanced down.

The necklace.

"Moki?" he said.

She motioned him to follow her to the lanai.

"He's wearing your fake," she whispered when they'd stopped at the railing. "And he's still . . . ?"

Bitter anguish dulled the animation in her eyes as she nodded. "Still the same."

"I'm sorry."

"Put it on," she whispered, touching the hand that held the necklace.

Jack thrust it into his pocket. "Better not. He'll notice."

"Put it on. You'll need it. Trust me."

Jack shook his head. "I'll be okay."

He looked out over the darkening valley. In the ocean beyond it he saw the white water of the whirlpool fading to gray. The maelstrom was slowing. Soon the geyser would begin and the air once again would fill with dying fish and hungry bugs.

But he still had time to make it to Kahului and take to the air.

He turned back to Kolabati. "What about the rest of it? What about you? Are you coming back to New York with me?"

"Do you trust me, Jack?" she said. Her gaze drilled into him. The answer seemed very important to her.

"Yes," he said, not completely sure of the truth here, but saying it anyway.

He sensed the new, improved Kolabati could be trusted further than the old, but how much further he couldn't say. He wasn't quite ready to stake his life on it.

"Good. Then I'll return to New York."

Jack couldn't resist hugging her. She truly had changed.

"Thank you, Bati. You don't know what this means to me, to everyone."

"Don't get the wrong idea, Jack," she said levelly. "It's good to have your arms around me again, but I'm not giving up my necklace. I have no intention of doing that. I'm going back to New York just to talk to this ancient man you've told me about. That and nothing more."

"That's fine. That's all I ask. I'll leave the rest up to Glaeken. I know he can work something out with you. But let's get moving. We haven't got much time."

"Not so fast. There's still tonight's ceremony."

Jack pushed her to arm's length but Kolabati clutched his forearms, refusing to let him go.

"Ceremony? You're going to let him kill another—?"

And then Jack remembered how last night Moki had let the Niihauan stab him first. Was that what she wanted? To see Moki die? Did she hate him that much for going crazy on her? He looked into her eyes and couldn't read them.

He would never understand this woman. Fine. But could he trust her? Her allegiances seemed as mercurial as her moods.

"That's my condition. After the ceremony, I'll return to New York. You have my word."

"Bati?" a voice called from inside.

And then Moki stepped out onto the lanai. His eyes flared when he saw the two of them touching. He took Kolabati by the arm and pulled her away.

"Come. We'll start the ceremony early tonight." He glared at Jack. "I'm especially looking forward to this one."

As Kolabati followed him into the house, she looked back at Jack and mouthed three words: *Wear . . . the . . . necklace.*

When they debarked from the Isuzu, Moki turned to Jack and jabbed his index finger at his chest.

"We came early because it will be *you* who faces Maui tonight."

Jack smiled. "I don't think so."

"If you can defeat me in the ceremony, you may have her. Otherwise she stays with me and you return to America."

Jack noticed how Moki had said "America" instead of "the mainland." Apparently his island had seceded from the union, at least in Moki's mind.

Jack looked at Kolabati. She returned his stare coolly.

"So . . . this is what you meant by 'after the ceremony.' Swell."

She nodded.

Moki gestured to the crater's edge. "Come. It's time."

Jack hesitated. This was happening too fast, and none of it in his plan. He didn't like surprises, and this was a particularly ugly one. Kolabati had known about it before when they were whispering on the lanai. Had she cooked it up with Moki, or was this all his idea?

At least Jack had one of the necklaces . . .

Or did he?

What was that around Moki's neck? Jack's fake, or the real thing? He cursed himself for not checking the one Kolabati had given him more closely. It didn't feel any different, and if he remembered correctly from years ago, the necklace had caused an unpleasant tingle the first time he'd touched it. But that sensation had dissipated after he'd worn it for a while. Was that why he felt nothing when he touched it now? Or was there nothing to feel because it was the fake?

"What's the matter?" Moki said, his grin broadening. "Afraid like your Asian friend?"

"Your ceremony sickened him last night."

"Perhaps you should have stayed behind with him—or better yet, left the island."

"I promised someone to get him back safely."

"Take off your shirt and follow me," Moki said, then turned and started up to the crater's edge.

Jack followed, removing his shirt as he went. The cold air raised and then flattened gooseflesh on his skin. He tossed his shirt to Kolabati as he passed. Her dark, almond eyes widened when she saw no necklace around his neck.

What had she wanted to do? Rattle Moki by letting him see that Jack wore a necklace exactly like his? Uh-uh. He wasn't playing her games.

She frowned at the three wide scars running diagonally across his chest. "Are those from—?"

"Yeah. Mementos from one of your pets."

He welcomed the heat from Haleakala's fires when they reached the ridge. Moki stopped and faced him. In the orange light he looked like a grinning demon as he produced two knives with slim, six-inch blades. The flames from below glinted off their polished surfaces. He handed one to Jack, wooden handle first. As Jack gripped it, a chorus of shouting erupted from below. He turned and saw the Niihauans approaching, angrily waving their arms.

"I was afraid of this," Moki said, sighing like an indulgent father watching his unruly children. "That's why I brought you up here early tonight. They want one of their own to defeat me, not some *malihini*. I'll have to tell them not to worry. They'll get their turn."

Moki stepped between the Niihauans and the crater rim. He spread his arms wide and spoke to them. Jack couldn't hear what he said over the roar of the inferno below, but finally they stepped back and waited.

"Now!" Moki said, returning. "Let's get on with it." He put his hands on his hips and puffed up his chest. "You strike first."

"First take off the necklace."

"Stop stalling. Is this the brave Repairman Jack Bati told me about?"

"Just 'Jack,' okay?"

"I think you're a coward."

"You won't take it off?"

"My necklace is not a subject for discussion. It is part of me. It will remain with me until I die. Which shall be never."

"Okay," Jack said slowly, "since we're on the subject of courage, let's give ourselves a real test: Each of us will pierce his *own* heart."

Moki stared at him with wide eyes. "You mean . . . I will plunge my knife into my chest and you will do the same into yours?"

"You got it. Simultaneously. It's one thing to stab somebody else, but it takes a *god* to stab himself."

Moki's grin widened. "I believe you are right. You are a worthy rival, Repairman Jack. I'll be sorry to see you die."

Not as sorry as I'll be if Kolabati has suckered me.

Moki positioned his knife over his chest, the point indenting the scarred area just to the left of the breastbone. Jack did the same. His sweaty palms slipped on the handle. The touch of the point sent a chill straight through to the organ beating barely an inch beneath it. It picked up its tempo in response.

This had to work.

"Ready?" Jack said. "On three. One . . . two . . ." He shouted the last number. *"Three!"*

Jack watched as Moki rammed the blade deep into his chest, saw his torso hunch, his grin vanish, his features constrict with sudden agony, watched his eyes fill with shock, horror, rage, betrayal as the sick realization of what had just happened to him filtered through the haze of pain.

He looked down at the knife protruding from his chest. Blood welled up against the hilt and ran down his skin. Then he looked at Jack's blade, still poised over his chest. His lips worked.

"You . . . didn't . . ."

"*You're* the crazy one, pal. Not me."

Moki glanced over to where Kolabati stood in the flame-flickered darkness. The hurt in his eyes was unsoundable. Jack almost felt sorry for him, until he remembered the brave Niihauan who hadn't had a chance against him last night. Jack followed his gaze and saw Kolabati's dismayed expression.

Sudden pain seared his chest. He staggered back and saw Moki go down on his knees, blood pumping from the slit in his chest, his bloody knife free in his hand. And across Jack's chest—a deep gash, bisecting the rakoshi scars. Moki had pulled his own knife from his wound and slashed Jack.

Jack pressed his hand against the gash but it had already stopped bleeding. The pain, too, was gone. And as he watched in amazement, the wound edges closed and began to knit.

He looked up and saw Moki watching too. Moki reached a bloody hand up to the metal encircling his neck. Ashen-faced now, he looked at Jack's unadorned throat, his eyes pleading for an explanation. He couldn't speak, but he could move his lips.

They said: *How?*

Jack pulled up the left cuff of his jeans to show where he'd wound the true necklace around his ankle.

"Just because they call it a necklace doesn't mean you have to wear it around your neck."

Moki pitched forward on his face, twitched, shuddered, then lay still.

Jack looked at the blade in his hand and tossed it onto the hardened lava beside Moki. Another victory for Rasalom, another talented human gone mad, and now dead.

Suddenly Jack felt exhausted, empty. Must it have ended like this? Couldn't he have found another way? Was the mad darkness in the air seeping into him as well? Or had he always carried a piece of it within? Was that what he felt twisting and thrashing against the walls of the cage he'd built for it?

Shouts made him turn. The Niihauans were charging up the slope. Jack backed away, unsure of their intent. But they ignored him, rushing directly to Moki's body. They prayed by it, then lifted him by his hands and feet and tossed his remains into Haleakala's fires.

As the others began to pray, the chief turned to Jack.

"Haleakala," he said, beaming. "The House of the Sun. Now that the false Maui is dead, the sun will return to the path that the true Maui taught it."

"When?" Jack said.

"Tomorrow. Tomorrow, you will see."

"I hope so," Jack said. He turned toward Kolabati. "All we've got to do is get back to the house and pick up Ba and—"

Kolabati was gone.

Jack spun this way and that, searching the darkness. Not a sign of her.

The Isuzu was still parked down the slope but no trace of her. He searched the area but all he found was his shirt, lying on the lava where she'd been standing. He pulled it on and hopped into the car.

Shit. She must have taken off on foot while he was listening to the old chief. Same old Kolabati. She'd lied to him. Should he have expected any less?

Me, of all people.

He'd spent most of his life lying. He mentally kicked himself for believing she'd changed. But she'd been so convincing. Had she ever had any intention of coming back to New York with him?

That's what you get for playing by the rules.

Maybe he and Ba simply should have tied up Moki and taken his necklace, then ripped Kolabati's from her throat and left her to die of old age in a few hours. Not that it hadn't occurred to him, yet everything within him balked at the plan. But maybe this hadn't been the time for niceties. Too much at stake.

He picked his way downhill, driving as quickly as he dared, while scanning the road ahead in the headlights and as far to each side as he could see in the dark. Nothing. Nothing moving but the wind. As he wound down from the crest, the wind abated and the fish and seawater began to rain from the sky, narrowing vision even further. An occasional bug began to harass the Isuzu.

Finally he came to the house. The lights were on and the generator was running, just as they'd been an hour ago. Jack leapt out and ran inside, stepping over a thrashing tuna along the way. Not many bugs around at the moment, and those seemed to be ignoring him. The necklace?

Once inside he ran through the halls, shouting Kolabati's name, and Ba's too.

Had to find her. Uncertainty gnawed at him. What if she hadn't returned to the house? What if she was hiding somewhere out on the hillside? He'd never find her.

And where was Ba?

He took the stairs to the upper floor, to the great room, but lurched to a stop when he heard the sound. Ahead, bleeding down the hall from the great room, a buzz, the unmistakable sound of oversize diaphanous wings, hundreds of them, beating madly.

He wanted to turn and run but forced himself to stand fast. Something about the buzzing . . . not wild and frenzied . . . calmer, smoother, almost . . . placid.

He stepped forward. He had to see what was going on. From back here he could see only the front end of the room. The lone lamp that still functioned gave off enough light for him to make out the details. What he saw sent his skin crawling.

Bugs . . . the great room was full of them, *mobbed* with them. They obscured the walls, perched on the furniture, floated in the air. All kinds of
bugs, from hovering chew wasps to drifting men-of-war, and all facing the
same direction, away from the smashed windows, toward the interior of the
room. Jack's legs urged him to get the hell out of here, but he had to see what
held them so spellbound.

He dropped to his knees and inched forward. The bugs remained oblivious to him. He stretched out on the bare floor and craned his neck around the
edge of the entryway to bring the rest of the room into view.

More bugs. So tightly packed he could barely see through the crush. Then
a gust of wind sluiced through the windows, undulating the hovering mass
enough for Jack to catch a look at the center of the great room.

They all faced the sculpture, Moki's final work—the only object in the
room on which the bugs had not perched. Its long, arching wooden spokes lay
bare for their entire length, from where they sprang from the walls to the jagged, unwieldy aggregate of black and red lava fragments at their center. The
bugs hovered about it, every one of them faced toward the center like rapt
churchgoers in silent benediction.

And the lava center . . . it pulsed with an unholy yellow light, slowly, as if
in time with the beat of a massive, hidden heart.

A single glimpse and then Jack's view was obscured again. But that
glimpse had been enough to break him out in a sweat and send him sliding
back along the floor. Something about that sculpture, the way it glowed, the
reverence of the bugs, the entire scene disturbed him on a level too deep to
comprehend or understand. Something within him, not from his personal experience, but some sort of racial memory, a warning carved on his hindbrain
or encoded in his genes, flooded him with circulating fear, leaving him unable
to react in any way but flight.

And when he was far enough down the hall, he rose to his feet and ran
around a corner where he stopped, panting. He resented the dread crawling under his skin. He prided himself on his ability to govern his fear, channel it, use
it. Now it was nearly out of control. He closed his eyes and took deep breaths,
willing himself to be calm. Half a minute of that and he was in control again.
But his fingers still trembled on their own in the adrenaline aftermath.

He moved toward the stairs—where he found Ba. And a woman struggling
in his iron grip.

Jack shook his head. "Bati . . . some things never change."

Ba had stayed behind in case something like this happened—or if Jack
didn't make it back.

"I was going back," she said through clenched teeth. "But *my* way!"

"I don't think you can get back, unless it's with us."

With her free hand she reached behind her neck and unclasped the necklace, then held it out to Jack.

"Take it then."

Jack blinked. "What?"

"And while you're at it," she said, tapping the center of her forehead, "put a bullet right here."

"Bati—" He didn't know what to say.

"You'd rather watch me die slowly?"

Damn her. Always manipulating. She knew he wouldn't shoot her, and knew he couldn't sit and watch her rot.

To Ba, he said, "Let her go." To Kolabati: "Put that back on, and get in the car. You can decide after you've met Glaeken, but you *are* coming with us."

"Yes," Ba said. "We must leave. I fear we might already be too late."

"Too late for what?"

A tortured look flickered across his features, all the more startling because of their usual waxy impenetrability.

"I do not know. I only know I must return to the Missus."

"Okay, Big Guy. We're on our way."

They escorted Kolabati to the Isuzu and put her in the passenger seat with Jack behind her where he could keep an eye on her. He wasn't letting her out of his sight.

They weathered the cascade of fish bouncing off the hood and roof as the car swerved through the downhill switchbacks. When Ba finally hit pavement he picked up speed. The wheels skidded on dead fish and clumps of wet seaweed.

"Easy, Ba. If we crack up, we may never get back to the plane, and then this whole trip will be for nothing. If it's not already."

"I must get back to the Missus. Quickly. She needs me."

Jack studied his grim, intent features in the dashboard glow. Ba was scared too. But not of bugs. Scared for his adopted family. Why? Why now? What was happening back there?

WEDNESDAY

In the Still of the Night

WFPW-FM

> **FREDDY:** It's a minute after midnight. A little over nine hours till the light.
> **JO:** We're almost halfway home. Hang in there, man.

Monroe, Long Island

Alan felt like a vampire.

Why not? He was living like one. Up all night, sleeping when he could during the light. Reminded him of his days as an intern. Thirty-six hours straight without a wink hadn't been at all unusual. But he was older now, and the stress of the nights—the insane paradiddles on the storm shutters, the incessant gnawing at the outer walls—carried over into the dwindling daytime, keeping his naps fitful and restless.

He was exhausted, plain and simple. But he couldn't let Sylvia know. She was a wreck as it was. The only time she got any rest herself was when she could curl up in the basement with Jeffy and Mess and Phemus, secure in the knowledge that Alan was patrolling the upper reaches of Toad Hall.

He was just finishing one of those patrols now, wheeling through the first-floor halls, checking the candles, replacing the ones that were guttering into glowing puddles. The power had failed around midday. He'd thought it might be just a local failure but the radio said LIPA was off-line for good. Another time it might have been romantic. Knowing what was outside, straining to get in, made it anything but.

So now with the midnight rounds completed and fresh candles flickering in every room, Alan settled himself down in the TV room and turned on the radio. Strange how a little adversity could change your habits. A week ago he wouldn't have thought twice about leaving the radio playing while he'd made his rounds. Now, with the power out and batteries scarce, he didn't leave it on a moment longer than necessary.

Jo and Freddy were still hanging in there, God bless 'em. Their voices were ragged, sometimes they were completely incoherent—their fatigue enhanced by a little herb, perhaps—as they broadcasted in shifts; their signal seemed at times like it was generated by a collection of frantic, wheel-spinning gerbils, but they weren't giving in to the fear. Neither was a fair share of their remaining listeners.

And neither was Alan.

Only problem was they didn't play doo-wop. They played good stuff, some new but mostly so-called "classic rock." As far as Alan was concerned, the real classic stuff had been sung on street corners—with the bass vocal and popping fingers for rhythm, and close, soaring, three- and four-part harmonies telling the story. That was where it all began. Some great stuff had come out of the sixties, and even the seventies, but the heart of it all, the *classic* end of the music, had begun in '55 and tapered into the sixties until the Brits began reinterpreting the music.

"Eight Miles High" came on. Alan could live with that. The Byrds knew their harmony—even if it was two-part masquerading as three-part—and he was losing himself in McGuinn's Coltranesque solo when he heard an unfamiliar sound from the front hall. He turned off the radio.

Splintering wood.

He pulled the tooth-studded billy from the pouch behind his backrest, laid it in his lap, and wheeled toward the front of the house. As soon as he entered the foyer he saw the problem. After nights of constant effort, the chew wasps finally had managed to rip off the metal weather strip from the bottom of the front door and were now busily at work gnawing rat holes at the floor line. Sharp-toothed lower jaws were visible in two spots, sawing relentlessly at the wood, gouging off pieces, building piles of splinters.

Not good. In no time they'd have a couple of holes big enough to wriggle through. And then Toad Hall would be full of chew wasps—and spearheads, too, no doubt.

All looking for Jeffy. But to get to Jeffy they'd have to go through Sylvia. The very thought of that sickened him.

But to get to Sylvia they've got to get through me.

Alan looked around for some sort of backup defense, something to shore up the weak point. He spotted the heavy brass étagère to the right of the door.

Perfect.

He rolled over to it, removed all the *netsuke* and piled them gently in the corner, then pulled the étagère over onto its side. He tried to let it down easy but it hit the floor with a clang. He found that maneuvering it against the door from his wheelchair was all but impossible, so he slid from the seat onto his knees and worked from the floor.

As he was guiding the thick brass back of the piece against the door, a chew wasp began to wriggle its head through the hole it had made. As its eyes lit on Alan, its movements became more frantic, its toothy jaws gnashed the air hungrily. Alan grabbed his club and bashed in the creature's skull with two blows. It wriggled for an instant, then lay still, its carcass wedged in the hole, blocking it.

Alan fitted the étagère snugly against the door, then pulled his wheelchair closer. He'd stocked its backrest pouch with the equivalent of a tool chest. Hammer, nails, saw, ax, pliers, screwdriver—anything he might need on short notice during the night.

He took out the hammer and began driving a half dozen of the biggest nails he had into the seams between the tiles along the outer edge of the étagère. Damn shame to mess up this beautiful marble but it could be replaced. The people besieged in Toad Hall could not.

Alan pulled himself back up into his chair and regarded his handiwork. It looked pretty stable. With only wing power behind them, he doubted the bugs were strong enough to push back the heavy brass piece even if he'd left it unsecured. But now, with nails acting as stoppers, he was certain they'd be frustrated until morning. He heard sharp little teeth scraping against the far side of the metal.

"Let's see you chew a hole in that."

Tomorrow, though, he'd have to find some way to reinforce the outer surface of the door.

Maybe Ba would be back by then. Alan hoped so. As much as he insisted on his own independence and refused to lean on anyone else, Toad Hall was awfully big. Too big to be adequately patrolled by one man in a wheelchair. With the welfare of Sylvia and Jeffy at stake, he couldn't let his pride endanger them. As long as Sylvia insisted on staying here, he'd do his best to protect her.

But he wished he had Ba for backup. Even more, he wished they'd all moved in with Glaeken last Saturday when the old guy had offered.

"Alan?"

He wheeled around and found Sylvia standing in the foyer entrance. She wore the loose sweater and baggy old jeans that were serving as her pajamas during the siege. Her face was pale and lined from the pillowcase. She did not look like the Sylvia Nash who'd once appeared in *The New York Times Magazine* with her unique bonsai art—her beautiful trees now lay smashed and broken in the shattered remains of the greenhouse—but Alan found her as beautiful as ever.

"Hey. You're supposed to be catching some sleep."

"I heard all that banging. I thought something was wrong."

"Sorry. I didn't mean to wake you, but the chewers have started to gnaw rat holes in the door."

She came over and dropped onto his lap; she slipped her arms around him and hugged.

"I wasn't sleeping. I couldn't. I'm worried about Ba. I'm afraid he won't come back. And if he doesn't, if he's . . . dead . . . it will be my fault for letting him go. I'll never forgive myself."

Alan put his arms around her waist. "We've been through this, and if anyone can take care of himself, it's Ba."

"But I'm worried about you too, Alan. When I'm down in the basement with Jeffy and you're up here alone I begin to think I've been very foolish, very selfish in insisting we stay here. But for some strange reason I feel it more than ever tonight. So I've made up my mind. Tomorrow we move in with Glaeken. Hopefully Ba will be back by then and we can all leave here as a group. I want our little family back together again, Alan. Toad Hall is our home, but we've got to survive. That comes first."

He squeezed her against him. "I know what this place means to you. I know how tough it is for you to leave it."

"It's like giving up." He could feel her jaw muscles bunch as she spoke. "I hate to give up."

"But it's not giving up or giving in. It's a strategic withdrawal so you can live to fight another day when you've marshaled your forces."

"I love you," she said, leaning her head against his. "Sometimes I wonder why you put up with me and my stubbornness."

"Maybe it's *because* of your stubbornness. Maybe I like a woman who don't take no shit from nobody, not even this Rasalom guy and his bugs."

Sylvia jerked her head up, fluttered her eyelids, and put on her Southern belle voice.

"Whah, Doctah Bulmuh! Ah don't believe Ah've evah heard you speak that way! Especially in front of a layday!"

"I only speak that way when I'm *under* a lady."

They kissed—simultaneously, spontaneously. Whether it was body language or the kind of telepathy that develops between soul mates, Alan didn't know. And didn't care. All he knew at that instant was that it was time for a kiss. And Sylvia knew it too. So they kissed. Simple.

"When was the last time we made love?" he heard her say as he nuzzled her neck and inhaled the scent of her.

"Too long."

They hadn't had a chance even to sleep together since the attacks.

"Another good reason to move in with Glaeken," she said. "An excellent reason."

They sat there for a while, Sylvia cradled on his lap, and held each other, listening to the bugs gnaw at the edges of the brass étagère. Alan realized again how much he loved this woman, how attuned he was to her, like no other person he had ever known. The thought of her coming to harm was unbearable. Tomorrow they'd move to Glaeken's and she'd be safe, as safe as anyone could be in this madness.

But first he had to see them through the night.

The Bunker

"What's that?"

Gia bolted upright in bed. A small night-light burned but otherwise the bunker was dark. Beyond the curtain, Abe snored. But between his loud, discordant rumbles . . . another sound.

Rasping . . . grinding . . .

Without disturbing Vicky, Gia slipped out of bed and padded around the curtain to where Abe slept. He lay on his back like a beached whale. She shook his shoulder once and he jolted awake.

"What? What is it?"

"Listen," she said.

And now, with the snoring silenced, the new sound came through loud and clear. She felt sick when she realized what it was.

"Something's chewing on the outer wall."

Abe shook his head. "No. Impossible."

"Listen! It's the burrowers. Has to be."

Abe listened.

"You may be right. They're trying to get in. But they haven't a chance. Like I said, four feet of steel-reinforced concrete—an atomic bomb they'll need. And even then . . ."

Gia shivered. It sounded good in theory, but what if whatever was out there kept it up all night, night after night, chewing up just a little wall at a time? Eventually they'd get through.

She hurried back to bed and snuggled against Vicky. But sleep was impossible. The noise . . . the grinding, the chewing . . . went on and on.

The Horror Channel's Drive-In Theatre—Special All-Day Edition
Flesh Feast (1970) Cine World Corp.
Twilight People (1972) New Worlds
Beyond Evil (1980) IFI-Scope III
The Night God Screamed (1973) Cinemation
From Hell It Came (1957) Allied Artists
The Unearthly (1957) Republic
Night of the Dark Full Moon (1972) Cannon
Bug (1977) Paramount
Creatures of Evil (1970) Hemisphere
The Unknown Terror (1957) 20th Century Fox
The Day the World Ended (1956) AIP
Scream and Scream Again (1970) Amicus/AIP
It's a Mad, Mad, Mad, Mad World (1963) United Artists

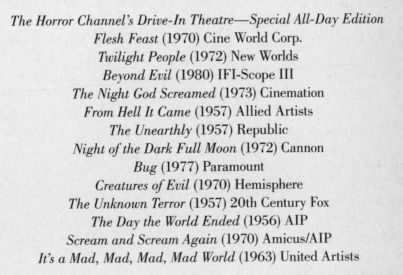

Monroe, Long Island

The scrape of metal on metal.

Alan snapped to full alert. Without hesitating he wheeled out of the game room and rolled toward the foyer. That was where it had come from. It sounded as if the étagère had moved. Alan didn't see how that was possible, but he had his toothed billy out and ready in his lap, just in case.

As he turned into the living room he heard the buzz of wings.

They're in!

His heart pumped dread but he kept on rolling. Maybe there were only a few. Maybe—

Something flashed toward him. He snapped his head back and it blew by his cheek, jaws grinding furiously.

Chew wasp.

Alan's heart pumped madly now. He fumbled in his lap for the billy. By the time the bug had banked around for a return run, he had it ready. Visibility wasn't great in the candlelight so he didn't swing at it. He simply held the billy between his face and the bug and braced himself.

The chew wasp ran into the club mouth first. It glanced off to the right and shredded its wing on the club's teeth in passing. Alan left it flopping around on the rug and wheeled into the foyer. It wasn't going anywhere with one wing and he could administer the *coup de grâce* later. Right now he needed to push that étagère back into place before any more of its friends got in.

He smelled them first—that rotten carrion odor. And as he rounded the corner from the living room into the foyer he saw two spearheads and another chew wasp wriggle free from behind the étagère and take flight. Either they didn't see him or they ignored him as they winged up the open curved stairway toward the darkness of the second floor.

Looking for Jeffy.

At top speed he rolled his chair over to the étagère. Not only had it been pushed away from the door, it had been moved with enough force to bend the nails onto their backs. It now rested atop them.

Alan shook his head. "What the . . . ?"

Time enough later to ponder how the little monsters had done this. Right now he had to plug the hole.

With a quick glance over his shoulder at the stairs, Alan slid off the wheelchair to his knees as he had before and threw his weight against the étagère. A squeaky scrape echoed through the foyer as it slid back over the nails and settled again on the floor, flush against the door. Alan turned and leaned his back against it.

Okay. No more could get in, at least for the moment. Now he had to find a way to secure it here until morning. He glanced at his watch: 6:22. Morning was still three hours away. Well, he could sit here all night, just like this; that would do it. Three hours on this marble floor wasn't forever; it would only seem that way. The problem with staying here was he was a sitting duck for the bugs that had already got in. He knew of at least three. Could be more.

He hefted the billy. At least he didn't have to concern himself with hunting them down. Sooner or later—most likely sooner—they'd come hunting him. He'd have to be—

The étagère bucked against his back.

Startled, Alan half turned and leaned hard against it with his shoulder. The piece slid back into place.

What the hell was that?

Uneasiness prickled his scalp. That was no chew wasp pushing through its hole. Too much power. Something big out there. Bigger than—

Alan remembered the dents in the storm shutter out front, and that long depression in the yard. He had a feeling whatever had been responsible was back.

Christ!

He didn't know what it was using to push the étagère but he'd been able to push it back, so maybe things weren't so bad as they seemed.

And then the étagère moved again, a good foot this time, sliding Alan along with it. He pushed back, his feet scraping along the marble floor, searching for purchase and finding little. And even if they had, he doubted he'd be able to do much.

If only I had two good legs! he thought as he brought all his upper body strength to bear on the étagère.

But what was this thing? How was it pushing the étagère?

As if in answer, a smooth black tentacle, glistening in the candlelight, slid up from the other side and unerringly darted toward his face. Alan ducked and swung at it with his club.

And missed. The tentacle had dodged the blow, almost as if it could see. It came for him again immediately and wrapped around his wrist. Its touch was cold and damp, but not slippery; Alan yanked back in revulsion but couldn't pull free. His skin was stuck, as if the tentacle were coated with glue. It began drawing him toward the door.

Thoroughly frightened now, he switched the club to his other hand and began pounding on the tentacle. The embedded teeth opened gashes that grew deeper and leaked foul-smelling black liquid with every blow. The traction eased, the grip loosened, and Alan was free again.

But only for a heartbeat. Another tentacle snaked in beside the damaged one and reached for him. Alan fell back and groped in his wheelchair pouch until he found the ax—a hatchet, really, with a short handle and a wedged head, no more than three inches along the cutting edge. But sharp. Alan got a good grip and swung it at the new tentacle. The blade sank deep, severing it clean through about a foot behind the tip. The proximal end whipped back immediately, spraying the foyer with its ebony equivalent of blood, while the free tip wriggled about.

All right!

He pushed the étagère out of the way and quick-crawled to the door, positioning himself to the right of the opening. The little holes had merged into one big one about eighteen inches wide and four inches high. He'd barely set himself when a third tentacle slithered through the near edge. He severed it with a single chop and that tip joined its brother on the floor. A fourth tentacle darted in, then a fifth. Alan hacked at them as soon as they appeared and they withdrew, wounded.

"Yes!" he said, the word hissing softly between his teeth. "Keep 'em coming, you bastards! It's circumcision time! Let's see if you've got more tentacles than I've got chops!"

He was pumped. He knew he was acting a little bit crazy, maybe because he was *feeling* a little bit crazy. Maybe he'd been in that wheelchair too long. Whatever, here he was, free of it, weapon in hand, defending Toad Hall. He hadn't felt this alive in years.

Suddenly a half dozen fresh tentacles surged through at once, rearing up, reaching for his arms, his face. He swung wildly, catching one in midair, one against the door. He was taking a bead on another when he heard buzzing wings and gnashing teeth above and behind him.

Bugs!

Instinctively, he ducked, but too late. Pain ripped through his left ear. He touched a hand to the side of his face. It came away red. Alan turned and grabbed the billy. Now he had a weapon in each hand—hatchet in right, club in left—and was eager to use them. The pain and the blood from his ear had released something within him. His fear was gone, replaced by a seething rage at these creatures who dared to invade his home and threaten the people he loved.

He chopped at an extended tentacle, severing its tip, then heard the buzz again and swung blindly at the air.

And connected. The broken, oozing body of the chew wasp—its jaws still smeared with blood from Alan's ear—bounced off the door and fell to the floor. Immediately, one of the tentacles coiled around its squirming form and yanked it outside.

Alan chopped at a particularly thick tentacle, severing it halfway through.

As he drew back to finish the job, something slammed against his back, shooting a blaze of pain through his right shoulder. He grunted with the sudden agony. As wings buzzed furiously by his ear, he dropped the billy and reached over his shoulder. When his questing fingers found the horny beak piercing his flesh, he knew a spearhead was trying to make him its next meal. It must have come in at an angle and glanced off his shoulder blade. A direct hit would have put it right through to his chest cavity. Had to get it out before it dug itself deeper and finished the job.

He wrapped his fingers around the twisting, gnawing beak and yanked. He was rewarded with another eruption of vision-dimming pain, but the spearhead came free. It writhed and twisted and wriggled and flapped madly as he brought it around front. But as he raised his hatchet to chop it in half, the tentacle he'd wounded seconds ago coiled around his right wrist and wrenched it toward the door. He groaned as the sudden movement sent a bolt of pain lancing down his arm from the shoulder wound. His fingers went numb momentarily; he lost his grip on the hatchet handle. But he couldn't worry about that. Had to get his right hand free. *Now.*

So Alan struck at the tentacle with the only weapon he had—the bug writhing in his left hand.

Using the spearhead's pointed beak as a knife, he stabbed and slashed madly, repeatedly. Desperate breaths hissed between his teeth. This was out of hand now. He'd lost the high ground and was on the defensive. He spotted a slew of new tentacles sliding under the door—how many did this thing *have?*

Had to retreat. He was going to be in very big trouble if he didn't pull free in the next few seconds and get out of reach.

He took a big swing with the spearhead, angling it so it cut into the open, oozing area he'd previously damaged with the hatchet. As the bug's sharp beak pierced through the far side, Alan pushed it deeper, cramming it into the tissues. It must have struck a vital nerve trunk because the distal end of the tentacle went into spasm, coiling and uncoiling wildly.

Alan pulled free of its grasp and rolled away from the door. Leaving his wheelchair behind, he rose to his hands and knees and scrambled across the foyer toward the living room.

He almost made it.

He cursed his legs as they slumped beneath him, slowing him down. His right arm was letting him down too. Had to depend on his arms for a good part of his speed, but the right was wounded. His left hand was just inches from the living room carpet when he felt something coil about his ankle. Even then, a good strong kick might have freed him, but his legs didn't have one in them.

He realized then that he should have tried for the stairs. If he'd been able to reach the newel post of the banister he'd have had something to hold on to.

As the tentacle dragged him back, Alan clawed at the marble floor, looking for a crack, a seam, anything to hold on to, but found nothing. It had been too expertly installed. He kicked feebly with his free leg but then felt another tentacle wrap around that ankle and worm its way up to his thigh.

Now he was being dragged back at a faster rate.

He spotted his hatchet where he'd dropped it. He tried to reach it. He stretched his good arm and fingers to the limit, until he thought his shoulder would dislocate, but could not get near it. Like a departing sailor gazing at his home port from the stern of a ship, he watched the hatchet slip farther and farther out of reach.

Next came his wheelchair. He grabbed at that, caught hold of a footrest, but it simply rolled with him. He clutched it because it was all he had to hold on to.

And then other tentacles, Alan couldn't count how many, looped and coiled around his legs, and no way he could kick free now, even if he'd had two good legs. He was helpless. Utterly helpless.

I'm going to die.

Although he never stopped struggling against the inexorable tug of the tentacles, the realization was a sudden cold weight in his heart. Fear and dread shot through him, but no panic. Mostly sadness. Tears sprang into his eyes, tears for all the things he'd never do, like walking again, or watching Jeffy grow up, or growing old with Sylvia. But most of all, for the way he'd be dying. He'd never feared the moment, but then he'd always imagined it arriving when he was gray and withered and bedfast, and that he'd welcome it with open arms.

The tentacles dragged his legs through the opening at the bottom of the door. The jagged wood raked the backs of his thighs and then dug into the flesh of his hips and buttocks as he became wedged into the opening.

He wasn't going to fit through. At least not in one piece.

Oh God, oh God, oh God, I don't want to die like this!

And suddenly amid the fear and the grief and the pain he realized that he had to die a certain way. He'd been given no choice in how death was coming to him, but he had a say in how he met it.

Silently.

He groaned as the traction on his legs increased and the ligaments and tendons and skin and muscles began to stretch past their tolerances.

Quiet!

He reached up and grabbed the thin cotton blanket from the wheelchair and stuffed it deep into his mouth, gagging as the fabric brushed the back of his throat.

Good. Gag. Then he couldn't scream. And he *mustn't* scream.

Oh God, the pain!

Had to be quiet because if he let out the pain and fear in a scream, Sylvia would wake and come for him . . . he knew her, knew if she thought he was in danger, she wouldn't hesitate, she'd charge, she'd wade through a storm of bugs and tentacles to get to him . . .

Alan screeched silently into his blanket-stuffed mouth as the ball at the head of his right femur twisted free and dislocated from the hip socket with a grinding explosion of agony, and screamed again as the left one followed.

Quiet, quiet, QUIET!

. . . because it was too late for him and if she came upstairs they'd have her too, and after they got Sylvia, they'd get Jeffy and then Glaeken wouldn't be able to assemble whatever it was he had to assemble and the Otherness would win it all and the bugs would feast on everybody . . . he just prayed he'd bought Sylvia and Jeffy enough time . . . prayed his body would stay wedged in the opening and block the bugs out for a while because soon Toad Hall would be swarming with them and if they had enough time they'd gnaw through the cellar door and all this agony would be for nothing . . . so he had to hold on and keep quiet for just a few more seconds because in just a few more seconds it would be over and . . .

Alan's blanket drank the howl that burst from his throat as his right leg ripped free of his body and slid away into the night and yet he smiled within as he felt his consciousness draining away in the warm red stream pumping from his ruptured femoral artery, smiled because nothing was quieter than a dead man.

"Alan?"

Sylvia awoke with a start and stared wildly around, momentarily disoriented in the darkness. Then she saw the candle flickering on the Ping-Pong table and remembered she was in the basement. She reached out a hand and found Jeffy's slumbering form curled next to her on the old Castro Convertible.

She squinted at the luminous dial on her watch: 7:30. Had she been asleep that long? She must have been more tired than she'd thought. At least the night had gone quickly. Daylight was due at 9:10. Another long, long night was drawing to a close. She stretched. Soon Alan would be knocking on the upstairs door, telling them all to rise and—

Then she heard it.

On the upstairs door—scratching. She leapt out of bed and hurried to the foot of the steps to listen again.

No—not scratching. *Gnawing.*

Trembling, chewing her upper lip, Sylvia crept up the stairs, telling herself with each tread that she was wrong, that it couldn't be, that her ears had to be playing dirty tricks on her. Halfway up she caught the smell and abruptly ran out of denials. She rushed the rest of the way to the door where she pressed her palms against the solid oak panels and felt the vibrations of countless teeth scoring the outer surface.

Alan! Dear God, where's Alan?

She turned the knob and gripped it with both hands. Bugs in Toad Hall. She had to see. She could hear them and smell them but she had to see them to believe so many had invaded her house. She edged the door open a crack and saw a sliver of hallway. The creatures immediately attacked the opening and she slammed the door shut. But she'd seen enough.

Bugs. The hall . . . choked with them—floating, drifting, darting, bumping, hanging on the walls.

Sylvia began to tremble. If the halls had been taken over, where was Alan? To invade Toad Hall they had to get past Alan.

"Alan?" she cried, her face against the vibrating door.

Maybe he'd reached the movie room and locked himself in. Maybe he was safe.

But those were only words. She could find no place in her heart and mind that truly believed them. A sob built in her throat and ripped free as a scream.

"ALAN!"

Homecomings

Monroe, Long Island

Ba heard Jack shout, "Watch out!" as Kolabati cried out.

He swerved to avoid the panel truck that had cut through the intersection ahead of them, missing it by inches.

"Christ, that was close. Ease up, Big Guy. If we T-bone someone we may not get there at all."

Ba could not ease up. He had commandeered the steering wheel at the Ashe brothers' airfield. He was unused to handling Jack's big car. He barely slowed for stop signs and none of the traffic lights were working. No matter. He had to get home. Now. The Missus needed him.

As the familiar streets and storefronts of downtown Monroe flashed by, his anxiety increased with every passing block. *Empty* streets, *smashed* storefronts, and only a few frightened people and fewer cars hurrying through the waning afternoon light. The town had deteriorated badly in the two days since he'd left.

Ba felt Bill Ryan's hand on his shoulder.

"Jack's right. Between us we've traveled more than halfway around the globe and back. Be a shame to crack up and die so close to home."

A new voice: "Yes. No need to hurry."

Who? The strange one, Nick, had spoken.

"What do you mean, Nick?" Bill said.

But Nick said no more.

No need to hurry . . .

Did that mean nothing to worry about? Or . . . too late to matter?

Ba had spent the entire trip from Maui in this state of anguished fear. He could not escape the feeling that something terrible was happening at Toad Hall without him. He had called the Missus time after time from the phone on the jet. Just a word or two from her was all he would have needed to ease his mind. But he could not make the connection.

Fortunately the trip had gone well. They had caught the jet stream and had made excellent time. Even more fortunate, Bill Ryan and Nick had already arrived and were waiting for them when they touched down.

Ba had tried to call again from the hangar phone but still no response. And so now he approached the scene of a tragedy. He knew it. He should not have left Toad Hall. If anything had happened to the Missus and her family . . .

Here was Shore Drive. Now the front wall of Toad Hall's grounds, the gate-posts, the curving driveway, the willows, Toad Hall itself, the front door—

"Oh, shit," Jack said softly. "Oh, no."

"Missus!"

The word escaped Ba when he saw how the bottom half of the front door had been smashed through and torn away. He was out the door and running toward the house, taking the front steps in a bound. The door hung open, angled on its hinges. He burst through and skidded to a halt in the foyer.

Carnage. Furniture strewn about, wallpaper hanging in tatters like peeling skin, the Doctor's wheelchair sitting empty in the middle of the floor, and blood. Dried blood puddled on the threshold and splattered the outer surface of the door.

Fear such as he'd never known gripped Ba's throat and squeezed. He'd battled the Cong and fought off pirates on the South China Sea, but they'd never made him feel weak and helpless like the sight of blood in Toad Hall.

He ran through the house then, calling for the Missus, the Doctor, Jeffy. Through the deserted upstairs, back down to the movie room, to another staggering halt before the cellar door. The door stood ajar, its finish gnawed off, its beveled panels splintered, nearly obliterated. Ba pulled it open the rest of the way and stood at the top of the stairs.

"Missus? Doctor? Jeffy?"

No answer from below. He spotted the flashlight lying on the second step. He picked it up and descended slowly, dreading what he'd find.

Or wouldn't find.

The basement was empty. A red candle had burned down to a puddle on the Ping-Pong table. Ba's finger trembled as he reached out and touched the pooled wax. Cold.

Feeling dead inside, he dragged himself up the stairs and wandered out to the front drive. Jack and Bill stood by the car. Kolabati and Nick waited within.

Bill said, "Are they . . . ?"

"Gone," Ba said. His voice was so low, he could barely hear himself.

"Hey, Ba," Jack said. "Maybe they left for—"

"There is blood. So much blood."

"Aw, jeez," Jack said softly.

Bill lowered his head and pressed a hand over his eyes.

"What do you want us to do, Ba?" Jack said. "You name it, we'll do it."

A good friend, this Jack. They had met only a few days ago and already he was acting like a brother. But nothing could ease the pain in Ba's heart, the growing grief, the bitter self-loathing for leaving the people he loved—his *family*—unguarded. Why had he—?

He whirled at the sound of a car engine starting in the garage at the rear of the house. He knew that engine. It belonged to the 1938 Graham—the Missus's favorite car.

Fighting a surging joy, afraid to acknowledge it for fear that it might be for nothing, Ba stumbled into a run toward the rear. He had gone only a few steps when the Graham's shark-nosed grille appeared around the corner of the house. The Missus was behind the wheel, Jeffy beside her. Her mouth formed an *O* when she saw him. The old car stalled as she braked and then she was out the door and running across the grass, arms outflung, face twisted in uncontrollable grief.

"Oh, Ba! Ba! We waited all day for you! I thought we'd lost you too!"

And then the Missus did something she had never done before. She threw her arms around Ba, clung to him, and began to sob against his chest.

Ba did not know what to do. He held his arms akimbo, not sure of where to put them. As overjoyed as he was to see her alive, it certainly was not his place to embrace the Missus. But her grief was so deep, so unrestrained . . . he had never seen her like this, never guessed she was capable of this magnitude of sorrow.

And then Jeffy ran up, and he too was crying. He threw his arms around Ba's left leg and hung there.

Gently, gingerly, hesitantly, Ba lowered one hand to the Missus's shoulder and the other to Jeffy's head. His elation at seeing them was tempered by the slowly dawning realization that the picture was incomplete.

Someone was missing.

"The Doctor, Missus?"

"Oh, Ba," she sobbed. "He's gone. Those . . . *things* . . . killed him and dragged him off! He's gone, Ba! Alan's gone and we'll never see him again!"

For a moment Ba thought he glimpsed the Doctor's face peering at him from the shadows in the backseat of the Graham, thought he felt the warmth of his easy smile, the aura of his deep honor and quiet courage.

And then he faded from view and something happened to Ba, something that hadn't happened since his boyhood days in the fishing village where he was born.

Ba Thuy Nguyen wept.

As the Change progresses above, so progresses the Change below.

Rasalom revels in his new form as it grows ever larger. Suspended in its cavern, he is the size of an elephant now. To make room for him, more earth drops away into the soft yellow glow of the bottomless pit below.

With his senses penetrating deep into the earth, Rasalom sees the Change progressing unimpeded, far ahead of schedule. Chaos reigns above. The sweet honey nectar of fear and misery, the ambrosia of rage and ruin continues to seep through the strata of the earth to nourish him, help him grow, make him ever stronger.

And in the center of the dying city, Glaeken's building stands unmolested, an island of tranquillity in a sea of torment. Members of his pathetic little company now rush back from trips here and there around the globe with their recovered bits and pieces of the first and second swords. All of them still clinging so doggedly to their hope.

Good. He wants to let that hope grow until it is the last great hope left for all humanity. Let them think they've been doing something important, something epochal. The higher their hope lifts them, the longer the fall when they learn they've struggled and died for nothing.

But Rasalom senses them taking comfort in their relative safety, drawing strength from their comradeship. Their peace, uneasy though it may be, is a burr in his hide. He cannot allow this to continue unchallenged. He does not wish to destroy them—yet. But he does wish to breach their insulation, unsettle them, vex them, start them looking over their shoulders.

One of them must die.

Not out in the streets, but in the heart of their safe haven. It must be an ugly death—nothing quick and clean, but slow and painful and messy. And to make the death as unsettling as possible, it must befall a dear member of their number, one who seems the most innocent, the most innocuous, one they never would expect him to single out for such degradation.

The new lips gestating within the sac twist into a semblance of a smile.

Time for a little fun.

In the tunnel leading to the cavern, Rasalom's skin, shed days ago, begins to move. It ripples, swells, fills out to living proportions. Then it rises and begins its journey toward the surface.

As it walks, it tests its voice.

"Mother."

Queens, New York

Ba should be driving, Bill thought as he raced along the deserted LIE, aiming the big Crown Vic for the Queens-Midtown Tunnel like a bullet from a gun. He glanced at his watch: 3:32. Less than forty minutes of light. He would have preferred the Queensboro Bridge but remembered that was impassable due to a gravity hole.

Jack rode shotgun—literally. He sat high in the passenger seat with this huge short-barreled thing—he'd called it a "Spas"—held up in plain sight. An exotic Indian woman was squeezed between them. Ba sat behind Bill with a similar shotgun in plain view. The two warriors were sending a message: Don't mess with this car. Nick sat behind Jack, Sylvia and the boy were squeezed in the middle, their cat on the boy's lap, their one-eyed dog panting on the floor.

That left the driving chore to Bill. He knew he wasn't the greatest driver, but if they ran into one of the roving gangs that had taken over the city during the day he figured he'd do better with a steering wheel than with a shotgun.

He glanced at Jack, who'd been withdrawn since their reunion at the airport. He was definitely on edge. Something eating at him, something he wasn't talking about.

Bill guessed if it concerned them, they'd find out soon enough.

The farther he drove into Queens, the more obstacles on the expressway; he wove as quickly as he dared around and through the litter of wrecked or abandoned cars. They slowed him and he wanted to fly.

Carol . . . he hungered for the sight of her, for the sound of her voice, the touch of her hand. She consumed his thoughts, his feelings. He wished he could have got a call through to her from the airport, just to let her know he'd made it back and was coming home.

"Better hurry," Nick said from the back.

"Going as fast as I can, Nick."

"Better go faster." His tone was as flat as when he'd told Ba he had no need to hurry. They'd learned what that had meant. What did this . . . ?

"Faster why?"

"It's Carol."

The car swerved slightly as Bill's fingers tightened on the wheel.

"What about Carol?"

"She's in trouble."

WNYW-TV

Manhattan

Carol found the head waiting in the kitchen.

She was on her way back from Magda's room, carrying her lunch tray, worrying about Bill and why she hadn't heard from him yet. She screamed and dropped the tray as she rounded the corner and saw it floating in the air. She recognized the face.

"Jimmy!" she cried, then got control of herself.

Not a head, just a face. And not Jimmy. Not her son. She'd almost stopped thinking of him as her son.

Rasalom. This was Rasalom.

The face smiled—an Arctic gale registered greater warmth. Then its lips moved, forming words, but the voice seemed to come from everywhere. Or was it inside her head?

"Hello, Mother."

Carol backed out of the kitchen. The face followed.

The tone turned mocking. *"Mommy, don't leave me!"*

Carol stopped retreating when her back came up against the dining room table. She looked around for Glaeken but knew he wouldn't be there. He'd gone out hours ago while she'd stayed to watch over Magda.

Carol swallowed and found her voice. "Don't call me that!"

"Why not? That's what you are."

She shook her head. "No. You grew inside me for nine months, but you were never my child. And I was never your mother."

Another smile, as cold as the first. *"I sympathize with your efforts to dissociate yourself from me. I understand them because I've tried to do the same in regard to you. Perhaps you've had more success than I."*

"What are you talking about?"

"The bond of flesh. Since the day I was conceived within you, I've worn the flesh you gave me. It links us. I don't like it any more than you do, but it is a fact, one that won't go away. One we both have to deal with."

"I've learned to deal with it—by not thinking about it."

"But that doesn't cancel it. I've given this a lot of thought and there's a better way to deal with it, a way that allows me to come to terms with my fleshy link to you. A way that can benefit you as well."

The voice in her head was so calm, so soothing. Almost mesmerizing. Carol shook herself.

"I—I don't want anything from you."

"Don't think just of yourself. Think of your friends. I'm offering you and some of them a safe harbor, a haven, a chance to survive the endless night."

"I don't trust you."

The smile again, rueful this time. *"I wouldn't trust me either. But hear me out. You have nothing to lose by listening to my proposal."*

Carol remembered what Bill had told her about a woman named Lisl who'd lost her soul and her life by listening to Rasalom. But what, besides sanity and dignity, did Carol have left to lose? Unless a miracle occurred, tomorrow would hold the world's last daylight. After Thursday's sundown she'd be in the same leaky life raft as the rest of the world.

"What do you mean by 'a haven'? And how many of my 'friends' can I take there?"

"A reasonable number."

"Glaeken among them?"

The face rotated back and forth, the equivalent of a headshake.

"No. Not Glaeken. Anyone else, but not Glaeken. I've waited too long to even my scores with him."

Carol didn't know what to think, what to do. If Rasalom had agreed to allow Glaeken safe harbor, she'd have known he was lying. No rivalry, no enmity in human history was as long and as bitter and as deeply ingrained as theirs. But he had excluded Glaeken. What did that mean? Could his offer be genuine? If she could save Bill and a few of the others . . .

"Come downstairs and we'll discuss it."

"Downstairs? Oh, no. I'm not leaving this building."

"I'm not asking you to. I'm one floor down. In your apartment."

"How—how did you get in?"

"Come now, Mother dear. I can do anything I wish. Anything. Come visit. We'll talk. I'll be there until darkness falls. After that I'll have other matters to attend to."

The face grew dim, became translucent, then disappeared. Gone as if it had never been.

Carol sagged back against the table. Expect the unexpected. Wasn't that what Glaeken had told her? Easy enough to say, but Rasalom's face—floating in the air, talking to her as casually as if they'd bumped into each other in an aisle at the A&P.

The ease with which he seemed to have entered the building was bad enough, but knowing he was waiting down in her apartment tied her in knots.

Should she go? That was the question. And what was this all about? Was she supposed to haggle with him? Barter for lives? The responsibility was numbing.

She had to risk it. If she could save even a few people . . .

But she didn't want to go alone. She knew she had to, but she didn't like it. She didn't have much time, either. If only she had a weapon of some sort. But what could she use against someone who could change the course of the sun and anything else he pleased?

As Carol picked up the broken dishes from the kitchen floor and threw them away, she spotted the knife rack over the sink. She pulled out the wide-bladed carving knife and tucked it into the folds of the old cardigan she'd borrowed from Glaeken. A laughable weapon, considering who she'd be facing. But the weight of the blade in her hand offered some tiny comfort.

She peeked in on Magda and found her sleeping soundly. Carol guessed it would be all right to leave her for a few minutes. Glaeken would be back soon, and Rasalom had said he'd wait only until dark.

She hurried downstairs.

Her apartment had an empty feel. The drapes stood open but because the windows faced north, the light was dusky.

Was he here? What was she supposed to call out? Jimmy? Rasalom? Certainly not *son*.

"Hello?" she said, settling on that. "Are you here?"

She walked through the living room and down the hall. Why didn't he answer? Was this some sort of a joke?

Suddenly he stepped out of the bedroom not three feet in front of her. In the flesh.

Naked flesh.

Carol cried out in shock and jumped back.

"Hello, *Mother*." His voice was coarse, raspy, more dead than alive.

He stepped toward her as she backed away. His left hand was missing. His slim body seemed faintly luminescent, and his genitals . . . he was hugely erect, pointing directly at her face. Suddenly he darted by her and positioned himself between her and the door.

She turned and faced him, her heart thudding, her palm slick on the handle of the knife in her sweater.

"Wh-what's this all about? I thought you wanted to talk."

He smiled. "Isn't it wonderful what desperation does to people? It paralyzes some, makes others brutish, and makes others *stupid*. You fall into that final category, *Mother*." He spat the last word. "What's this about? It's about a love note to Glaeken and the rest. It's about defilement and slow, painful death, Mother. Incestuous rape and matricide. In other words, you and me."

He leapt at her. Reflexively Carol pulled out the knife and held it before her with both hands. She felt the impact as Rasalom's body struck it, felt the skin part before the point, felt the blade sink deep into his flesh. He grunted and stepped back. He looked down in wonder at the knife handle protruding from his upper abdomen, just below the breastbone. He touched the handle with a finger, then looked up at her.

"Mother . . . you shock me. I guess there are still a few surprises left in this world."

"Oh, God!"

"He won't help you. He was never there. But I am here now. And I am your God. Think of it, Mother. You are about to be raped by God. And afterward . . ." He caressed the handle like a priapic tool . . . "I shall use this to skin you alive. Won't that be a nice gift to hang in Glaeken's closet? Your skin."

Carol screamed and tried to dash past him but he caught her with his only hand and slammed her back against the wall. The breath whooshed out of her with the impact. As she tried to regain it, the door burst open.

"Carol!"

A group of men—some of them armed—burst in, with Bill in the lead. He leapt to her side and Carol clung to him, sobbing.

"Oh, Bill, oh, Bill, thank God you're here!"

"You!" Bill glared at Rasalom, who had stepped back and appeared to be surveying the scene with amusement.

Jack stepped forward and faced Rasalom, a shotgun of some sort cradled in his arms. Ba stood by the door, similarly armed, while Nick stood behind him in the hall.

"Who the hell are you?" Jack said.

"I once knew him as Rafe Losmara," Bill said. "But his real name is Rasalom."

Rasalom bowed, unfazed by the intruders. "At your service."

Jack's expression was skeptical as he glanced at Bill, then back to Rasalom's slim, naked figure.

"Doesn't look like the Rasalom I've met."

"I am many things to many people."

Bill was staring at the handle protruding from Rasalom's abdomen.

"Is that a knife . . . ?"

The sight of the knife seemed to unsettle Jack. "I've just been through this movie."

As Carol wondered what Jack meant, Rasalom smiled at him and said, "Have much success on your trip to Maui, *Heir*?"

Heir? What was happening here? Jack looked ready to explode as Rasalom turned to Bill and yanked the blade free.

"Please don't be concerned, Father. I'm a rapid healer."

"Yeah?" Jack's face was tight with rage. In a single smooth, swift motion he had his shotgun extended to arm's length, its muzzle inches from Rasalom's face. "Heal this."

The explosion was deafening. Close against her Bill cried out in shock as Carol screamed and turned away, but not before she saw Rasalom's head disintegrate behind the muzzle flash.

A moment later, Bill's hushed, awed whisper slipped past the ringing in her ears.

"Look at that!"

Carol turned and saw Rasalom's headless body lying on the floor. It seemed to be shrinking, deflating. And then she saw why. Loose soil was pouring from the stump of his neck.

"Dirt," Jack said. "This wasn't him, just skin filled with dirt." His eyes were more than a little wild as he gave the remains an angry kick. "Dirtbag."

Glaeken hobbled through the doorway then.

"What has happened here?"

Carol quickly ran over the events of the past twenty minutes. Glaeken nodded with slow resignation.

"Leave your skin in my closet, he told you?"

Carol felt Bill tighten his grip around her shoulders.

"Why?" Bill said. "What does it mean?"

"More of his games. A diversion while he waits for the Change to be complete. One more thing to confound, confuse, sicken, and terrify us. He probably meant to leave Carol's skin and his own. A grisly reminder to me that his Change is far along to completion."

Glaeken went to Rasalom's remains and lifted the skin by both feet. Jack helped. Together they shook the last of the dirt from within. It felt dry and light, almost like an oversize set of a child's footed pajamas. Glaeken rolled it up, then tucked it under his arm and started for the door.

"Come upstairs. I want to get rid of this once and for all. Then we have work to do."

She noticed Jack looking around with a panicked expression.

"Hey! Where's Kolabati?"

Rasalom's skin smoked, twisted, browned, blackened, and burned in the fire-place. Carol watched as Glaeken pushed it deeper into the flames with the poker. As the ashes curled and rose through the flue, he turned and surveyed the gathering of his inner circle.

Carol surveyed it as well. The newcomers were Sylvia Nash and her son, huddled against her. Pale, distant, remote in her grief, Sylvia sat quietly in a corner of the huge sofa. Carol's heart went out to her. Alan was missing. Bill had told her what had happened. She hadn't got to know that man in the wheelchair, but during their brief contact last Saturday Carol had sensed something fine and strong within him. And now, looking at Sylvia, she could sense a comparable rebellious strength within her. This woman had been bat-tered but refused to bow. Ba stood tall behind her like some preternatural guardian.

Carol leaned against Bill; Nick sat stiff and straight but inattentive on Bill's far side.

Jack had disappeared, searching for a woman he'd brought back from Hawaii.

"Well," Glaeken said, jamming his hands into his pockets as he looked at Bill and Nick, "our wanderers have returned. What have you brought back?"

Bill reached into a sack and pulled out a few odd-shaped pieces of rusted metal. He dropped them onto the marble-topped coffee table.

"This is the best I could do."

Glaeken picked up the pieces, examined them closely, then nodded.

"Amazing. These are from the blade. How—?"

"Nick helped. I'd never have found them without him. But are they . . . is it enough?"

"These are fine. We need only a sample of the metal. I—"

Jack burst in then, his expression bleak. "She's gone! Disappeared! I can't find a trace of her."

Glaeken stared at him. "But how—?"

"Rasalom's skin . . . walking around . . . I got distracted . . . shit!"

He tossed a heavy, intricately carved necklace onto the table. It rolled and skidded to a stop in front of Glaeken. He didn't pick it up to examine it. He seemed to know it was right merely by looking at it.

"The other?"

Jack lowered his gaze. "Where do you think? Kolabati's got it."

Carol noticed Glaeken's complexion fade two or three shades toward white. He seated himself—carefully.

"And she's gone?"

"I got suckered," he said. "Twice. Let myself get distracted. But there's enough here to do your thing, right? I mean, you've got the kid, pieces of the old sword, and one of the necklaces. That's enough, right?"

Glaeken sat motionless for an endless moment, then he shook his head, slowly, painfully.

"No, Jack. I wish it were, but we need the combined power within the pair of necklaces to make this work."

Jack shot to his feet and began to pace the room. Carol had learned something about him from Glaeken during the past few days, how he made his living working for people who had been let down by everyone else. Now he obviously felt he'd let them all down and his failure was eating him alive.

"I don't know where she is. She took off into the city. She could be anywhere. She could be dead."

"It's all right, Jack," Glaeken said. "You brought her back."

"But I didn't get it done. That's the bottom line: I didn't get it *done*!"

"I doubt if anyone else on earth could have returned with even one of the necklaces."

"All fine and good. But you're telling me one necklace doesn't cut it, so the whole trip was a waste of time. That makes Bill's trip a waste of time. And I took Ba with me, and maybe if he'd stayed home . . ."

Jack didn't finish the thought. He stopped and faced the group. His eyes were tortured. It took him a moment to find his voice again.

"I blew it. And because of that, there's no way out now, for any of us. I've let everybody down. I'm sorry."

He turned and started for the door. Carol tried to think of something to say that would ease his pain, lighten his load, but before she could call out to him, she saw Sylvia reach out and grab his arm as he passed. He stopped and stared down at her. She rose wordlessly, slipped her arms around him, and hugged him.

For a moment Jack stood stiffly, looking baffled, then he lifted his arms and returned the embrace. He closed his eyes as if in pain.

Bill rose to his feet and Carol rose with him.

"It's okay, Jack," Bill said. "Really. We know you gave it your best shot.

We trust in that. And if that's the way it is, then that's the way it is. We go on from here as best we can."

He stepped toward Jack and extended his hand.

Jack eased away from Sylvia and gripped Bill's hand, then Carol hugged him, then Glaeken offered his own hand.

His throat working, his voice on the verge of crumbling, Jack stepped back and stared at the semicircle that had formed around him.

"You people . . . you people. Where'd you all come from? Where've you been all my life?"

His voice seemed to fail him then. He took a deep breath, held it, then let it out as he turned to Glaeken.

"I'll keep searching for her, but she knows this city. She's lived here. If she doesn't want to be found, then . . ."

Shaking his head, he turned and walked out the door.

When he was gone, they all stood and stared at each other in silence.

"There's no hope then?" Carol said.

Glaeken heaved a sigh, slow and heavy, as he shook his head. His eyes were remote, his disappointment palpable.

"If there is, it depends on Kolabati having a change of heart. And that . . ." He shook his head again.

"That's it?" she said. "We've lost? What do we do now?"

"We do what we've always done," Bill said. "We don't back down. And we refuse to be anything less than we are."

Carol looked at him standing tall and defiant. He'd told her what he'd been through in the past five years, and if that hadn't broken him, she doubted anything could. She realized in a blaze of heat how much she loved Bill Ryan.

Glaeken too seemed to draw strength from him.

"You're right, of course. We can make Rasalom come for us rather than crumble and fall toward him. That will be a victory of sorts." He extended his elbow toward Sylvia. "Mrs. Nash, if you'll allow me, I'll show you the apartment I've been holding for you."

As they left, Bill turned to Nick.

"Want me to take you back to your room?"

Nick was staring at the flames in the fireplace. To Carol's surprise, he answered.

"I want to watch the fire. I want to see where all the ashes go."

Carol dared a quick glance at the fireplace, ready to turn away if Rasalom's skin was still there. But it wasn't—at least not recognizably so. Just burning logs.

"They go up the chimney and float away, Nick," Carol said.

"Not all of them. Some are on the window."

Carol turned and for the first time noticed the ashes sticking to the picture window. She gasped and clutched Bill's arm when she saw how they clung in a gray, feathery pattern—the shape of a headless man, spread-eagled against the dying light.

Bill hurried to the wall and touched a button. The drapes slid closed.

"Maybe I'd better walk you home."

"I can't go back there."

The thought of that pile of dirt on the rug, the memory of what he'd planned to do—it sickened her.

"Sorry," he said. "I wasn't thinking."

Carol looked at him. She didn't know how else to put this, other than come right out and say it.

"Can't I stay with you?"

He stared at her for a long moment, then reached out, pulled her close, and kissed her.

"I've been wanting to do that for days." He sighed. "For years. For decades. Forever, I think."

She looked up at him, into his clear blue eyes.

"It's time, isn't it?"

He nodded. "Yes. Long past time, I think."

He took her hand and led her toward his apartment.

The Bunker

"Really, Jack," Gia said into the shortwave microphone. "We're okay. Everything's a mess topside, but we're fine down here."

With the coming of daylight, the grinding had stopped. Why, she couldn't say. Maybe the burrowers returned to the hole, maybe they went dormant during the light time. All Gia knew was that the damned noise had stopped.

But with darkness upon them, she was sure it would start again.

"You don't sound so sure."

I'm trying my best, she thought.

She didn't want to give Jack even a hint about the burrowers. She knew if he thought they were in the slightest danger he'd hop in the first car he could find and rush to them.

And never make it. Jack was as tough and resourceful as they come, but even he couldn't prevail against the horrors of the night. They'd never see or hear from him again. So she couldn't let him suspect a thing.

"You're the one who doesn't sound good," she said, deflecting the talk from herself.

"Yeah, well, I came up short on the Maui trip."

When he'd called earlier to tell her he'd landed safely, he hadn't mentioned success or failure. Now she heard the full story. Kolabati . . . that bitch.

"One isn't enough. I need to find the second."

"You're not thinking of going out tonight."

"I may be crazy, but I'm not insane. Speaking of night, are you sealed in?"

"All three hatches locked up tight."

But the threat wouldn't come by way of the hatch. It would come through the walls.

Somehow they had to hold out through tonight.

Until tonight, Carol had made love to only two men in her life, both of them husbands. Bill was the third and by far the most anxious. His hands trembled as he undressed her, as he helped her remove his own clothes, as he caressed her.

"I'm not very practiced at this," he told her when they were lying skin-to-skin, and even his voice trembled.

"I am," Carol said, and drew him into her.

What he lacked in technique he more than made up for with the intensity of his passion. Their lovemaking rocked the mattress. Hot, fierce, and over too soon for Carol, but somehow it left her as breathless as Bill. She hugged him tight against her, reveled in his being warm and wet within her.

And then she heard him sobbing softly on her shoulder.

"Bill? Are you okay?"

"No. Yes. I don't know. It's just . . . I keep thinking . . . what a waste. This is so wonderful. I've never felt so close to another human being in my entire life. I'm way past my prime, Carol. We can all count the rest of our days on one hand, and I'm just now learning what it's like to make love. All those years— wasted! My *life*—wasted! What an idiot!"

"Don't you say that, Bill Ryan. Don't you ever let me hear you say that!" She shared his hurt, but she was angry at him too. "You did *not* waste your life. Maybe your beliefs were misplaced, but not your actions. You spent your life being a father, a real father, to hundreds of lost and abandoned boys, the first and maybe the best father they ever knew. You couldn't have done that if you'd had a wife and children of your own. You couldn't have been there twenty-four hours a day for them like you were. So it wasn't wasted at all. You made a difference, Bill. A big difference. A lot of grown men are walking around who still remember you, who still have a warm place in their hearts for their beloved Father Bill, who are maybe good to their own kids because you were good to them, because you showed them how it's done. That's a legacy, Bill, one that might have gone on for generations if Rasalom wasn't trying to bring all our generations to an end. So don't you dare say you've wasted your life—at least not in front of me."

After a long pause, Bill lifted his head and kissed her.

"I love you," he said. "I puppy-loved you in high school and then buried it in an unused corner like a bone. But it never went away. I think I've always loved you."

"And I think part of me always loved you, a little bit. But now all of me loves you—a lot."

"Good. Does that mean we do this again? Soon?"

"How soon?"

"Now?"

And then she realized that he was hard again inside her.

"Oh my."

The Final Piece

WFPW-FM

> FREDDY: The Internet's definitely down again, folks. Talk about a bummer.
>
> JO: And worse, it's four o'clock in the afternoon, ten minutes of light left.
>
> FREDDY: Yeah. According to the Sapir curve, this is the next to last sunset. Let's all hope he's wrong, man.

Glaeken, feeling as low as he'd ever felt in all his millennia, had settled Sylvia Nash and her son in her apartment and was on his way back to his apartment.

"Yo, G!"

He looked up and saw Julio, the muscular little bar owner, hurrying his way down the hall.

"A lady downstair lookin' for Jack."

"What does she want? You let her in, I hope."

Night had fallen. The streets would be lethal. Where had she come from?

"Yeah, but I got Doug and Nadia staying in the lobby with her. Thing is, I can't find Jack nowhere an' she's real crazy 'bout seeing him."

"Is it the woman he sent into hiding?"

"Gia? No way. I know Gia. This lady's dark. Says her name's Cola-body or som' like that."

Glaeken closed his eyes and steadied himself, making sure he'd really heard that last sentence. Could it be? Could it truly be her? Or could this be another of Rasalom's games?

Well, he'd know soon enough.

"Bring her to the top floor. Immediately."

A few moments later, Glaeken was waiting by the door to his apartment when Julio ushered a slim, dark, raven-haired woman from the elevator. Her clothes were torn, her hands and face smudged with grime, the dark almonds of her eyes were wide, wild, exhausted. Not at all the way Glaeken had pictured her, but he sensed the years crowded beneath the smooth youth of her skin.

He could barely drag his eyes from the necklace encircling her throat. He had to have it. How he was going to get it, he did not know, but he could not allow her to leave here with that necklace.

"Miss Bahkti?"

She nodded. "And you're the man Jack told me about, the old one?"

The old one. He hid his smile. Is that how he speaks of me? Well, it's true, isn't it?

"Yes, that would be me. Call me Glaeken. Come in."

He nodded his thanks to Julio and ushered Kolabati into his apartment. She stumbled crossing the threshold and almost fell, but Glaeken caught her under the arm.

"Are you all right?"

She shook her head. "No. Not in the least."

He led her to the sofa. She all but fell into it. She rubbed a trembling hand over her eyes and sighed. She looked utterly exhausted.

"Jack told me what was happening to the world. I thought he was lying, trying to trick me. It couldn't be as bad as he said." She paused and looked up at Glaeken with haunted eyes. "But it's worse. Much worse."

Glaeken nodded, watching her closely. She seemed dazed.

"And worse is yet to come."

She stared up at him. "Worse? Outside . . . one street over . . . something huge and black and slimy . . . so big it had to squeeze against the buildings on both sides to get down the street. It was covered with tentacles and it was reaching into the windows and pulling out anything it found. I heard people—children—screaming."

"A long dark night of the soul for the survivors," Glaeken said.

Kolabati shifted her gaze toward the fire and fingered her necklace.

"Did Jack give you the other necklace?"

"Yes."

"Is it sufficient for your needs?"

"No." Where was this leading?

"Then you still need this one?"

"Yes."

"Will it make a difference?"

"It may. It may be too late now for anything to make a difference, but it is our only chance, our only hope. We must try it."

She continued to stare at the fire. Her voice was barely audible.

"All right then. You may have it."

A wave of relief struck Glaeken. The impact forced him to sit. But before he could speak, Jack burst into the room.

"It *is* you!" he said, glaring at Kolabati.

"Jack—" Her lips curved halfway to a smile but Jack was in her face before they reached it.

"You lied to me! You agree to come back here and talk to Glaeken, then you pull a vanishing act."

Glaeken wanted to stop Jack before he said anything rash, but noticed that Kolabati was unfazed by the outburst. So he kept quiet.

"That's true," she said. "And I am here. And I've been talking to Glaeken."

Jack hovered over her, his anger visibly evaporating.

"Oh. Yeah, but—"

"I said I'd come back—but on my terms, not yours. I am no one's prisoner, Jack. Ever."

Glaeken studied Jack and Kolabati as they faced off. He sensed more going on between these two than met the eye, but he had no time to concern himself with that. He jumped into the momentary lull.

"Miss Bahkti has agreed to give us her necklace."

"We already have it. You said it wasn't enough."

"No," Glaeken said softly. "The one she is wearing."

Jack's eyes narrowed with suspicion. "What's the catch?"

"No catch, Jack," she said, her voice laden with exhaustion. "What I've seen here has convinced me: You were not exaggerating. Everything is falling apart. This is not a world I wish to live in. If I keep the necklace, I'll go on living in it—indefinitely. That would be horrible beyond imagining. So I've decided to surrender it to someone who can make better use of it."

"But you'll die."

She stared at him. "I'm well aware of that. But I wish to end my life the way I've lived it—on my own terms."

"Fine. But charity isn't in your nature, Bati. You're a *quid pro quo* type—just like me. What's the *quid* here? Is it losing its power? What aren't you telling us?"

"Please, Jack," Glaeken said, offended by his unyielding hostility. "She's agreed to give us the necklace, the rest is really none—"

"I've always been upfront with Bati," Jack said, half-turning toward Glaeken. "She knows that. She knows not to expect anything less." He turned back to Kolabati. "What's the rest of it?"

She rose and stepped to the window. She stared into the living darkness for a long moment.

"Karma," she said. "What's happening out there threatens the turning of the Karmic Wheel."

She turned and faced Jack. Glaeken felt as if he'd been forgotten.

"You know the stains on my karma, Jack. Kusum shared those stains. The weight of that karmic burden drove him to the acts that led to his death at your hands. I've long feared dying because of the retribution my karma will earn me in the next life. Now . . . now I fear living more than dying." She touched her necklace again. "And perhaps . . . if giving this up will allow the Great Wheel to keep turning . . . perhaps this deed will undo all the others. Perhaps this act will purify my karma."

Jack nodded his understanding. Glaeken, too, thought he understood: Kolabati was making a deal with her gods—forgiveness of her karmic burden in return for the necklace. Glaeken wondered if truly there might be a Karmic Wheel. He doubted it. In all his many years he had seen no evidence of it. But he was not about to say anything that might dissuade Kolabati from surrendering that necklace.

Without warning, she reached both hands behind her neck, unfastened the necklace, and handed it to Jack.

"There," she said, her voice husky, her eyes glittering. "This is what you wanted."

Then she turned and headed for the door.

Jack stared a moment at the necklace in his hand, then started after her.

"Bati, wait. Where're you going?"

"Outside. It will end quickly there."

Glaeken rose and followed Jack. He passed him and caught up to Kolabati at the door. He grabbed her arm and stopped her.

"No. I cannot allow you to die like that. Not out there. Not alone."

"Everyone dies alone." Her eyes looked frightened, terrified of what lay beyond, waiting for her. "I'm used to being alone."

"So was I. But I've learned to draw strength from companionship. Let the years take you. It will be gentle—far gentler than out there."

"I'll stay with you, Bati," Jack said. "I'll sit with you to the . . . the end."

"No!" she said, her voice rising. "I don't want you to see me—I don't want *any*one to see me."

A proud woman, Glaeken thought. And vain, too, certainly. But that was her privilege. He loosened his grip on her arm and clasped her hand. He found it cold, moist, trembling.

"I know a place where you can be alone and comfortable. Where no one will see you. Come."

As he began to lead her through the door, Jack stepped forward.

"Wait."

For the first time since Glaeken had met him, Jack looked awkward. His catlike grace was gone. The necklace hung in his hand like a leaden weight. He seemed at a loss for words.

"Please, Jack," Kolabati said, turning to him, "I haven't much time."

"I know. I know. I just wanted to tell you that I've thought some awful things about you for the past few years, but what you're doing now . . . it takes courage. More courage than I think I'd have if positions were reversed. I think you're the bravest woman I know." He reached for her hand and raised it to his lips. "I . . . we all owe you. And we won't forget you."

Kolabati nodded slowly. "I know I don't have your love, so I guess I'll have to settle for that." She stretched up and kissed him on the cheek. "Good-bye, Jack."

"Yeah," Jack said, his expression stricken. "Good-bye."

Glaeken led Kolabati down to Carol's apartment—*former* apartment. Carol would not re-enter it. He guided her to the bedroom but did not turn on the light.

"It's quiet here. Safe and dark. No one will disturb you."

He heard the springs squeak as she sat on the bed.

"Will you stay with me?" she said in a small voice.

"I thought—?"

"That was Jack. I couldn't be comfortable with him here. But you're different. Your years stretch far beyond mine. I think you understand."

Glaeken found a chair and pulled it up beside the bed.

"I understand."

His sentiments echoed Jack's: This was one brave woman. He took her hand again as he had upstairs.

"Talk to me. Tell me about the India of your childhood—the temple, the rakoshi. Tell me how you spent your days before you came to wear the necklace."

"It seems I was never young."

Glaeken sighed. "I know. But tell me what you can, and then I will tell you of my youth, what little I remember of it."

And so Kolabati spoke of her girlhood, of her parents, of her fear of the flesh-eating demons that roamed the tunnels beneath the Temple-in-the-Hills. But as she talked on, her voice grew hoarse, raspy. The air in the room grew moist and sour as her tissues returned their vital fluids to the world. Her voice continued to weaken until speech seemed a terrible effort. Finally . . .

"I'm so tired," she said, panting.

"Lie back."

He guided her to a recumbent position, gripping her shoulders and lifting her knees. Beneath her clothes her flesh felt wizened, perilously close to the bone.

"I'm cold."

He covered her with a blanket.

"I'm so afraid. Please don't leave me."

He held her hand again.

"I won't."

"Not until it's completely over. Do you promise?"

"I promise."

She did not speak again. After a time her breathing became harsh and rapid, rising steadily to a ragged crescendo. Her bony fingers squeezed Glaeken's in a final spasm—

And then relaxed.

All quiet.

Kolabati was gone.

Glaeken released her hand and stepped into the hall outside the apartment. Jack sat cross-legged on the floor next to the door. He looked up.

"Is she—?"

Glaeken nodded and Jack lowered his head.

"Collect both necklaces and the blade fragments and be ready to leave for Monroe as soon as it's light."

Jack shot to his feet. "Monroe? Uh-uh. I'm done here. I'm heading out to Abe's place. Gia and Vicky—"

"Will be much better served by your delivering the necklaces and the fragments to an enclave of smallfolk in Monroe."

He shook his head. "No can do. They're scared. I could hear it in their voices. They need me."

Glaeken leaned heavily against the wall. No. This could not be happening. He could not allow Jack to leave. Not now. It hadn't mattered when the refashioning seemed impossible. But now . . . Jack had to be here. To activate the weapon . . . to claim it and have it claim him . . . to transform from Heir to Sentinel . . . Defender . . . to step into Glaeken's worn and empty shoes.

"We—the world needs you more, Jack. This must be done. Alan and Kolabati gave their lives to make this possible. If you use the last daylight to go to Gia instead of the smallfolk, their sacrifices will have been for nothing."

"But Ba—"

"Will not leave Sylvia and Jeffy again. It's up to you—you and Bill together."

He punched the wall. "Shit!"

"Jack, if there were any other way—"

"Yeah-yeah." He waved him off. "Okay, I'll do it. Just stop jawing about it."

"Very well." He twisted the knob and opened the door.

Jack frowned at him. "What are you up to?"

"I promised I'd stay until the end."

Jack nodded and walked away.

Back in the bedroom, the scent of rot was vague in the air. He resumed his seat and found Kolabati's hand again. He would hold it until the skin was cold, dry, as flaky as filo dough, until it crumbled to dust and ran through his fingers. And when the sky began to lighten, he would draw the curtains, close the door, and lock the apartment.

The Bunker

"Mommy, make it stop!"

Vicky had her hands over her ears and a pleading look on her face. Gia seated herself on the bed next to her and enfolded her in a bear hug.

"I wish I could, honey."

The grinding sound gradually had grown from background noise to scratchy

Muzak to cacophony. The bunker walls seemed to act as an amplifier and echo chamber. As far as Gia was concerned, the increasing noise could mean only one thing: Whatever they were, there were a lot of them. And they were digging through the concrete.

Gia felt so trapped she wanted to scream. If Vicky weren't here, she'd be in the middle of one right now, her throat rawed from the ones before it. No way out. The bugs above, the burrowers on all sides and maybe even beneath. They'd been digging their way closer and closer all night.

And worse . . . worst of all . . . Jack had called and said Glaeken needed him for some crucial task that only he could do, and that maybe the end result would bring back the light. He'd said he didn't think he'd have time to do what Glaeken needed and drive out here. He'd asked her what to do, saying if she wanted him to come out, he'd blow off Glaeken to be with her and Vicky.

How could she allow that? If what he had to do offered even the slimmest chance of returning things to normal, she had to let him take it. She'd told him to do what he thought would turn out best for them, for everyone.

The hardest words she'd ever had to say.

She'd ended the transmission feeling almost certain that they'd never see each other again.

And now she watched Abe standing in the center of the bunker floor, turning in a slow circle. When he faced Gia he stopped and gestured to her.

"A word, please, Gia."

She gave Vicky a parting squeeze. "Be right back, sweetie."

When she reached Abe he turned her so their backs were to Vicky.

"The night's almost over," he said in a hushed voice. "If we can hold out just a little longer, light will come and they'll leave us alone."

"Thank God."

"Thanks we shouldn't give yet. I have a feeling a few of them are very close."

"I thought you said this place could withstand an atomic bomb."

"It can. It can withstand anything man or nature can throw at it. But whatever these things are, from man or nature they ain't."

"What do we do?"

"Work your way along the walls with your hands. Look for vibrations. If something's getting close, you should be able to feel it."

"And if I find something—then what?"

"I don't know, but at least we'll know where to stay away from."

"Okay," Gia said slowly. The idea sounded crazy but . . . not as if she had much else to do. "I'll give it a shot."

She started by the entry chimney and moved to her right, rubbing her hands up and down the concrete. The whole wall seemed to be trembling. How was she going to find one spot vibrating more than—

"Oh, God!" she cried as she felt an area of concrete fairly shuddering beneath her palms. "Something's happening here!" She pressed harder. "I think—"

And then a foot-wide circle of wall exploded, showering her with gray powder and bits of concrete.

Gia cried out and tumbled backward as a tapered snout, glistening white, wriggled into the room. Row upon concentric row of black teeth ringed its central mouth and ground away the concrete as the head twisted back and forth, ninety degrees this way and that. From somewhere behind her she heard Vicky's high-pitched scream.

Movement to her right—Abe, moving faster than she'd have thought possible.

"Hold your ears, ladies!" he shouted as he stepped up to the creature and jammed one of his shotguns into the opening in its snout.

Gia slapped her palms over her ears, barely in time to muffle the thunderous *boom!* as he pulled the trigger. He jerked back from the recoil, then another *boom!* as he fired again.

The thing thrashed and bucked, and then, leaking thick yellow goo, backed away, withdrawing into its burrow.

Two more thundering reports as he fired twice more into the opening.

Then he backed into the center of the space and did a slow turn. His lips were moving. She lowered her hands to hear him.

"Any others, Gia? I can't tell. My ears are ringing too much."

Gia scrambled to her feet and listened. She heard Vicky sobbing, but the grinding had stopped.

"I don't hear anything. Do . . . do you think you scared them away?"

He shook his head. "I hurt that one, but the rest . . . I can only think it's the light. It's dawn and they've gone to do whatever they do when it's light."

Gia hurried over to where Vicky cowered on the bed and wrapped her arms around her quaking shoulders. She watched Abe standing alone with his shotgun. He couldn't defend them alone. And Jack wasn't coming.

She made a decision.

"Abe . . . remember your offer of shooting lessons?"

"Yes?"

"I'm going to take you up on it."

His face lit. "Really?"

She nodded. "I need to be able to do what you just did."

THURSDAY

The Last House on the Left

Monroe, Long Island

"You sure these are the directions he gave you?"

Jack stopped his Vic in the middle of the road and peered about in the gloomy light. Bill Ryan sat in the passenger seat, a pair of shotguns propped between his knees. The two necklaces, the katana, and the blade fragments sat between them in a long, carved wooden box.

Bill peered at the hastily scribbled note in his hand.

"Positive."

Jack would have preferred to have Ba along on this trek but Bill seemed different today. He had an odd air of peace about him that Jack found strangely comforting.

And he needed comfort, damn it. He should have been heading west today instead of east. Gia's voice had sounded strange this morning. She'd said they'd had a quiet night . . . why was he having trouble believing her?

And it had taken goddamn forever to make their way through the carnage in and around the city.

"You grew up in Monroe, didn't you?" he asked, not because he gave a damn, but to fill the void.

"Yeah, but in all those years I never ventured out here. I don't think I ever knew there *was* an out here. This is nowhere."

Nowhere. Perfect description, Jack thought.

But he'd been here before. Two years ago—damn near to the day—he'd discovered Scar-lip, the last rakosh, in a freak show that had set up out here in the far northeast corner of Monroe.

He was following a dirt road through the heart of a vast salt marsh. To their left, under a low, leaden, overcast sky, Monroe Harbor sat smooth and flat and still and gray as slate. Somewhere dead ahead lay the Long Island Sound. Nothing moved. Not an insect, not a bird, not even a breeze to stir the reeds and tall grass to either side. Like being caught in the middle of a monochrome marshscape.

The only break in the monotony was the file of utility poles marching along the east flank of the road toward what looked like an oversize outhouse near the water at its far end.

"That's got to be the place," Bill said.

"Can't be."

"You see anything else around? We're supposed to follow this road out to the house at its end. That's the place."

Jack doubted it but put the Vic in gear again and started forward. As they approached the shack, Jack noticed smoke rising from behind it.

"Whoever he is, he's got a fire going."

"I hope he builds a better fire than he builds a house," Bill said.

"Right. Must be the original crooked man and this must be the original crooked house."

The shack did not seem to have one true upright. The entire one-story structure canted left, leaning against the peeling propane tank on its flank; its crumbling brick chimney canted right; and the aerial atop that canted left again.

But this had to be it: the house at the end of the road.

A battered, antediluvian Torino sat in front. Except for the fire in the back, the place looked deserted.

"You know," Bill said as they neared it, "that's not just a plain old fire back there. I don't know much about that sort of thing, but it looks to me like he's got some kind of forge going full blast."

As Jack made a left into the small graveled front yard he noticed ripped and tattered screens, smashed windows—like every other house they'd passed on their way out from the city.

"This doesn't look good."

Bill shrugged. "The fire's going, and Glaeken said . . ."

"Yeah. Glaeken said."

He parked and took the wooden box with him when he got out. Bill accompanied him to the door. To the right lay what appeared to be a small vegetable garden, but nothing was growing. The front door opened before they reached the steps and a grizzled old man glared at them through the remnants of the screen in the upper half of the storm door.

"Took your time getting here."

His shock of gray hair stuck out in all directions. He needed a shave like his stained undershirt needed to be washed—or better yet, tossed out and replaced.

Jack remembered him from two years ago: George Haskins, the man they were looking for. Except now he looked . . . younger. No matter. This was the guy.

"You're expecting us?" Jack said.

How could that be? The phones had been out for days.

"Yeah. You got the metal?"

"May we come in?" Bill said.

"I don't think they'd like that. You see—"

Jack heard a garbled babble from somewhere behind the solid lower half of the storm door.

Haskins looked down and spoke toward the floor. "All right, all right!" Then he looked up at Jack again and thrust his hand through the opening. "They're real anxious to get started. Gimme the metal."

Jack handed him the box. Haskins pulled it inside and handed it to someone down by his feet.

"There! You happy now? You gonna shut up and leave me alone now? Good!" He looked up at Jack again. "They been driving me crazy waiting for this stuff."

"Who?"

"My tenants. I been spending my nights down in the crawlspace with 'em. They been keepin' the cooters out. If it hadn't—"

More babbling.

"Okay, okay. They say come back in about four hours. If they really rush it, they should be done by then."

Curious, Jack stepped up on the stoop and peeked through the opening. He saw maybe a dozen scurrying forms, like midgets, only they couldn't have been more than eighteen inches tall. And they looked furry.

"What the—?"

Haskins moved to block his view.

"Four hours. They'll have it for you then."

"Yeah, but who are 'they'?" Jacked remembered Glaeken mentioning "smallfolk."

"My tenants. Been with me since a little before the Beatles broke up, just waitin' for this day—'when time is unfurled and we're called by the world,' as they put it. Seems to me like time and ever'thing else is unfurled these days. So go away and come back later. They don't want nobody around while they're workin'."

He closed the door.

"Four hours," Bill said, looking at his watch as they returned to the car. "It's a little after eleven now. That'll be after dark."

Jack sat behind the wheel, unease gnawing at his stomach. Bill was right. According to the Sapir curve, this morning's sunrise had been the last. After four hours and forty-two minutes of light, the sun would set for the last time at 3:01 P.M. No more day forever after. Only night.

And then there'd be no quarter from the "cooters," as Haskins called them.

Damn. Could have been to Abe's by now.

"How the hell are we going to get back?"

Jack started the car. "Drive. How else?"

He pulled out and headed back down the road, wondering how to kill the time. No point in heading back to the city. They'd have to spend it in Monroe.

"What is it with this town?" Jack said.

"Village," Bill said. "North Shore towns like to refer to themselves as villages."

"Fine. Village. But what gives here? Every time I turn around, the name pops up. You're from Monroe, Carol's from Monroe, the doc, the Nash lady and her boy are from Monroe. And now we're back out here again making a delivery to some old coot with a house full of furry dwarfs. And I don't want to get started on what I've been through out here in the past few years."

"I've wondered about that myself, and I think I know."

"The 'burst of Otherness' people have told me about?"

Bill frowned. "Haven't heard that. Take a right at the end of the road down here and I'll show you."

Bill guided him to a residential neighborhood, to Collier Street. They stopped in front of number 124, a three-bedroom ranch.

"This is where it happened," Bill said, his voice strangely husky as he stared at the house through his side window. "This is where Rasalom re-entered the world more than a quarter century after Glaeken thought he'd killed him. It was in the house that used to stand on this lot—the original was set afire— that Carol conceived the child whose body was usurped by Rasalom. That single event has left a stain on this town, given it some sort of psychic pheromone that draws odd people and creates a fertile environment for weird and strange occurrences."

"Like those dwarfs out in the marsh."

"Right. They must have sensed Rasalom's return, must have known they'd be needed, so they've been camped out there with George Haskins for decades, waiting for their moment. Now it's come. Same with the *Dat-tay-vao*. It traveled halfway around the world to end up in Monroe, where it lived for a while in Alan Bulmer, then moved on to Jeffy. From what I can gather, that journey began about the time Rasalom was reconceived."

"So it must have known that it would be needed too."

"So it seems. But there were other occurrences back in that first year, a cluster of hideously deformed children born in November and early December. No one could explain it then, but now I can see that they all must have been conceived around the same time as Rasalom. His very presence in town must have mutated them in embryo."

Jack nodded. He'd heard about that cluster of deformities and, to his regret, had even met some of them.

"That must have been the 'burst of Otherness' I mentioned."

"Seems likely." Bill shook his head. "Those deformed children . . . major tragedies for the families involved but merely warnings of what was to come."

Jack mulled that as Bill guided him through the town, past the high school where he'd been a football star, past the new house built on the site of his family home, burned to the ground, killing both of his elderly parents.

"I'm sure Rasalom was responsible for that too," he said in a low voice, thick with emotion. He ground a fist into his palm. "So many others—friends, acquaintances, *children*! My folks, Jim, Lisl, Renny, Nick, and Danny—dear God, Danny! Damn, I've got scores to settle!"

Jack put a hand on Bill's shoulder and gave it a reassuring squeeze.

"We'll get the bastard. We'll make him pay."

Sure we will.

"Meanwhile, let me show you something—if I can find it."

It took Jack ten minutes of scouting before he recognized the street. He turned onto it and found the vacant lot.

"Two years ago, one of those holes opened here—but only for a few minutes."

Bill rolled down his window and stared. "Wasn't that—? Yes! That used to be the old Rubin place. But where's the house? And I seem to remember a big oak."

"House and most of the tree—down the hole."

Bill turned to Jack, eyes wide. "The disappearing house! I remember hearing about it but thought it was a *Weekly World News* story or something along those lines. I never dreamed it happened in Monroe." He stared out the window again. "The Rubin place . . . I can't believe it. But how did you—?"

Jack put the car in gear. "Long story. But we've got time."

Jack told it as they wandered around Monroe. The town—village—seemed all but deserted. No bodies lay about. No bodies anywhere. Probably because unlike the bugs, which merely sucked the juices from their victims, the newer, bigger hole-things devoured their kills. Occasionally Jack spotted fearful faces peering at them from darkened rooms through shattered windows. As they cruised the main drag through the remnants of the downtown harbor-front area, a gang of lupine scavengers began to approach the car.

Bill lifted one of the Spas-12s.

Jack looked at him. "You know how to work that thing?"

"It's not rocket science, and I almost hope they try something." He spoke through thin, tight lips. "I'm feeling *real* mean at the moment."

At sight of the shotgun they lost interest and trotted away.

Jack stared at him. "Even you."

"What?"

"It's getting to you. Even you're starting to feel the effects of this craziness."

"And you're not?"

"Nah. I've made my living waiting for guys like that to start something. You're just beginning to window-shop in the neighborhood where I've spent my adult life."

Abe's Place

"Like a rifle it's not. Not like a pistol even. Those you must caress, treat gently. A shotgun is a brute that throws not single well-aimed punches, but flurries."

She thought of her father and his hunting shotguns, but they were nothing compared to this. The barrels were longer and smaller gauge. She prayed he and mom were all right.

Focus, she told herself.

She couldn't help them, but she could do everything in her power to protect Vicky. And if that meant learning to shoot . . .

Gia tried to relax but found it impossible. The surprising weight of the weapon in her hands, the evidence of its destructive power—she was looking at the holes Abe had blown in the barn wall—had her insides coiled into tight little knots.

And now it was her turn to pull the trigger.

She and Abe stood side by side in the ravaged barn, three feet or so from its north wall. Vicky watched from a good twenty feet behind them.

"Okay," Abe said. "In your hands you hold a fine weapon: a twelve-gauge Benelli M1 Super 90 semiautomatic shotgun. Jack has used one on occasion."

Gia didn't ask what occasion.

"Its magazine holds seven rounds. With one in the chamber, you've got eight shots. We have two of these—one for you and one for me—and lots and lots of double-ought and hardball shells, so don't worry about saving ammo."

"Don't I have to pump something?" In the movies they always seemed to pump the barrel between shots.

"Like I said, it's semiauto. You just pull the trigger when you need to, and if you feel another shot is called for, you pull the trigger again."

"What happens when I run out?"

"I'll show you how to reload later. First we get you comfortable pulling the trigger. Ready?"

No, but she nodded anyway.

"Okay. That hole in the wall there is the worm's mouth. You do what I did last night: Jam the barrel in there and pull the trigger. Pull it twice. I've got you loaded with alternating shot and hardball shells. Give it one of each. That seemed to be enough to back it up last night. Got it? Barrel in, two quick shots, then back up and see if it needs more."

Gia nodded. "Got it."

"I'll get your earmuffs on, then go to it. And remember to be ready for the recoil."

The ear protectors looked like oversize plastic headphones. Abe adjusted a pair on Gia's head, then his own, then he turned and signaled Vicky to hold her ears.

When he nodded the go-ahead, Gia swallowed. God, how guns scared her. But those burrowers scared her more.

She poked the muzzle into the hole, closed her eyes, and pulled the trigger.

—and almost wound up on her butt from the recoil.

Abe had warned her but she hadn't appreciated how strong it would be. She saw him urging her forward, so she rammed the barrel back into the hole and fired again. This time she was ready and held the weapon steady during discharge.

Abe was smiling and she knew she was grinning too. She'd done it, and damn if it hadn't felt good.

Abe was motioning toward the hole and she faintly heard him shouting, "It's another one! Get it! Get it!"

And got it she did.

They ran the scenario twice more and she blew away two more imaginary worms.

Yes!

Then she saw Abe reaching for the shotgun. Was he kidding? She pulled her Benelli out of reach.

Yes, suddenly it was *her* Benelli. She *loved* it. She thought of that bumper sticker she'd always snickered at: *You can have my gun when you pry it from my cold, dead hands.* Now she thought she understood.

Abe looked puzzled as his lips moved. She removed her ear wear.

"It's got to be reloaded," he said.

"*I'll* reload it. Show me."

"All right already, but—"

He reached again but she wouldn't give it up. She *liked* the way it made her feel. She had power. She wouldn't be helpless against those things. When they came for her and Vicky, she could strike back and drive them off.

She didn't want *ever* to let go of her Benelli. At least not until this was over, one way or another.

The Horror Channel's Drive-In Theatre—Special All-Day Edition
And Soon the Darkness (1970) Levitt/Rickman
When Time Ran Out (1980) Warner Brothers
Nothing but the Night (1972) Cinema Systems
Doomed to Die (1940) Monogram
Night Must Fall (1937) MGM
The Dark (1979) Film Ventures
Dark Star (1972) Bryanston
Dead of Night (1946) Universal
Fade to Black (1980) Compass International
Don't Be Afraid of the Dark (1973) TV
Night World (1932) Universal

Abe's Place

She stood with Abe and Vicky on the stone outcropping and stared at the hole in the valley below. Her arms ached from the repeated recoil of the practice, but she was comfortable with the Benelli now, and could reload almost as fast as Abe.

In the fading light she could make out scores of mounds radiating from the hole. But the ones that had started off in the other direction had curved around and were now pointed toward them.

"They must have sent out a signal," Abe muttered. "They all know we're here."

Gia shivered. That meant even more of them gnawing at the bunker tonight. She prayed whatever Jack was involved in would work.

And soon.

Monroe, Long Island

By 2:30 they were back at Haskins's place. The fire was still burning in the forge in the back, though not as brightly as before. The clang of metal upon metal filled the air.

"You're early," Haskins said at the door, still not inviting them in.

"We know," Bill said, "but the dark's coming and we want to get moving as soon as we can."

"Can't say as I blame you. Just as well you did show up. They're almost done. Wait in the car and I'll bring it out to you."

Jack hesitated asking, then figured, what the hell. "You wouldn't happen to have a shortwave, would you?"

"What fer? Don't know nobody anywheres."

"I do," Jack said.

He led the way back to the car. Bill got inside and began fiddling with the radio, trying to find a broadcast of any sort. Jack paced in front, his gut twisting steadily tighter as the gray sky faded toward black.

"Listen," Bill said, sticking his head out the window. "The clanging's stopped."

"Doesn't matter," Jack said. "Too late. We're not going to make it back. Even if we had a goddamn *plane* we couldn't make it back in one piece."

The storm door slammed then, and out came old George Haskins lugging two blanket-wrapped objects in his arms like sick children.

"There you go," he said, dumping them into Jack's waiting hands.

One bundle was square and bulky, the other long and slim. And they were *heavy*. Bill took the smaller one and together they placed them on the back-seat, then Jack was diving for the steering wheel.

"It's been great talking to you, George, but we've gotta run."

"Good luck, boys," Haskins said, heading back to his front door. "I don't know what this all means, but I sure hope it works out."

The rear wheels kicked gravel as Jack accelerated down the road. He glanced at the rearview mirror and saw Haskins standing on the stoop, watching them go. He couldn't be sure in the dim light but he thought he saw a group of knee-high figures clustered around him. Then Haskins waved—they *all* waved.

Blinking his eyes to clear them, Jack concentrated on the road.

Somewhere beyond the mists that masked the sky, the sun was setting for the last time.

"We're not going to make it," he said. "No way we can get back alive."

"We've got to give it our best shot. We don't have any other options that I can see."

"Oh, we'll give it a shot, Billy boy. One *hell* of a shot."

But we're not going to make it.

He wished again that he hadn't sent Gia and Vicky off with Abe. He needed to see them again, hold them in his arms—one last time before the end.

WFPW-FM

JO: This is it, folks. It's 3:01 in the afternoon. Supposedly the last sunset, man. If Sapir's curve is right, the last time we'll ever see daylight.

FREDDY: Yeah. Nobody's offered us any hope, so we can't pass any on to you. We wish we could, but—

JO: And don't ask us why we're here because we don't know ourselves. Maybe 'cause it's the only thing we know how to do.

FREDDY: Whatever, we'll keep on doing it as long as the generators hold out, so keep us on as long as you've got batteries to spare. If we hear anything we'll let you know. And if you hear anything, call us on the CB and we'll pass it on.

JO: Any way you look at it, it's gonna be a long night.

PART THREE

NIGHT

Aaaahh! NIGHT. Endless night. Everlasting darkness.

Rasalom turns within his fluid-filled chrysalis and revels in the fresh waves of panic seeping through from the nightworld above. Darkness reigns. His dominion is established beyond all doubt. A fait accompli.

Except for one flaw, one minuscule spot of hope—Glaeken's building. But that is a calculated flaw. That too will fade once its residents realize that all their puny efforts to reassemble the weapon are for naught. It is too late—too late for anything. The juices from those crushed hopes will be SWEET.

All Rasalom need do now is await the completion of the Change at the undawn tomorrow, then break free from this shell to lay claim to this world.

His world.

And he is nearly there. He feels the final strands of the metamorphosis drawing tight around and through him. And when it is done, he will rise to the surface and allow Glaeken to gaze on the new Rasalom, to shrink in awe and fear from his magnificence before the life is slowly crushed from his body.

Soon now.

Very soon.

END PLAY

Manhattan

"Where can they *be*?"

Carol knew she was being a pest, that no one in the room—neither Sylvia, nor Jeffy, nor Ba, nor Nick, not even Glaeken himself—could answer the question she'd repeated at least two dozen times in the past hour, but she couldn't help herself.

"I know I'm not supposed to be afraid, I know that's what Rasalom wants, but I can't help it. I'm scared to death something's happened to Bill. And Jack."

"That's not fear," Glaeken said. "That's concern. There's an enormous difference. The fear that Rasalom thrives on is the dread, the panic, the terror, the fear for one's self that paralyzes you, makes you hate and distrust everyone around you, that forces you either to lash out at whoever is within reach or to crawl into a hole and huddle alone and miserable in the dark. The fear that cuts you off from hope and from each other, that's what he savors. This isn't fear you're feeling, Carol. It's anxiety, and it springs from love."

Carol nodded. That was all fine and good . . .

"But where *are* they?"

"They're gone," Nick said.

Carol's stomach plummeted as she turned toward him. Glaeken, too, was staring at him.

Nick hadn't answered her all the other times she'd asked the same question. Why now?

"Wh-what do you mean?"

"They're gone," he repeated, his voice quavering. "They're not out there. Father Bill and the other one—they've disappeared."

Carol watched in horror as a tear slid down Nick's cheek. She turned to Glaeken.

"What does he mean?"

"He's wrong," Glaeken said, but his eyes did not hold the conviction of his words. "He has to be."

"But he sees things we don't. And he hasn't been wrong yet. Oh, God!"

She began to sob. She couldn't help it. Lying in Bill's arms last night had been the first time since Jim's death that she had felt like a complete, fully functioning human being. She couldn't bear to lose him now.

Or was this part of a plan?

She swallowed her sobs and wiped away her tears.

"Is this another of Rasalom's games? Feed us a little hope, let us taste a little happiness, make us ache for a future and then crush us by snatching it all away?"

Glaeken nodded. "That is certainly his style."

"No!" she screamed.

The outburst shocked her. She never raised her voice. Never felt it necessary. But this had leapt from her—and it seemed right. It capsulized the anger she felt. She glanced over to where Jeffy sat reading a picture book with Sylvia. Sylvia was looking at her with a curious expression, but the boy wasn't paying attention. Carol turned back to Glaeken.

"No," she said again, in a lower voice. "He's not getting anything from me. I won't be afraid, I won't lose hope, I won't give up."

She went to the huge curved sofa, picked up a magazine, and sat down to read it. But she couldn't see the trembling page through her freshly welling tears.

The Horror Channel
<no transmission>

"Got to be those things in the backseat," Jack said in a hushed voice.

Bill said nothing. He held his breath and leaned away from the passenger-side window as countless tentacles brushed across its surface.

Hurry up!

A giant, tentacled slug blocked their way on Broadway as it squeezed into 47th Street. He mentally urged it to keep moving and get out of their way.

"This happened to me once before," Jack went on. "With the rakoshi. As long as I was wearing one of the necklaces, they couldn't see me. One or both of those things Haskins gave us was made from the necklaces. This has got to be the same kind of effect. I mean, look at that slug. It's ignoring us like we don't even exist."

The whole trip had been like a dream, an interminable nightmare. The horrors from the holes had taken over—completely. Their movements had lost the frantic urgency of all past nights. Now they were more deliberate, no longer an invading army, but more like an occupying force.

Bill and Jack had traveled in from the Island through swarms of bugs and crawlers large and small—but they had traveled unnoticed. An occasional horror would flutter against one of the windows or crash into a door or a fender, but each was accidental contact. Still, their progress had been slow through the dark dreamscape, and when they arrived at the Midtown Tunnel, they'd found it impassable—choked with countless giant millipede-like creatures. They'd finally found their way across the miraculously intact Brooklyn Bridge and had been making good time heading uptown on Broadway. The wide avenue had run downtown in the days when it had been a thoroughfare for cars instead of crawlers, but no one seemed to be writing tickets tonight.

Bill watched Jack. "You wanted to keep on going west, didn't you."

Jack glanced at him, then looked away. "Say what?"

"When we hit Manhattan and it was clear we weren't going to be attacked, you wanted to cut straight across and into Jersey. Am I right?"

"Crossed my mind."

"You could have dumped me, reached the people you care about, and used these things to protect them. Why didn't you?"

He shrugged. "Not the right thing to do. And Gia would have sent me back anyway." He grinned. "A colossal waste of gas."

Bill thought he finally understood why Glaeken placed such stock in this violent, enigmatic man.

The slug's back end finally cleared enough pavement to allow Jack to scoot around behind it and they were moving again. Another fifteen minutes of picking their way around abandoned cars and the larger crawlers and they arrived at Glaeken's building.

Bill unlocked his door and reached for the handle as Jack drove up on the sidewalk.

"Better not get out empty-handed," Jack said. "You might not make it to the door."

Good thought. Bill grabbed the boxier of the two blanket-wrapped objects and hopped out. Julio was at the lobby door, holding it open.

"Where you guys been?" he said as Bill rushed through. "We been worried sick 'bout you."

Bill patted him on the shoulder as he passed.

"Elevator still working?"

"Slow as shit, but it gets there."

Bill hopped in and waited for Jack only because it would have been a slap in the face to leave him behind. The need to be with Carol was a desperate, gnawing urgency. He wanted to see her, hold her, let her know he was all right. She had to be sick with worry by now.

Jack hit a button short of the top.

"Got to make a stop."

Bill knew it wasn't for the bathroom.

"Hope they're okay."

"Yeah." His voice was tight. "So do I."

Jack got out and seconds later Bill reached the top floor alone. He fairly ran for Glaeken's apartment, and there she was, the wonder and joy and relief in her eyes so real, and just for him. She sobbed when he wrapped his free arm around her. He wanted to carry her back to the bedroom right now but knew that would have to wait.

"Nick said you were dead!"

Bill straightened and looked at her. "He did? Dead?"

"Well, not dead. But he said you were gone—not there anymore."

"Why would he—?"

And then Bill thought he understood. Just as he and Jack had been invisible to the bugs on their trip home, so they must have been invisible to Nick as well.

He realized that he and Carol were the center of attention—Sylvia, Jeffy, Ba, Glaeken—everyone but Nick was staring at them. He released Carol and showed his blanket-wrapped bundle to Glaeken.

"We got it. Those smallfolk you mentioned were there. They took the necklaces and scraps and gave us this and another package in return."

"Where's the other?"

"Jack has it. He's making a call. He'll be here in a minute."

Glaeken pointed to the bundle, then the coffee table.

"Unwrap it and place it there, if you will."

Bill searched through the many folds until his hand came in contact with cold metal. He wriggled it free and held it up.

Bill's gasp was echoed by the others in the room.

"A cross!" Carol said in hushed tones.

Yes. A cross, identical to the ones that studded the walls of the keep back in Romania. But the colors surprised him most. He'd expected something made of iron, a dull flat gray similar to the necklaces they had delivered to Haskins this morning. Not this. Not an upright of solid gold and a crosspiece of shining silver, reflecting the dancing light of the flames in the fireplace.

Bill tore his eyes away from its gleaming surface and looked at Glaeken. "Is this it? A cross?"

Glaeken had stepped back, placing a section of the sofa between Bill and himself. He shook his head.

"Not a cross. But it is the source, the reason the cross is such an important symbol throughout the world. In truth it is merely the hilt of a sword."

Bill ran his fingers over its surface and felt something like a tingle.

"But what happened to the iron from the necklaces?"

"You're touching it," Glaeken said. "The smallfolk have a way with metals."

"I guess they do."

Glaeken looked around. "What's taking Jack so long?"

The Bunker

Nightmare.

The only word for it.

Vicky crouched in the center of the floor, fingers jammed into her ears, shoulders quaking as she sobbed in terror. Abe knelt next to her, reloading his shotgun while Gia rotated in a slow circle. Sweat soaked her hair, dripped down her face, drenched the long-sleeve T-shirt she wore. Her insides quaked, her fingers twitched, and her palms felt sweaty against the stock as she waited for the next burrower to show its snout.

The strategy, if it could be called that, was Abe's: One of them would shoot until only one round—the one in the chamber—remained; then the other would take over while the first reloaded.

The burrowers hadn't waited long after dark before resuming their incessant grinding. Gia had expected one to pop through the existing hole, but it remained empty. Maybe the burrower that had made it backed up and died after Abe had shot it, blocking the passage. She could only guess, and feel relieved.

But that didn't last. Others must have been close to breaking through before they'd quit with the coming of the light, because it didn't take long before new holes began opening in the walls and horrid snouts pushing into the bunker.

Abe took the lead, pumping two shots each into the first two, then three into the third. Each time, they writhed and retreated, leaving their holes empty. But more were on the way. Gia couldn't hear them through her ear protectors, but she knew they were coming.

Abe had insisted on wearing the protectors, saying they'd be virtually deaf after a few shots if they didn't. And they might need their hearing.

He tapped her calf and pointed to her right. Gia looked and saw the concrete begin to flake and bulge. She swallowed her fear and hurried over. She reached the spot just in time to see the snout break through. Again, a close look at the concentric rows of black grinding teeth ringing the snout, but this time she got a look inside the round, gnashing mouth and saw more rings of teeth, diamond clear like chew wasps', angled inward for tearing.

Fighting her rising gorge she jammed the muzzle in among those teeth, took a breath, and pulled the trigger—once, twice. The creature twisted, shuddered, then withdrew.

I did it! I got one!

But she couldn't celebrate. Another was breaking through a dozen feet to her right. She ran over and blasted that one twice.

As she looked around for the next invader, she saw a light on the shortwave radio flashing red. An incoming signal. That could only be Jack calling. As she debated answering she felt something tickle the back of her neck. She rubbed it and looked at her hand: fine white powder mixed with sweat.

Cement!

She looked up in time to see a burrower break through the ceiling directly above her. They were coming from all directions!

She screamed and lifted the shotgun. As she rammed the muzzle into the snout she thought of Jack's call. No way they could answer. She prayed he was calling with good news, to say he'd been successful. But if so, she saw no sign of a letup here.

Whatever he was involved in had to work, and work soon.

Very soon.

Or she and Vicky and Abe were goners.

Manhattan

Jack finally stepped into the room carrying the longer package. Something in his face . . .

Bill gripped his arm. "Everything okay?"

He shook his head. "No . . . don't know. Couldn't get an answer. Let's get this done." He hefted his burden. "What's in here?"

"The rest of the instrument," Glaeken said. "Be careful. It will be sharp."

Another intake of breath across the room as the layers of blanket fell away to reveal a gleaming length of carved steel.

"The blade," Jack breathed.

The muscles in his forearm rippled as he held it by the butt spike and raised it in the air, turning it back and forth, letting the light leap and run across the runes carved along its length.

The blade . . . magnificent. The sight of it warmed one part of Bill and chilled another. Something alien and unsettling about those runes. He slipped his arm around Carol and held her closer.

Bill still held the hilt in his free hand. He'd noticed a deep slot in the center of its upper surface—a perfect receptacle for the blade's butt spike.

"Should we put them together?" he asked Glaeken.

The old man shook his head. "No. Not yet. Please place the hilt on the table."

As Bill complied, Jack lowered the blade.

"This too?"

"Drive its point into the floor, if you will."

Jack shot him a questioning look, then shrugged. He upended the blade, grabbed the butt spike with both hands, then drove it through the carpet and deep into the hardwood floor beneath. It quivered and swayed a moment, then stood straight and still.

Glaeken turned to Sylvia. His eyes opaque, his expression grave.

"Mrs. Nash . . . it is time."

Sylvia stared at the gold-and-silver cross gleaming on the table not five feet away and felt all her strength desert her in a rush.

Everything was happening—changing—too quickly. She'd gone to bed last night thinking she'd been freed of the burden of deciding. Jack had only one necklace and it wasn't enough. The instrument could not be reassembled, Jeffy would not be called on to give up the *Dat-tay-vao*. She had been frightened, terrified of the near future, and ashamed at the relief she had felt at being spared the burden of risking her son's mind.

This morning she'd awakened to find everything changed. Glaeken had both necklaces and the original plan was back in motion.

Sylvia had been preparing herself for this moment all day but still wasn't close to ready. How could she ever be ready for this?

She sensed Ba looming behind her and didn't have to look to know that whatever she decided he would be with her 100 percent. But the rest of them . . . she glanced around the room. Carol, Bill, Jack, Glaeken—all their eyes intent upon her.

How could they ask her to do this? She'd already lost Alan. How could they ask her to risk Jeffy?

But they could. And they were. And considering all that was at stake, how could they *not* ask?

Jeffy too seemed to notice their stares. He drew his gaze from the hilt—he'd been fixated on it since Bill had unwrapped it—and turned to Sylvia.

"Why are they all looking at us, Mom?"

Sylvia tried to speak but no sound came. She cleared her throat and tried again.

"They want you to do something, Jeffy."

He looked around at the expectant faces. "What?"

"They want you to—" She looked up at Glaeken. "What does he have to do?"

"Just touch it," Glaeken said. "That is all it will take."

"They want you to touch that cross. It will—"

"Oh, sure!"

Jeffy pulled away from her, eager to get his hands on the shiny object. Sylvia hauled him back.

"Wait, honey. You should know . . . it might hurt you."

"It didn't hurt that man," he said, pointing to Bill.

"True. But it will be different for you. The cross will take something from you, and after you lose that something you . . . you might not be the same."

He gave her a puzzled look.

"You may be like you were before, in the time you can't remember." How to explain autism to a nine-year-old? "You didn't speak then; you barely knew your name. I . . . don't want you to be like that again."

His smile was bright, almost blinding. "Don't worry, Mommy. I'll be okay."

Sylvia wished she could share even a fraction of his confidence, but she had a dreadful feeling about this. Yet if she held him back, didn't let him near the hilt, then what had Alan died for? He'd gone to his death protecting Jeffy and her. How could she hold Jeffy back now and condemn him—condemn everyone—to a short life and a brutal death in a world of eternal darkness?

Yet the risk was Jeffy losing the light of intelligence in those eyes and living on as an autistic child.

Certain darkness without, a chance of darkness within.

What do I do?

She forced her hands to release him. She spoke before she had a chance to change her mind.

"Go, Jeffy. Do it. Touch it."

He lurched away from her, eager to get to the bright metal thing on the table. He covered the distance in seconds, reached out and, without hesitation, curled his tiny fingers around the grip of the hilt.

For an instant his hand seemed to glow, then he cried out in a high-pitched voice. A violent shudder passed through him, then he was still.

What is that?

A disturbance. An aberrant ripple races across Rasalom's consciousness, disrupting the seething perfection of the ambient fear and agony.

Something has happened.

Rasalom searches the upper reaches, sensing out the cause. Only one possible place it could have originated—Glaeken's building.

And there he finds the source.

The weapon. Glaeken has managed to reassemble its components. He has actually recharged it. That is what Rasalom felt.

But even now the sensation is fading.

Such hope concentrated in that room, an unbearable amount. Yet exquisite misery is incipient there. How wonderful it will be to catch the falling flakes of that hope as it crystallizes in the cold blast of fear and terror when they realize they have failed.

For it is too late for them. Far, far too late. This world is sealed away from Glaeken's Ally. Let him assemble a hundred such weapons, a thousand. It will not matter. The endless night is upon the world. A dark, impenetrable barrier. There can be no contact, no reunion of Glaeken with the opposing force.

Let him try. Let his pathetic circle hope. It will make their final failure all the more painful.

There now. The disturbing ripple is gone, swallowed by the thick insulating layers of night that surround it like a shroud.

Rasalom returns to his repose and awaits the undawn.

"Jeffy?"

Her little boy stood stone still with his hand on the hilt, staring at it. His cry of pain had pierced her like a spear and she'd leapt to his side. Now she hovered over him, almost afraid to touch him.

"Jeffy, are you all right?"

He did not move, did not speak.

Sylvia felt a rime of fear crystallize along the chambers of her heart.

No! Please, God, no! Don't let this happen!

She grabbed him by the shoulders and twisted him toward her, caught his chin with her thumb and forefinger and turned it up. She stared into his eyes.

And his eyes . . .

"Jeffy!" she cried, barely able to keep her voice under control. "Jeffy, say something! Do you know who I am? Who am I, Jeffy? *Who am I?*"

Jeffy's gaze wandered off her face to a spot over her shoulder, lingered there a few seconds, then drifted on. His eyes were empty. *Empty.*

She knew that face.

She fought off the encroaching blackness that her mind hungered to escape to. She'd lived with that vacant expression for too many years not to know it now. Jeffy was back to the way he used to be.

"Oh, no!" Sylvia moaned as she slipped her arms around him and pulled him close. "Oh, no . . . oh, no . . . oh, no!"

This can't be! she thought, holding his unresisting, disinterested body tight against her. First Alan and now Jeffy . . . I can't lose them both! I *can't*!

She glared across the room at Glaeken, who stood watching her with a stricken expression. She had never felt so lost, so alone, so utterly miserable in her life, and it was all his fault.

"Is this the way it has to be?" she cried. "Is this it? Am I to lose everything? Why? Why me? Why Jeffy?"

She gathered Jeffy up in her arms and carried him from the room, hurling
one final question at Glaeken and everyone else there as she left.

"Why not *you*?"

The heaviness in Glaeken's chest grew as he stood at the far end of the living
room and watched poor Sylvia flee with her relapsed child.

Because this is war, he thought in answer to her parting question. And
every war exacts its price, on the victors as well as the vanquished.

Even in the unlikely event we win this, we will all be changed forever.
None of us will come through unscathed.

That knowledge did not make him grieve any less for the loss of that poor
boy's awareness.

A single sob burst from Carol and echoed like a shot in the mortuary
silence. Bill slipped his arms around her. Jack stood with his hands in his
pockets, staring at the floor. Ba looked simply . . . lost. And tortured. Glaeken
knew anything that hurt his mistress hurt him doubly. His pain-filled eyes
reflected the war within—torn between following Sylvia or staying here. He
took a step toward the door, then turned back and leaned against the wall.

Glaeken faced the others. "We are ready."

"How can you be so cold?" Carol said, glaring at him.

"I am not immune to their torment. I ache for that child, but even more for
his mother. He may have lost his awareness and his ability to respond to the
world around him, but he has lost his perspective as well—he doesn't know
what he has lost. Sylvia does. She bears the pain for both of them. But we must
save our grief for later. If the price the child has paid is to have meaning, we
must take the final step."

"Okay," Jack said. "What do we do?"

"Put the hilt and the blade together."

"That's it? Then what?"

"Then the signal reaches the Ally or it does not. And then the Ally re-
sponds or it does not."

"Do or die, eh?"

"Quite literally."

"Then let's get to it. We've waited long enough. Let's get this over with."

Jack seemed in a terrible hurry. Why?

He picked up the hilt, hefted it, and turned toward the blade where it jutted from the floor.

"Wait," Glaeken said. "There's something you should know."

Jack was the Heir. The Ally hadn't hung a sign on him saying so, but Glaeken sensed it, and everything pointed to it. Even Rasalom had referred to him as such. He was destined to take on the role of Sentinel, Defender, Guardian when Glaeken died. A natural progression.

But Rasalom's ascension and the initiation of the Change while Glaeken still lived had changed all that. What should have been a simple progression now required an initiation. The Heir would have to participate in the process. When Jack rammed the hilt onto the blade's butt spike, he would become a different sort of being—ageless, potent, powerful.

And so the easiest thing for Glaeken would have been to allow Jack to join the two parts of the weapon and have done with it.

But he felt compelled to warn the man what he was getting into. Glaeken wished someone had warned him countless years ago before his own first encounter with the weapon.

But I was so reckless and headstrong then. Would it have made a difference?

Jack stood by the blade, waiting.

"If this works," Glaeken said, "when you join the two halves you will be, in a very real sense, joining yourself to the weapon and the force that fuels it."

Jack looked at him. "Just by putting it together? No spells or incantations or any of that stuff?"

"None of that *stuff*," Glaeken said, allowing himself a tiny smile. "Because that's just what it is—*stuff*. Showbiz. This is the real thing. Know that it is an intimate bond, permanent, one you will not be able to break no matter how much you desire to."

He noticed that Jack seemed to have lost some of his enthusiasm for joining the hilt to the blade.

"What about you?" he said. "Didn't this used to be yours? Shouldn't you be handling this?"

Glaeken fought the urge to retreat to the farthest corner of the room.

"No. It's over for me. This is not my age. I'm from another time, a long-dead time. This is your age. I saved mine. Someone from your time must save yours."

"So you're saying if this works I'll be the new Sentinel or whatever?"
Glaeken nodded. "You are, after all, the Heir."

The Bunker

Gia saw Vicky leap to her feet and lurch away from her spot, her face a mask
of terror. And then Gia knew why: A snout burst through the floor inches away
from where she'd been crouching. Vicky slipped and fell and the snout stretched
toward her.

"No!" Gia screamed, leaping forward.

She rammed the muzzle of her Benelli into its maw and yanked the trigger
three times in rapid succession.

"Fuck you!" she shouted in a burst of rage and horror. "FUCK you!"

Spurting goo, the thing slipped back into its hole.

Too close. She shuddered. Too, too close.

Vicky was staring at her. "Mom, you said the F-word."

"Did I?" She hadn't realized. "Well, when some slimy worm is trying to
eat your little girl, you're allowed."

She looked around. The situation was deteriorating. Some of the burrowers in the walls and ceiling were starting to wriggle from their holes, revealing
white, bulbous bodies, ringed with bristling ridges. They reminded Gia of
maggots—glistening, human-size maggots.

So many now. Too many. She and Abe simply couldn't reach them all.

But they had to try.

Gia ran over to one that jutted three feet into the room. As she neared, it
whipped toward her, stretching like an accordion. She fell back in shock
and it snapped at her shotgun. She fired and missed, gouging a deep pock
in the ceiling. Another pull of the trigger and this time the shot shredded
an area behind the head. The burrower writhed and twisted, spraying thick
yellow goo, but it kept coming, pushing itself farther and farther into the
room.

Around her she saw others doing the same.

Manhattan

His mouth dry as sand, Jack could only stare at Glaeken. The moment he'd been dreading had arrived.

Or had it?

"But I'm not supposed to . . . at least I was told that I don't take over till you're gone."

"The Change alters the rules. I'm as good as gone. My sword was broken and I have aged. Now there's a new sword, and it needs a new champion, a new Sentinel to wield it. By completing the weapon you accept the role."

Jack thought of Gia and Vicky . . . if they'd somehow survived, taking Glaeken's place meant losing them. Because he wouldn't be Jack anymore. He'd be the new Sentinel, the immortal watchman. He remembered what Glaeken had told him about how his own past relationships had deteriorated as the women grew old and he did not. He'd had to watch his wives, his children, his grandchildren age and wither and die, until he'd decided to have no more wives or children, or even long-term relationships.

Until he'd been freed . . . until he'd known that he and Magda could grow old together.

Watching Gia and Vicky age and die while he stayed young . . . Jack had been struggling for years to find a way to make it work with them, and now Glaeken wanted him to throw everything away—assuming anything was left.

He laid the hilt on the table.

"I'm going to take a rain check."

Glaeken's expression slackened. "Jack, you can't—"

"I can, and I am. What makes you so sure it's me?"

"You know as well as I that you're the Heir."

Looking around, he saw all eyes fixed on him. Confused eyes . . . they didn't know what had gone down these past years, what he and Glaeken were talking about—that he'd been drafted into this cosmic war and, without being given a choice or a say, tagged for the generalship when the time came. Glaeken was saying the time was now. Jack couldn't buy that—*wouldn't* buy that.

"Maybe it's someone else here."

Glaeken sighed. "You know very well it is not. The weapon chooses who shall wield it—and it shall choose you."

"*It* has a say?"

"Of course. What you've known as the *Dat-tay-vao* now resides within the hilt. That is not an inert amalgam of metals, it is very much alive—almost sentient."

"Then let's see if it chooses someone else."

"One of *us*?" Bill said.

Jack turned to him. "Why not?" He was grasping at straws, he knew, but what if there was more than one potential Heir? "None of you is an accidental bystander. You've all played a part in the events leading up to this moment."

He turned to Ba.

"If there was ever a natural-born warrior, it's you, Ba. Maybe you were cured by the *Dat-tay-vao* so you'd be able to travel halfway around the world to wind up here in this room at this time."

Plus, Jack realized, all this had become personal for Ba. No way he couldn't be carrying an incandescent grudge against Rasalom after what happened to his friend Alan and now to Jeffy. Righteous fury—the perfect fuel.

The big Asian's expression remained calm but Jack noticed a tightening in the muscles of his throat. His nod was almost imperceptible.

"I will do this."

Ba stepped forward with no hint of hesitation. Jack glanced around and noticed Sylvia slipping back into the room. She stood in a corner holding her listless Jeffy by the hand. She watched grim-faced as Ba took the hilt from the table and lined it up over the butt spike.

Ba paused and looked at Glaeken. "What will happen?"

"Maybe nothing. It may be too late for anything to work. Rasalom may have us sealed off too completely for the signal to break through."

"But if it does work, how will I know?"

"Oh, you'll know," Glaeken said. "Believe me, we'll all know."

Ba continued to stare at him questioningly.

"For one thing, Ba, the blade and hilt will fuse. That will be your confirmation that the sword has accepted you."

Ba nodded.

Jack noticed that Glaeken took a surreptitious backward step and looked away as Ba inhaled deeply and rammed the hilt home.

Nothing happened . . . nothing that Jack could see.

After a few heartbeats Ba said, "I do not feel different." He pulled up on the hilt, slipping it free of the butt spike. "And they have not become one. It has refused me."

Jack couldn't read his expression. Relief, or disappointment that he would not have this weapon to protect Sylvia and Jeffy?

Jack ground his teeth and hid his frustration. The big guy would have been perfect.

Without a word, Ba held out the hilt to Bill.

Bill blinked. "Me? But I can't . . . I mean, I'm not . . ."

Jack jumped in. "Why not? I mean, from what you told me in the car, you've been Rasalom's nemesis since his rebirth—since *before* his rebirth. Is there anyone alive today besides Glaeken who Rasalom hates more? Look what he did to your life." Jack's life had been shattered too, but not by Rasalom. "That sets you up as someone ready to administer major payback."

Yes. It could be Bill. *Had* to be. He was perfect—a holy man's soul and a warrior's heart. Bill had drawn blood and had withstood the death, misery, and horror of Rasalom's vicious campaign to break him.

They were *made* to face off against each other.

At the moment, however, Bill looked anything but the fearless standard-bearer.

Carol was clutching his arm, but he pulled free and stepped forward. She stood back with her eyes fixed on the hilt and both hands pressed tight against her face, covering her mouth. The ex-priest approached Ba as if he were holding a poisonous snake. Slowly, hesitantly, he reached out with trembling hands and took the hilt from him.

"It can't be me."

Ba stepped aside, clearing the path.

Like a sleepwalker, Bill shuffled to the blade, fitted the tip of the spike into the opening—and paused. He looked around.

"It's not me. I know it's not." But his hoarse voice lacked conviction.

Bill didn't shove the hilt down, he merely let it fall upon the spike. Once again, Jack noticed Glaeken averting his eyes.

But nothing happened—again.

Bill removed the hilt and stepped back from the instrument, his body trembling from head to foot.

Jack closed his eyes and swallowed a surge of bile. He'd run out of denials.

It's me. Christ, it's me.

Glaeken's eyes bored into his, penetrating to his soul. Bill and Ba too were staring at him.

But their faces were replaced by Gia's and Vicky's. Even if, somehow, they were still alive, if he cut and run now they'd have no chance. If this hilt-and-blade thing worked—still a big if—things could never be the same between him and them, but at least he'd be able to give them a chance of survival.

"Damn it!" he said through his clenched teeth. "God*damn* it!" He stepped forward and snatched the hilt from Bill. "No sense in wasting any more time. Let's get this shit over with."

With a single swift motion he positioned the hilt over the spike and— paused. He didn't want this.

But if it's gotta be, it's gotta be.

He set his jaw and pushed the hilt onto the spike.

And waited.

And waited.

He jiggled the hilt. Loose. No fusion.

He didn't know whether to laugh or cry. Maybe cry. Because the inescapable truth was that the instrument, the sword, whatever it was, didn't work. No signal would be going out.

We're all screwed.

He looked up and saw Glaeken gaping at him.

Glaeken balled his fists to keep from shouting.

No! This couldn't be! He'd done everything right! The sword was fresh, new, and ready! Why didn't—?

"Well, then, who is it?" he heard Carol say in a high voice verging on rage. "It's got to be somebody!" She turned to Glaeken. "And who said it has to be a man?"

Glaeken had no answer for that, and Carol wasn't waiting for one anyway. She reached past Jack, lifted the hilt, and slammed it back down.

With no more effect than anyone before her.

"Don't tell me we went through all this for nothing!" she said. "It's got to—" She turned to the figure watching from the far end of the room. "Sylvia! Sylvia, you try it. Please."

Sylvia wiped away a tear. "I don't . . ."

"Just come over and do it."

Leading Jeffy by the hand, Sylvia approached the instrument. She made eye contact with no one.

"This is a waste of time," she said.

The words proved too true. She released Jeffy, lifted the hilt, and rammed it home.

Nothing.

How pathetic they are.

Rasalom's expanded consciousness has witnessed the members of Glaeken's circle stride up to the odd conglomeration of metals and spirit standing in the center of the room, each so full of hope and noble purpose, and watched each of them fail. He relishes the growing despair in the room, thickening and congealing until it is almost palpable.

And something else growing there . . . anger.

When their trite little totem fails, they will begin to turn on each other. Luscious.

The Bunker

Burrowers, living and dead and dying, littered the floor. They ran six to seven feet in length and moved with an obscene, undulating motion. They'd backed Gia, Vicky, and Abe into the corner by the bathroom. Gia had Vicky hidden behind the bathroom door while she and Abe did what damage they could to the invaders. The burrowers would have overrun them by now if the live ones hadn't paused to taste the dead and the nearly so.

Gia's gorge rose at the sight of them tearing into their inert brothers, knowing they'd soon be doing the same to the three humans down here. The dying burrowers jerked and spasmed as they were eaten. Unbidden images of Vicky at their mercy, eaten alive, flashed through her brain.

For the first time in her life she almost felt it might be a good thing that Emma hadn't made it.

Almost.

She couldn't imagine, couldn't allow her child to die like this. Better a quick clean death than . . .

But could she do it? Even if it was the best thing for Vicky, a merciful gift, could she aim this shotgun at her daughter and pull the trigger?

Listen to me. I've got us dead already. And we're not. Jack and Glaeken are still out there. They'll come up with something. They've got to.

But when? Oh God, *when?*

Manhattan

Glaeken watched Sylvia tug the hilt free of the spike and turn in a slow circle. This time she made eye contact—and her gaze was withering.

"This is it?" her voice bitter, brittle. "This is all we get? Alan loses his life, Jeffy sinks back into autism, all for what? For nothing?"

"Maybe it's Nick," Bill said.

"No," Sylvia said, her voice rimed with disdain. "It's not Nick."

Jack shook his head. "Maybe it wasn't refurbished right. Or like Glaeken said, maybe it's too late. Maybe the signal can't get through."

"Oh, it's too late all right." She continued her slow turn. "Too late for Alan and Jeffy." Finally she stopped and glared at him. "But it's not too late for you, is it?"

Glaeken felt his mouth going dry. "I'm afraid I don't understand."

"Yes, you do." She lifted the hilt higher, straining against its weight. "This is yours, isn't it?"

"Its predecessor was, before it was melted down and—"

"It's *still* yours, isn't it?"

Glaeken swallowed. Sylvia was trespassing along a path he dearly wished her to avoid.

"Not anymore. Someone new must take it up now."

"But it wants you."

"No." What was she *saying*? "I served my time—*more* than my time. Someone else—"

"But what if no one but the wonderful *Glaeken* will do?" She spat his name.

"That's not possible."

She lifted the hilt still higher, her expression fierce.

"Try it. Just try it. Let's see what happens. Then we'll know for sure."

"You don't understand," Glaeken said. His arthritic lower back was shooting pain down his left leg so he eased himself into the straight-back chair against the wall behind him. "It can't be me. It's not possible."

He saw Jack step closer to Sylvia. He kept his voice low but Glaeken made out the words.

"Chill, Sylvia. Look at him. He's all rusted up. Even if he's the one it wants, what can he do against all that's going on out there?"

Sylvia stared Glaeken's way a moment longer, then shook her head.

"Maybe. But there's something else going on here." She handed the hilt to Jack. "You figure it out."

Jack glanced down at the gold and silver hilt in his hand, then looked at Bill. "Only one other person left to try. It's crazy, but what's new about that?"

As they led Nick to the blade, wrapped his hands around the hilt, and guided it over the butt spike, Glaeken rose stiffly and walked down the hall to the rear of the apartment. He needed to be alone, away from the oppressive despair in the living room.

He stopped at Magda's bedroom and looked in. She was sleeping. That was all she seemed to do these days. Maybe it was a blessing. He took a seat at her bedside and held her hand.

Sylvia and the others didn't—couldn't—understand. He was *tired*. They didn't know how tired one could be after all this living. To have engineered one last victory, or merely to have launched a final battle against Rasalom would have been wonderful. He could have gone blissfully to his death then. But that was not to be. He would die in the darkness like everyone else—no . . . *worse* than everyone else. Rasalom had something special reserved for him.

Still, he couldn't risk even going near the instrument. Who knew what the reaction might be? It might start everything over again, and once more he would be in the thrall of the ally power. Its champion. Its slave. Forever.

I've done my part. I've contributed more than my share. They cannot ask for more.

Someone *else* had to carry on the fight.

The Bunker

"Are we going to die?"

Gia looked down into Vicky's wide, terrified blue eyes. Abe had pushed her into the bathroom with Vicky, saying he'd hold off the burrowers as long as he could, then come in and join them for a final defense.

She could hear him out there, back to the door, firing round after round at the advancing creatures; she imagined the flying bits of maggot flesh, the splattering yellow goo. Part of her felt she should be out there with him, but another knew her place was here as her daughter's last defense.

"No. We're not going to die." She hoped she sounded convincing. "We've got Jack working on it. Remember?"

She nodded but didn't smile. She almost always smiled at the mention of Jack's name. "Yeah, Jack. He'll fix it."

Oh, the faith of youth.

"He sure will. And when—"

Gia yelped and Vicky screamed as something heavy slammed against the steel door, rattling it on its hinges and leaving a soccer ball–size dent.

The gunfire from the other side stopped.

"Abe?" Gia banged on the door. Oh, no! *"Abe!"*

Manhattan

"Where's my Glenn?"

Startled by the words, spoken in Hungarian, Glaeken looked down and found Magda awake, staring at him. Their litany was about to begin. Her memories were mired in the Second World War, when they both had been young and fresh and newly in love.

"I'm right here, Magda."

She pulled her hand away. "No. You're not him. You're old. My Glenn is young and strong!"

"But I've grown old, my dear, like you."

"You're not him!" she said, her voice rising. "Glenn is out there fighting the darkness."

The darkness. Some part of her jumbled mind was aware of the horrors outside, and knew Rasalom was involved.

"No, he isn't. He's right here beside you."

"No! Not my Glenn! He's out there! He'd never let the dark win! Never! Now get away from me, you old fool! Away!"

Glaeken didn't want her to start screaming, so he rose and left her.

"And if you see Glenn, tell him his Magda loves him and knows he won't let the darkness get away with this."

The words stung, setting their barbs into the flesh of his neck and shoulders and trailing him down the hall toward the living room.

The living room . . . it looked like a wake. The seven silent occupants, though separated by only a few feet of space, were miles apart, each closed off, locked behind the walls of their own thoughts. And fears.

Even here.

Nick and Jeffy stared at the air. Ba sat cross-legged against the far wall, eyes closed, silent. Jack and Sylvia stood at opposite ends of the long window, each gazing out at the eternal blackness. Even Bill and Carol sat apart, silent and separate on the couch.

And here am I, he thought, separated from them and from my wife, as cut off from the rest of humanity as I've ever been.

Rasalom had won outside, and he was winning in here.

And then Glaeken saw Jeffy move. The boy approached the coffee table and dropped to his knees before it. He gripped the hilt where it lay and pressed his cheek down against it, as if some part of him knew that what he was missing was locked within the cold reaches of the metal.

All their sacrifices . . . all their faith in him . . . Rasalom eternally victorious . . .

Anger erupted within Glaeken like one of the long-dormant volcanoes in the Pacific, exploding in his chest, engulfing him in its fiery heart.

Rasalom winning . . . having the last laugh . . .

It comes down to that, doesn't it? Me against him. That's what it's always been. Always the two of them pitted against each other.

He couldn't allow Rasalom to win. If there was one chance, no matter how slim, he had to take it.

He found himself moving, crossing the room toward Jeffy, lifting him gently away from the hilt.

"Sylvia," he said, keeping his voice calm. "Take him and stand back."

Sylvia rushed over and pulled Jeffy away.

"Why? What's happened?"

"Nothing yet. And perhaps nothing will. But just in case . . ."

Glaeken stared down at the hilt.

Is this what it wants? he said, speaking silently to the power within the metal, wondering if it could hear him. It let me go and now it wants me back? Will no one else do?

The hilt lay silent, gleaming coldly in the flickering light of the breathless room. Wondering which he hated more, Rasalom or the power to which he had allied himself ages ago, Glaeken reached down and wrapped his gnarled fingers around the hilt.

Memories surged through him at the metal's touch. Yes, the hilt was alive. The entity that had been the *Dat-tay-vao* welcomed him back. The smallfolk had done their job well.

And as much as he hated to admit it, the hilt felt as if it *belonged* in his hands.

He turned toward the blade.

"Everybody back."

What is that?

Rasalom is disturbed by another ripple through the enveloping chaos above. Bigger. A wavelet this time.

He spreads his consciousness. It's that instrument again. And this time Glaeken himself is holding it. It's the reunion of the man and the living metal that is disturbing. No matter. A minor ruffle, and short lived.

"Too late, Glaeken!" he shouts into the subterranean dark. "Too late!"

"Don't look," Glaeken said.

But Carol had to look. For as soon as Glaeken had touched the hilt the air of the living room became charged.

She'd risen and followed Bill to the far side of the sofa where they now stood with their arms wrapped around each other watching as Glaeken poised the hilt over the butt spike.

Something was going to happen. How could she turn away?

She watched the old man set his feet, take a deep breath, then ram the hilt downward.

Light such as she had never seen or imagined, *light* like the hearts of the Hiroshima and Nagasaki and the Bikinis and all the Yucca Flats bombs rolled into one, *light* like the Big Bang itself exploded from the hilt, engulfing Glaeken and searing the room. Hot light, cold light, new light, ancient light, it blasted through the room in a wave.

In that initial flash Carol saw Glaeken's bones silhouetted through his flesh and clothes, saw the springs and inner supports of the sofa before her, then the *light* was upon her, making her retinas scream and her irises spasm and her lids clamp down tight to shut out the *light* but it was no use because the *light* would not be denied and it poured through her, suffusing each cell of each tissue in a perceptible wave of warmth as it passed.

She heard cries of wonder and astonishment from the others and was startled by a deafening crash as the glass in the picture windows blew out. Gusts of night air stormed through the room as Carol fought to open her eyes against the glare.

The light was still there, more diffuse now, and splotched with purple from the afterburns on her retinas. It had stopped expanding and had begun to contract, rushing back from the edges of the room to concentrate again at the center, coalescing into a column with Glaeken at its heart. Carol had to raise a protecting arm across her face and half turn away as it consolidated and amplified its power into a narrower beam, shooting upward, burning through the ceiling, through the roof, into the blackness above. And faintly through the brilliance she could still make out the figure of a man standing in the heart of the light.

She turned to Bill. "The roof! We've got to go up to the roof!"

He blinked at her, half dazed. "Why?"

She didn't know why exactly. A deep part of her was responding to the light, almost as if she recognized it. Whatever the reason, she felt compelled to be up where she could watch this beam of light challenge the darkness.

"Never mind why." She grabbed his hand. "Let's go!" She turned to the others in the room. "Everybody—the roof! The roof!"

Rasalom writhes in his chrysalis.

What is happening? A sudden squall of light in the upper reaches of Glaeken's building.

The instrument! He's activated it!

Rasalom remains calm. The light being shed is a discomfort, an irritant. No more.

This is not a setback. Glaeken may be able to cause some trouble with this, but he can be no more than an inconvenience. The Change is too far along. It cannot be reversed.

The Bunker

Finally, Abe's voice, weak and shaky, filtered through the door.

"I'm okay, but don't come out."

Relief flooded Gia. "Why not?"

"Because the things, the burrowers . . . they're still here."

Gia pressed her ear against the door. She didn't understand.

"Then why . . . ?"

"Why am I not shooting? Because they're not doing anything. They're just . . ."

Gia couldn't stay in the bathroom. She had to see, had to know what he was talking about. She pulled open the door . . . and gaped.

Abe, drenched in sweat and slime, slumped on the floor with his back against the wall. A rearing burrower loomed over him . . . but was facing away. Gia looked around and saw that the two dozen or so surviving burrowers had all reared up and were facing in the same direction.

"What . . . what happened?"

"I don't know." Abe didn't try to rise, just lay there panting. "They had me. I'd emptied every weapon I have, and then suddenly they stopped and turned."

"What are they doing?"

"I don't know. It almost seems as if they're waiting."

Gia noticed that they all faced the wall to the right of the hatch chimney. She did a quick calculation of the direction.

"They're facing east."

"What? They're Muslims?"

"Toward New York."

Jack . . . Glaeken . . .

Someone had done something. But was it enough?

Manhattan

Carol led the way up, throwing her shoulder against the door at the top of the stairs and bursting out into the cold night air. She was vaguely aware of the hungry buzz and flutter of the night things swooping through the darkness beyond the edges of the building; she barely heard the rooftop gravel crunch under her feet, or noticed the others crowding out behind her. She was locked on the bright beam spearing into the heavens—straight and true, unwavering, a narrow tower of light shooting upward, ever upward until it pierced the sky.

And then it faded.

"It's gone," Bill said close behind her.

"No!" She pointed up. "Look. There's still a bright spot up there. Like a star."

The only star in the sky.

"Never mind the star," Bill said. "Check out the roof."

Carol saw a smoldering hole where the light had burst through. She approached it cautiously and looked down into the living room below, afraid of what she might see there, afraid that Glaeken had been harmed somehow by the blaze of light.

But no charred, blackened remains lay crumbled on the rug below. No Glaeken either. Instead, a stranger stood in his place—in Glaeken's clothes—clutching the hilt that sat upon the blade.

"Look!" Carol whispered. "Who's that?"

He was taller than Glaeken. He had the old man's broad build but was much younger, perhaps Jack's age. And fiery red hair. His shoulders and upper arms stretched the seams of the shirt he wore. Who—?

And then she caught a glimpse of his blue eyes and knew beyond all question—

"It's Glaeken!"

She felt an arm slip around her shoulder as she heard Bill's hoarse whisper beside her.

"But he's so young! He can't be more than thirty-five!"

"Right," she said as understanding grew. "The same age as when he first took up the battle."

Carol could not take her eyes off him. The way he moved as he tore the blade free of the floor and swung it before him. He was—she could find no other word for him—magnificent.

And then he looked up at them through the opening and Carol recoiled at the grim set of his mouth and the rage that flashed in his eyes. He lifted the weapon and reduced the coffee table to marble gravel and kindling with one blow, then he strode from sight. Seconds later they heard the apartment door shatter.

"He is *pissed*," Jack said.

Bill shook his head. "I hope it's not at us."

"No," Jack said. "It's Rasalom. Got to be Rasalom."

"Then I'm glad I'm not Rasalom."

Jack spun and ran toward the doorway.

"Where——?" Carol began, but he was already out of earshot.

"Probably headed to Pennsylvania. I know he's been worried sick about his ladies and his friend."

Carol shivered in the cold wind and looked back up at the point of light the beam had left in the sky. It looked brighter—and bigger.

She pointed. "It's growing."

"I think you're right," Bill said, squinting upward at the rapidly expanding spot. "It almost looks like——" He yanked her back, away from the hole in the roof. "Run! It's coming back!"

Carol shook him off and stood waiting for the brilliance falling from the heavens. It wouldn't hurt her—she *knew* it wouldn't hurt her. She spread her arms, waiting for it, welcoming it.

And suddenly she was bathed in light—the whole rooftop awash in blindingly white light. Warm, clean, almost like——

"Sunlight!"

The entire building stood in a cone of brilliance that challenged the darkness from the point source far overhead—as if a pinhole had been poked into the inverted bowl of Rasalom's night and a single, daring ray of sunlight had ventured through.

Carol ran to the edge of the roof and leaned over the low parapet. Below, on the bright sidewalk, the crawlers were scuttling away into the darkness, fleeing the glare.

She heard a crash as bright fragments of glass exploded onto the pavement. And suddenly Glaeken was there, striding across the street toward the park, his red hair flying as he swung the blade before him, as if daring something to challenge him. And as he stepped from the light into the darkness beyond——

"Bill!" Carol cried. "Oh, God, Bill, come look! You've got to see this!"

The light followed Glaeken, clinging to the sword and to his body like some sort of viscous fluid, trailing after him, creating a luminescent tunnel through the darkness.

"Where's he going?" Bill said as he, Ba, Sylvia, and Jeffy joined her at the edge.

Carol thought she knew but Ba answered first.

"To the hole. The one he seeks is there."

They quickly lost sight of Glaeken, but together they stood on the roof and watched the tube of light channel its way into the inky depths of the park.

And then something else—some*one* else: another figure, bristling with weapons, running along the path of light.

"Who on Earth——?" Carol began, but didn't have to finish.

No one felt the need to answer. They all knew who it was, the only one it could be.

WFPW-FM

FREDDY: Something's happened out there, man. We just got a call on the CB that there's a beam of light coming out of the sky over Central Park West. We can't see it from here so we don't know for sure if it's true.

    JO: Hey, the guy who called's been pretty reliable all through this mess, but you know we've all been getting, like, a little funky since the sun went out, man, so if you've got a CB and you're anywhere near Central Park, peek out what's left of your windows and let us know what you see.

Rasalom relaxes within his chrysalis.

    Only a pinhole, nothing more. All that effort expended by Glaeken's circle and to what end? A pinhole in the night cover. Laughable. It changes nothing.

    Except Glaeken. He's been changed, returned to the way he was when he and Rasalom first squared off against each other. Little did either of them know that they would be locked in battle for ages.

    But Rasalom cheers Glaeken's rejuvenation. It would have been almost embarrassing to crush the life out of the feeble old man he had become. Destroying the reborn Glaeken—young, agile, angry—will be so much more satisfying.

    And best yet, he doesn't even have to seek out Glaeken. The idiot is coming to him. How convenient.

    Their last meeting . . . so like their first. The circle shall be complete. It shall end as it began—in a cavern.

Glaeken stood in the dark on the rim of the Sheep Meadow hole and gazed into the abyss.

Somewhere down there, Rasalom waited. Glaeken could feel him, sense him, *smell* his stink. He would not be hard to find.

But he had to hurry. A rude, insistent urgency crowded against his back, nudging him forward. In spite of it, he turned and stared back at the cone of brilliance that pinned his apartment house like a prop on a stage, at the worm of light that had trailed him from the cone. Because of it, the night things had avoided him on his trek to this spot. They'd been clustered along the edge here but had slithered away at his approach.

He wished they hadn't—wished something had challenged him, blocked his path. He hungered to hurt something—to slash, cut, maim, crush under his heel, destroy.

I was free! he thought. *Free!*

And now he was caught again, trapped once more in the service of— what? The power he'd served had no name, had never presented a physical manifestation. It simply was *there*—and it wanted him *here*.

The rage seething and boiling within him was beyond anything he had experienced in all his countless years. A living thing, like a berserk warrior, wild, deranged, psychotic, slavering for an object—anyone, any*thing* on which to vent the steam of its pent-up fury. His whole body trembled as the beast within howled to be let loose.

Save it. Save it for Rasalom.

He was sure he'd need it then. All of it.

He turned back to the pit and swung the weapon. Damn the Ally, but it felt good to feel good, to have his muscles and joints so strong and lithe, to be able to fling his arms freely in all directions, to twist and bend without stiffness and stabs of pain.

And the weapon—he hated to admit how *right* it felt in his grasp as a deeper part of him remembered and responded to the heavy feel of the hilt tight against his palms and fingers. The warrior in him smelled blood.

He sensed movement behind him and whirled. Had one of the creatures dared—?

No. A lone figure approached, trotting toward him. He had a strange-looking shotgun strapped across his back, an assault rifle in his hands, and a pair of pistols stuck in his belt.

Jack.

"Take your back?" he said as he stopped before him.

Glaeken's bitterness eased at the words, balmed by the man's casual courage.

"You shouldn't be here, Jack—you're the Heir. You should be back with the others."

He held back from telling him that he was a liability here—that Rasalom might find a way to use Jack against him.

Jack shook his head. "You're not the only one with a score to settle."

Yes . . . the Connells . . . Weezy and Eddie. Especially Weezy. Glaeken had loved her too.

"I understand, but I'm the only one who can do the settling." He pointed to Jack's weapons. "Bullets are useless here." He hefted the sword. "This is the only thing that can put an end to Rasalom."

Or maybe not. Maybe he's too powerful now even for the sword.

"You'll help me best by waiting with the others. All my dangers lay straight ahead. It's not my back I'm worried about—it's you."

"All right. You go ahead. But I'm not going back. I'm waiting right here—just in case."

"Just in case what?"

"You never know."

Glaeken had no more time to waste. He nodded to Jack, slipped the weapon through the back of his belt, and lowered himself over the edge to begin his descent.

WFPW-FM

JO: Awright, man. We've had confirmation. A few other good people have CB'd in to tell us that yes, there is some heavy light coming out of the sky on Central Park West up near the Sheep Meadow.

FREDDY: Yeah, and if you remember, that's near where the first of those nasty bug holes opened up. We don't know if there's a connection so you might want to be careful, but the folks who've contacted us say they're going to try to get over to it and check it out.

JO: We'll keep you informed. As long as we've got juice from the generator, we'll be here. So keep us on.

Carol pointed into the dark blob that was Central Park. The thread of light that wove through the blackness there had not lengthened in the past few minutes.

"Glaeken must have stopped moving," she said. "Do you think something's wrong?"

"I don't think we'll see it move any farther," Bill said. "It looks like it's reached the hole. He's probably out of sight now, moving down."

"I hope the light's still following him. And where's Jack?"

No one had an answer.

Carol glanced down at the sidewalks below in time to see a battered car skid to a halt against the curb. It was covered—smothered—with night things, but they slipped away when the car penetrated the edge of the light. The door flew open and a half dozen people—a man, two women, and three kids— tumbled out. They began to run for the door of the building but slowed to a stop as they realized they were no longer being pursued. They looked up at the light, spread their arms, laughed, and began to hug each other.

Another car flew out of the darkness and bounded over the curb before it came to a stop. Another group of people jumped out. The first greeted them with cheers and they all embraced.

"I don't know if I like this," Bill said.

Carol looked at him. "They're coming to the light."

"That could be trouble. Think we ought to get downstairs, Ba?"

The big Asian stood behind Sylvia and Jeffy. He shook his head.

"I don't think there's anything to worry about," Carol said. "I mean, I think we should share the light."

Bill nodded. "I do too. As long as that's all they want."

Carol looked down again. More people had reached the light, some apparently on foot from neighboring buildings. She noticed something.

"Bill? Remember when we first looked down? Wasn't the light just to the edge of the sidewalk?"

Bill shrugged. "I don't know. I didn't notice."

Carol stared down at the rim of shadow that encircled the building. It now reached a good yard beyond the curb on the asphalt of the street.

A hundred or so feet down the western wall, Glaeken found the mouth of the lateral passage—a dozen feet across and the only break in the smooth granite surface. He swung inward and landed on his feet. He pulled the weapon free and started walking. He needed no signpost to tell him that Rasalom lay ahead.

The light followed, filling the tunnel in his wake, stretching his shadow far ahead, sending dark things scuttling and slithering and fluttering out of the way.

He pushed on, not running, but moving swiftly with quick, long strides. The sense of urgency clung to his back, propelling him forward. He swung the blade back and forth, splashing the air with bright arcs of light, then waded through them.

But as he progressed deeper and farther along the tunnel, he noticed a dimming of the light. He turned and looked back along his path. Back there the light looked as thick and bright as before, but down here it seemed attenuated, diluted, tainted . . .

It could only mean he was nearing his goal, the heart of the darkness.

Not much farther on, the light loosened its embrace and pulled free; it hung back, abandoning him to penetrate the beckoning blackness of the tunnel ahead alone.

Glaeken kept moving, slower now, stepping more carefully. Only the blade was glowing now, and that faintly, struggling against the thickening blackness that devoured its light. Soon its light failed too. Glaeken stood in a featureless black limbo, cold, silent, expectant. Darkness complete, victorious.

And then, as he knew it would, came the voice, the loathed voice, speaking into his mind.

"Welcome, Glaeken. Welcome to a place where your light cannot go. My place. A place of no light. Remind you of anywhere from the past?"

Glaeken refused to reply.

"Keep walking, Glaeken. I won't stop you. There's light of sorts ahead. A different light, the kind I choose to allow here. No traps or tricks, I promise. I want you here. I've been waiting for you. The Change is almost complete. I want you to marvel at my new form. I want you to be the first to see me. I want to be the very last thing you see."

Glaeken felt his palms dampen. He was in another country now, where Rasalom made all the rules. Tightening his grip on the hilt, he stepped forward into the black.

WFPW-FM

JO: Okay. We've had somebody CB us from right inside the beam of light over on Central Park West and they say it's the real thing. Bright, warm, and the bugs won't

go near it. Nobody knows how long it'll last, but it's there now and these folks think it might be there to stay.

FREDDY: So look, here's what we're gonna do. We're gonna make this loop and set it going, then we're outta here. We're heading there ourselves. We'll have a message on the tape, then we'll follow it with a Travelin' Wilburys song, and the whole deal will play over and over.

JO: And here's the message: Get to the light. Get over to Central Park West any way you can and get into the light. Get moving and good luck. And while you're on the move, here's some appropriate traveling music. See you there, man.

<cue "Heading for the Light">

Dim light ahead, oozing around the next bend in the passage.

Unhealthy light. A sickly, wan, greasy glow, clinging to the tunnel walls like grime, casting no shadows. No hope dwelt in that light, no succor from the night, merely a confirmation of the dark's superiority.

As Glaeken moved toward the feeble glow, the air grew colder; an acrid odor stung his nostrils. He rounded the bend and stopped.

In the center of a huge granite cavern, a hundred feet across, Rasalom's new form hung suspended over a softly glowing abyss. Four gleaming ebony pillars reached from the corners of the chamber, arching across the chasm to fuse over its center. A huge sac, bulging, pendulous, nearly the size of a small warehouse, hung suspended from that central fusion. Glaeken could make out no details of the shape floating within its inky amnion. He didn't need to see Rasalom to know it was he, undergoing the final stage of his transformation.

"Welcome to my womb, Glaeken."

Glaeken did not reply. Instead, he leapt upon the nearest support where it sprang from the wall and strode along its upper surface toward the center where Rasalom hung.

"Glaeken, wait! Stop!" Rasalom's voice took on a panicky edge in his head. *"What are you doing?"*

Glaeken kept moving toward the center, the weapon raised before him.

"There's no need for this, Glaeken! I'm so close! You'll ruin everything!"

Glaeken slowed, alerted by the anxious tone. This was the Adversary's time, and Rasalom's natural arrogance must have ballooned to gargantuan proportions by now. Glaeken could count on any sign of uncertainty being a sham, a lure to draw him closer, not put him off.

He'd cautiously progressed to within a dozen feet of the sac when the surface of the support suddenly softened and erupted in hundreds of fine tendrils that wrapped around his ankles, snaring them, encasing them in a squirming mass, then recrystallized to rocklike hardness. He pulled and strained but his feet were locked down. He chopped with the blade but remained trapped like a fly on a pest strip.

He stared down at the sac hanging within spitting distance below. A huge eye rolled against the inner surface of the membrane and stopped to stare back at him.

"That is quite far enough."

"Perhaps you're right."

He shifted his grip on the hilt and raised the weapon over his shoulder like a spear, its point directed at the eye. Rasalom's voice screamed in his brain.

"No! Glaeken, wait! I can help you!"

That didn't sound feigned. Was Rasalom vulnerable while not fully reshaped?

"No deals, Rasalom."

He reared back to hurl the weapon.

"I can make her whole again!"

Glaeken hesitated. He couldn't help it.

"Whole again? Who?"

"Your woman. That Hungarian Jewess who stole your heart. I can give her back her mind—and make her young again."

"No. You can't. Not even the *Dat-tay-vao*—"

"I'm far more powerful than that puny elemental. This is my world now. When I complete the Change I can do whatever I wish. I will be making the rules here, Glaeken. All the rules. And if I say the woman called Magda shall be thirty again and sound of mind and body forever—forever—then so it shall be."

Magda . . . alert, young, healthy, *sane* . . . the vision of the two of them together as they used to be . . .

He shook it off.

"No. Not in this world."

"It doesn't have to be this world. You can have your own corner of the globe, your own island, your own archipelago. All to yourselves. You can even take some of your friends. The sun will shine there forever. You can live on in idyllic splendor."

"While the rest of the world . . . ?"

"Is mine. All you have to do is acknowledge me as master of this sphere and drop your weapon into the abyss. After that I shall see to all your comforts."

For a heartbeat he half considered it—and the realization rocked Glaeken.

Did he want Magda back that much? And Magda—she'd never forgive him. He'd have to live on with her abhorrence, her loathing.

He tightened his grip on the weapon.

"No deals."

Putting all his arm and as much of his foot-locked body as he could behind it, Glaeken hurled the weapon at the sac. The huge eye ducked away as Rasalom's voice screamed in his mind.

"NOOOOOOOOOOOOOOOOOOOO!"

The point of the blade pierced the membrane, penetrated about a foot, then stopped, quivering. Rasalom's voice became a howl of pain as inky fluid spurted out around the blade, coating it, congealing around it, sealing the wound and encasing the weapon until the entire blade and all but the pommel of the hilt were mired in a hardening tarry mass.

And then Rasalom's howl of pain segued into a peal of laughter. The single huge eye once again pressed against the inner surface of the membrane and regarded him coldly.

"Ah, Glaeken. Noble to the end. Just as well, I suppose. You probably knew you'd never see the tropical idyll I promised. But did you truly think you could hurt me? Here in the heart of my domain, in the seat of my power? Your arrogance is insufferable. It is too late to harm me, Glaeken—too late for a long time."

Glaeken tried once more to pull his feet free but they would not budge. He took a deep breath and stood quietly, waiting, listening to the hated voice in his mind.

"You knew it was too late, Glaeken. You must have known all along. Yet knowing it was useless, still you took up the weapon and came to me instead of waiting for me to come to you. I don't understand that. Can you explain your madness, your arrogance? We have some time. Speak."

"If the answer is not apparent to you, no amount of talking will make you understand. Where do we go from here?"

"We wait. I'm almost ready. At the undawn I will be complete. When I emerge from my chrysalis I shall leave you here and move to the surface where I shall deal with your little circle of allies. And as I gut them I shall let you see it all through my eyes. And as for your wife, I shall keep my promise to you: I will restore her youth and her mind before her end—after all, we wouldn't want her to die without knowing exactly what is happening. When all that is done, I'll return for you. And then the fun shall truly begin."

Glaeken said nothing. No use in asking for mercy for himself or the others when none was to be had. So he closed his eyes and willed his insides to stone to inure them from the sick dread coiling through him.

He'd failed.

"And while we wait, I believe I'll close that tiny wound in my perfect night. Too many people are taking undue pleasure in it. Imagine their fear and dismay when it starts to fade and they realize that they are naked prey to all the night things encircling them. Yes, I like that idea. I should have thought of the pinhole myself. Allow a little cone of light through here and there about the world, let the locals run to it like moths to a flame, let it shine long enough to lift hopes, and then douse it. Thank you, Glaeken. You've given me a new game."

"Look at them all," Carol said. "Must be thousands down there."

She'd returned with the others to the living room of Glaeken's apartment and now she gazed down through the broken windows at the crowd below, listening to the noise floating up as each new arrival was greeted with cheers and hugs. A good sound, the noise of people breaking from unrelenting fear.

"It's the radio," Bill said. "The only station still on air in town is playing a message sending everybody here."

Suddenly it went quiet below.

"What happened?" Carol's heart thudded with alarm and she clutched his arm. "I think the light just dimmed. Tell me I'm wrong, Bill. Tell me I'm *wrong!*"

Bill glanced at her, then back out the windows.

"No . . . I'm afraid you're right. Look—it just dimmed a little more!"

"It's Glaeken's fault," said a familiar voice.

They all turned. Nick was still sitting on the couch where they'd left him, still facing the dead fireplace.

"Glaeken has lost. Rasalom is ascendant."

"Glaeken is . . . dead?" Sylvia said, stepping forward, hovering over Nick.

Carol was surprised at her concern. She'd thought Sylvia blamed Glaeken for Jeffy's condition.

"Not yet," Nick said. "But soon. We'll die. Then he'll die. Slowly."

Carol heard a new sound well up from the crowd outside—murmurs of fear, wails of panic. She turned back to the window and had the sudden impression that their cries of despair seemed to chase the light. She watched with growing dread as it faded from midday glare to twilight glow.

They're afraid again.

"Afraid!" she cried. "Maybe that's it." Suddenly she knew what had to be done—or thought she knew. "Bill, Sylvia, everybody—downstairs. Now!"

She didn't wait to explain and she didn't wait for the elevator. Filled with a growing excitement and a desperate urgency, she galloped down the dizzying flights to the ground floor, dashed through the lobby, and out into the crowd on the twilit sidewalk.

Bill was right behind her, then Ba, carrying Jeffy and guiding Sylvia through the restless, panicky people. Carol led them to the edge of the fading light, right to the shadow border facing the park, then grabbed Bill's hand in her right and took a stranger's—a frightened-looking black woman's—in her left.

"I won't be afraid anymore!" Carol shouted at the huge outer darkness that tried to stare her down. She squeezed the woman's hand. "Say it," she told her. "I won't be afraid anymore! Grab somebody's hand and say it as loud as you can." She turned to Bill. "Shout it, Bill. Mean it. Take a hand and get them to say it!"

Bill stared at her. "What's this—?"

"Just do it. *Please!* There's not much time."

Bill shrugged and grabbed someone's hand and began repeating the phrase. She noticed that the black woman to her left had taken a young man's hand and was repeating the phrase to him. Carol turned and saw a very grim Sylvia standing behind her, arms folded across her chest.

"Come on, Sylvia!"

She shook her head. "This is nuts. It's—it's hippie bullshit. Like those peaceniks back in the sixties trying to levitate the Pentagon. You can't chant Rasalom away."

"I know that. But maybe we can put a kink in his plans. His whole thrust has been to isolate us from each other, to use fear to break us up into separate, frightened little islands. But look what's happened here. One little ray of light and we've suddenly got a crowded little island. What if we refuse to play his game anymore? What if we refuse to run screaming in fear back to our hidey-holes? What if we stand here as a group and defy him? There's a defect up there, a hole in Rasalom's night. Maybe we can keep it open. Maybe we can even widen it. What have we got to lose that's not already lost?"

"Not one damn thing!" a nearby bedraggled, middle-aged woman said. She pulled Sylvia's arm away from her chest and grabbed her hand. "I won't be afraid anymore!"

"Okay, okay," Sylvia said through tightly clenched teeth as she clutched Jeffy's arm in one hand and the woman's in the other. "Do your worst—I *won't* be afraid anymore!"

Carol felt her throat tighten at the defiance in her voice.

The chant was becoming more organized, picking up a rhythm as it spread through the crowd, growing in volume as more and more voices chimed in . . .

And then the light around them brightened. The increase was barely noticeable, but it *was* noticed. A cheer rose from the crowd and suddenly *everyone* was a believer. The chant doubled, tripled in volume.

Carol laughed as tears sprang into her eyes. She heard Sylvia's voice behind her.

"It's working! It's *working!*"

Everyone in the crowd was involved now, shouting at the tops of their lungs. And the light continued to brighten. Carol had no doubt now that the glow was growing stronger. Even the light in the channel that had trailed Glaeken into the park was growing brighter.

But more than that, the cone of light was growing *wider,* inching across the pavement toward the park, pumping pulses of brightness along the luminous channel that led to the Sheep Meadow hole.

And more people were coming, running to the light, swelling the crowd, swelling the sound of defiance.

Something was happening.

Rasalom had been uncharacteristically silent. And his huge new form did not lie quiet in its amniotic sac. The membrane rippled now and again, like a chill running over fevered skin, and occasionally it bulged in places as Rasalom shifted within.

Glaeken closed his eyes and tried to sense what was going on. He stood perfectly still, listening, feeling.

Warmth.

Light . . . light growing above. Not visible here, but he sensed it. Light and warmth, seeping into the earth above the cavern. And behind . . .

He turned and looked down the passageway. Where he'd left perfect darkness, he now saw the faintest glow. An illusion? Or the harbinger of a tiny dawn?

Glaeken turned back to his ancient enemy.

"What's happening upstairs, Rasalom? Tell me!"

But now it was Rasalom's turn to be silent.

Sylvia watched the scene from a second-floor window. The noise, the press of people had begun to frighten Jeffy so she'd brought him inside.

The cone of light had returned to noontime brightness and was widening steadily now, creeping uptown and down along the street, invading the park. The crowd, too, was swelling steadily, the light and the noise attracting thousands more. The Manhattan mix was there, red, yellow, Central African ebony to Norwegian white and every shade between.

The chant Carol had started still reverberated loud and clear, but here and there in the crowd Sylvia noticed pockets of people singing and dancing. A couple of MP3 ghetto blasters had appeared and different kinds of music, from hip-hop to salsa, were each attracting their own fans. A couple of guys were leading a big group in singing "Happy Together." She guessed that was just as effective. You didn't have to proclaim your lack of fear when you were singing and dancing. And from directly below her window, uncertain harmonies drifted up as a ragtag group tried to find a comfortable key for "The Closer You Are."

Sylvia thought of Alan then and how he'd loved doo-wop and suddenly she was crying.

Oh, Alan. My God, how I miss you. You belong here, not me. You loved people so much more than I. I should be dead and you should be here.

Alan . . . after he'd pulled out of the coma from the *Dat-tay-vao,* she'd come to think of him as indestructible. An indisputable assumption: Alan would be around forever. She'd never considered the possibility of life without him. And now he was gone—no body, no grave, no trace, just *gone*—and she hadn't even had a chance to say good-bye.

She hugged Jeffy closer. It was all so damn unfair.

For a brief while she had blamed Glaeken, but knew now that he, too, was paying a terrible price. She'd seen it in his eyes as he'd picked up the hilt and told her to get Jeffy clear—the anger, the frustration, the vulnerability, the weary resignation. All in a single glance. The weight of the terrible responsibility he was shouldering once more had struck her like a blow. She'd instantly regretted all the angry things she'd said to him.

And now maybe he was gone too.

She watched the arc of light edging through the park—well into the Sheep Meadow now, almost to the rim of the hole. Did that mean they were winning, or was this just a false hope?

Sylvia closed her eyes and hugged Jeffy tighter.

If you're still alive down there, Glaeken, please know that you're in our thoughts. If there's anything you can do, do it. Get him, Glaeken. Don't let him get away with what he's done to us. GET HIM!

Yes, light was seeping down the tunnel. Glaeken was sure of it now. Growing steadily. And Rasalom . . . Rasalom was thrashing about in his amniotic sac.

What was happening up on the surface? The weapon was here, useless, encased in hardened fluid from the sack. What in the name of anything could exert such a disturbing effect on Rasalom?

Suddenly a thunderous rumble from the tunnel behind him. The support shuddered beneath Glaeken's feet. He twisted and saw the growing glow disappear as the roof of the tunnel collapsed, choking the passage with rubble. As the tunnel mouth belched a cloud of dust, Rasalom's voice returned.

"Once again you've chosen a vexing group of friends, Glaeken."

A warm glow of pride lit within him, along with a glimmer of—did he dare?—hope.

"They're a tough bunch. What have they done?"

"Nothing that will matter in the long run, but for the present they've created an annoyance, an inconvenience."

"What?"

"They've enlarged the pinhole in the night-cover made by your puny little weapon."

Glaeken steadied himself, choked down the shout of triumph that surged against his vocal cords. He maintained a calm exterior.

"How?"

"How is irrelevant. Their success is irrelevant. The entire world is in darkness. A single cone of sunlight, no matter how bright, is laughably insignificant."

Glaeken sensed the weight of all that Rasalom had left unsaid.

"Sunlight, Rasalom? Since when have you been afraid of sunlight?"

"I fear nothing, Glaeken. I am master of this sphere. It fears me."

"It's not sunlight, is it, Rasalom. It's another kind of light. Light from your enemy. And it comes at a time and place that's more than 'inconvenient.' It's shining directly above your little nest, and it has arrived at a time when you're vulnerable, before your new form has matured."

"Nonsense, Glaeken. Pure wishful thinking on your part. When my gestation is through, and that is only a matter of hours now, I shall personally plug that hole in my perfect night. Then you will see how 'vulnerable' I am."

Glaeken noticed a growing warmth at his back. He twisted again toward the rubble-strewn tunnel. Something happening there.

And then he saw it. A gleaming pinpoint, a tiny bead no larger than a grain of sand, glowing near the top of the debris, growing bigger, growing brighter. The light seemed to be worming its way through the rubble, as if it had a mind of its own. But how was that possible?

"Don't allow yourself to hope, Glaeken. It cannot harm me."

Yet Glaeken did allow himself to hope, could not help but hope when he saw the bead brighten suddenly and shoot out toward the pit in a narrow beam of brilliance, like a needle-thin blue-white laser streaming toward Rasalom. But it came up short against the support under Glaeken's feet, spraying and splashing like water against a stone wall.

The beam persisted, though. Like a living thing with a will of its own, it split, one half sliding upward, the other down around the support. The light crept to the top just inches ahead of Glaeken's trapped feet. As soon as it crested the support it raced downward to rejoin its other half. They fused and once again shot out toward Rasalom's amniotic sac.

But the beam did not strike the sac. Instead it flashed toward the weapon, igniting the exposed butt of the hilt. The pommel blazed with blinding fire, and dimly, through the encrustations, Glaeken could see bolts of light flashing along the length of the blade.

Rasalom howled in Glaeken's mind as he writhed and thrashed within his sac. Glaeken had a feeling that this time was no act.

The weapon began to vibrate, the encrustations cracked and fell away like old skin, and suddenly the hilt was free, blazing with white light.

Another beam of radiance broke through the rubble and flashed across the cavern. It too found the weapon and added its power to it.

But how . . . how could the light pass through the rubble?

And then he heard a stone tumble off the debris pile. Something— some*one*—was disturbing the rubble, clearing a passage along its top.

Glaeken knew of only one person with the indomitable will necessary to reach this spot.

As Rasalom's howl rose to a shriek, Glaeken felt the tendrils wrapped around his legs begin to soften, their hold weaken. He bent and tore at them, straining to pull free. No time to lose. Rasalom's thrashings were shaking the weapon within the wound it had made. The beam of light stayed with it, moving whenever it did, but if the weapon slipped loose it would fall into the pit. And then Rasalom's victory would be assured.

With a final surge, Glaeken yanked his legs free and leapt to the central disk where the four arched supports fused. He dropped to his belly, hung precariously over the edge, and reached for the weapon.

Cold-fire eternity beckoned below.

He fought a surge of vertigo and stretched his right arm to its limits, violently thrusting it down to force the ligaments to give him the tiny extra increment of length he needed to reach the jittering hilt. His fingertips brushed the pommel twice, and then with a final, agonizing thrust, he hooked two fingers around it. At his touch the weapon seemed to move on its own, slamming the grip of the hilt against his palm. Power surged up his arm and throughout his body and once more the weapon was his.

As he was the weapon's.

He stood and looked about. The original beams of light and new ones from the rubble stayed with the blade, fueling it, following wherever he moved it. He couldn't reach Rasalom or his sac, so he decided to try the next best thing.

Reversing his grip, he lifted the weapon high and drove the point down into the center of the nearest of the supporting arches. A blinding flash lit the cavern as the blade cut deep into the flinty substance. The material of the support began to bubble and smoke as the blade melted its way through it like a hot knife cutting frozen butter. Foul, greasy smoke, reeking of seared flesh, engulfed him. More flashes followed as Glaeken worked the blade back and forth, widening the gash as he deepened it, strobing the cavern with bursts of light and stretching weird shadows against its walls.

Rasalom howled.

"*No, Glaeken! I command you to stop! Stop now or you'll pay dearly. And so will your friends!*"

Without pausing an instant in his labors, Glaeken glanced down at the huge eye pressed furiously against the membrane.

"You've already promised that, Rasalom. What have I got to lose?"

"*I* won't *kill you, Glaeken! I'll let you live on, just barely. I'll make you witness, see, feel everything that happens in my new world.*"

Glaeken said nothing. He had almost cut through the first arch. With a final thrust, the blade angled through the underside and came free.

The central portion suddenly sagged a half a foot under him. Glaeken hurried to his left, toward the next support.

"Glaeken, NO! That island I promised you—you and the woman and your friends—"

Glaeken shut his mind to Rasalom's rantings and drove the blade into the second arch. More flashes and oily smoke. He worked the blade ferociously, gasping with the stench and the exertion, and eventually it worked its way through.

The center sagged again, its free edge lurching downward almost two feet this time. The supports he had cut wept dark fluid from their truncated ends as they remained suspended above the void like severed arms reaching for something they would never again possess.

Supported now by only two arches, the center tilted at an angle. Glaeken's feet slipped on the smooth surface as he hurried toward the nearer of the remaining arches.

And again he drove the blade deep into the substance. But as he worked it through, he felt an impact on his right leg. Searing pain flashed up to his hip. He caught a blur of movement and rolled away.

A huge hand had reared up from the underside of the center, but it resembled a hand in only the vaguest sense—black as the night above, with three fingers as thick around as Glaeken's waist, each terminating in a sharp yellow talon. Crimson fluid stained one of those—his blood.

Rasalom—in his new form. Glaeken could not see the rest of him, most of which was no doubt still in the sac below. Had his new form finally matured, or was he breaking free before the process was completed in order to stop Glaeken?

It made another swipe, blindly, in his direction. Glaeken ducked under the talons. The sudden move sent a fresh surge of agony through his wounded leg. As it came for him again, he slashed with the weapon and felt the blade dig deep into the inky flesh.

Light exploded around him, a flash of brilliance that dwarfed all those before it. In his mind he heard Rasalom cry out in shock and pain. When his vision cleared he saw the taloned hand waving above him, one of its thick fingers swinging madly back and forth as it dangled from a smoking stump by a few remaining intact tendons.

Glaeken straightened and limped to the other support. He had been able to cut only partway through the third and was unlikely to get a chance to finish the job within Rasalom's reach. He'd attack the fourth—but not near the center.

His move must have surprised Rasalom because Glaeken was halfway along the arch before the voice sounded in his brain.

"Don't run off, Glaeken. We've only begun to play."

Glaeken didn't look back. He continued his torturous trek toward the far end of the arch. Within a dozen feet of its origin he stopped and turned.

Rasalom's amniotic sac still hung from its lopsided platform like a gargantuan punching bag, but now a sinewed arm with a wounded hand protruded from the rent made by the weapon. It raked the air above it with its two remaining talons. And the eye . . . that malevolent eye still pressed against the membrane, glaring at him.

"I'm not running far."

With another burst of light and bloom of oily smoke, he drove the weapon deep into the arch beneath him and began to work it back and forth. The support was thicker here near its base, but he could afford the extra time it would take because he was out of Rasalom's reach.

"Glaeken," Rasalom said to his mind, *"you'll never learn. You are forcing me to . . ."*

Ahead, over the center of the pit, another arm clawed free of the membrane, then ripped a talon down the surface of the sac, opening it like a zipper. Tons of ebony fluid poured from the rent, spilling into the bottomless glow of the depths below. The rent parted, widened, and then . . .

Something emerged from the membrane.

Glaeken knew who it was, but could not be certain *what* it was. It had arms, that he knew. And a huge eye at its upper end. But in the dim glow leaking up from the pit below he could be sure of little else as it crawled from the sac and hoisted itself onto the sagging central platform. Legs . . . now he could see legs, four bristling, segmented stalks like a tarantula's, but the rest was encased in an oozing gelatinous mass that dripped off the platform in amorphous globs and tumbled into infinity. A larger shape lurked within the mass, something with a head and a torso, but Glaeken could make out no details. And now a pair of thick, sucker-studded tentacles wriggled free of the gelatin below the arms to twist and coil in the air.

Glaeken flashed back to the q'qrs with their extra, tentacle-like upper limbs, but he had a feeling this shape, this avatar possessed far more appendages.

It began moving his way, crawling toward him along the slope of the fourth arch.

Glaeken redoubled his efforts with the weapon, widening, deepening the cut in the upper surface, thrusting the blade through to the underside. Rasalom's incomplete new form was cumbersome, his progress slow, but he was sliding steadily closer. He soon would have Glaeken within reach of those talons.

Suddenly an explosive crack echoed through the cavern as the fourth arch shook beneath Glaeken's feet and broke partway through like a green sapling. Its distal segment sagged. Glaeken paused and watched Rasalom claw frantically for purchase as he slipped back along the decline toward the central disk. He gave the monstrous form no time to recover, however; immediately he renewed his hacking assault at the remaining splinters holding the arch together.

"Give it up, Glaeken! This is an exercise in futility! You cannot win!"

Rasalom's words were no longer in his mind. His new form was speaking in a startlingly powerful voice. Even muffled by the gelatinous coating, it shook the walls of the cavern.

Glaeken ignored it and forced his wearying arms to maintain the assault on the arch. The reflexes were still there, the arms knew what to do, but the unconditioned muscles were sagging with fatigue. Yet he couldn't rest, couldn't even slow his pace. He closed his eyes to blot out all distractions and kept hacking.

"GLAEKEN!"

The stark terror in the voice and the ripping sound that accompanied it jolted Glaeken. He looked up.

Rasalom was near, clinging to the arch with his tentacles, his outstretched talons only a few feet from Glaeken's face, yet he was receding, falling away. And then he saw why. Glaeken had cut through the remnant of the fourth support and now Rasalom was dangling over the pit, clutching the swiftly tilting remnant with arms, legs, and tentacles.

The entire structure—the central disk, the new Rasalom, and the remnant of his saclike chrysalis—was now supported entirely by the third arch. And Glaeken had already damaged that near its union with the disk.

After all these ages, Rasalom's end was at hand.

Or was it?

Rasalom was suspended head down over the pit, but he was scrabbling backward along the remnant of the newly severed arch, up toward the disk.

"You cannot win, Glaeken! Not this time! It cannot happen! I'm too close!"

His movements were shaking the entire structure, exerting enormous pressure on the lone arch. It began to bob like a fishing pole that had hooked an enormous great white. As Glaeken hobbled back to the rim of the cavern and made his way toward the final arch, he heard it begin to crack where he had started his cut.

Rasalom must have realized it too, because even in this dim light Glaeken could discern a frantic desperation in his movements. But too late. The end of the arch was splitting, angling down at its wounded tip. Breaking . . .

A cannon-shot crack signaled the end. The disk lurched downward to a vertical angle, twisted crazily. Rasalom remained, clutching the disk's upper edge with his taloned fingers. Other appendages, spiny, rickety arms with clawed tips had broken free of the gel along his flank and were blindly questing for purchase while his tentacles stretched toward the end of the arch, reaching.

And then the final threads of the final arch gave way and the disk, the sac, and Rasalom too, plunged into the abyss.

No—not Rasalom.

Glaeken groaned as he realized Rasalom was still there. The rest had fallen away but he was clinging to the remnant of the final support by one of his tentacles—and pulling himself up.

"What can I do?"

Glaeken whirled at the sound of the voice and saw a dirt- and dust-caked Jack silhouetted in the light from the tunnel. He must have crawled through.

"Nothing! Go back!"

"Not likely."

"You've done more than enough. This is my fight!"

"Like hell!"

"*YOU!*"

Jack focused on Rasalom. "Jesus Christ, look at you! You spent thousands of years and put us through all this shit so you could look like *that*? You've gotta be the biggest asshole in the multiverse!"

He raised his automatic rifle and began firing at Rasalom's tentacles. The bullets had no more effect than gnats. He quickly ran out his magazine.

Glaeken forced his wounded leg to move, to half run, half stagger along the ledge to the base of the third arch, climb upon it, and hobble along its wavering length. He didn't have time to cut through this one. He had to meet Rasalom at its terminus and stop him there before he regained his footing.

"This is what it's always come down to, hasn't it, Rasalom. You and I. Just you and I."

Rasalom's reply was to snake his other tentacle upward and loop it around the shaft next to the first. He used them to hoist himself higher until his taloned hands could grip the arch. That done, new tentacles began to spring from the great gelatinous mass of his body to join the others.

He's going to make it!

Glaeken clenched his teeth against the pain in his leg and increased his speed. He didn't hesitate when he reached the shaft. He stepped out on its swaying, sloping surface and slashed the first tentacles with the weapon. The air filled with blinding flashes, greasy smoke, and thick, dark fluid spurting from the amputated ends. The world narrowed to Glaeken, Rasalom, the arch, and the weapon. Slitting his eyes against the flashes, choking on the smoke, he slipped into a fugue of pain and motion, moving in a fog, operating on reflexes as he severed coil after coil and kicked their writhing remnants aside, then moved on to the next group.

From below him came a thunderous roar as Rasalom kicked and thrashed in inarticulate pain and rage.

Spiny, spidery, pincer-tipped arms rose on both sides and snapped at him. Glaeken lashed out left and right, scything through them as he kept inching forward.

Something coiled about his ankle and pulled him off his feet. He fell and landed hard, almost losing his grip on the sword. Ahead of him, Rasalom's yellow-taloned hands found purchase. He began to lever himself up onto the support. If he made it—

Something boomed in the cavern and the area of the support beneath the hand with the missing finger exploded, the flinty surface dissolving into a spray of fragments. The two talons slipped, leaving Rasalom dangling by one arm.

Glaeken glanced over his shoulder and saw Jack aiming a large-bore weapon like a grenade launcher his way. Only he hadn't fired a grenade, more like a huge shotgun shell. The pellets couldn't harm Rasalom, but the support was another matter.

Another *boom* and another explosion as the shot tore up the support beneath the remaining set of talons. They slipped but held.

Glaeken rolled, severed the tentacle holding him, then crawled to the end of the arch where Rasalom swung below, suspended by only three talons dug into its surface.

"Glaeken . . . no . . . please! Don't—"

And in the instant of that plea Rasalom yanked his body upward and lashed at Glaeken with the two talons of his damaged hand. Glaeken ducked as they raked the air inches away, the breeze of their passing ruffling his hair. He swung the weapon upward, over his head. The impact with Rasalom's wrist and the simultaneous detonation of brilliance as the blade sliced through skin and muscle and tendon and bone nearly knocked Glaeken off the arch. He threw himself flat and hung on as Rasalom thrashed and howled and waved his partially severed, black-spurting wrist in the air.

Up ahead, near the shattered tip of the arch, Glaeken saw that Rasalom's only remaining hold on it was the three talons of his surviving hand.

"Kinda like déjà vu, huh?" said a voice close behind him.

Glaeken turned. Jack, his expression fierce, his eyes ablaze, had stepped onto the arch and was addressing Rasalom.

"You again!"

"Yeah, me again. Looks like you've lost *another* hand." Jack edged past Glaeken, then held out his own hand. "I need a piece of this son of a bitch."

Glaeken understood. He handed Jack the sword. Jack hefted it, then looked down at Rasalom.

"You really wanted to look like that? You think you're scary? Seriously? What an asshole."

His face changed, becoming a mask of rage as he raised the sword over the clutching talons.

"NO!"

A flash as Jack swung the blade and severed one of the fingers. Rasalom howled incoherently.

"That was for Eddie and Weezy!" Jack screamed in a raw voice Glaeken didn't recognize. His throat worked as his tone softened. "Especially Weezy."

Another flash, another scream as he swung and sliced through a second. The severed tip tumbled into oblivion.

"And that was for whatever you did or tried to do to three very important people."

Rasalom howled as the talon of the last digit scraped along the surface of the arch, scratching a deep furrow as it slipped slowly toward eternity. Then it caught in a small pit near the edge.

Jack seemed to be blinking back tears as he handed the sword to Glaeken.

"The last one is yours. You must have one helluva list."

Glaeken, still prone, nodded. "It would take me all day to recite it."

"The Lady there?"

"She's number one."

"Glaeken!" came the muffled, agonized voice from below. "You can't! This can't be happening! Don't!"

Glaeken pointed to the partially choked tunnel where Jack had entered.

"Back up."

Jack nodded and retreated. Glaeken rose to his knees and lifted the weapon to sever that last digit.

"GLAEKEN! Surely after all these millennia we can find a tiny piece of common ground, come to some kind of accord!"

He lowered the blade.

"Never."

Instead of using the weapon, he swiveled his body, flexing his good leg all the way to his abdomen.

His foot shot out and knocked the talon over the edge.

No final farewell to Rasalom, no verbal send-off. Nothing more than a contemptuous kick. Just what he deserved.

Rasalom's scream was loud, almost painfully so. It echoed up from the glowing depths long after his tumbling, mutilated form had been swallowed by the mists.

But Glaeken did not wait and watch and listen as he dearly would have loved. Instead, as soon as the arch slowed its bobbing from the release of Rasalom's enormous weight, he began crawling back toward the cavern rim as fast as his limbs would allow.

Rasalom was falling into eternity. When he passed the point where his presence no longer influenced this sphere, the old laws would begin to reassert themselves. Nature would awaken from its Rasalom-induced coma and begin its recovery, regain its control.

And this cavern had no place in nature.

As he reached the end of the arch, the walls began to shake. He saw Jack knocked off his feet to tumble back into the tunnel. Glaeken knew if he could reach that tunnel, he might survive.

He was almost there when the cavern rim gave way. He fought for purchase but his hands found only loose earth. He tried to raise his good leg, find some sort of foothold, but no use. His upper torso angled back as he began to tumble after Rasalom. Eternity beckoned below . . .

And then a hand closed about his ankle.

The Bunker

Vicky screamed as the burrowers broke from their paralysis and lurched into motion again. But they ignored the humans as they moved . . . away.

Gia watched in awe as they wriggled back into the holes that Swiss-cheesed the walls—something frantic about their movements—and disappeared.

"What's happening?"

Abe shook his head. "I don't know, but I bet You-Know-Who has some-thing to do with it."

Vicky frowned. "Who's You-Know-Who?"

Gia nudged her and gave her a look. "Who do you think?"

The little girl beamed. "Ohhhh yeaaaah."

Manhattan

The crowd quieted as a new sound overwhelmed their chants and songs. Carol's voice had given out a while ago, so she was already silent.

They'd spilled across the street and into the illuminated sections of the park, and were swelling farther. But the sound had frozen them all in their tracks; and now they stood half crouched, looking up, looking around, looking at each other. Carol hushed those near her.

A basso drone, a thunderous buzz, a monstrous flapping in the air all around the widening cone of light, growing louder, vibrating the streets, the sidewalks, the buildings.

"It's the bugs!" someone cried. "They're coming back! Coming to get us!"

"No!" Carol cried, her voice a ragged blare above the growing fearful murmur of those about her. "Don't be afraid. They hate the light. As long as we stay in the light they won't come near us."

She, too, was afraid, but she hid it. What was happening? She glanced at Bill and he shrugged and held her close.

Then she saw them. Bugs. An immense horde of them, thickening the air and swarming along the ground around the cone of light. Some of them were forced to dip into the light by the crowding but their wings and bodies began to smoke where the light touched them and they darted back out.

No concerted attack, no suicidal kamikaze bug rush to wipe them out. Rather, a mad, blind, panicked dash toward the hole. The cone of light had reached the edge of the bottomless opening and she could see the countless horrors diving into the depths beyond the light, the winged ones spiraling down, the crawlers leaping from the edge.

"They're going back!" Carol said, as much to herself as to Bill. "They're going back into the hole!"

As a cheer roared from the crowd and she pressed forward for a better look, the earth began to shake. Cheers turned to screams as people were

knocked off their feet. Carol's hoarse shout of alarm rose with the others as she
was hurled to the pavement with Bill atop her.

From the blown-out windows of the top floor, Sylvia watched the pandemonium
below with growing alarm. She clutched the sill with one hand and Jeffy with
the other as the building shook and creaked and groaned around them.

An earthquake! she thought. She remembered the 2011 tremor, but this
was much worse.

And there, down on the near edge of the Sheep Meadow, the earth was
cracking open.

Another hole!

This was it, then. The growing light, the sense of impending victory, the
return of the bugs en masse to the original hole—all a false hope, an empty
promise. A new hole, unafraid of the light, was opening closer to the building.
What new horror was going to issue from that?

The sudden changes could mean only one thing: Glaeken had failed.

The tremors worsened as a deep rumble issued from the first hole in the
center of the Sheep Meadow. Clouds of what looked like dust or smoke were
spewing from the opening. Sylvia reached for the field glasses and focused on
the hole. The edges looked ragged—they seemed to be crumbling, breaking
away, sliding into the opening, choking it.

Yes! It was closing! And below—she shifted the glasses—what was happening with the new hole?

But it wasn't a hole yet. Maybe it never would be. More like a depression,
a cave-in of some sort.

The tremors stopped.

Then silence. Sylvia lowered the field glasses and paused, listening. Silence like no silence she could ever recall. Not a bird, not an insect, not a
breeze was stirring. She could hear the rush of her own blood through her arteries, but nothing else. All the world, all of nature paused, frozen, stunned,
afraid to move, afraid to breathe.

It lasted one prolonged agonized moment. And then, for the second time
tonight, the light began to fade.

The silence was shattered by a burst of cries of renewed terror from below,
then the chant began again. She heard Ba begin to repeat the words behind

her. Sylvia joined him, whispering the litany as she raised the glasses and scanned the roiling crowd for Carol or Bill or Jack—anyone she knew.

The chant was failing this time. Despite thousands of throats shouting the words at the tops of their lungs, the light continued to fade.

We've lost!

Somehow in the dying light she managed to pick out Carol's familiar figure at the edge of the new hole, or depression, or wherever it was. She wanted to shout down to her to get away from there. That was where the new threat would arise. But Carol was right on the edge, pointing down at the bottom of the depression. She was pacing back and forth, hugging Bill, hugging everyone within reach. What—?

Sylvia refocused on the bottom of the pit. Something moving there, struggling in the loose dirt. She strained to see in the last of the light.

A man. A man with red hair. And another man, helping him, pulling him free.

Glaeken? Jack? Alive? But . . . if they'd survived down there, it could only mean—

Suddenly Ba was at her side, pointing across the park toward the East Side. "Look, Missus! *Look!*"

In all their years together, she had never heard such naked excitement in his voice. She looked.

The crowd below couldn't see it yet, but from this elevation there could be no doubt. Sylvia didn't need the field glasses. Straight ahead, down at the far end of one of the streets, a bright orange glow was firing the eastern sky, reaching for them along the concrete canyons that ran to the East River.

Manhattanhenge.

"The sun, Missus! The sun is rising!"

PART FOUR

DAWN

FRIDAY

In The Beginning . . .

Manhattan

Carol stood on Glaeken's rooftop in the bright morning sunlight and wished she had the nerve to remove her blouse. Jack and Bill had pulled off their shirts as soon as they'd stepped out the door. Carol envied the males their casual ability to expose so much surface area to the warm light pouring through the cloudless sky.

Why not me? she thought, reaching for the top buttons on her blouse. After all we've been through together, what difference would it make?

But she stopped after two buttons. If it was just Bill, maybe. But not with Jack here.

I know I've been changed by all this—but not that much. An uptight Catholic girl still lived somewhere within her.

"Still hard to believe it's over," Jack said.

Bill stared out over the city. "What a mess."

Carol followed his gaze. There didn't seem to be an unbroken window in the city. Ruined buildings were everywhere, some torn apart by gravity holes, some crushed by debris falling from other gravity holes. Above them, pillars of smoke rose from fires still raging here and there about the boroughs. Below, a rare car picked its way through the cluttered streets. Dazed-looking people wandered the sidewalks or stood around the huge depression that only hours ago had been the Sheep Meadow hole.

"It's not all bad," Jack said. "When was the last time midtown air smelled this clean?"

He seemed a new man, energized. She knew why: The shortwave had come alive. He'd contacted his loved ones.

Bill nodded. "You've got a point. I'm just wondering how we'll ever rebuild this."

Jack made a face. "Who said we should?"

"We have to," Carol said. "We now have a chance to start from scratch and do it right this time."

Bill nodded. "Or at least give it our best shot."

"Oh, wow!" Jack said through a laugh. "Polly, meet Anna. Anna, meet Polly."

Carol turned to him. "What's wrong with that?"

"Pie in the sky. Sure, there'll be lots of talk about a new world and a new brotherhood, but believe me it won't be long before we're all back to the same old shit: The truly capable people, the ones you'd be proud to call leader, will be devoting all their time to the actual rebuilding, while the usual crew of blowhard leeches incapable of building anything will be pretending to lead while they position themselves for a driver seat once things get rolling again."

"I disagree," Carol said. "I think we can and will do better. And as for leaders . . ." She gestured below. "Do you think anyone down there knows what you two did?"

"No," Jack said sharply. He suddenly seemed uneasy. He began slipping back into his shirt. "And let's leave it that way."

"Don't want to be a hero?" Bill said, smiling.

"I don't even want to be *noticed*." He turned and started walking away.

"Leaving?" Carol said.

"Yeah. Soon as I find a car with gas I'm heading out to Pennsylvania." A light glowed in his eyes. "Abe's bringing Gia and Vicky back. I'm going to provide the escort."

"Good luck," Bill said.

Carol watched Jack go. As he reached the stairs, a little girl, maybe seven or eight with curly blond hair, approached him. She held a puppy. How on Earth had she got up here?

Jack skidded to a stop before her. They stared at each other. Jack spoke, the child nodded. Then Jack did the strangest thing: He dropped to one knee before her, wrapped her in his arms, and hugged her.

"Do you see that?" Carol said.

Bill nodded, frowning. "Are those tears in his eyes?"

Carol was pretty sure they were. "I wonder who she is?"

As she watched Jack wipe his eyes, something swooped through the air and landed on the little girl's head: a pale blue parakeet.

Carol heard Jack cry, "Parabellum?" then laugh. "I'll be damned!"

He took the child by the hand and led her, the dog, and the bird downstairs.

"What was that all about?"

Carol shook her head. "I don't think that's the little girl he's been talking about."

"No," Bill said. "Something different—something very unchildlike about that child."

"Whoever she is, he seems very protective. Heaven help anyone who tries to harm her."

Bill slipped his arm around her waist and turned her toward the ruined cityscape before them.

"I doubt heaven helps anybody."

"Just a figure of speech. But I do wonder who or what will get the credit for the sunrise."

Bill laughed. "I heard a bunch of guys singing 'Here Comes the Sun' over and over. I'll bet that becomes a new religious hymn. But you're right. A whole new mythology could rise out of this. A new round of sun worship, that's for sure. It'll be interesting to see what develops."

"But whatever it is, it will be wrong. They'll be looking for some deity to praise and thank."

"That's nothing new."

"But what about you? You deserve part of the credit."

Bill shook his head. "No. I just ran an errand." He looked into her eyes. "You're the one who found the real key and put it to use. You saw that the answer was inside us rather than outside."

"It's always been that way, hasn't it? We've always been in charge but we've never taken control. We just let ourselves get pushed this way and that."

"Fear is like a disease, and I guess some of us have better immune systems than others. Sometimes we need a little help from others, but we all have the power to step aside and say I'm not going to be a part of this anymore."

She locked her arms around his waist and smoothed his wind-ruffled gray hair.

"Do you think things will be different?"

He shook his head. "I like to think I'm more optimistic than Jack, but I fear he's right. Nothing changes."

"That's not true, Bill. I'm changed, you're changed, we've all been changed by this."

"Especially Glaeken."

Yes, she thought with a pang of anguish. Especially poor Glaeken. What would he do, where would he go when Magda was gone?

And Sylvia and Jeffy—what about them? And Nick . . . would he ever re-cover?

So many questions, so many uncertainties.

She locked her arms around Bill's waist and snuggled against him.

At least there were a few things of which she could be sure—her love for Bill, for one, and the certainty that no one alive today would ever again take sunrise for granted.

And beneath their feet, in the apartment directly below, a red-haired man with an ageless thirty-five-year-old body spoon-feeds applesauce to the twisted, empty-minded woman he loved so dearly and with whom he had hoped to grow old. A little girl, older than Glaeken, enters with a puppy in her arms. Glaeken embraces her. The Veilleur household has just expanded.

THE SECRET HISTORY OF THE WORLD

The preponderance of my work deals with a history of the world that remains undiscovered, unexplored, and unknown to most of humanity. Some of this secret history has been revealed in the Adversary Cycle, some in the Repairman Jack novels, and bits and pieces in other, seemingly unconnected works. Taken together, even these millions of words barely scratch the surface of what has been going on behind the scenes, hidden from the workaday world. I've listed them below in the chronological order in which the events in them occur.

Note: "Year Zero" is the end of civilization as we know it; "Year Zero Minus One" is the year preceding it, etc.

THE PAST
"Demonsong" (prehistory)
"Aryans and Absinthe"** (1923–1924)
Black Wind (1926–1945)
The Keep (1941)
Reborn (February–March 1968)
"Dat Tay Vao" + (March 1968)
Jack: Secret Histories (1983)
Jack: Secret Circles (1983)
Jack: Secret Vengeance (1983)
"Faces"* (1989)

YEAR ZERO MINUS THREE
Sibs (February)
The Tomb (summer)
"The Barrens"* (ends in September)
"A Day in the Life"* (October)
"The Long Way Home" ++
Legacies (December)

YEAR ZERO MINUS TWO
"Interlude at Duane's"** (April)
Conspiracies (April) (includes "Home Repairs" ++)
All the Rage (May) (includes "The Last Rakosh" ++)

Hosts (June)
The Haunted Air (August)
Gateways (September)
Crisscross (November)
Infernal (December)

YEAR ZERO MINUS ONE
Harbingers (January)
Bloodline (April)
By the Sword (May)
Ground Zero (July)
The Touch (ends in August)
The Peabody-Ozymandias Traveling Circus & Oddity Emporium (ends in
   September)
"Tenants"*

YEAR ZERO
"Pelts"*
Reprisal (ends in February)
Fatal Error (February) (includes "The Wringer" ++)
The Dark at the End (March)
Nightworld (May)

* available in *The Barrens and Others*
** available in *Aftershock & Others*
+ available in the 2009 reissue of *The Touch*
++ available in *Quick Fixes—Tales of Repairman Jack*